PUBLISHED BY
KaBOOM!

ROSS RICHIE CEO & Founder

JACK CUMMINS President

MARK SMYLIE Founder of Archaia

MATT GAGNON Editor-in-Chief

FILIP SABLIK VP of Publishing & Marketing

STEPHEN CHRISTY VP of Development

LANCE KREITER VP of Licensing & Merchandising

PHIL BARBARO VP of Finance

BRYCE CARLSON Managing Editor

MEL CAYLO Marketing Manager

SCOTT NEWMAN Production Design Manager

IRENE BRADISH Operations Manager

DAFNA PLEBAN Editor

SHANNON WATTERS Editor

ERIC HARBURN Editor

REBECCA TAYLOR Editor

IAN BRILL Editor

CHRIS ROSA Assistant Editor

ALEX GALER Assistant Editor

WHITNEY LEOPARD Assistant Editor

JASMINE AMIRI Assistant Editor

CAMERON CHITTOCK Assistant Editor

HANNAH NANCE PARTLOW Production Designer

KELSEY DIETERICH Production Designer

EMI YONEMURA BROWN Production Designer

DEVIN FUNCHES E-Commerce & Inventory Coordinator

ANDY LIEGL Event Coordinator

BRIANNA HART Executive Assistant

AARON FERRARA Operations Assistant

JOSÉ MEZA Sales Assistant

ELIZABETH LOUGHRIDGE Accounting Assistant

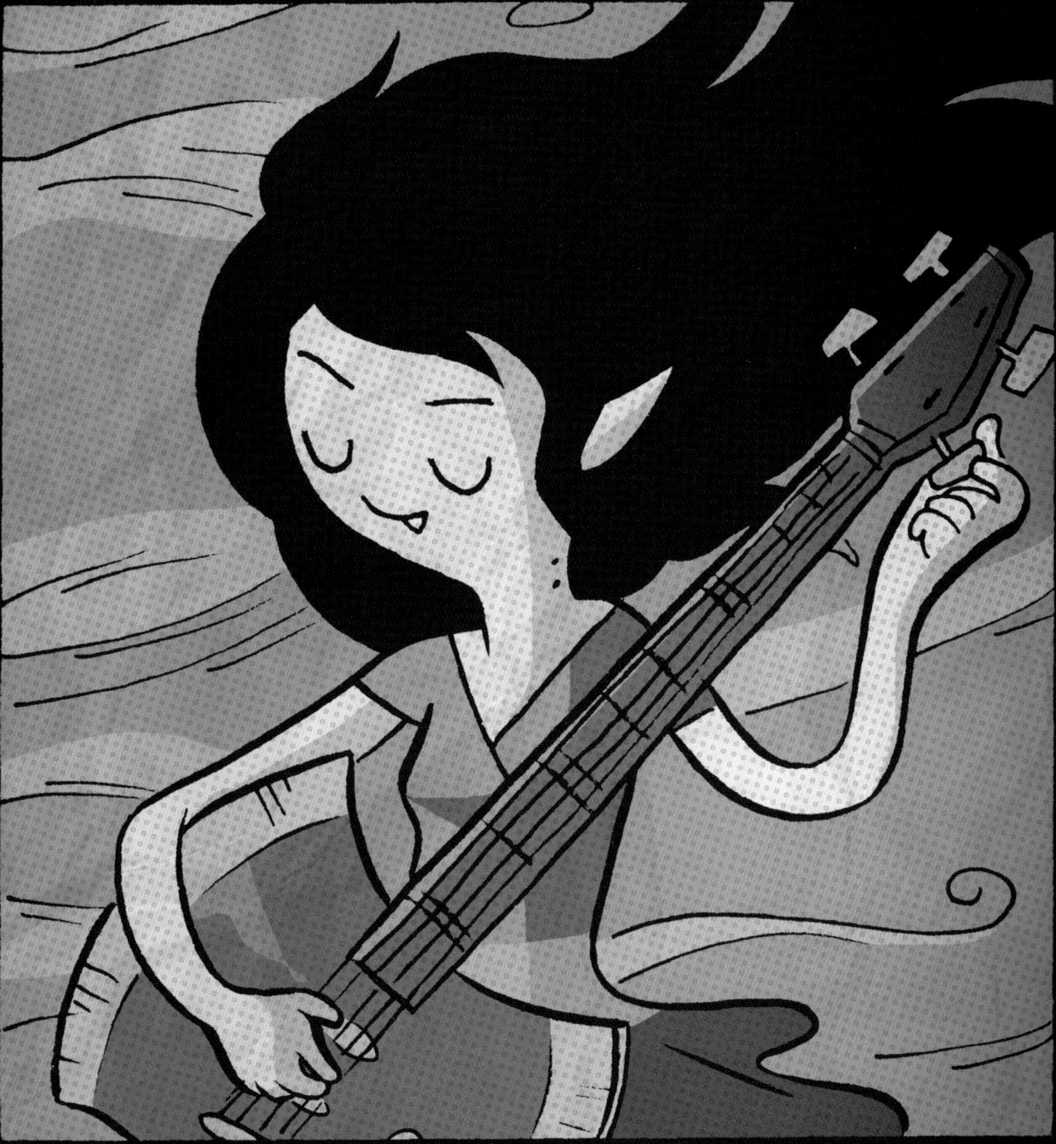

Adventure Time Presents Marceline and the Scream Queens

kaboom!
Cartoon Network
Frederator

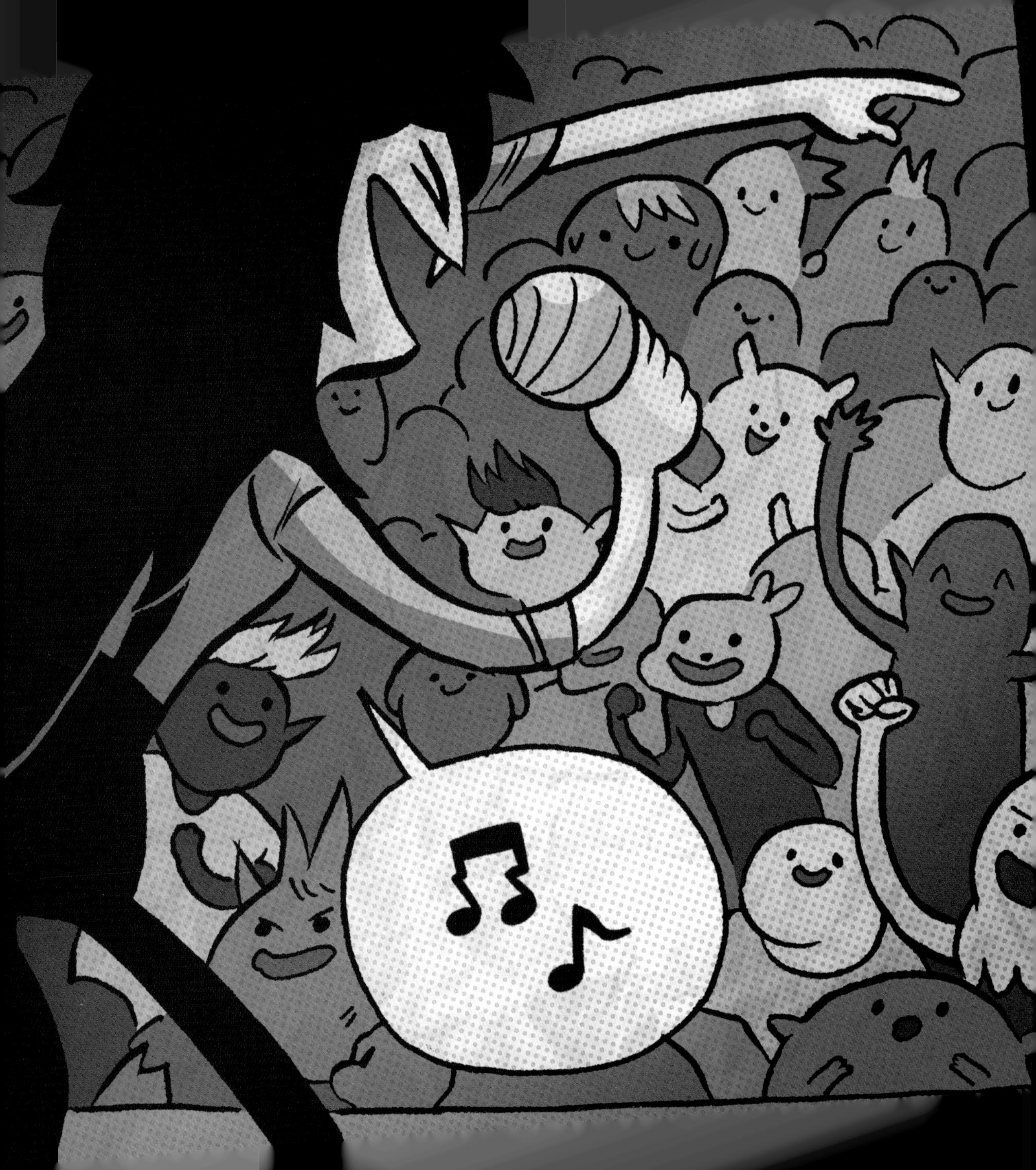

ADVENTURE TIME™

Created by
PENDLETON WARD

Written & Illustrated by
MEREDITH GRAN

Colors by
LISA MOORE

Letters by
STEVE WANDS

Collection and Cover Design by
HANNAH NANCE PARTLOW

Enchiridion Edition Cover by
ZACHARY STERLING

San Diego Comic-Con
Exclusive Cover by
CLAIRE SULLIVAN

"RESURRECTION SONG"
Written & Illustrated by JEN WANG

Designer HANNAH NANCE PARTLOW

Assistant Editor WHITNEY LEOPARD

Editor SHANNON WATTERS

SPECIAL THANKS TO MARISA MARIONAKIS, RICK BLANCO, CURTIS LELASH, LAURIE
ONO, KEITH MACK, KELLY CREWS AND THE WONDERFUL FOLKS AT CARTOON NETWORK.

"GRUMPY BUTT"
Written & Illustrated by FAITH ERIN HICKS
Colors by MIRKA ANDOLFO

"FRUIT SALAD DAYS"
Written & Illustrated by LIZ PRINCE

"THE BOOTLEGGER"
Written by YUKO OTA & ANANTH PANAGARIYA
Illustrated by YUKO OTA

"TREASURES UNTOLD"
Written & Illustrated by KATE LETH

"COMMUNICATION ISSUES"
Written & Illustrated by POLLY GUO

"COFFIN BREAK"
Written & Illustrated
by RICH TOMMASO

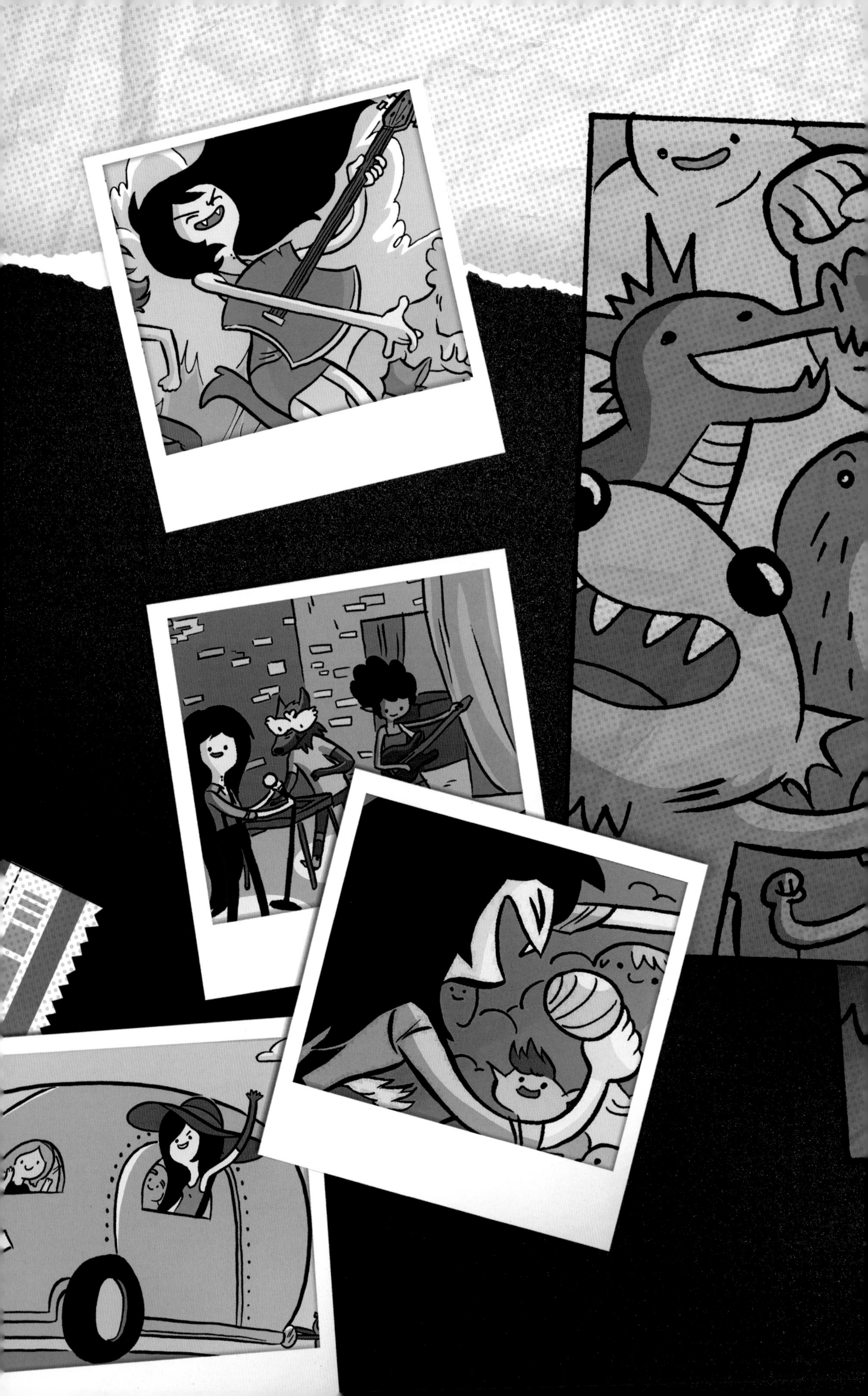

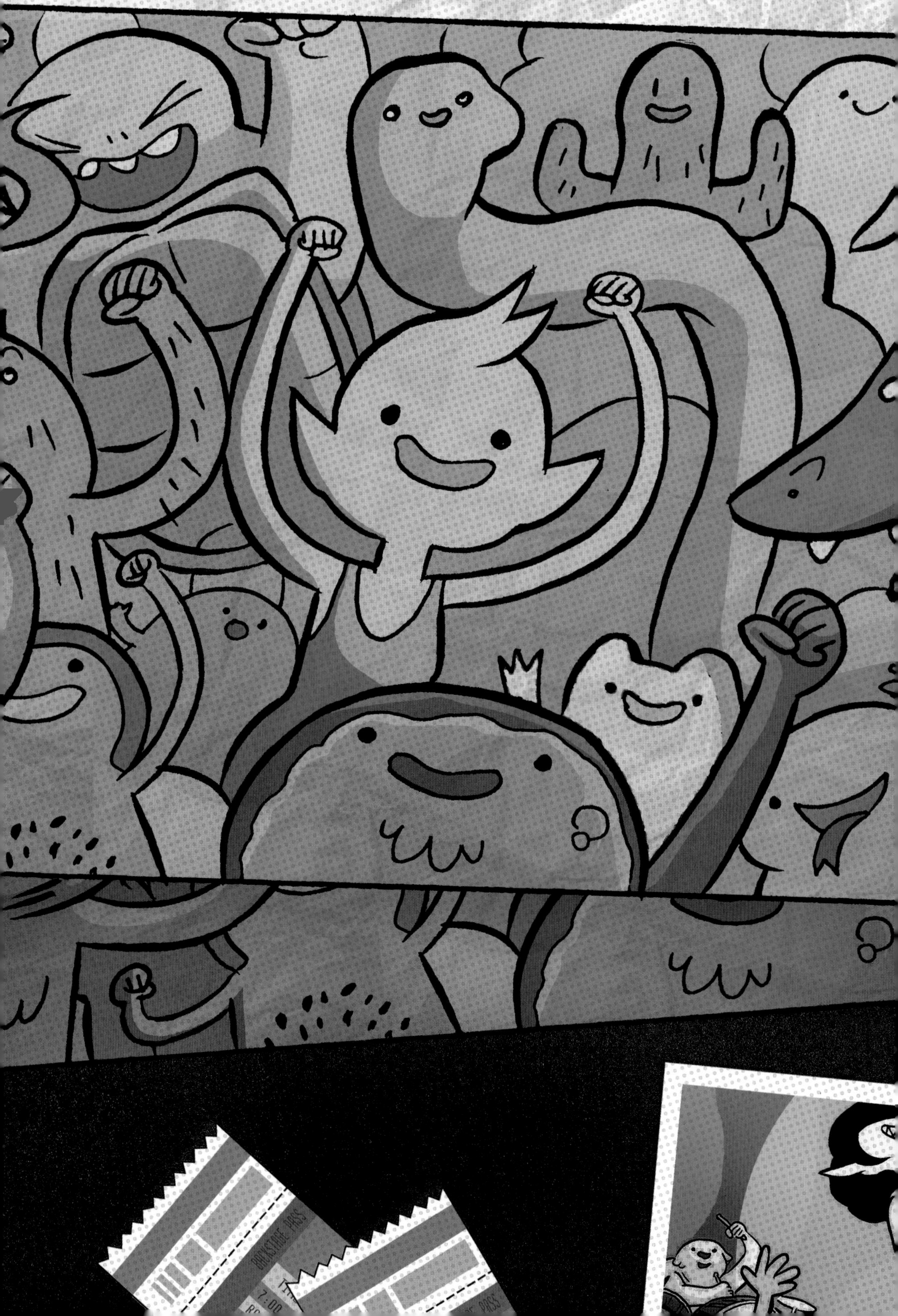
BACKSTAGE PASS
7:00

CHAPTER ON

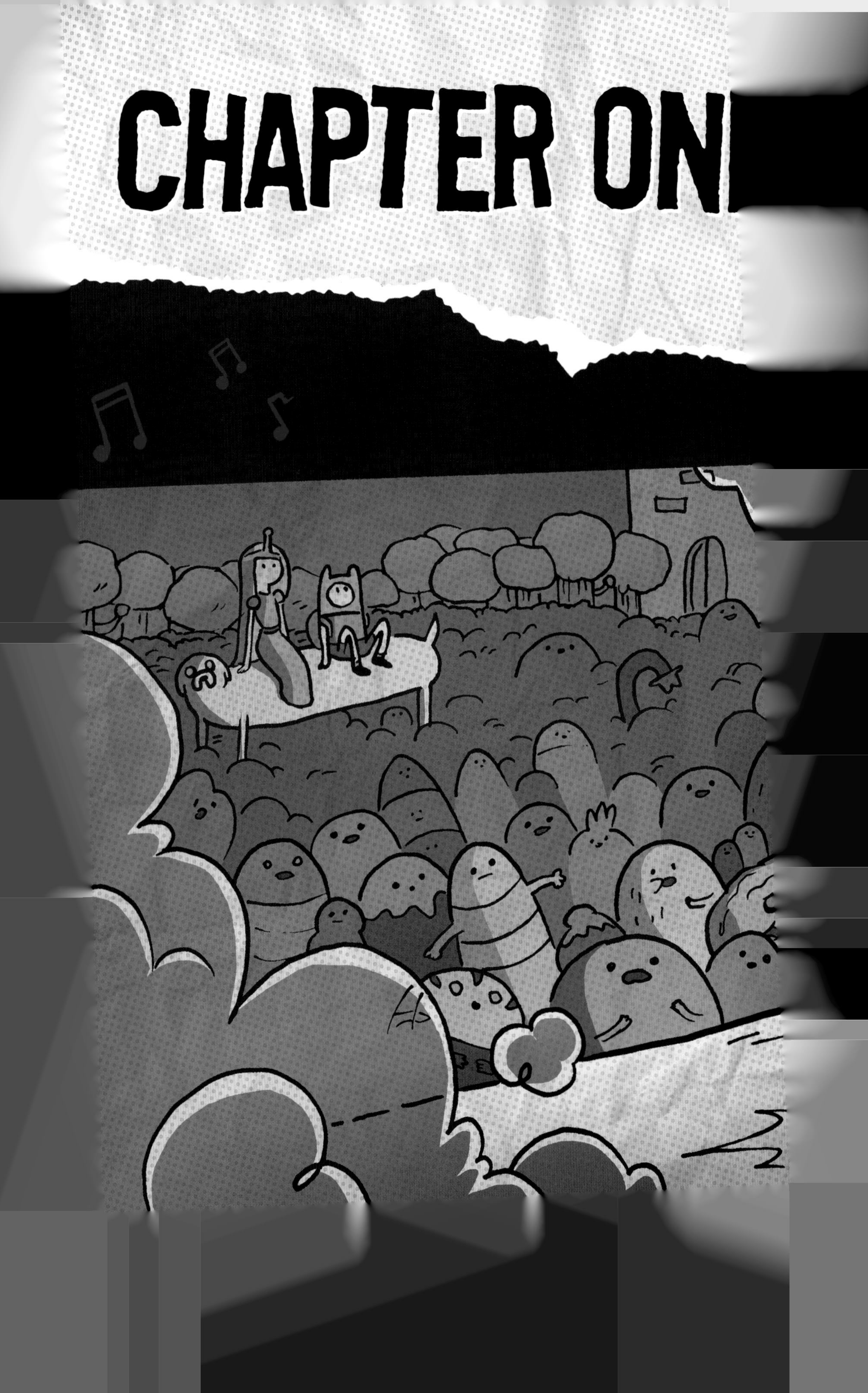

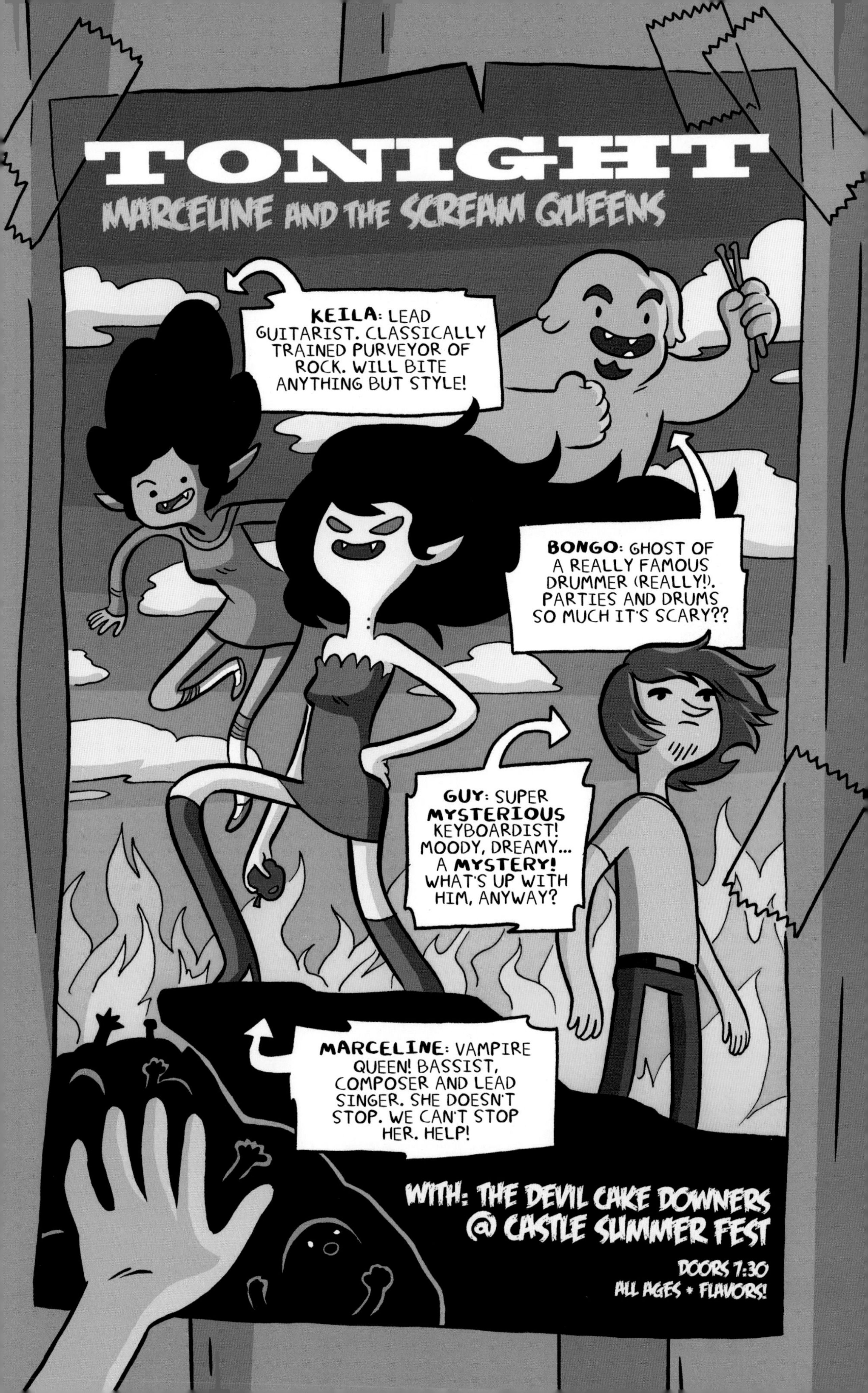
TONIGHT
MARCELINE AND THE SCREAM QUEENS
KEILA: LEAD GUITARIST. CLASSICALLY TRAINED PURVEYOR OF ROCK. WILL BITE ANYTHING BUT STYLE!
BONGO: GHOST OF A REALLY FAMOUS DRUMMER (REALLY!). PARTIES AND DRUMS SO MUCH IT'S SCARY??
GUY: SUPER MYSTERIOUS KEYBOARDIST! MOODY, DREAMY... A MYSTERY! WHAT'S UP WITH HIM, ANYWAY?
MARCELINE: VAMPIRE QUEEN! BASSIST, COMPOSER AND LEAD SINGER. SHE DOESN'T STOP. WE CAN'T STOP HER. HELP!
WITH: THE DEVIL CAKE DOWNERS
@ CASTLE SUMMER FEST
DOORS 7:30
ALL AGES + FLAVORS!

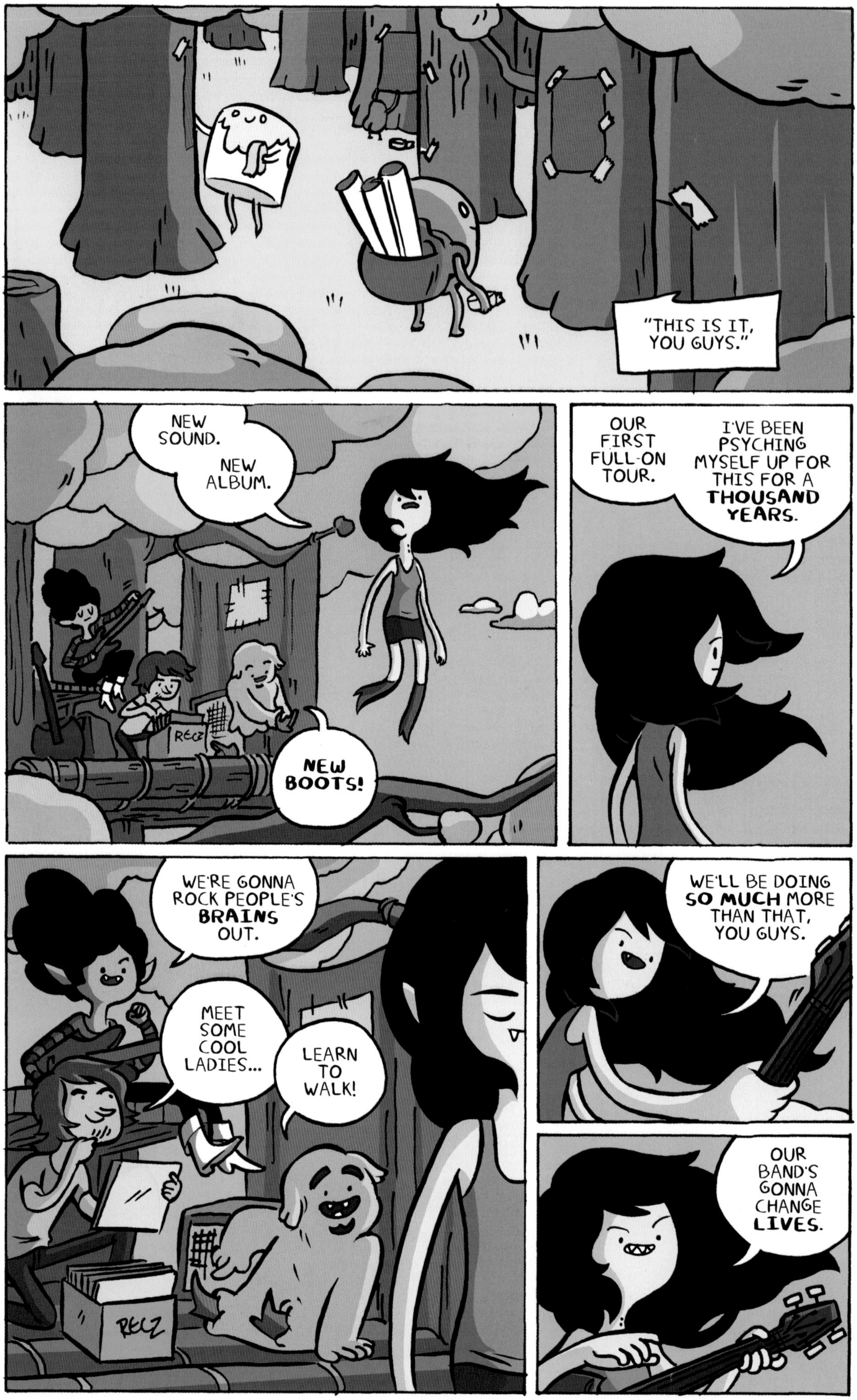
"THIS IS IT, YOU GUYS."
NEW SOUND.
NEW ALBUM.
NEW BOOTS!
OUR FIRST FULL-ON TOUR.
I'VE BEEN PSYCHING MYSELF UP FOR THIS FOR A THOUSAND YEARS.
WE'RE GONNA ROCK PEOPLE'S BRAINS OUT.
MEET SOME COOL LADIES...
LEARN TO WALK!
WE'LL BE DOING SO MUCH MORE THAN THAT, YOU GUYS.
OUR BAND'S GONNA CHANGE LIVES.

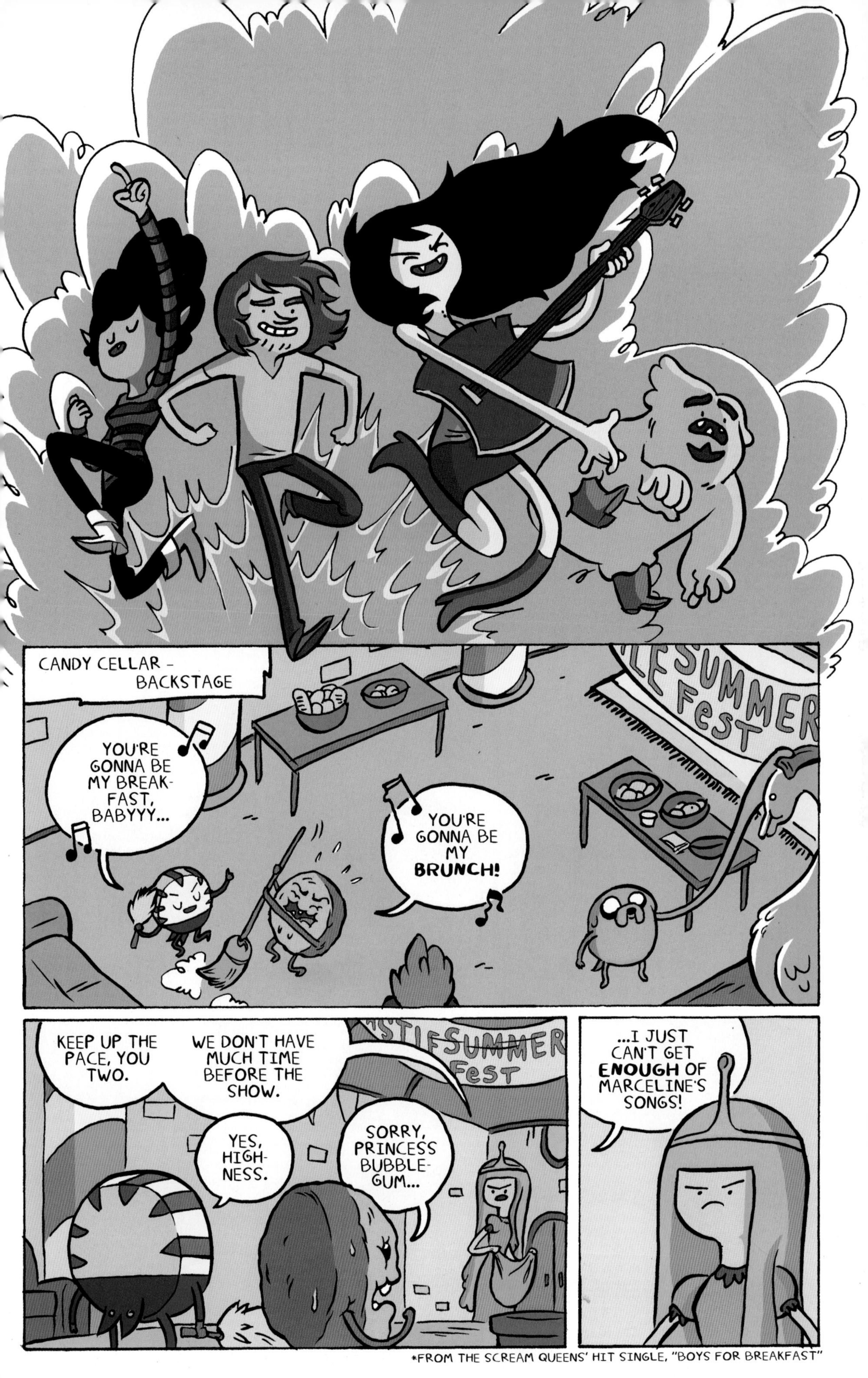

CANDY CELLAR – BACKSTAGE
YOU'RE GONNA BE MY BREAK-FAST, BABYYY...
SUMMER Fest
YOU'RE GONNA BE MY **BRUNCH!**
KEEP UP THE PACE, YOU TWO.
WE DON'T HAVE MUCH TIME BEFORE THE SHOW.
YES, HIGH-NESS.
SORRY, PRINCESS BUBBLE-GUM...
...I JUST CAN'T GET **ENOUGH** OF MARCELINE'S SONGS!

*FROM THE SCREAM QUEENS' HIT SINGLE, "BOYS FOR BREAKFAST"

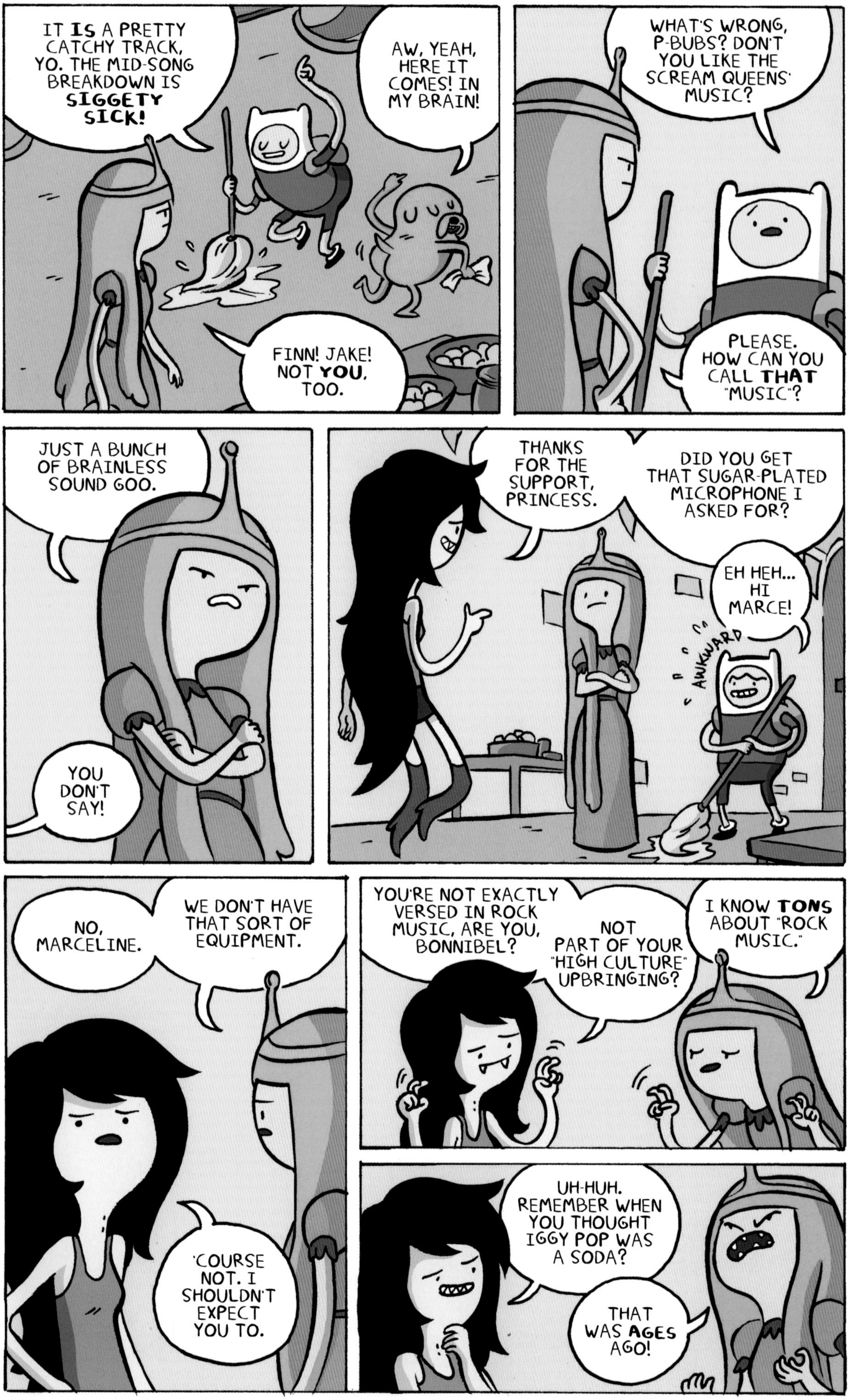
IT **IS** A PRETTY CATCHY TRACK, YO. THE MID-SONG BREAKDOWN IS **SIGGETY SICK!**
AW, YEAH, HERE IT COMES! IN MY BRAIN!
FINN! JAKE! NOT **YOU**, TOO.
WHAT'S WRONG, P-BUBS? DON'T YOU LIKE THE SCREAM QUEENS' MUSIC?
PLEASE. HOW CAN YOU CALL **THAT** "MUSIC"?
JUST A BUNCH OF BRAINLESS SOUND GOO.
YOU DON'T SAY!
THANKS FOR THE SUPPORT, PRINCESS.
DID YOU GET THAT SUGAR-PLATED MICROPHONE I ASKED FOR?
EH HEH... HI MARCE!
AWKWARD
NO, MARCELINE.
WE DON'T HAVE THAT SORT OF EQUIPMENT.
'COURSE NOT. I SHOULDN'T EXPECT YOU TO.
YOU'RE NOT EXACTLY VERSED IN ROCK MUSIC, ARE YOU, BONNIBEL?
NOT PART OF YOUR "HIGH CULTURE" UPBRINGING?
I KNOW **TONS** ABOUT "ROCK MUSIC."
UH-HUH. REMEMBER WHEN YOU THOUGHT IGGY POP WAS A SODA?
THAT WAS **AGES** AGO!

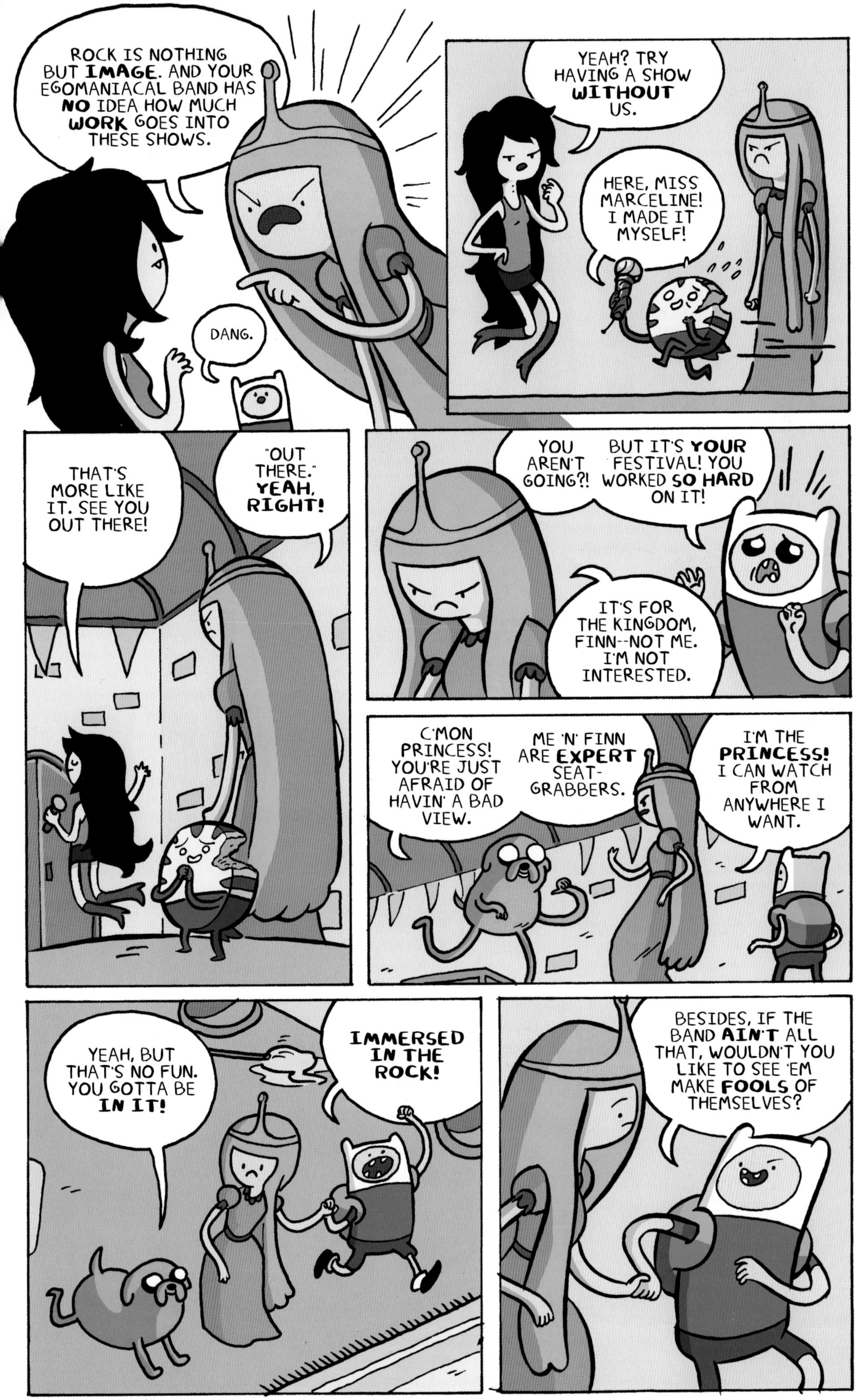
ROCK IS NOTHING BUT IMAGE. AND YOUR EGOMANIACAL BAND HAS NO IDEA HOW MUCH WORK GOES INTO THESE SHOWS.
DANG.
YEAH? TRY HAVING A SHOW WITHOUT US.
HERE, MISS MARCELINE! I MADE IT MYSELF!
THAT'S MORE LIKE IT. SEE YOU OUT THERE!
"OUT THERE." YEAH, RIGHT!
YOU AREN'T GOING?!
BUT IT'S YOUR FESTIVAL! YOU WORKED SO HARD ON IT!
IT'S FOR THE KINGDOM, FINN--NOT ME. I'M NOT INTERESTED.
C'MON PRINCESS! YOU'RE JUST AFRAID OF HAVIN' A BAD VIEW.
ME 'N' FINN ARE EXPERT SEAT-GRABBERS.
I'M THE PRINCESS! I CAN WATCH FROM ANYWHERE I WANT.
YEAH, BUT THAT'S NO FUN. YOU GOTTA BE IN IT!
IMMERSED IN THE ROCK!
BESIDES, IF THE BAND AIN'T ALL THAT, WOULDN'T YOU LIKE TO SEE 'EM MAKE FOOLS OF THEMSELVES?

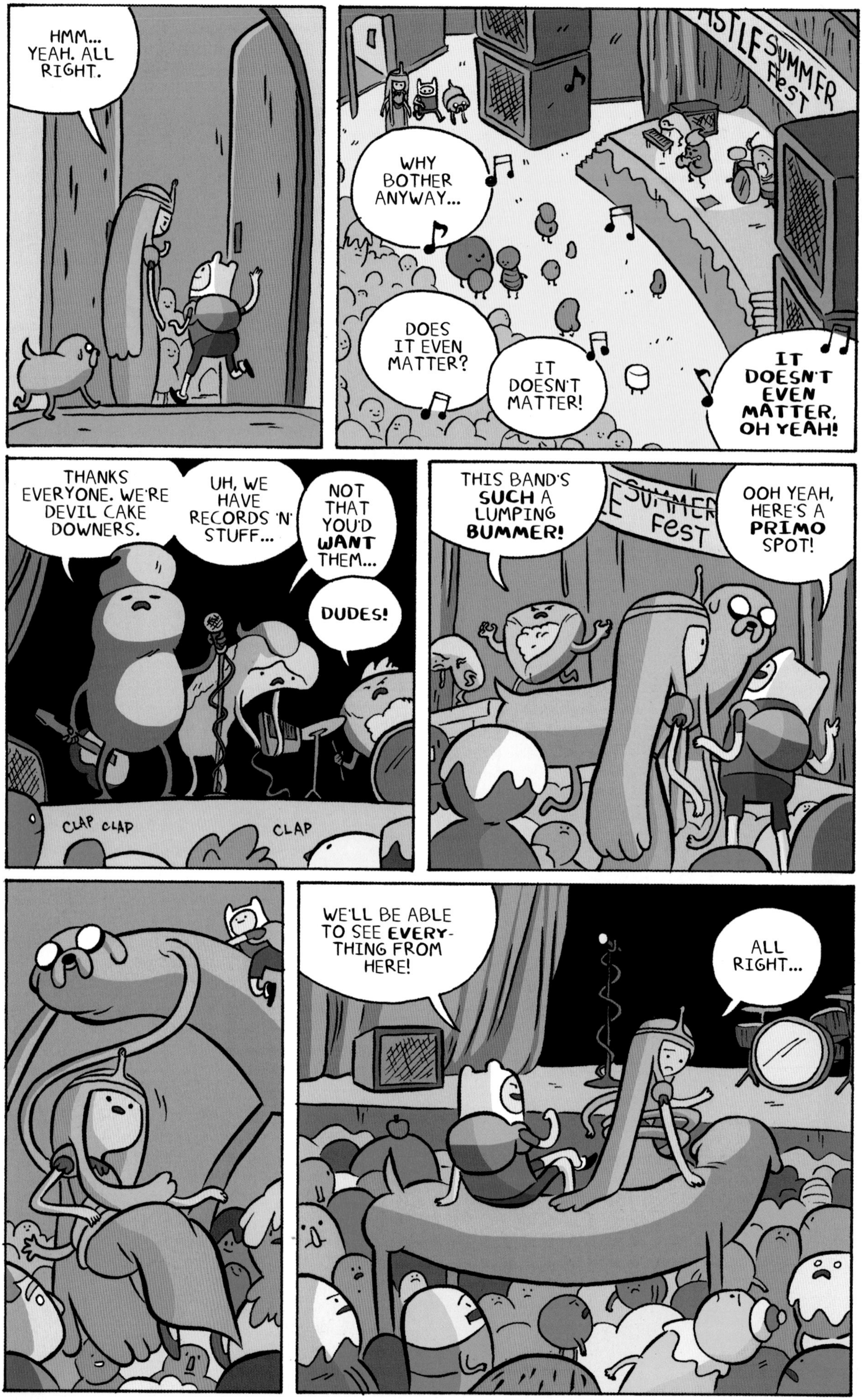
HMM... YEAH. ALL RIGHT.
ASTLE SUMMER FEST
WHY BOTHER ANYWAY...
DOES IT EVEN MATTER?
IT DOESN'T MATTER!
IT DOESN'T EVEN MATTER, OH YEAH!
THANKS EVERYONE. WE'RE DEVIL CAKE DOWNERS.
UH, WE HAVE RECORDS 'N' STUFF...
NOT THAT YOU'D WANT THEM...
DUDES!
CLAP CLAP
CLAP
THIS BAND'S SUCH A LUMPING BUMMER!
SUMMER FEST
OOH YEAH, HERE'S A PRIMO SPOT!
WE'LL BE ABLE TO SEE EVERYTHING FROM HERE!
ALL RIGHT...

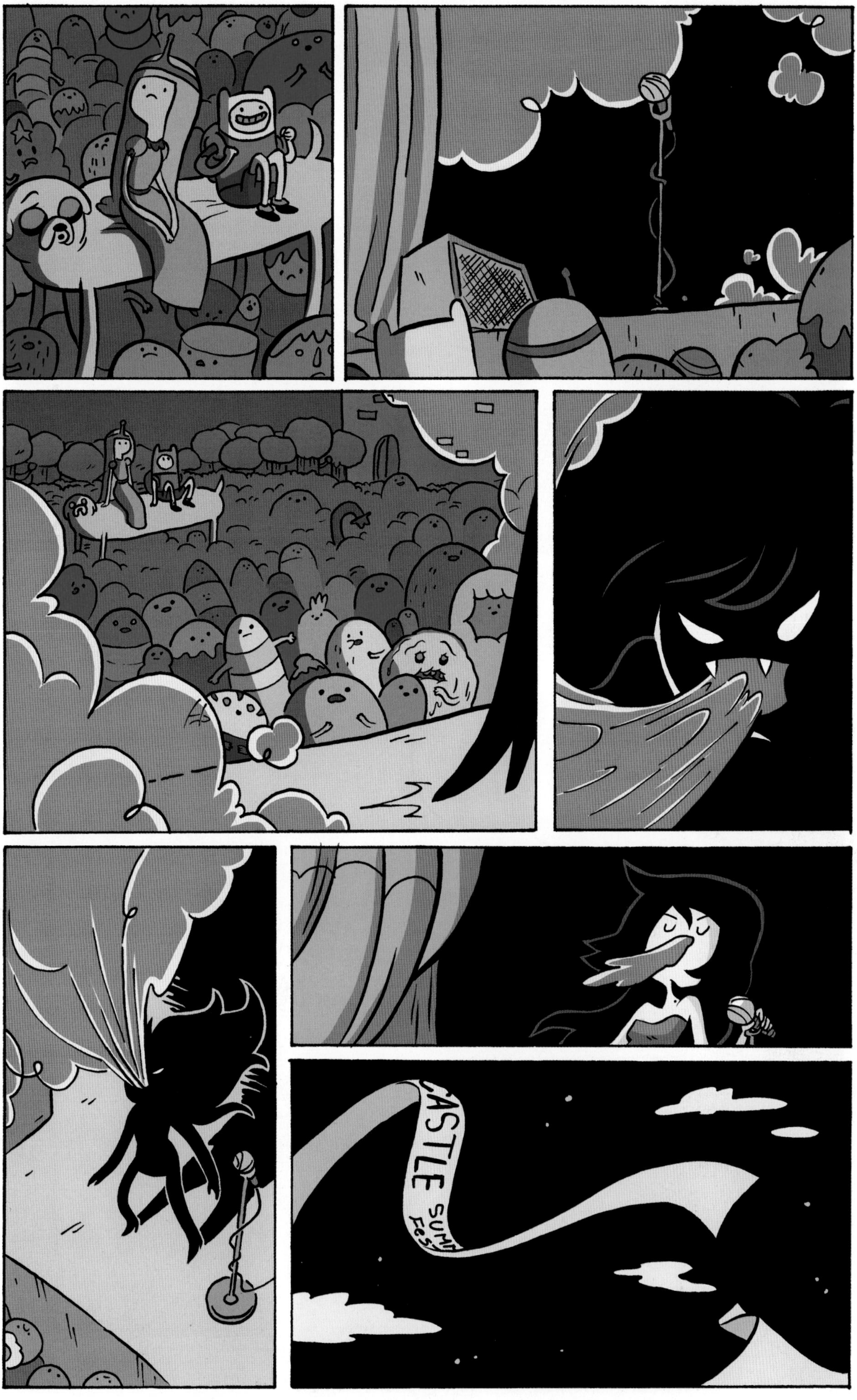
CASTLE

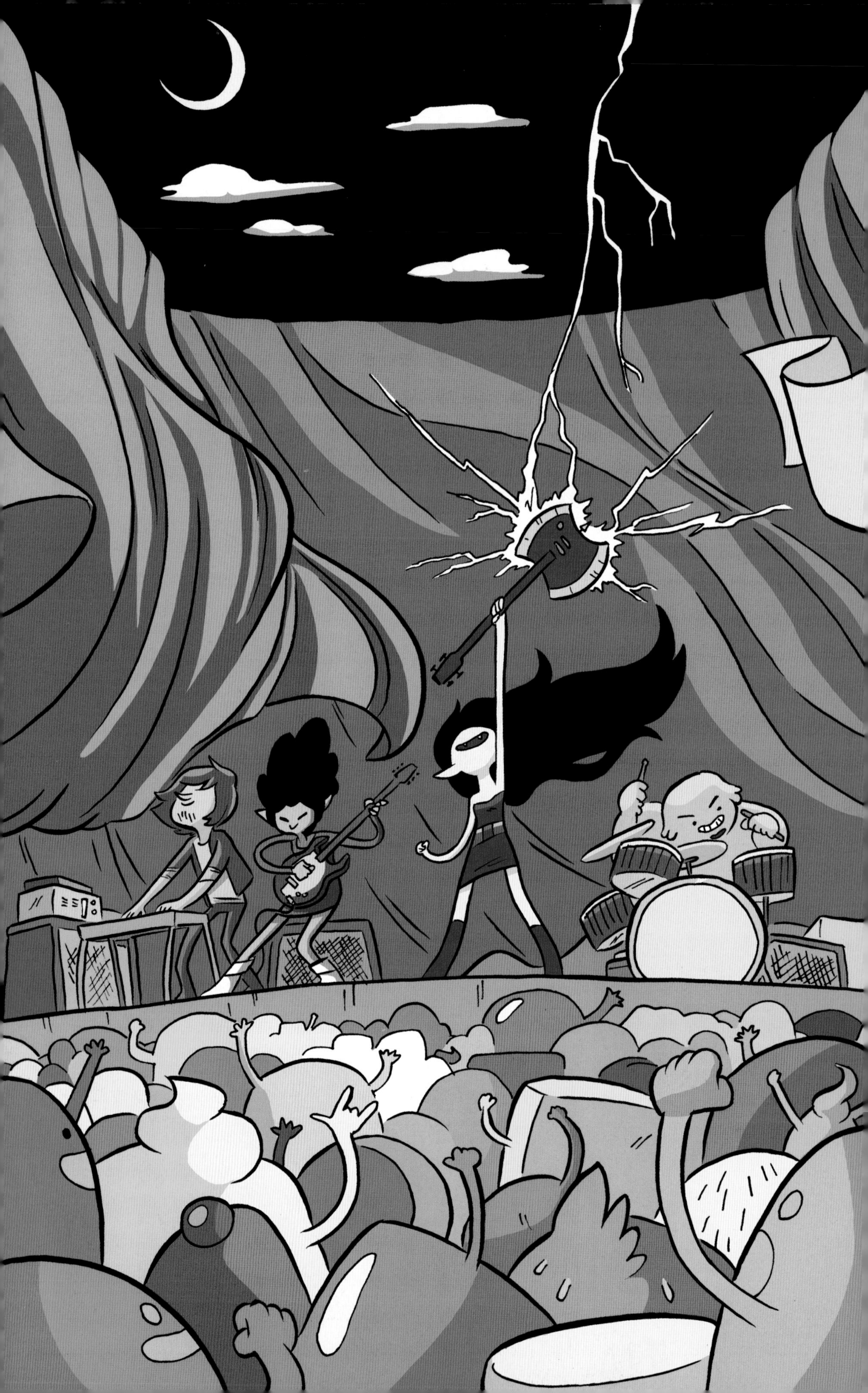

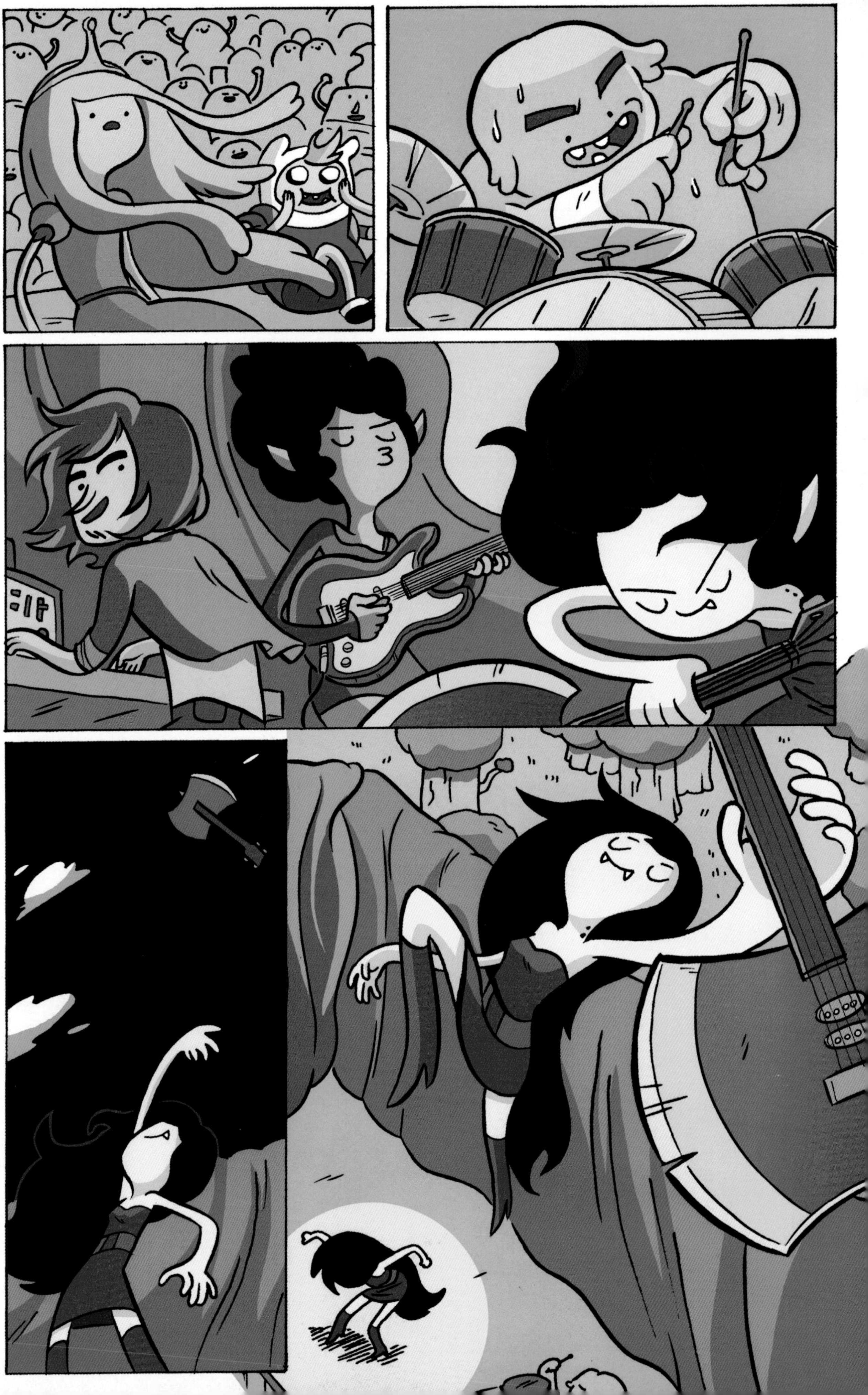

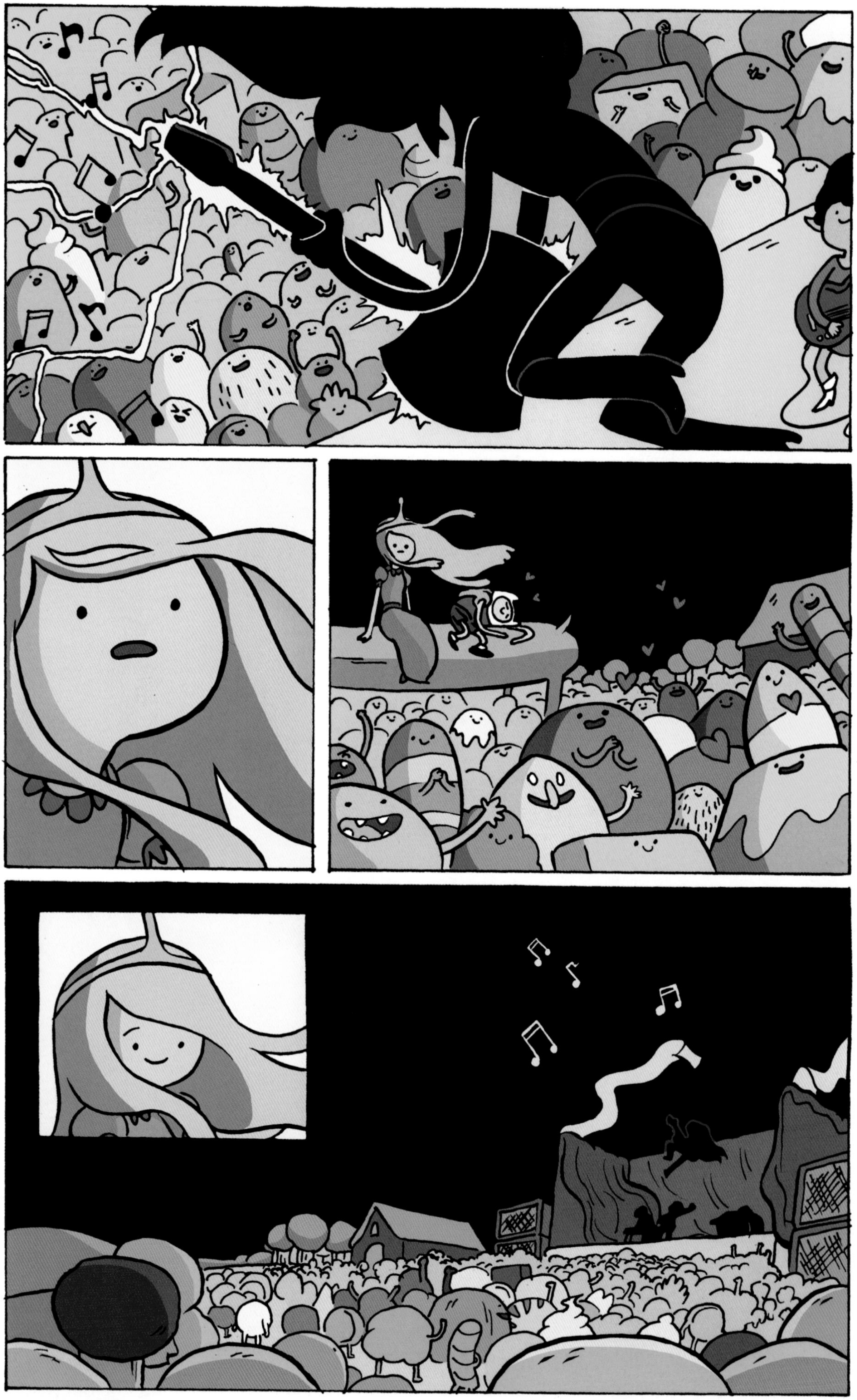

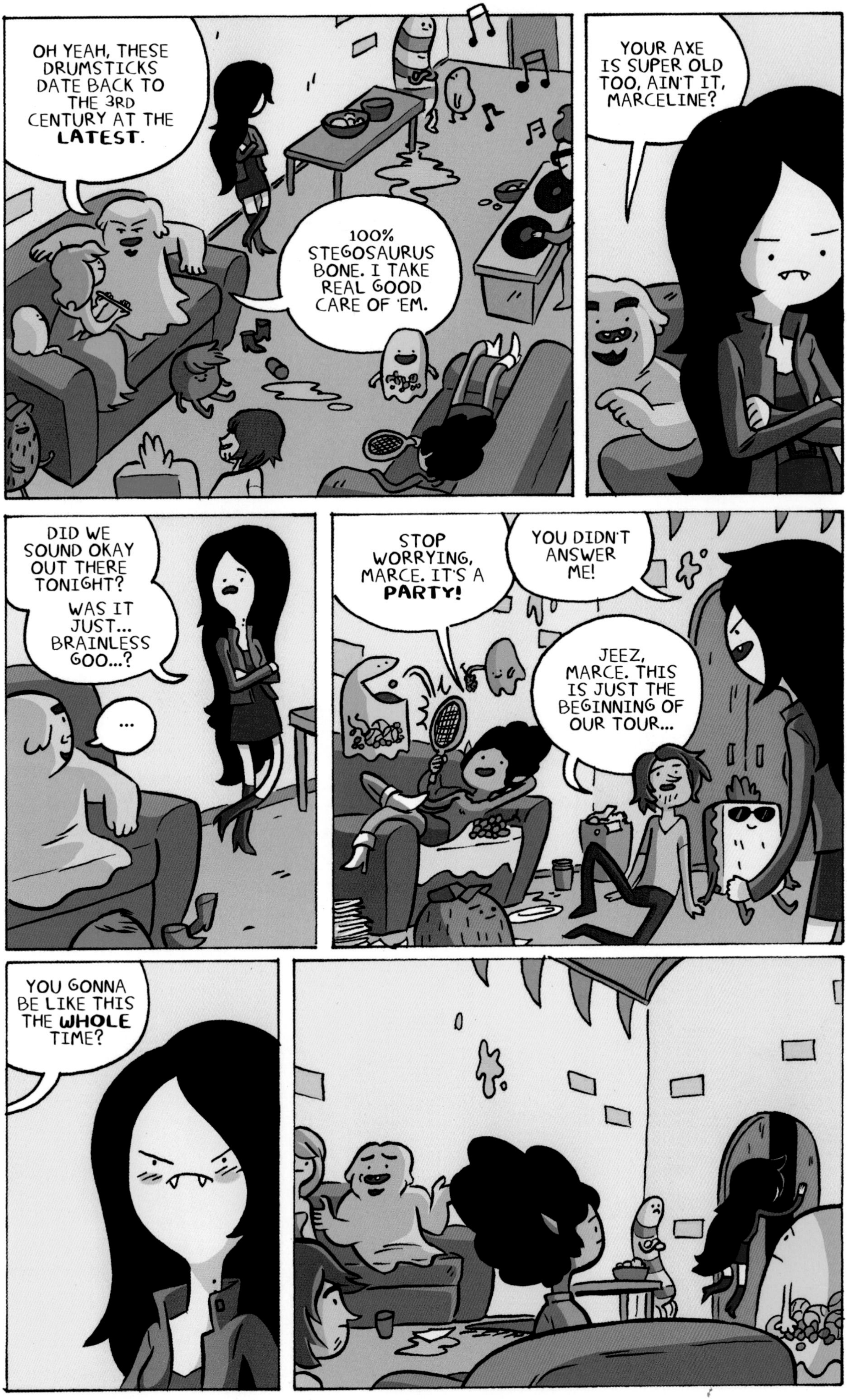

OH YEAH, THESE DRUMSTICKS DATE BACK TO THE 3RD CENTURY AT THE **LATEST**.
100% STEGOSAURUS BONE. I TAKE REAL GOOD CARE OF 'EM.
YOUR AXE IS SUPER OLD TOO, AIN'T IT, MARCELINE?
DID WE SOUND OKAY OUT THERE TONIGHT?
WAS IT JUST... BRAINLESS GOO...?
...
STOP WORRYING, MARCE. IT'S A **PARTY!**
YOU DIDN'T ANSWER ME!
JEEZ, MARCE. THIS IS JUST THE BEGINNING OF OUR TOUR...
YOU GONNA BE LIKE THIS THE **WHOLE** TIME?

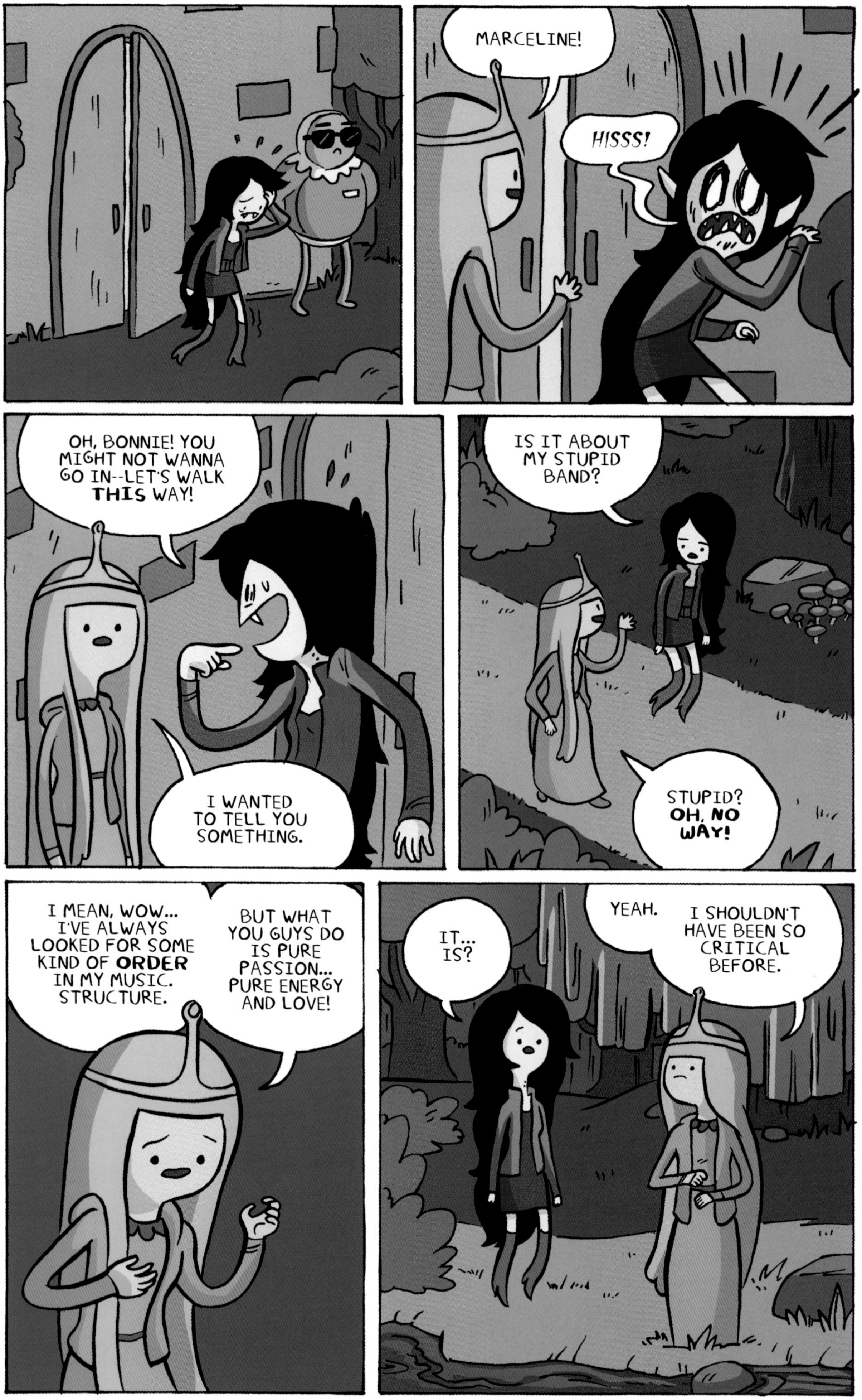

MARCELINE!
HISSS!
OH, BONNIE! YOU MIGHT NOT WANNA GO IN--LET'S WALK **THIS** WAY!
I WANTED TO TELL YOU SOMETHING.
IS IT ABOUT MY STUPID BAND?
STUPID? **OH, NO WAY!**
I MEAN, WOW... I'VE ALWAYS LOOKED FOR SOME KIND OF **ORDER** IN MY MUSIC. STRUCTURE.
BUT WHAT YOU GUYS DO IS PURE PASSION... PURE ENERGY AND LOVE!
IT... IS?
YEAH.
I SHOULDN'T HAVE BEEN SO CRITICAL BEFORE.

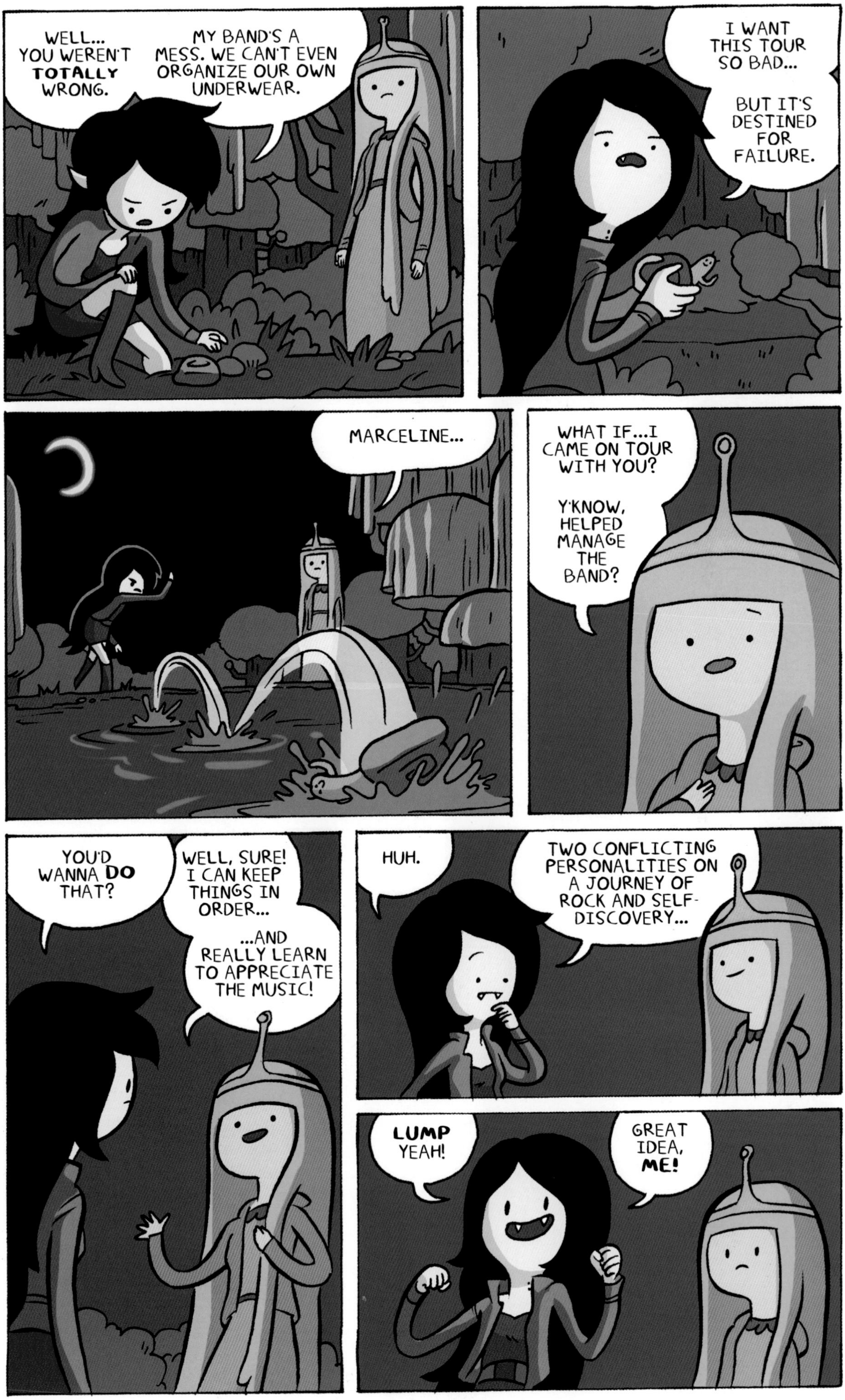
WELL... YOU WEREN'T **TOTALLY** WRONG.
MY BAND'S A MESS. WE CAN'T EVEN ORGANIZE OUR OWN UNDERWEAR.
I WANT THIS TOUR SO BAD...
BUT IT'S DESTINED FOR FAILURE.
MARCELINE...
WHAT IF...I CAME ON TOUR WITH YOU?
Y'KNOW, HELPED MANAGE THE BAND?
YOU'D WANNA **DO** THAT?
WELL, SURE! I CAN KEEP THINGS IN ORDER...
...AND REALLY LEARN TO APPRECIATE THE MUSIC!
HUH.
TWO CONFLICTING PERSONALITIES ON A JOURNEY OF ROCK AND SELF-DISCOVERY...
LUMP YEAH!
GREAT IDEA, **ME!**

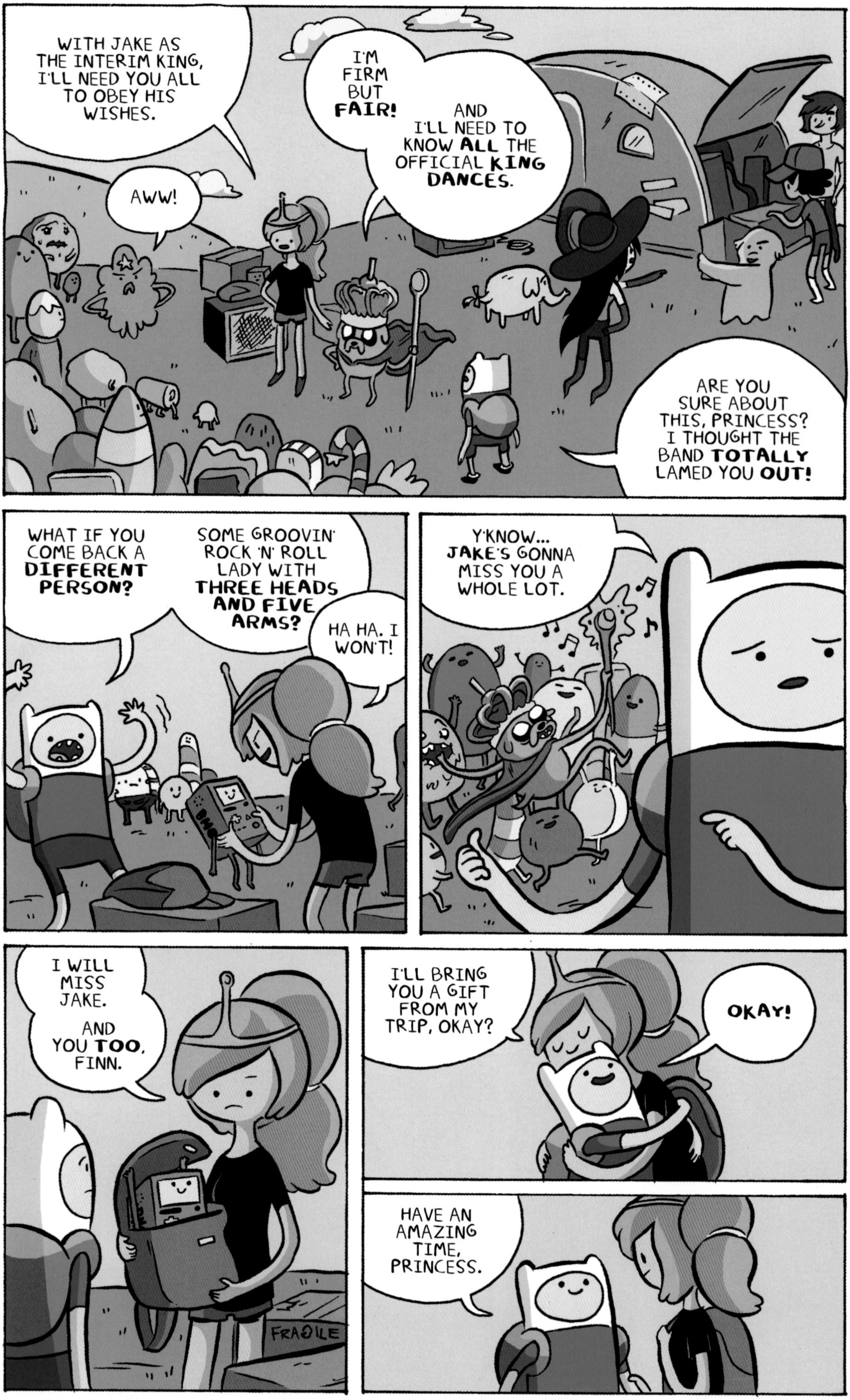
WITH JAKE AS THE INTERIM KING, I'LL NEED YOU ALL TO OBEY HIS WISHES.
I'M FIRM BUT FAIR!
AND I'LL NEED TO KNOW ALL THE OFFICIAL KING DANCES.
AWW!
ARE YOU SURE ABOUT THIS, PRINCESS? I THOUGHT THE BAND TOTALLY LAMED YOU OUT!
WHAT IF YOU COME BACK A DIFFERENT PERSON?
SOME GROOVIN' ROCK 'N' ROLL LADY WITH THREE HEADS AND FIVE ARMS?
HA HA. I WON'T!
Y'KNOW... JAKE'S GONNA MISS YOU A WHOLE LOT.
I WILL MISS JAKE.
AND YOU TOO, FINN.
FRAGILE
I'LL BRING YOU A GIFT FROM MY TRIP, OKAY?
OKAY!
HAVE AN AMAZING TIME, PRINCESS.

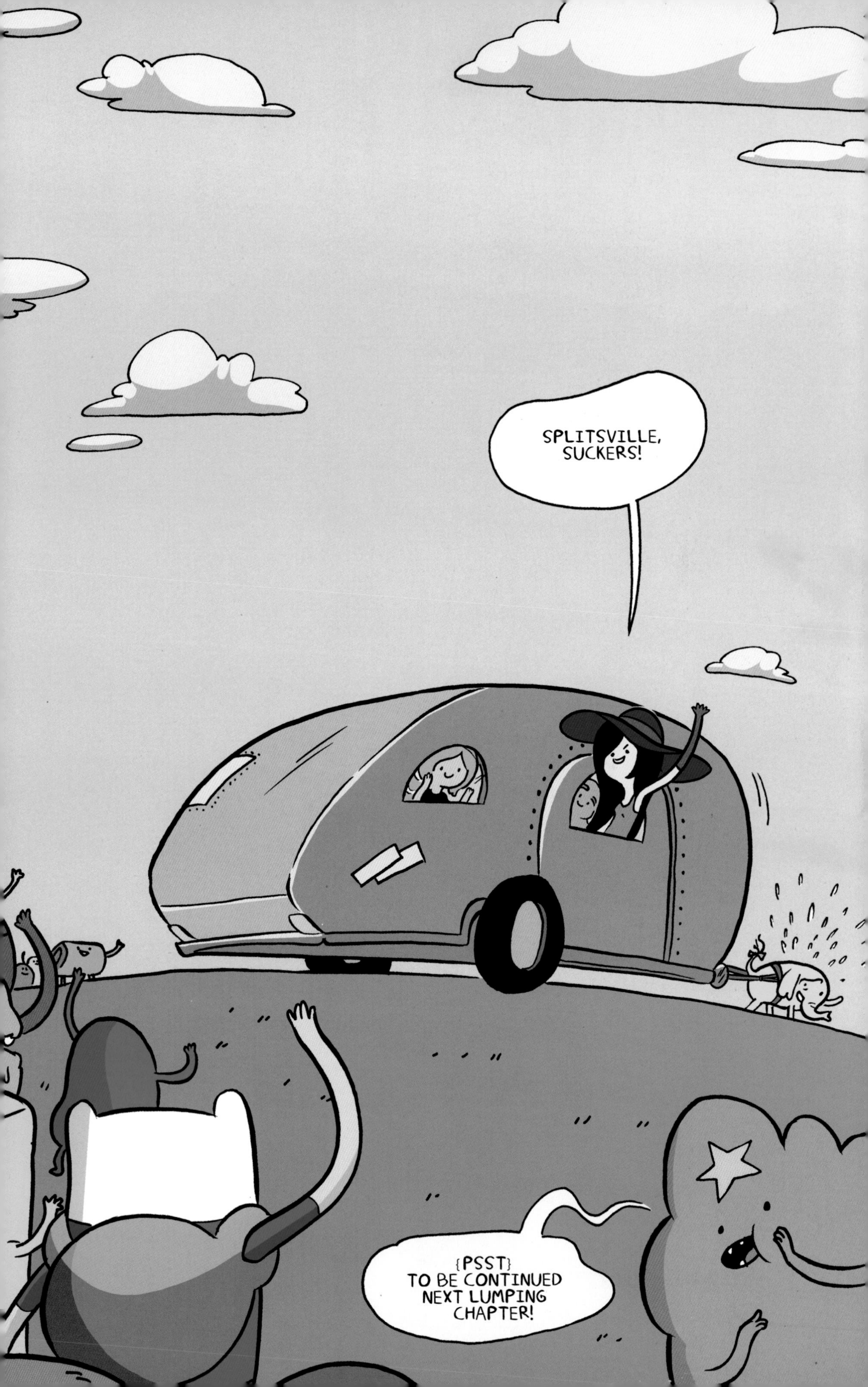
SPLITSVILLE, SUCKERS!
{PSST} TO BE CONTINUED NEXT LUMPING CHAPTER!

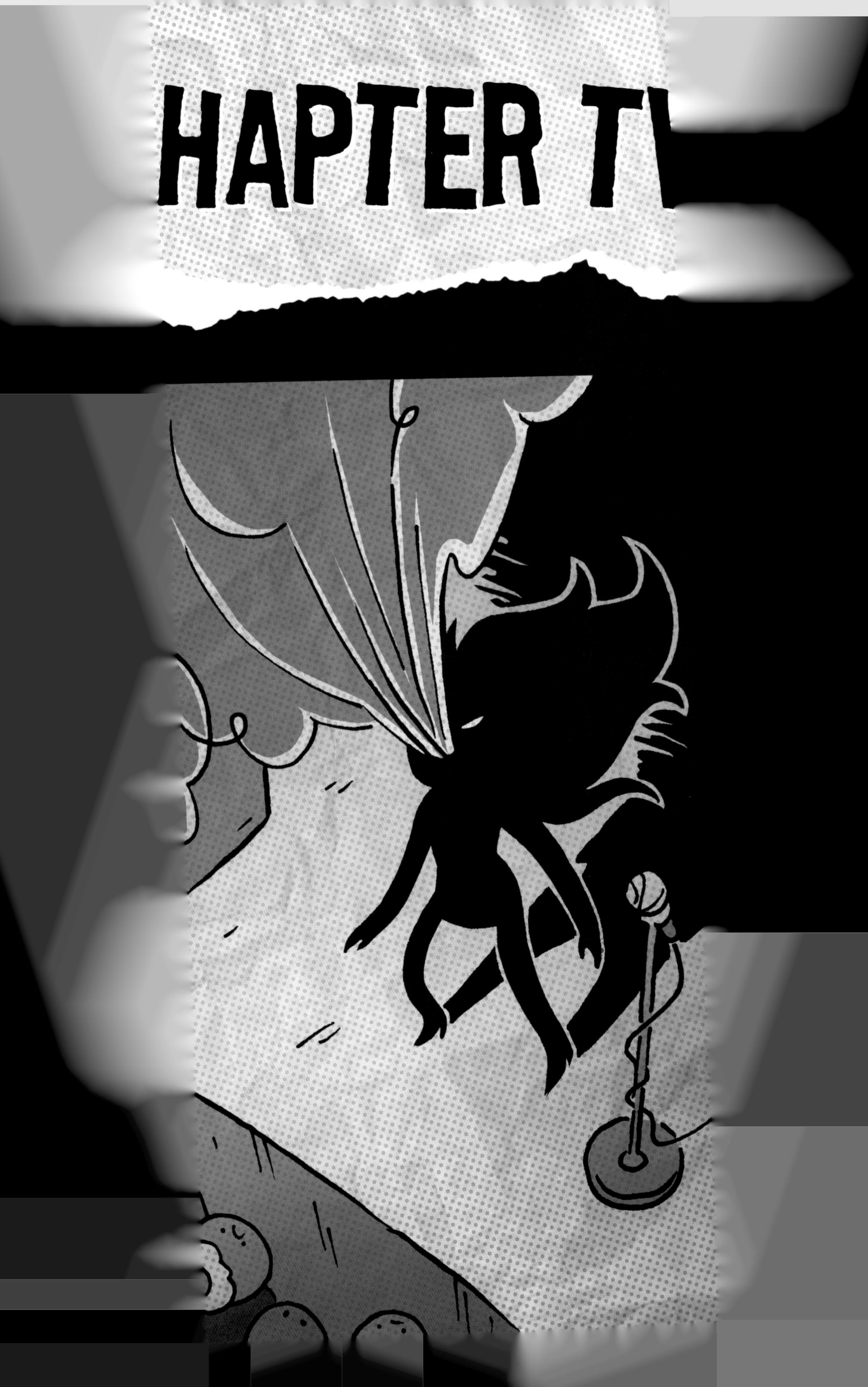
HAPTER T

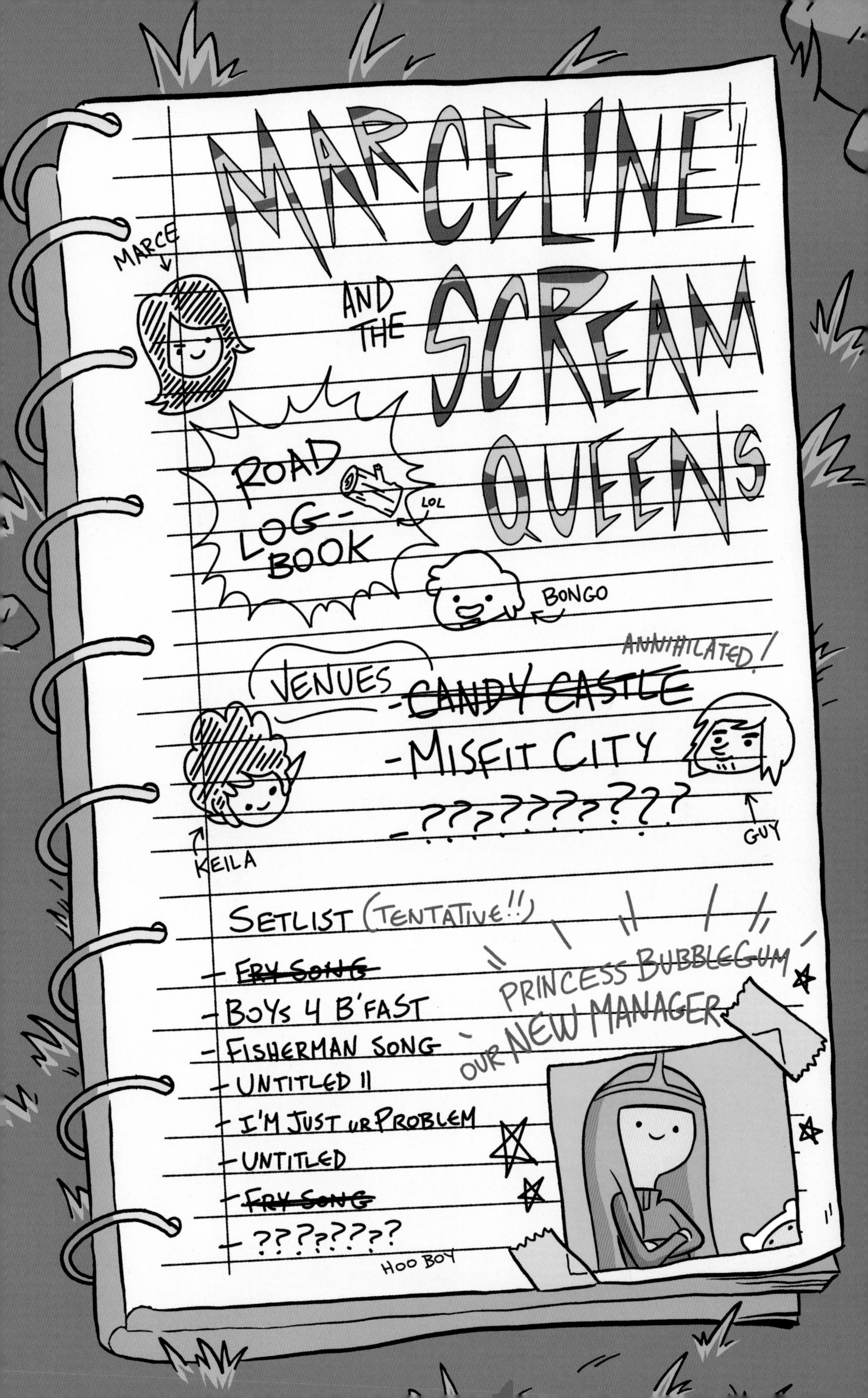

MARCELINE AND THE SCREAM QUEENS
MARCE
ROAD LOG BOOK
LOL
BONGO
VENUES
-CANDY CASTLE
ANNIHILATED!
-MISFIT CITY
-??????????
KEILA
GUY
SETLIST (TENTATIVE!!)
-FRY SONG
-BOYS 4 B'FAST
-FISHERMAN SONG
-UNTITLED II
-I'M JUST UR PROBLEM
-UNTITLED
-FRY SONG
-????????
HOO BOY
PRINCESS BUBBLEGUM
OUR NEW MANAGER

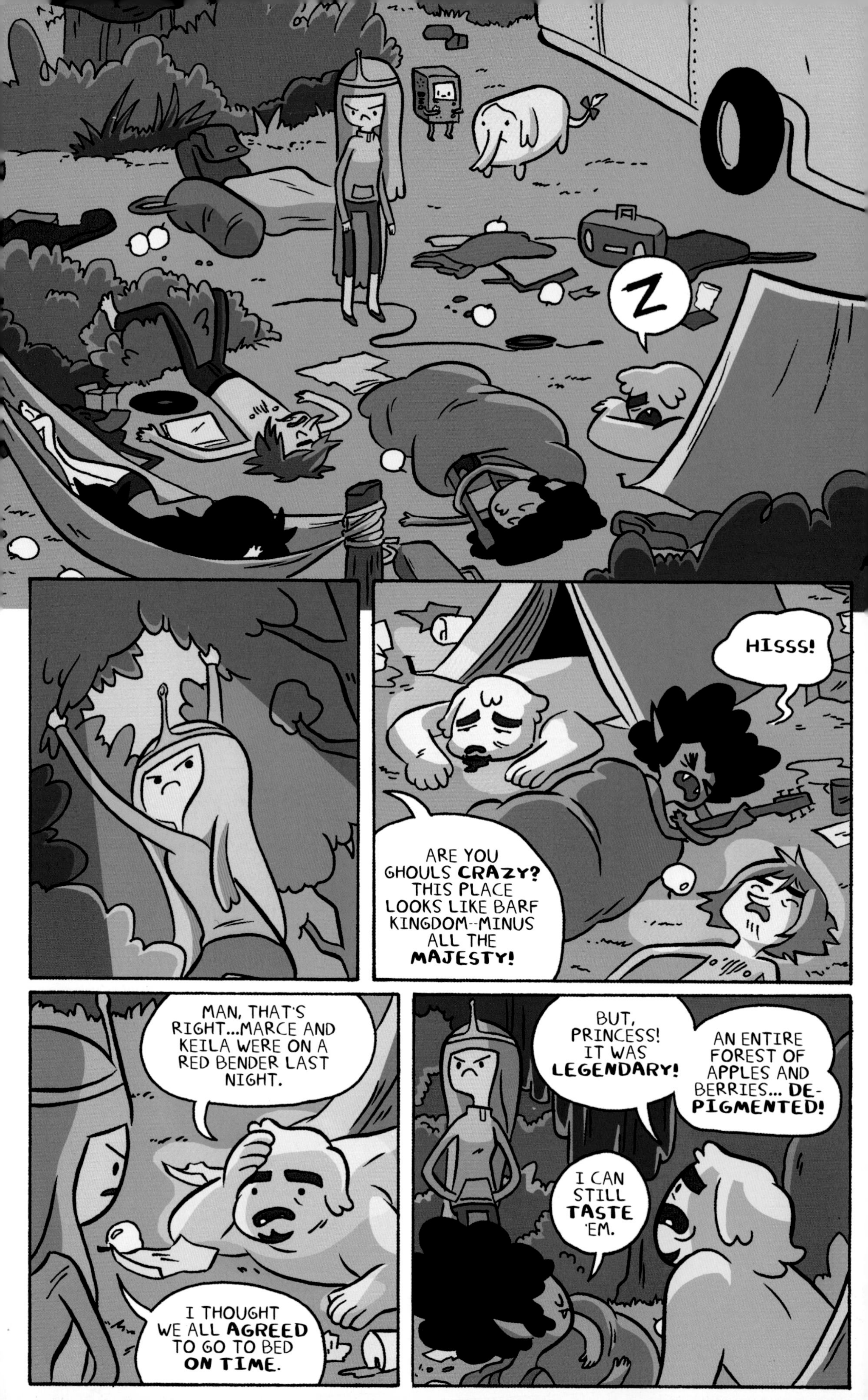
Z
HISSS!
ARE YOU GHOULS CRAZY? THIS PLACE LOOKS LIKE BARF KINGDOM--MINUS ALL THE MAJESTY!
MAN, THAT'S RIGHT...MARCE AND KEILA WERE ON A RED BENDER LAST NIGHT.
I THOUGHT WE ALL AGREED TO GO TO BED ON TIME.
BUT, PRINCESS! IT WAS LEGENDARY!
AN ENTIRE FOREST OF APPLES AND BERRIES... DE-PIGMENTED!
I CAN STILL TASTE 'EM.

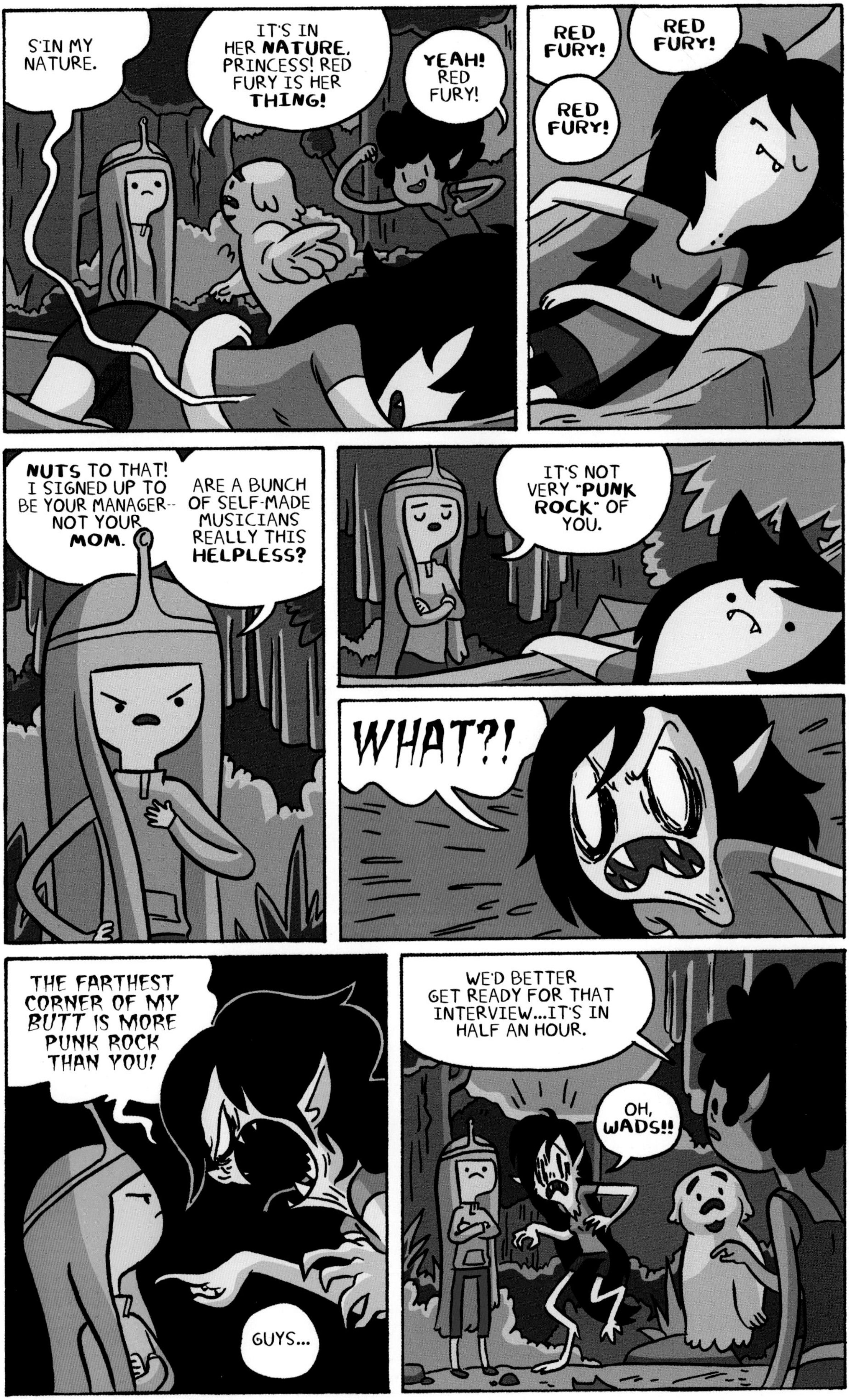

S'IN MY NATURE.
IT'S IN HER NATURE, PRINCESS! RED FURY IS HER THING!
YEAH! RED FURY!
RED FURY!
RED FURY!
RED FURY!
NUTS TO THAT! I SIGNED UP TO BE YOUR MANAGER-- NOT YOUR MOM.
ARE A BUNCH OF SELF-MADE MUSICIANS REALLY THIS HELPLESS?
IT'S NOT VERY "PUNK ROCK" OF YOU.
WHAT?!
THE FARTHEST CORNER OF MY BUTT IS MORE PUNK ROCK THAN YOU!
GUYS...
WE'D BETTER GET READY FOR THAT INTERVIEW...IT'S IN HALF AN HOUR.
OH, WADS!!

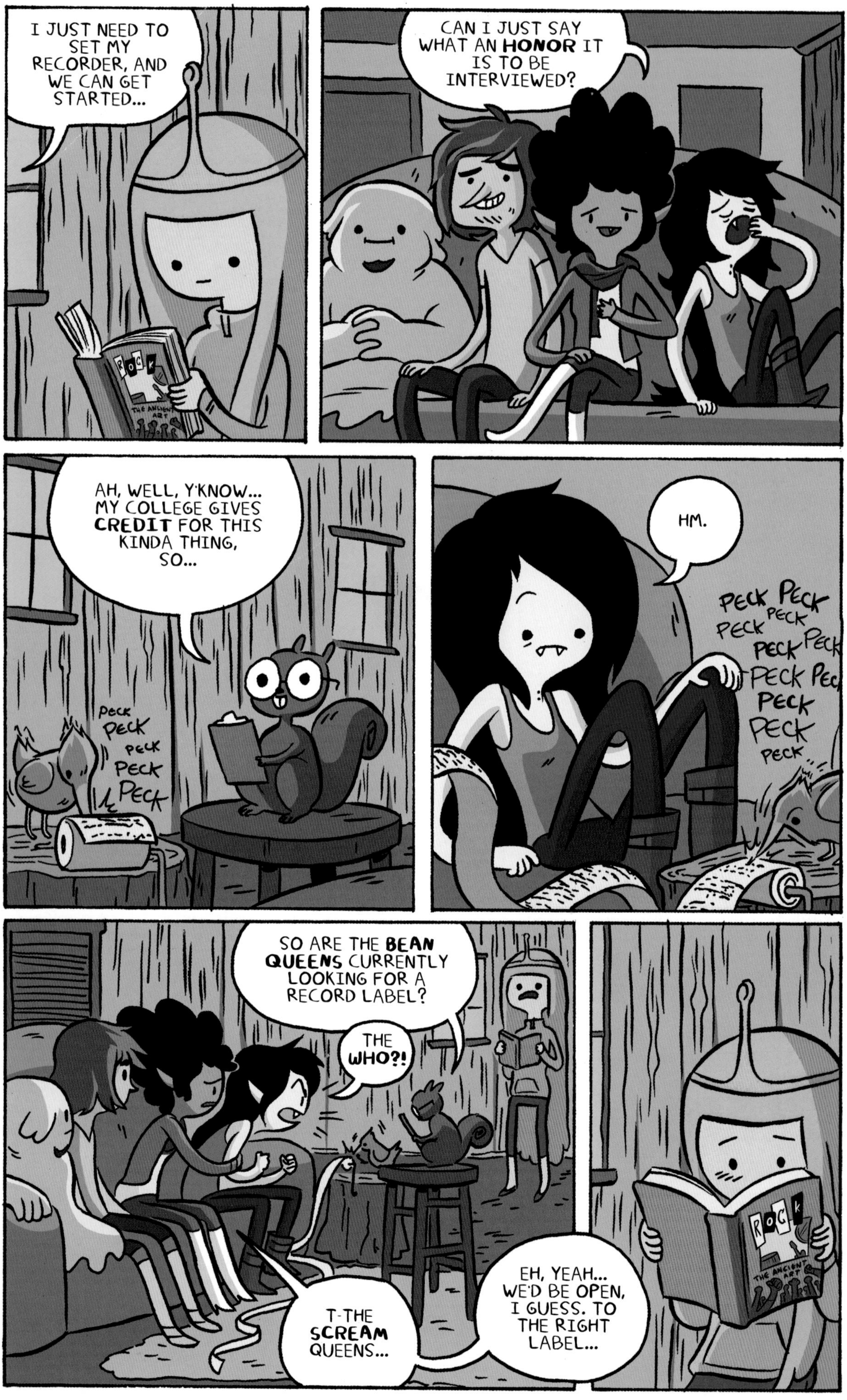
I JUST NEED TO SET MY RECORDER, AND WE CAN GET STARTED...
ROCK
THE ANCIENT ART
CAN I JUST SAY WHAT AN **HONOR** IT IS TO BE INTERVIEWED?
AH, WELL, Y'KNOW... MY COLLEGE GIVES **CREDIT** FOR THIS KINDA THING, SO...
PECK PECK PECK PECK PECK
HM.
PECK PECK PECK PECK PECK PECK PECK PECK PECK PECK PECK PECK
SO ARE THE **BEAN QUEENS** CURRENTLY LOOKING FOR A RECORD LABEL?
THE **WHO?!**
T-THE **SCREAM** QUEENS...
EH, YEAH... WE'D BE OPEN, I GUESS. TO THE RIGHT LABEL...
ROCK
THE ANCIENT ART

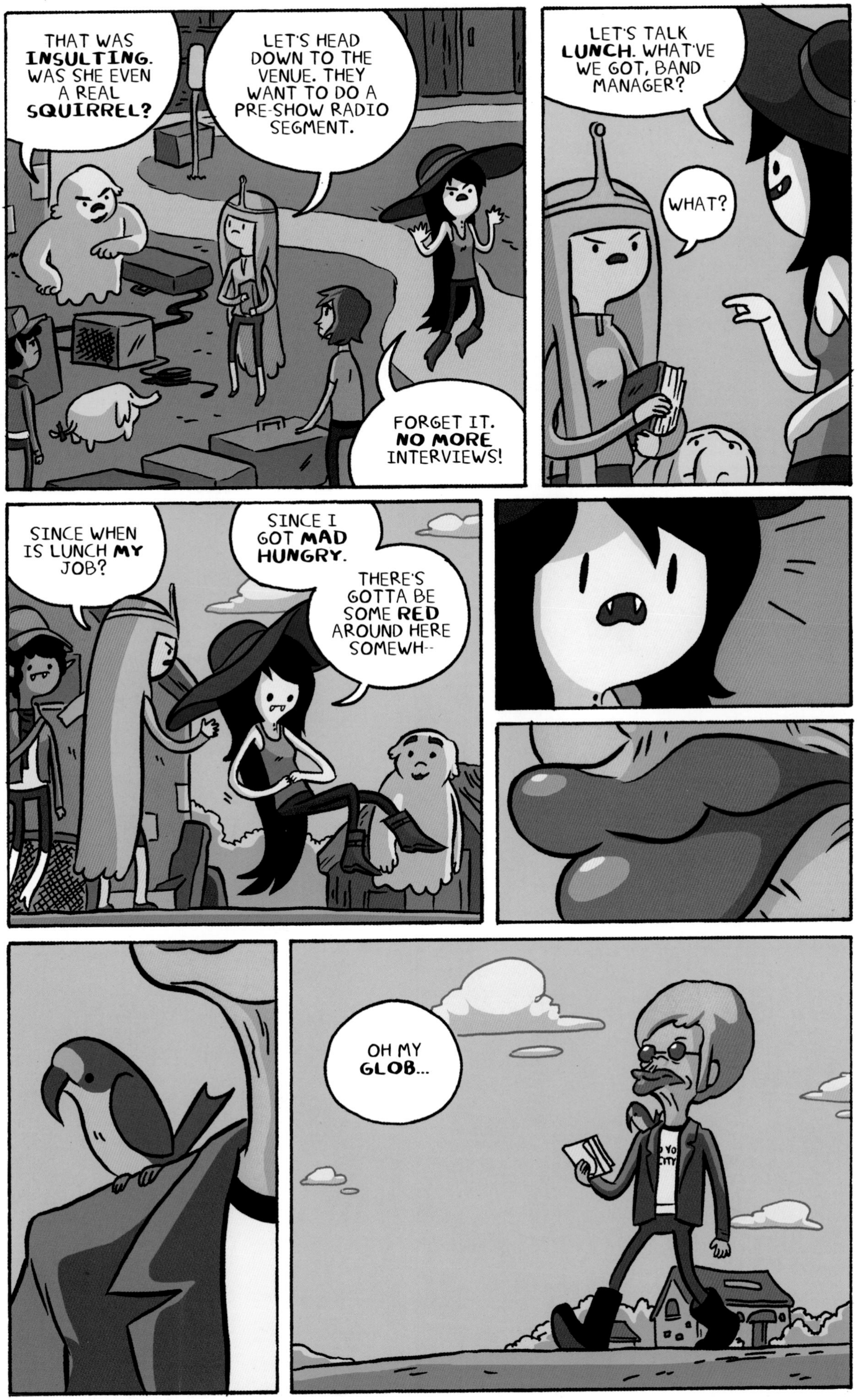
THAT WAS **INSULTING**. WAS SHE EVEN A REAL **SQUIRREL?**
LET'S HEAD DOWN TO THE VENUE. THEY WANT TO DO A PRE-SHOW RADIO SEGMENT.
FORGET IT. **NO MORE** INTERVIEWS!
LET'S TALK **LUNCH**. WHAT'VE WE GOT, BAND MANAGER?
WHAT?
SINCE WHEN IS LUNCH **MY** JOB?
SINCE I GOT **MAD HUNGRY**.
THERE'S GOTTA BE SOME **RED** AROUND HERE SOMEWH--
OH MY **GLOB**...

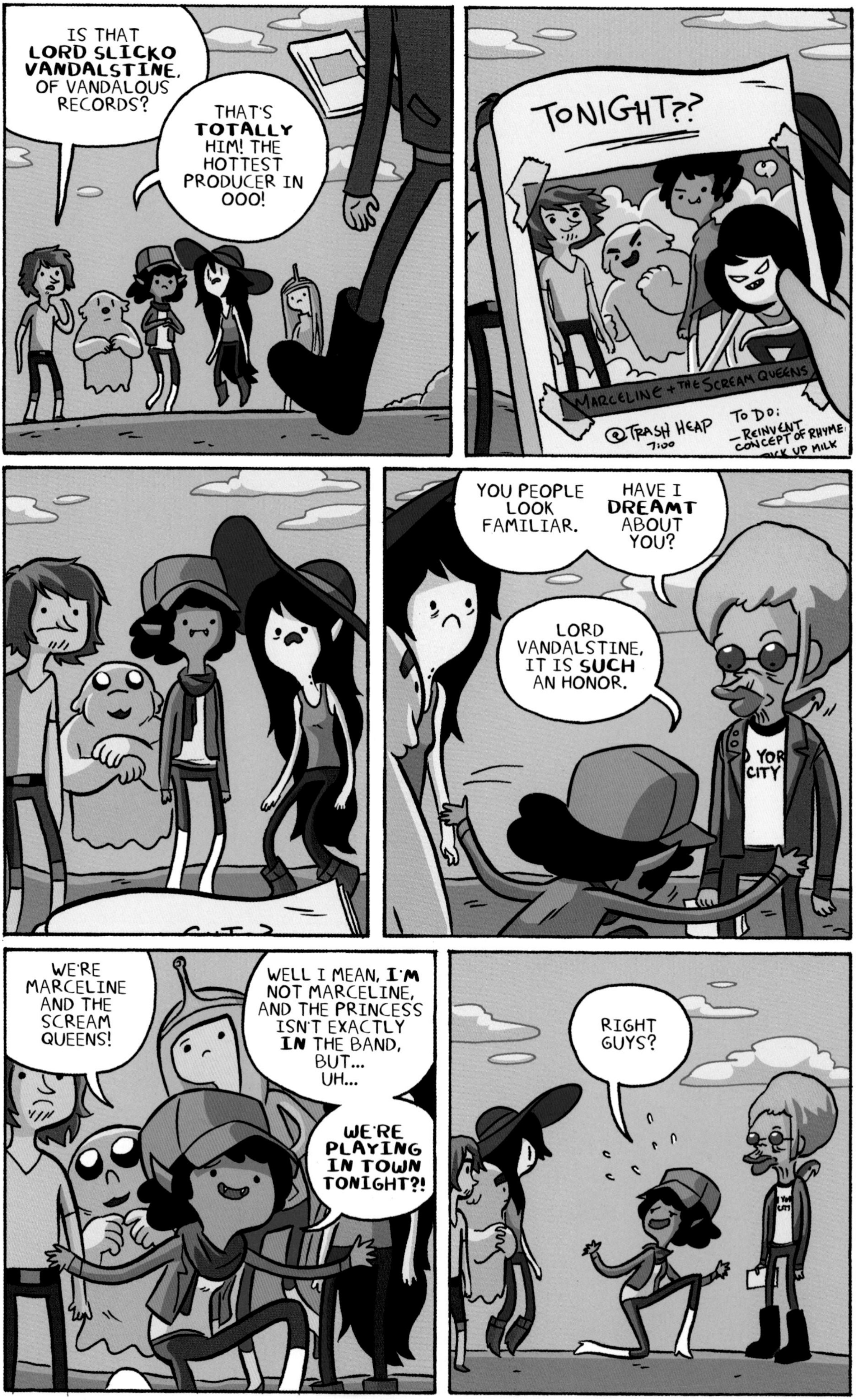
IS THAT **LORD SLICKO VANDALSTINE**, OF VANDALOUS RECORDS?
THAT'S **TOTALLY** HIM! THE HOTTEST PRODUCER IN OOO!
TONIGHT??
MARCELINE + THE SCREAM QUEENS
@ TRASH HEAP 7:00
TO DO: —REINVENT CONCEPT OF RHYME
YOU PEOPLE LOOK FAMILIAR.
HAVE I **DREAMT** ABOUT YOU?
LORD VANDALSTINE, IT IS **SUCH** AN HONOR.
WE'RE MARCELINE AND THE SCREAM QUEENS!
WELL I MEAN, **I'M** NOT MARCELINE, AND THE PRINCESS ISN'T EXACTLY **IN** THE BAND, BUT... UH...
WE'RE PLAYING IN TOWN TONIGHT?!
RIGHT GUYS?

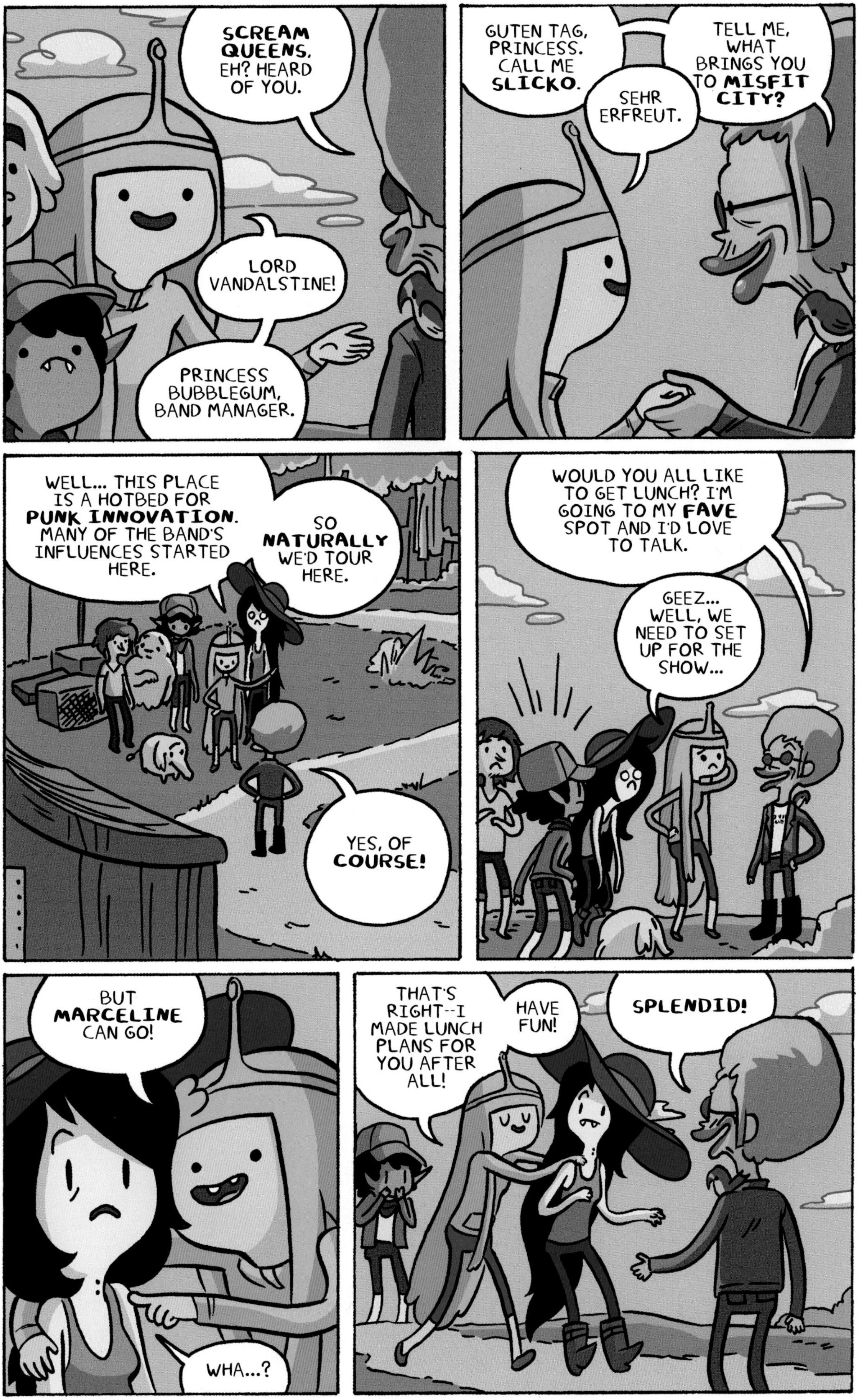
SCREAM QUEENS, EH? HEARD OF YOU.
LORD VANDALSTINE!
PRINCESS BUBBLEGUM, BAND MANAGER.
GUTEN TAG, PRINCESS. CALL ME SLICKO.
SEHR ERFREUT.
TELL ME, WHAT BRINGS YOU TO MISFIT CITY?
WELL... THIS PLACE IS A HOTBED FOR PUNK INNOVATION. MANY OF THE BAND'S INFLUENCES STARTED HERE.
SO NATURALLY WE'D TOUR HERE.
YES, OF COURSE!
WOULD YOU ALL LIKE TO GET LUNCH? I'M GOING TO MY FAVE SPOT AND I'D LOVE TO TALK.
GEEZ... WELL, WE NEED TO SET UP FOR THE SHOW...
BUT MARCELINE CAN GO!
WHA...?
THAT'S RIGHT--I MADE LUNCH PLANS FOR YOU AFTER ALL!
HAVE FUN!
SPLENDID!

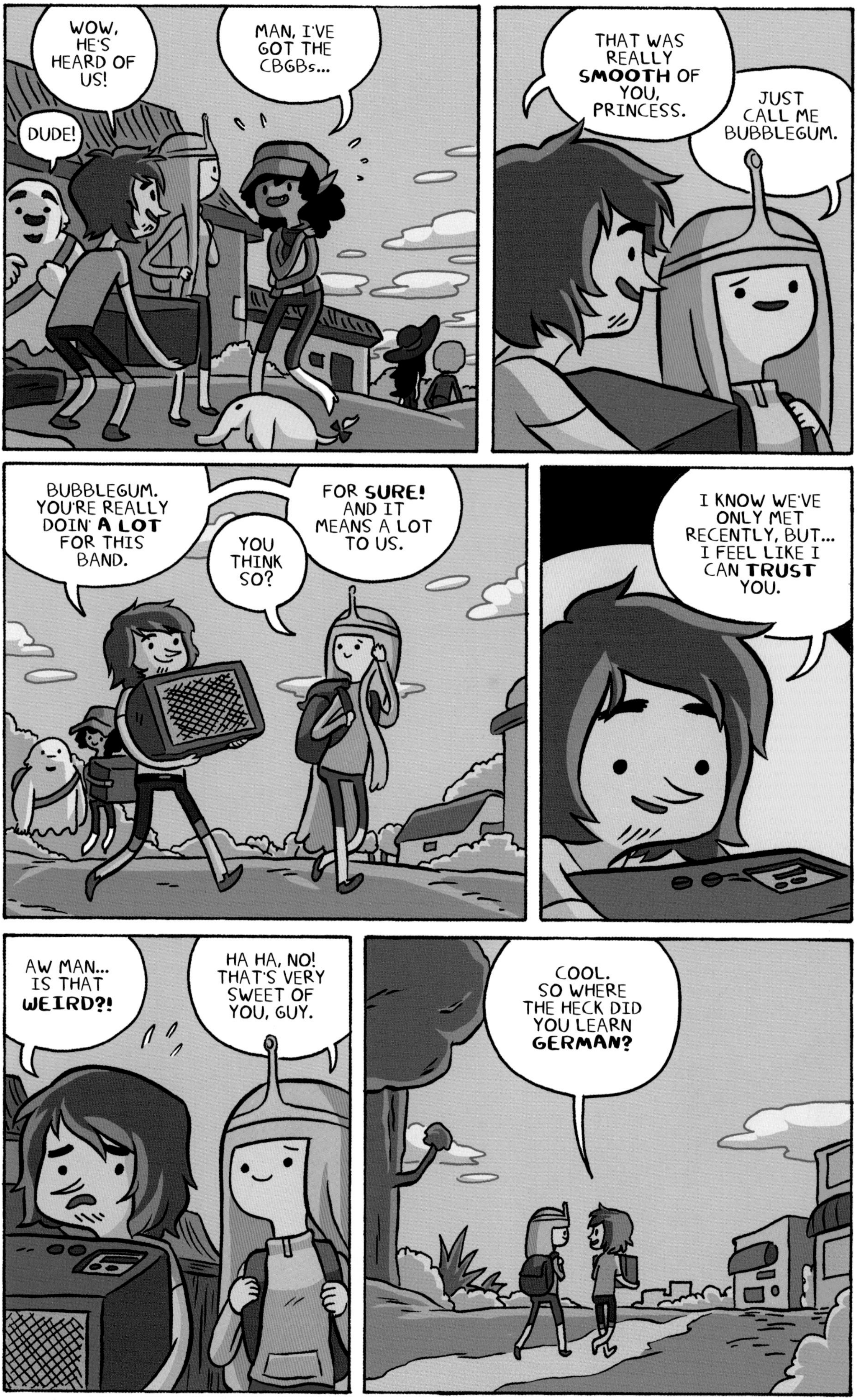

WOW, HE'S HEARD OF US!
DUDE!
MAN, I'VE GOT THE CBGBs...
THAT WAS REALLY **SMOOTH** OF YOU, PRINCESS.
JUST CALL ME BUBBLEGUM.
BUBBLEGUM. YOU'RE REALLY DOIN' **A LOT** FOR THIS BAND.
YOU THINK SO?
FOR **SURE!** AND IT MEANS A LOT TO US.
I KNOW WE'VE ONLY MET RECENTLY, BUT... I FEEL LIKE I CAN **TRUST** YOU.
AW MAN... IS THAT **WEIRD?!**
HA HA, NO! THAT'S VERY SWEET OF YOU, GUY.
COOL. SO WHERE THE HECK DID YOU LEARN **GERMAN?**

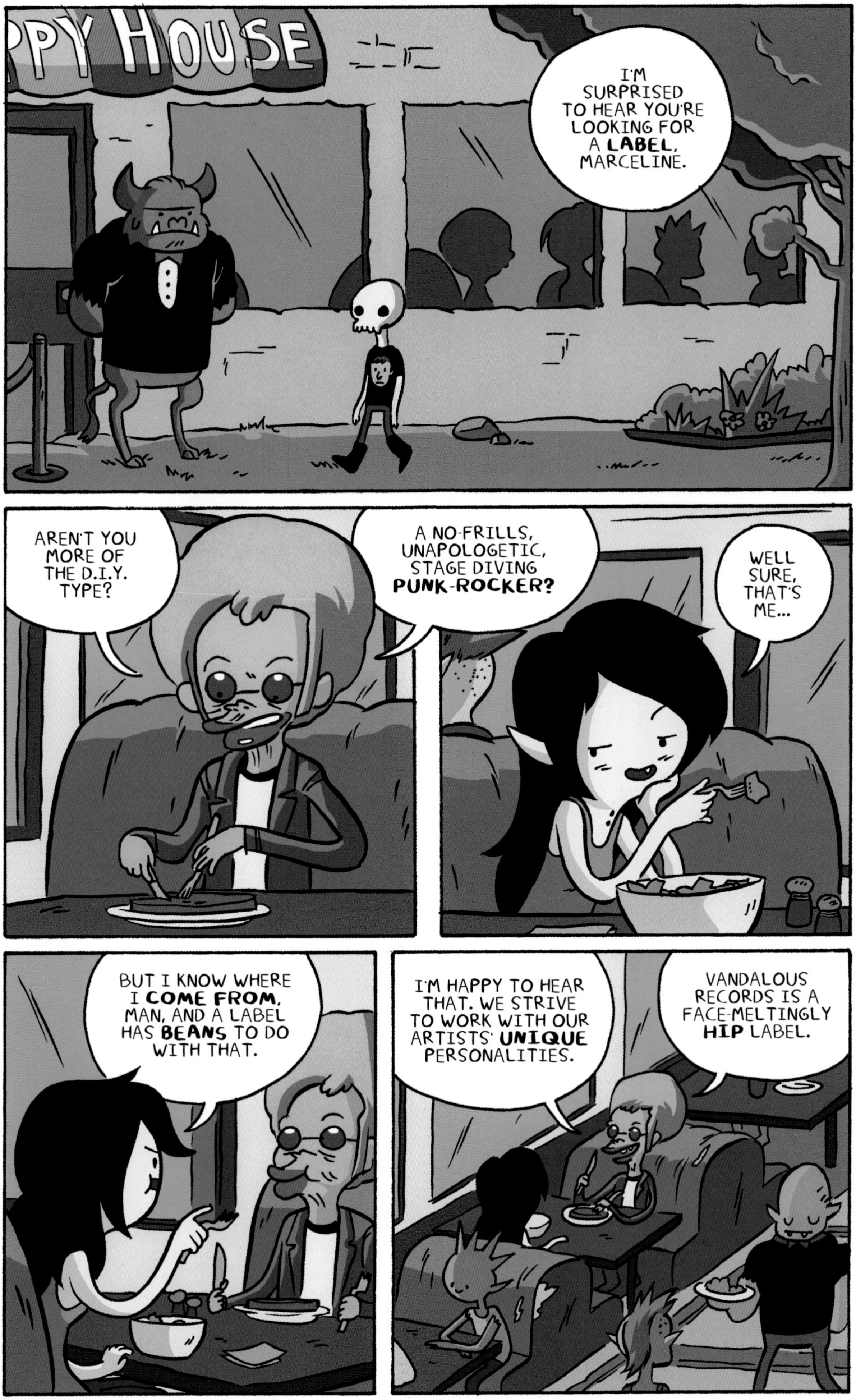
PPY HOUSE
I'M SURPRISED TO HEAR YOU'RE LOOKING FOR A **LABEL**, MARCELINE.
AREN'T YOU MORE OF THE D.I.Y. TYPE?
A NO-FRILLS, UNAPOLOGETIC, STAGE DIVING **PUNK-ROCKER?**
WELL SURE, THAT'S ME...
BUT I KNOW WHERE I **COME FROM**, MAN, AND A LABEL HAS **BEANS** TO DO WITH THAT.
I'M HAPPY TO HEAR THAT. WE STRIVE TO WORK WITH OUR ARTISTS' **UNIQUE** PERSONALITIES.
VANDALOUS RECORDS IS A FACE-MELTINGLY **HIP** LABEL.

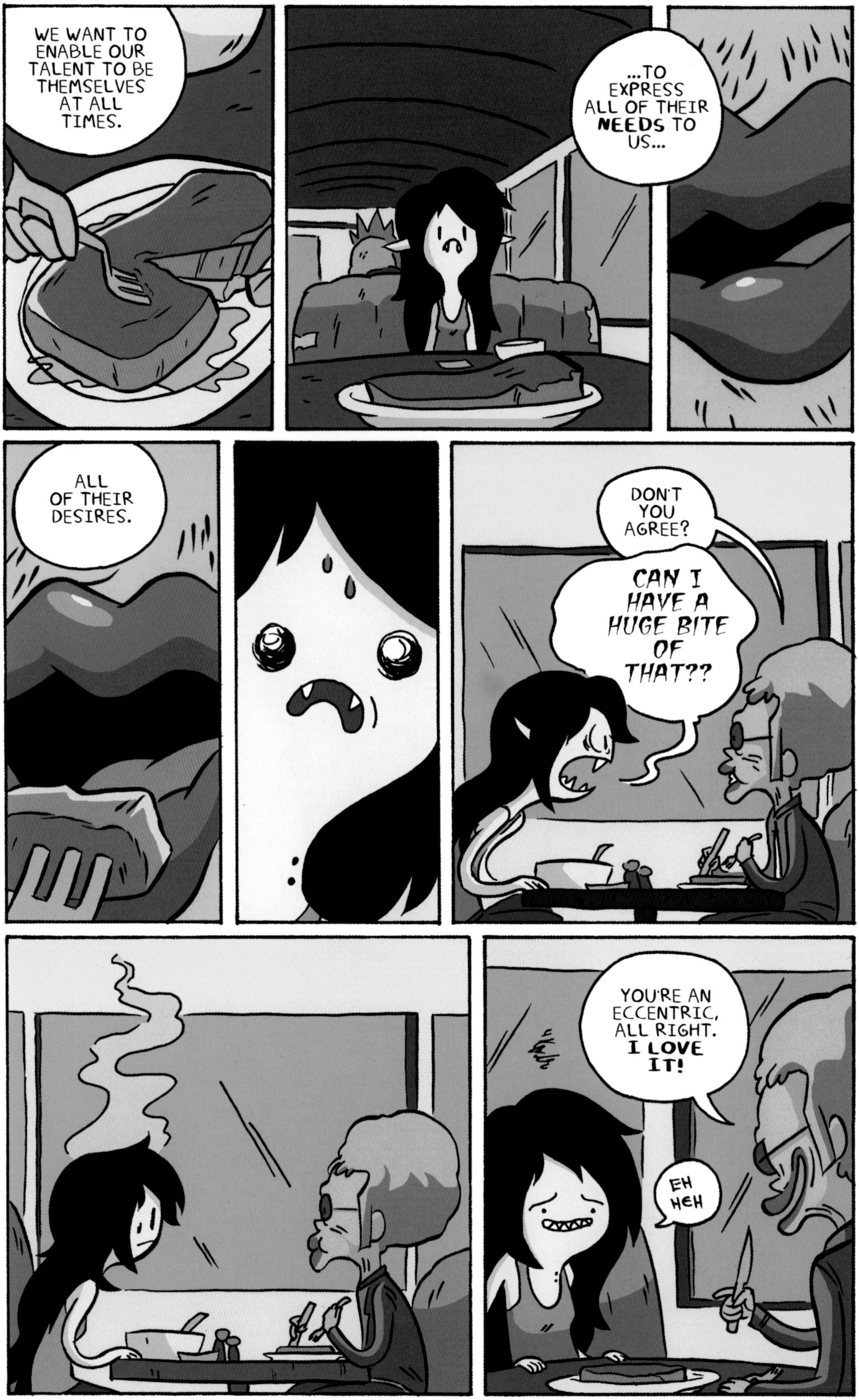
WE WANT TO ENABLE OUR TALENT TO BE THEMSELVES AT ALL TIMES.
...TO EXPRESS ALL OF THEIR NEEDS TO US...
ALL OF THEIR DESIRES.
DON'T YOU AGREE?
CAN I HAVE A HUGE BITE OF THAT??
YOU'RE AN ECCENTRIC, ALL RIGHT. I LOVE IT!
EH HEH

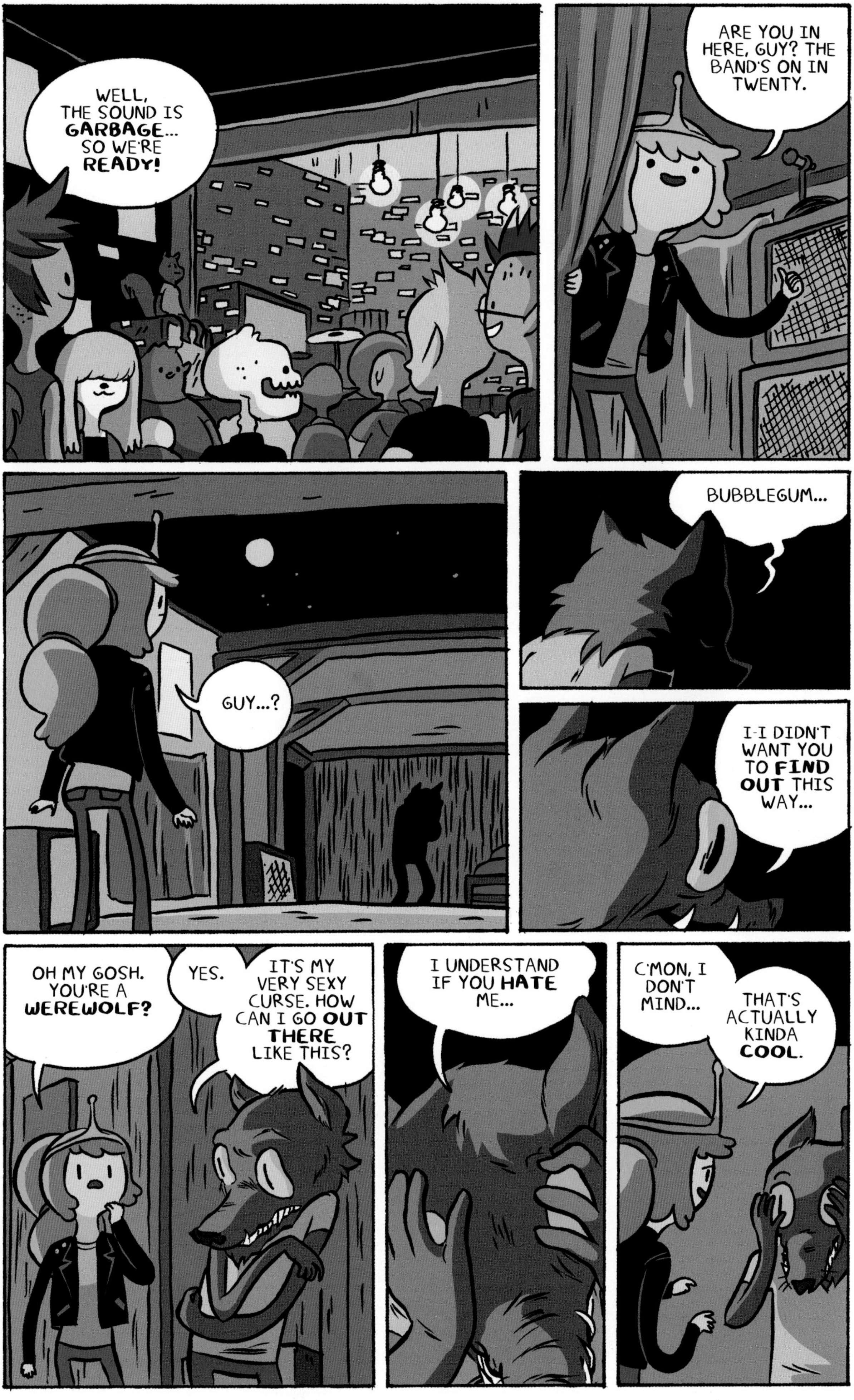
WELL, THE SOUND IS **GARBAGE**... SO WE'RE **READY!**
ARE YOU IN HERE, GUY? THE BAND'S ON IN TWENTY.
GUY...?
BUBBLEGUM...
I-I DIDN'T WANT YOU TO **FIND OUT** THIS WAY...
OH MY GOSH. YOU'RE A **WEREWOLF?**
YES.
IT'S MY VERY SEXY CURSE. HOW CAN I GO **OUT THERE** LIKE THIS?
I UNDERSTAND IF YOU **HATE** ME...
C'MON, I DON'T MIND...
THAT'S ACTUALLY KINDA **COOL**.

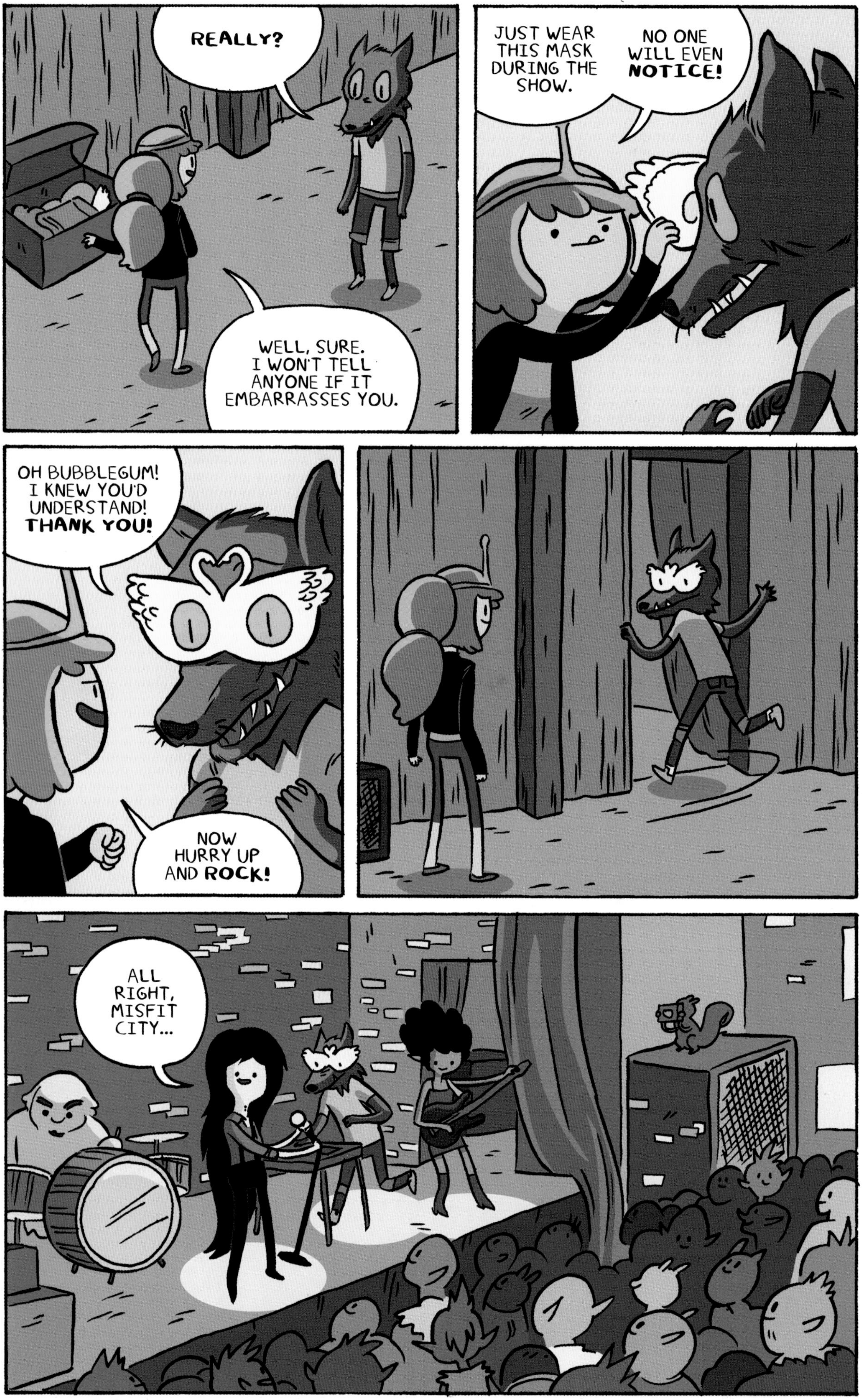
REALLY?
WELL, SURE. I WON'T TELL ANYONE IF IT EMBARRASSES YOU.
JUST WEAR THIS MASK DURING THE SHOW.
NO ONE WILL EVEN **NOTICE!**
OH BUBBLEGUM! I KNEW YOU'D UNDERSTAND! **THANK YOU!**
NOW HURRY UP AND **ROCK!**
ALL RIGHT, MISFIT CITY...

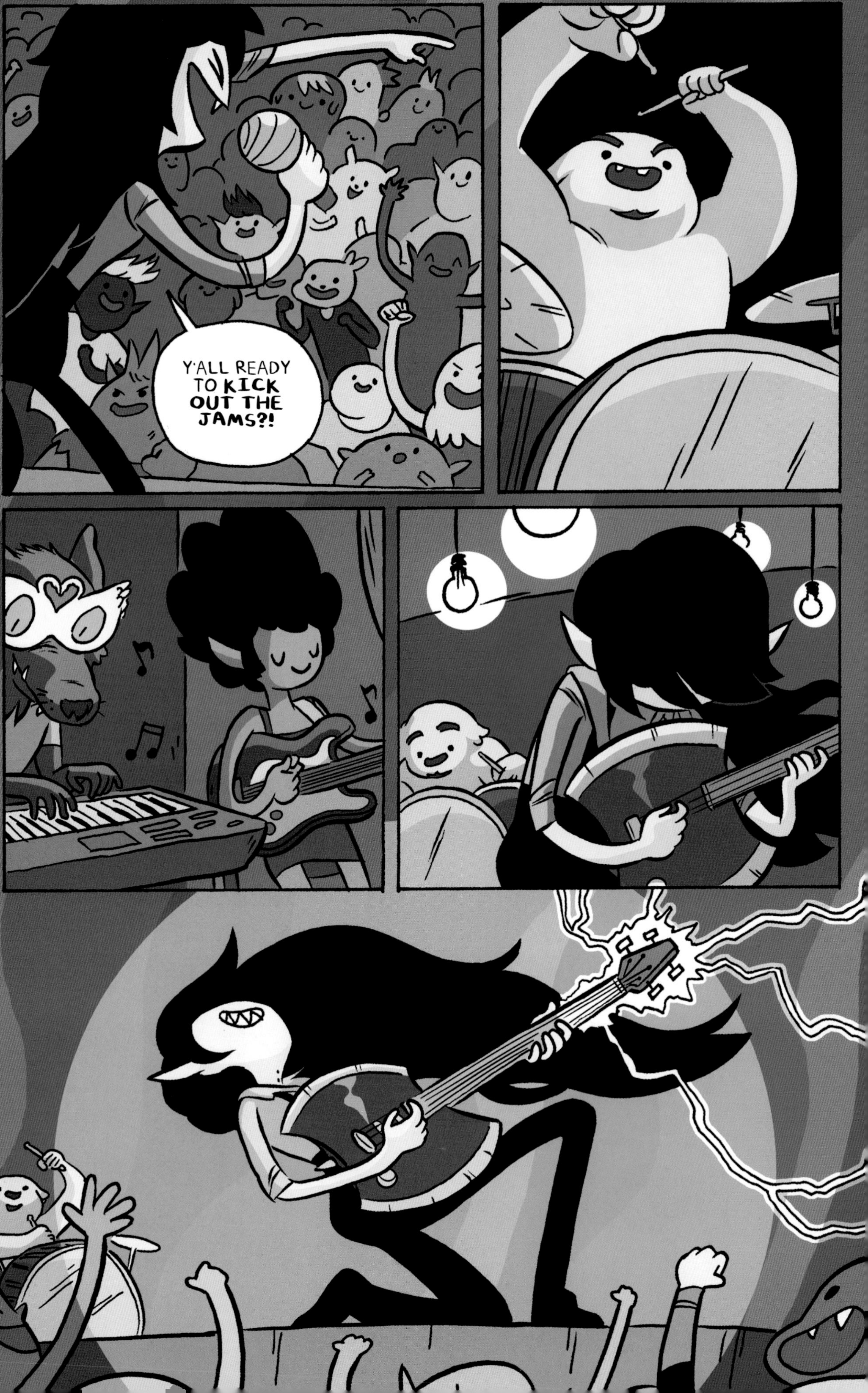
Y'ALL READY TO KICK OUT THE JAMS?!

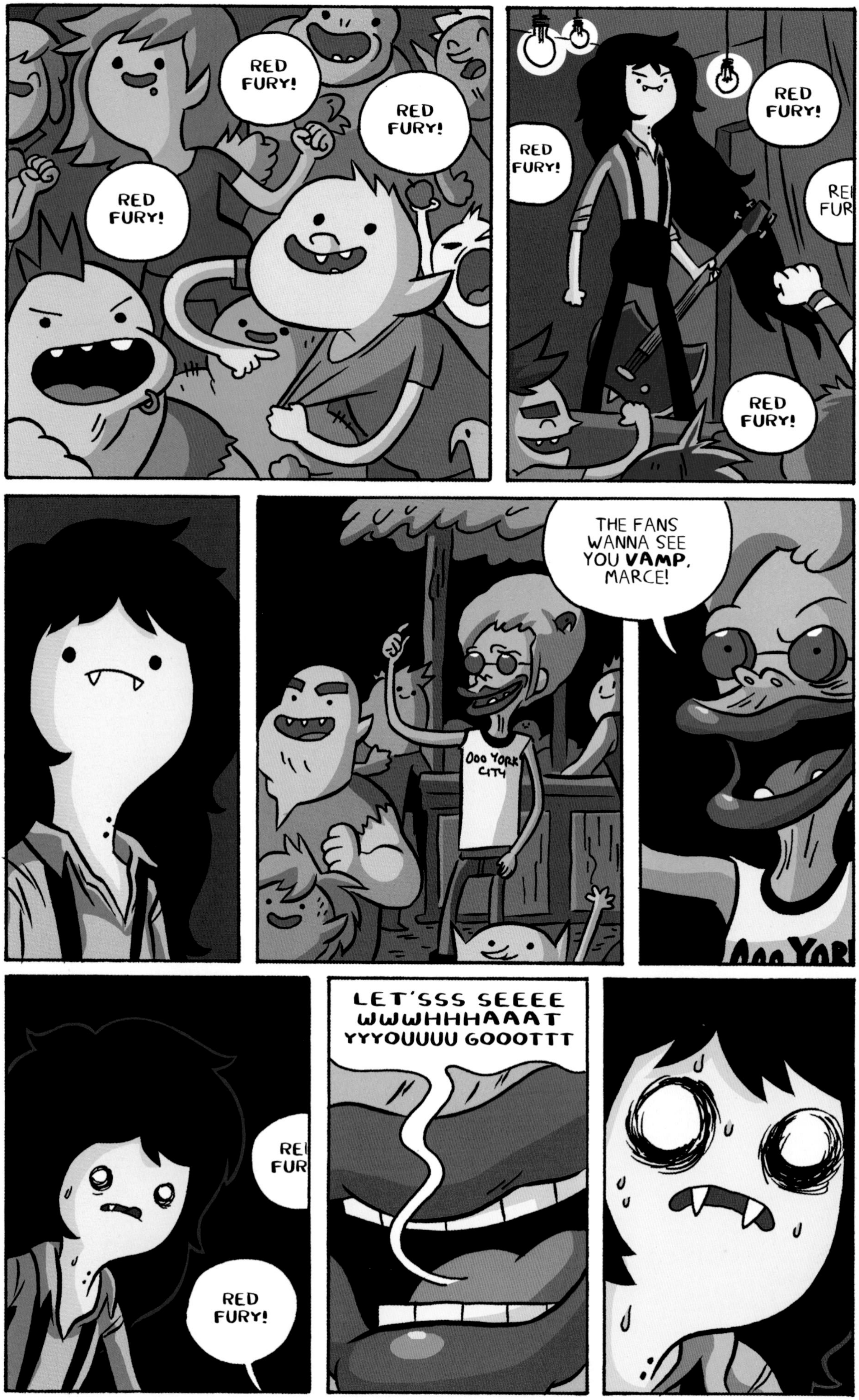
RED FURY!
RED FURY!
RED FURY!
RED FURY!
RED FURY!
RED FURY!
THE FANS WANNA SEE YOU VAMP, MARCE!
OOO YORK CITY
RED FURY!
LET'SSS SEEEE WWWHHHAAAT YYYOUUUU GOOOTTT

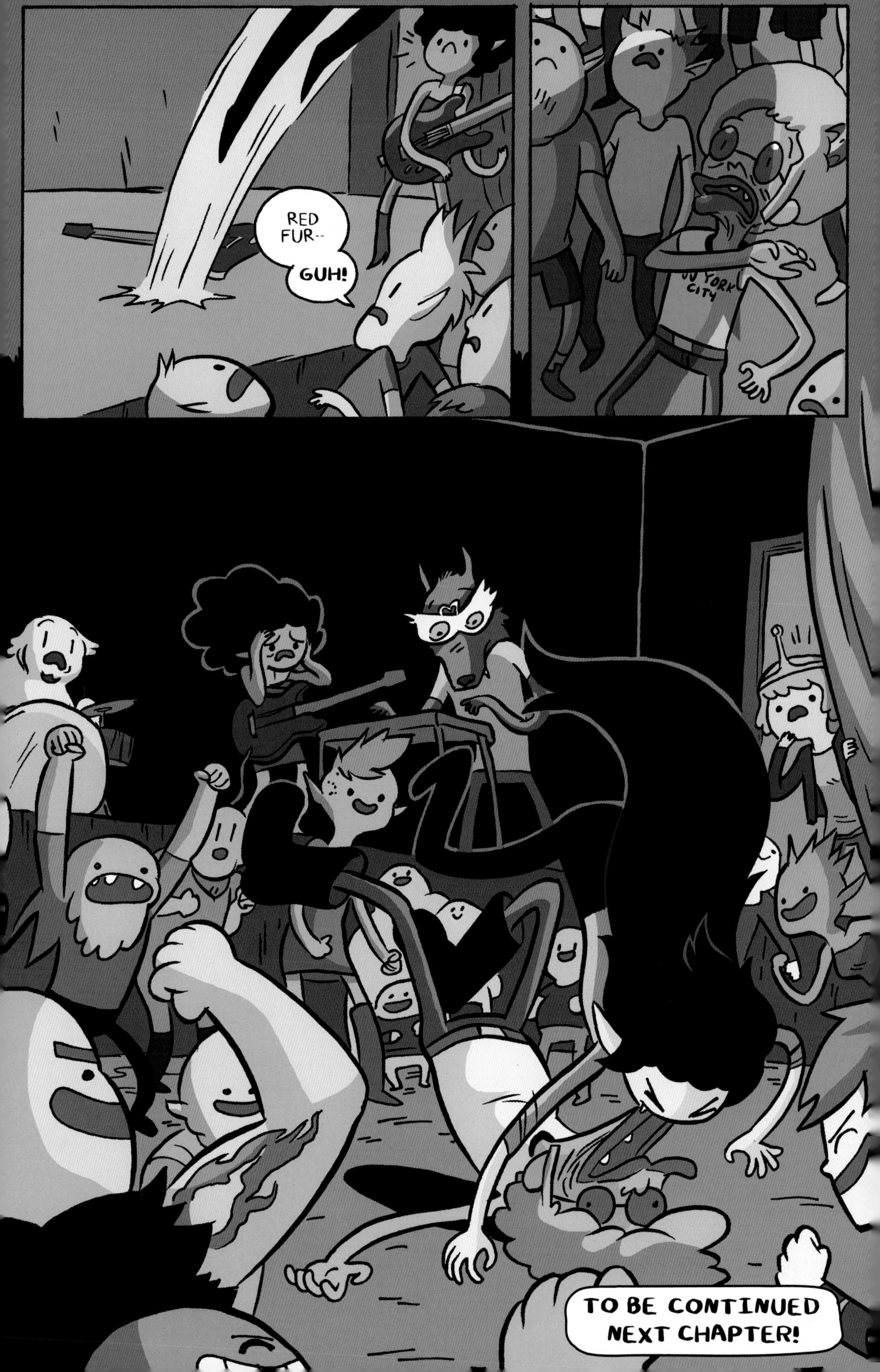
RED FUR--
GUH!
YORK CITY
TO BE CONTINUED NEXT CHAPTER!

CHAPTER THREE

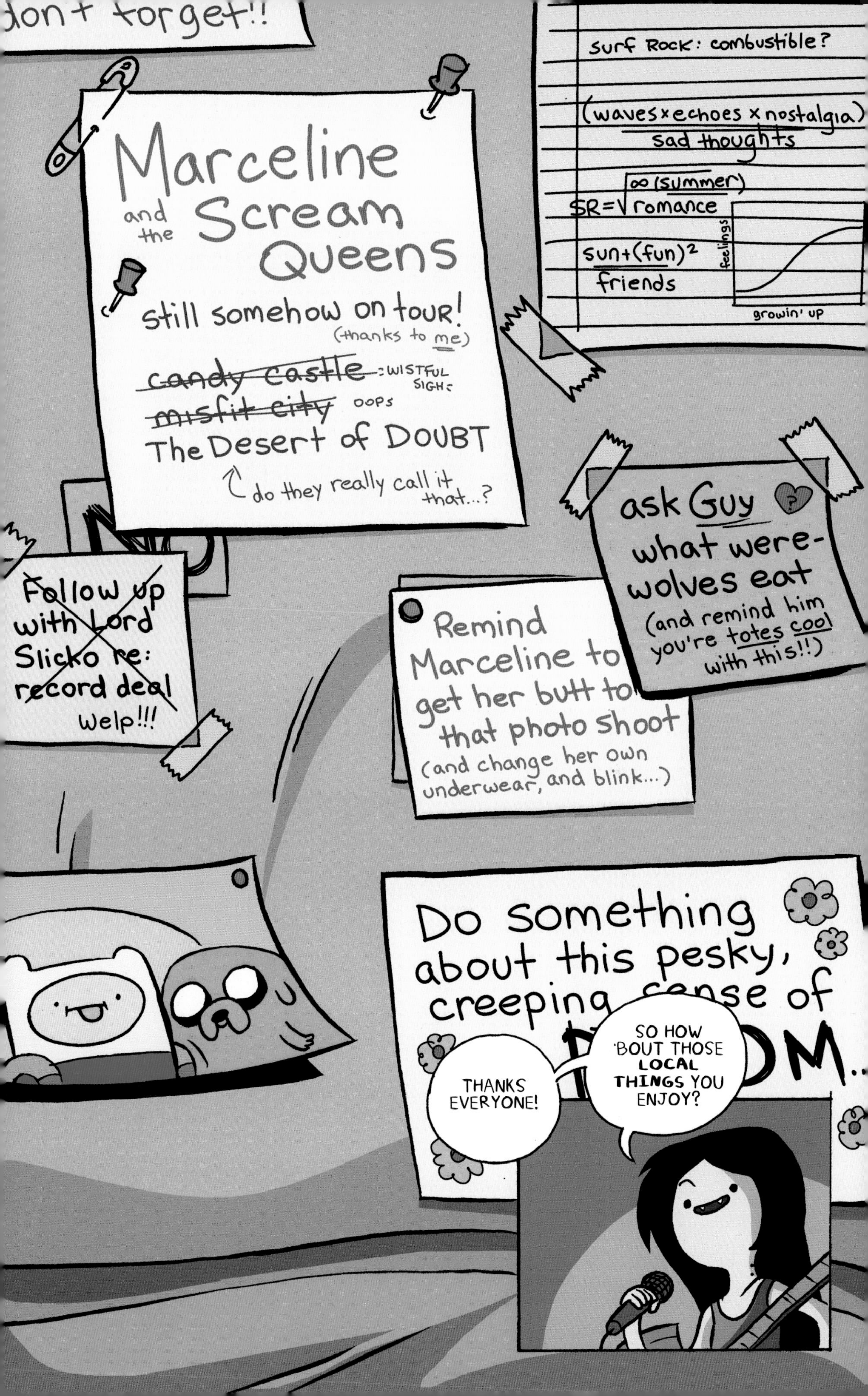

don't forget!!
Surf Rock: combustible?
(waves x echoes x nostalgia) / sad thoughts
SR = √(∞(summer) / romance)
sun+(fun)² / friends
feelings
growin' up
Marceline and the Scream Queens
still somehow on tour!
(thanks to me)
candy castle :wistful sigh:
misfit city oops
The Desert of DOUBT
do they really call it that...?
Follow up with Lord Slicko re: record deal
Welp!!!
Remind Marceline to get her butt to that photo shoot (and change her own underwear, and blink...)
ask Guy what were-wolves eat (and remind him you're totes cool with this!!)
Do something about this pesky, creeping sense of
D OM...
THANKS EVERYONE!
SO HOW 'BOUT THOSE LOCAL THINGS YOU ENJOY?

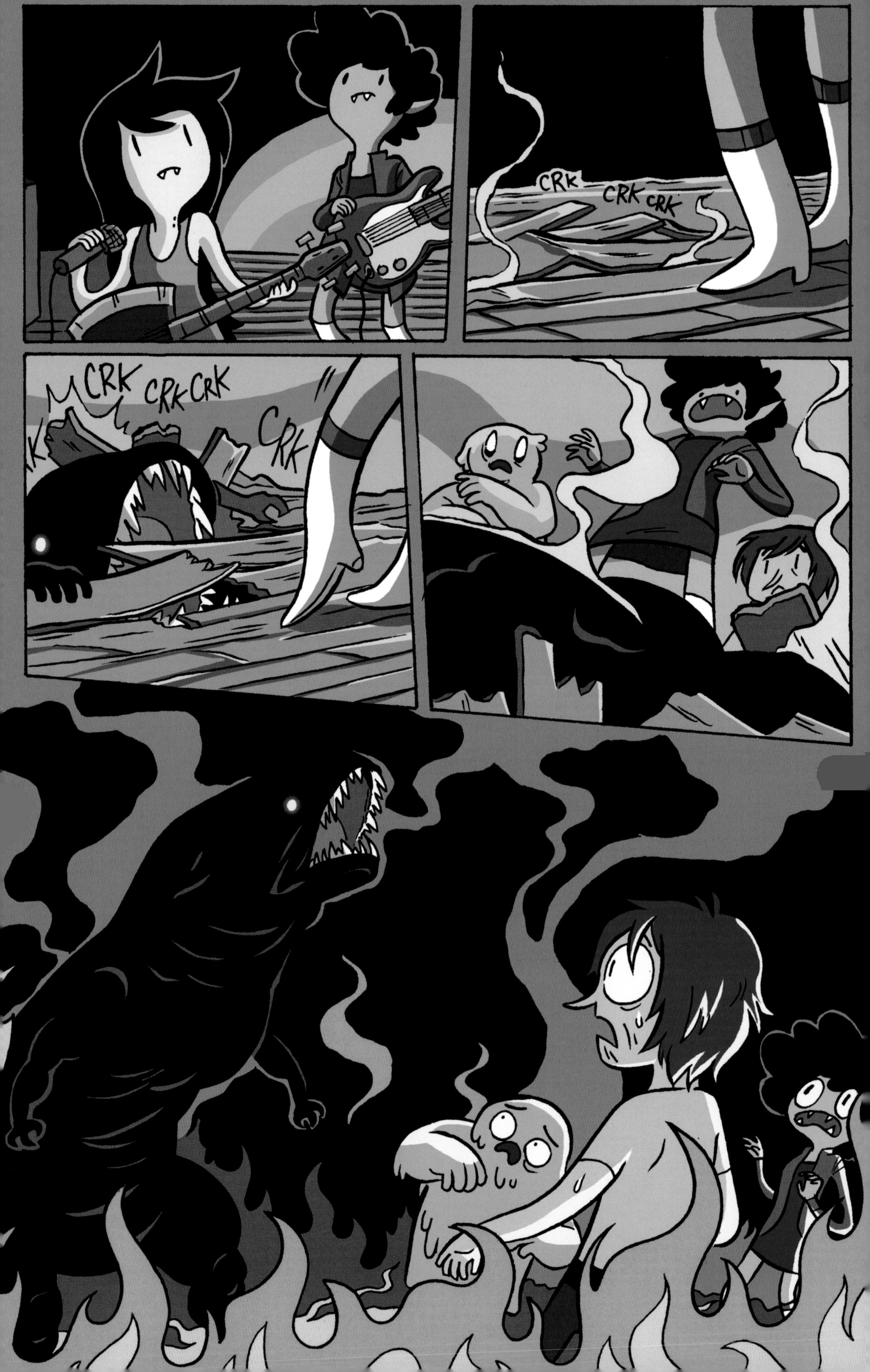
CRK
CRK CRK
CRK CRK-CRK
CRK

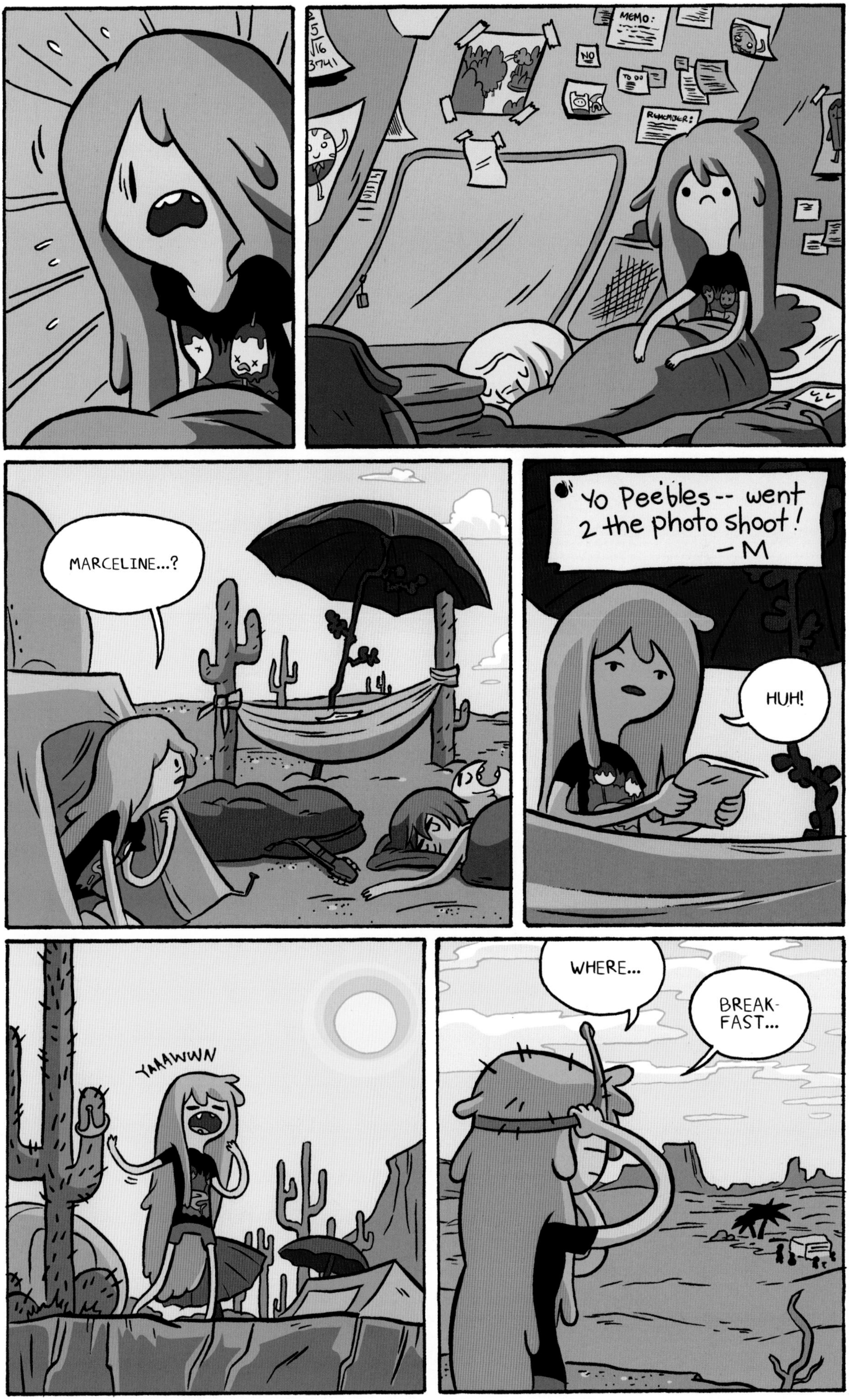
MEMO:
NO
TO DO
REMEMBER:
MARCELINE...?
Yo Peebles -- went 2 the photo shoot! -M
HUH!
YAAAWWN
WHERE...
BREAK-FAST...

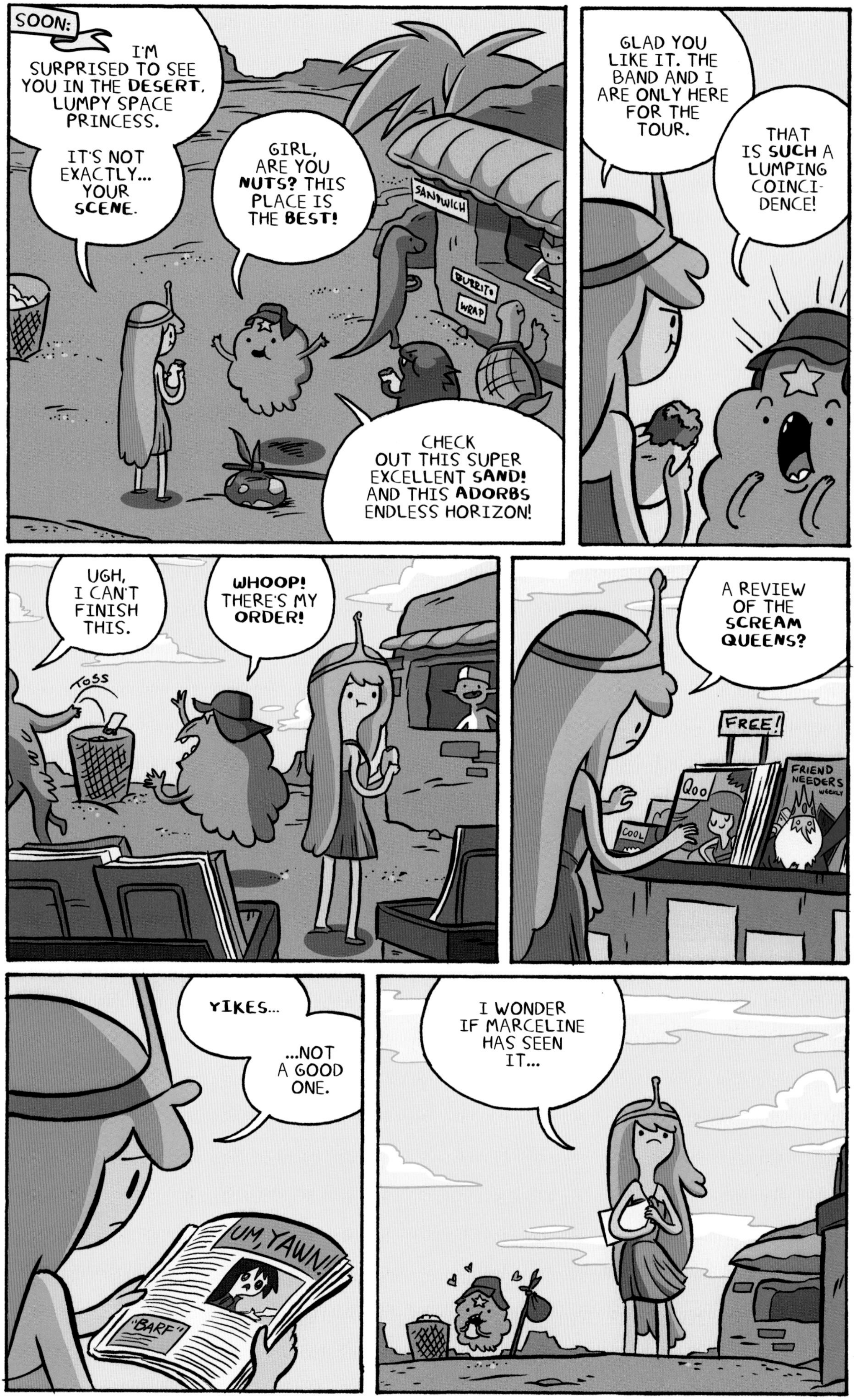
SOON:
I'M SURPRISED TO SEE YOU IN THE DESERT, LUMPY SPACE PRINCESS.
IT'S NOT EXACTLY... YOUR SCENE.
GIRL, ARE YOU NUTS? THIS PLACE IS THE BEST!
SANDWICH
BURRITO
WRAP
CHECK OUT THIS SUPER EXCELLENT SAND! AND THIS ADORBS ENDLESS HORIZON!
GLAD YOU LIKE IT. THE BAND AND I ARE ONLY HERE FOR THE TOUR.
THAT IS SUCH A LUMPING COINCI-DENCE!
UGH, I CAN'T FINISH THIS.
TOSS
WHOOP! THERE'S MY ORDER!
A REVIEW OF THE SCREAM QUEENS?
FREE!
FRIEND NEEDERS
WEEKLY
Qoo
COOL
YIKES...
...NOT A GOOD ONE.
UM, YAWN!
"BARF"
I WONDER IF MARCELINE HAS SEEN IT...

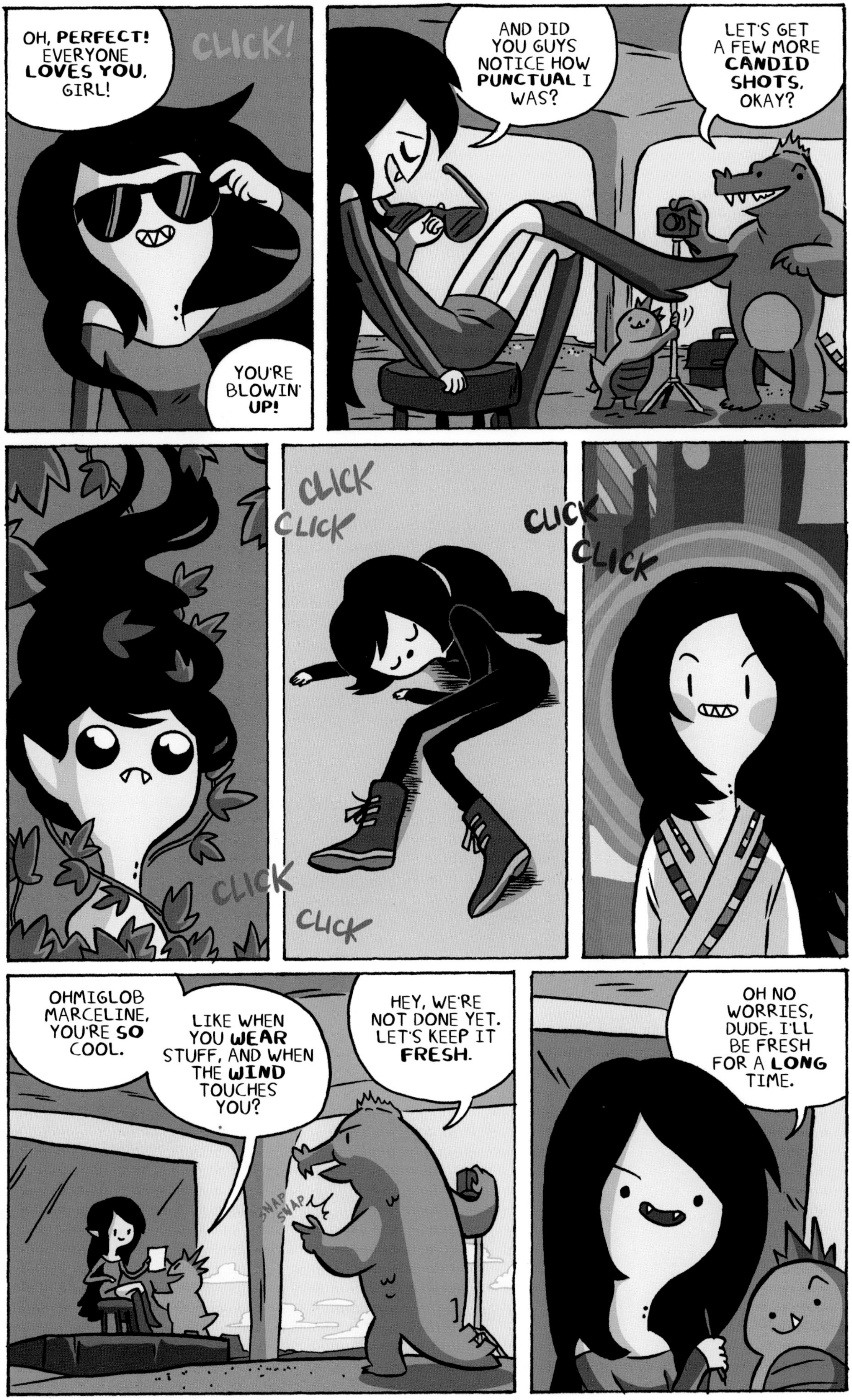
OH, **PERFECT!** EVERYONE **LOVES YOU,** GIRL!
CLICK!
YOU'RE BLOWIN' **UP!**
AND DID YOU GUYS NOTICE HOW **PUNCTUAL** I WAS?
LET'S GET A FEW MORE **CANDID SHOTS,** OKAY?
CLICK
CLICK
CLICK
CLICK
CLICK
CLICK
OHMIGLOB MARCELINE, YOU'RE **SO** COOL.
LIKE WHEN YOU **WEAR** STUFF, AND WHEN THE **WIND** TOUCHES YOU?
HEY, WE'RE NOT DONE YET. LET'S KEEP IT **FRESH**.
SNAP SNAP
OH NO WORRIES, DUDE. I'LL BE FRESH FOR A **LONG** TIME.

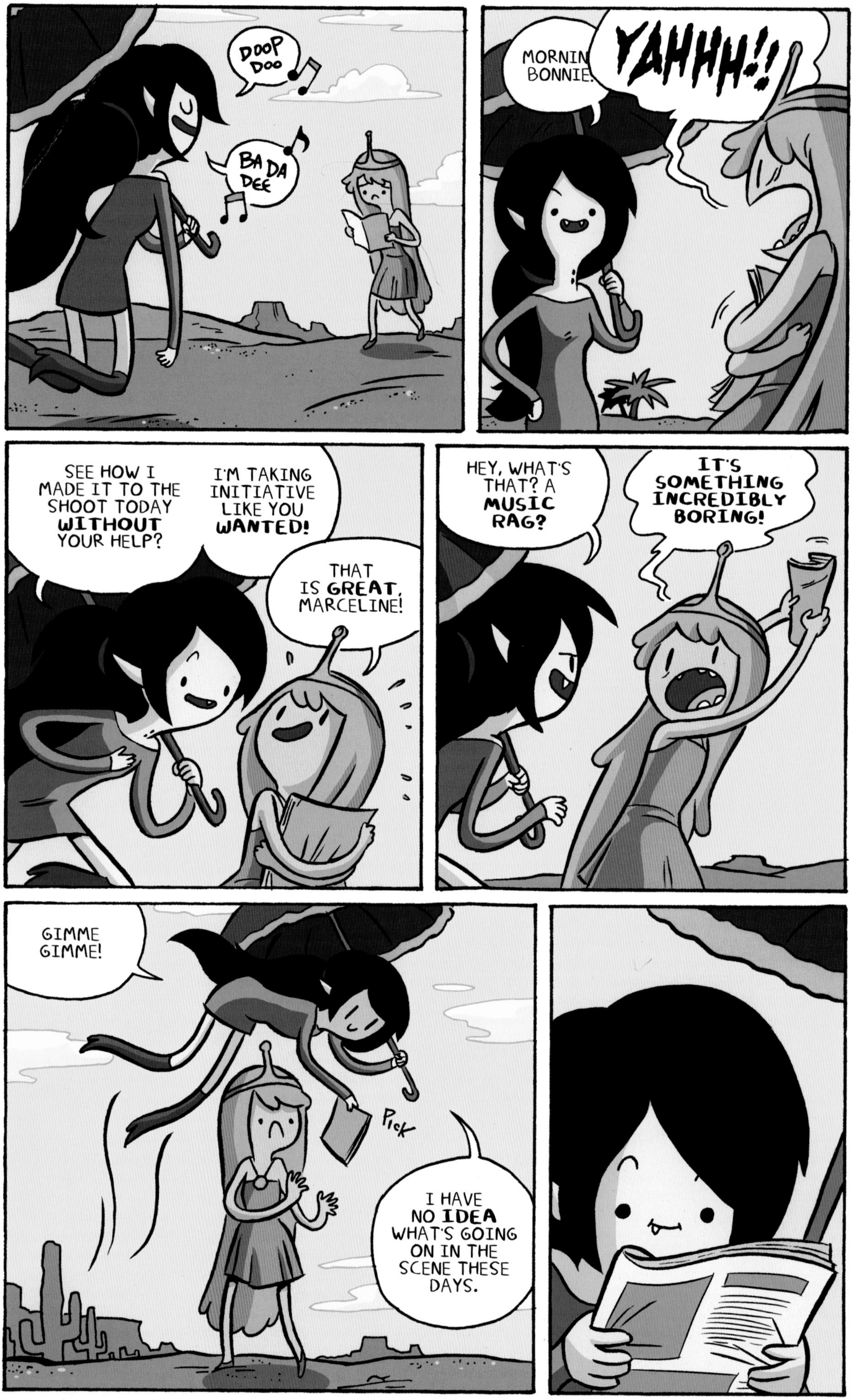
DOOP DOO
BA DA DEE
MORNIN BONNIE!
YAHHH!!
SEE HOW I MADE IT TO THE SHOOT TODAY WITHOUT YOUR HELP?
I'M TAKING INITIATIVE LIKE YOU WANTED!
THAT IS GREAT, MARCELINE!
HEY, WHAT'S THAT? A MUSIC RAG?
IT'S SOMETHING INCREDIBLY BORING!
GIMME GIMME!
PICK
I HAVE NO IDEA WHAT'S GOING ON IN THE SCENE THESE DAYS.

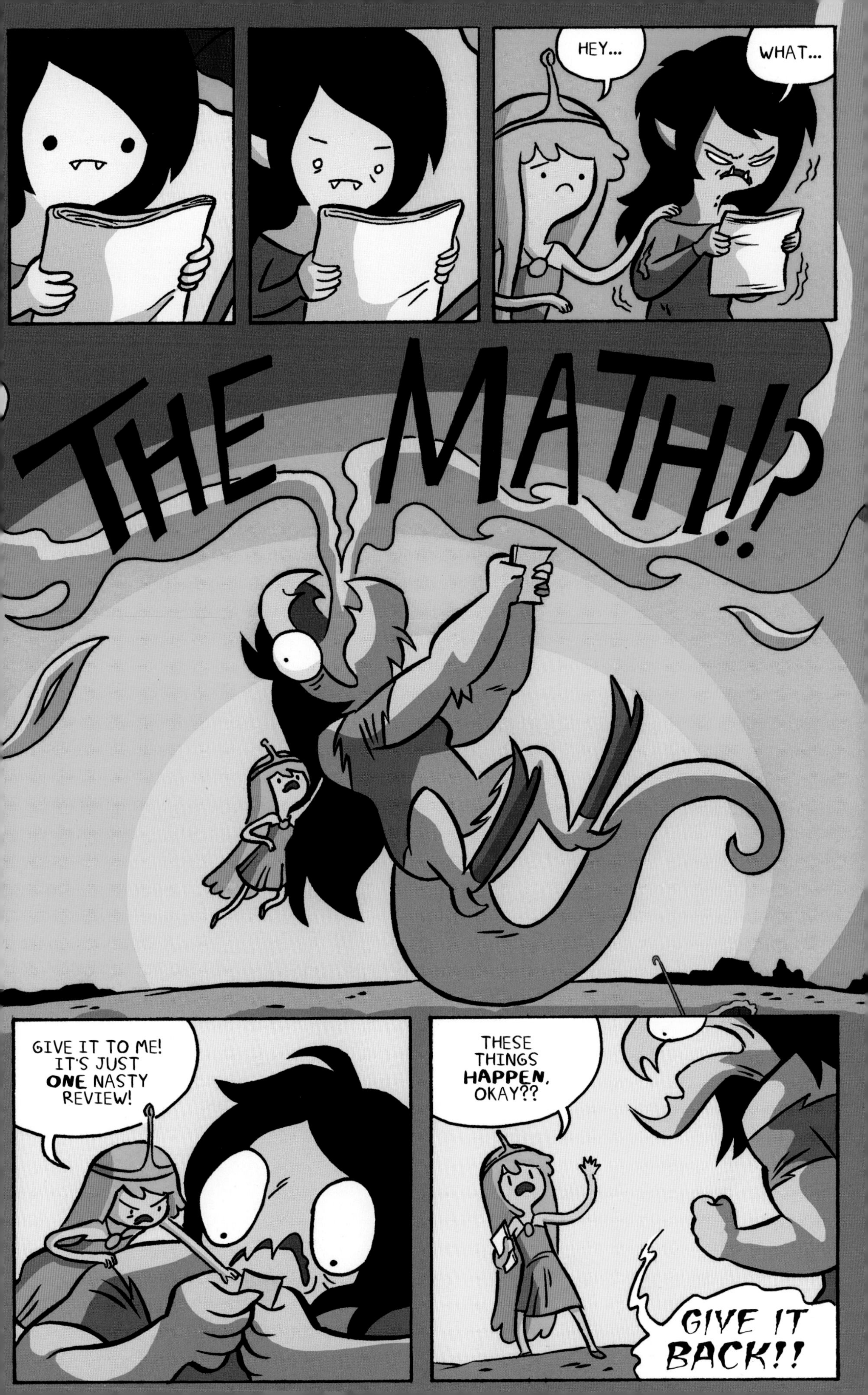
HEY...
WHAT...
THE MATH!?!
GIVE IT TO ME! IT'S JUST **ONE** NASTY REVIEW!
THESE THINGS **HAPPEN**, OKAY??
GIVE IT BACK!!

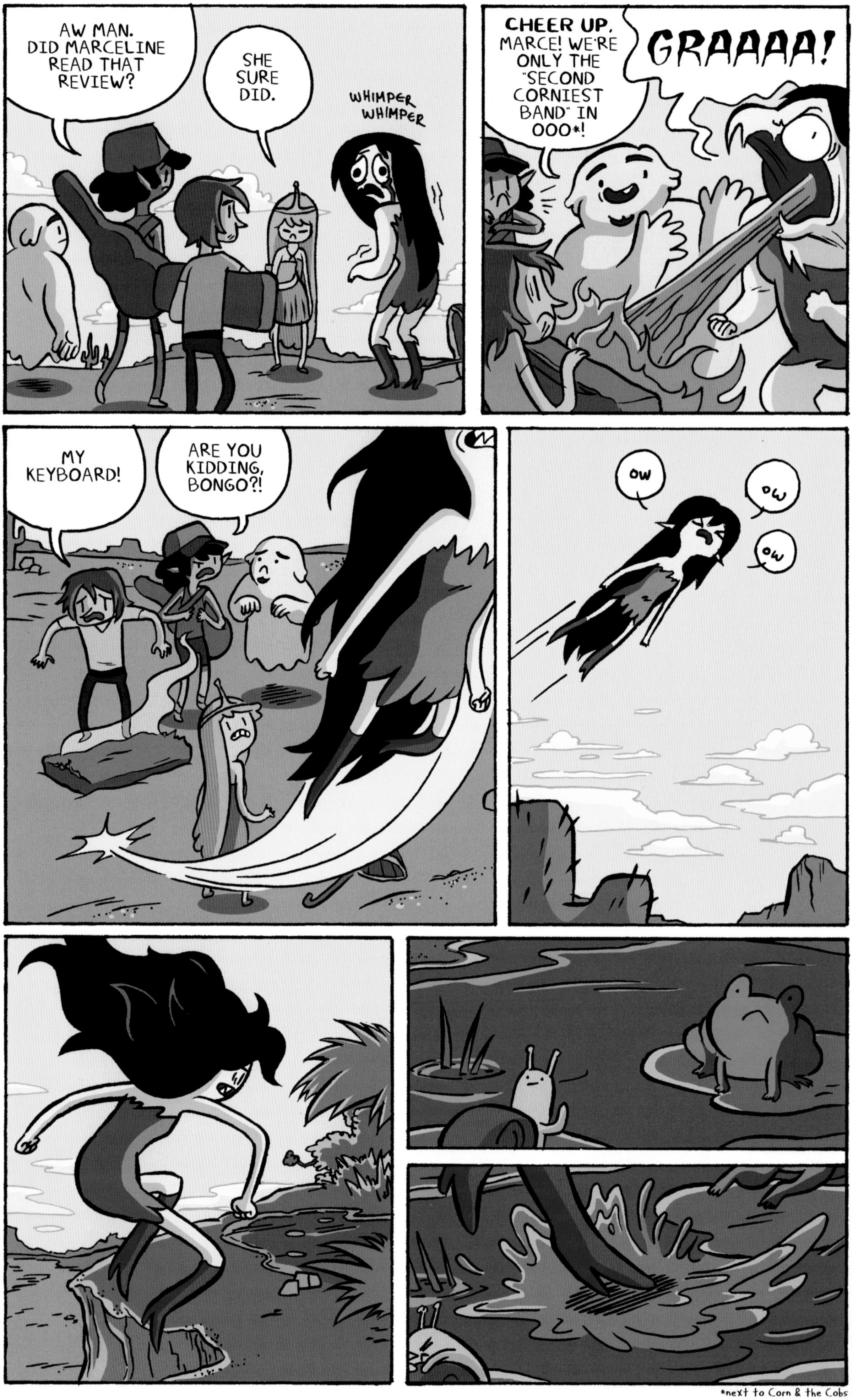
AW MAN. DID MARCELINE READ THAT REVIEW?
SHE SURE DID.
WHIMPER WHIMPER
CHEER UP, MARCE! WE'RE ONLY THE "SECOND CORNIEST BAND" IN OOO*!
GRAAAA!
MY KEYBOARD!
ARE YOU KIDDING, BONGO?!
OW
OW
OW

*next to Corn & the Cobs

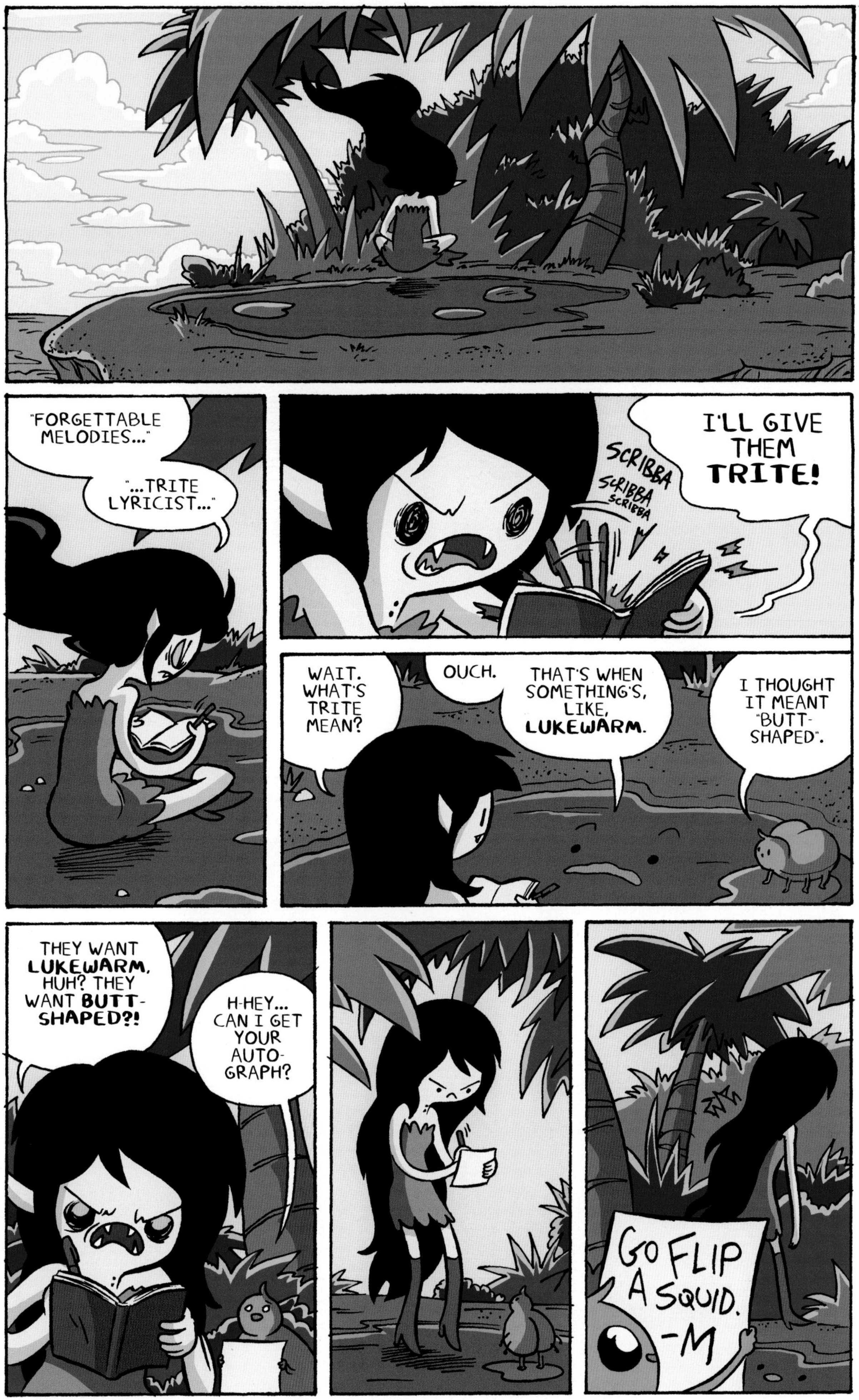

"FORGETTABLE MELODIES..."
"...TRITE LYRICIST..."
SCRIBBA SCRIBBA SCRIBBA
I'LL GIVE THEM **TRITE!**
WAIT. WHAT'S TRITE MEAN?
OUCH.
THAT'S WHEN SOMETHING'S, LIKE, **LUKEWARM**.
I THOUGHT IT MEANT "BUTT-SHAPED".
THEY WANT **LUKEWARM**, HUH? THEY WANT **BUTT-SHAPED?!**
H-HEY... CAN I GET YOUR AUTO-GRAPH?
GO FLIP A SQUID. -M

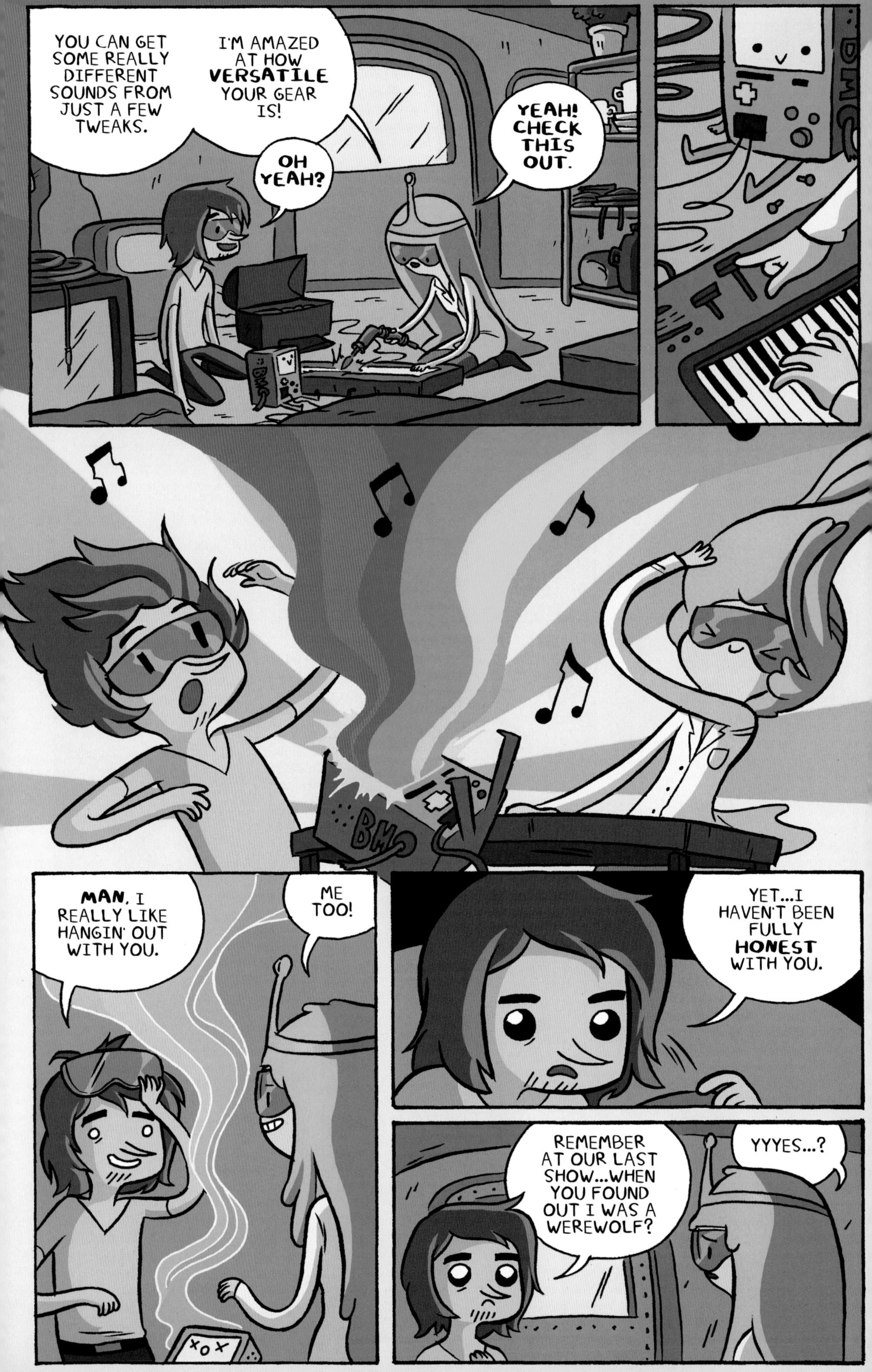
YOU CAN GET SOME REALLY DIFFERENT SOUNDS FROM JUST A FEW TWEAKS.
I'M AMAZED AT HOW **VERSATILE** YOUR GEAR IS!
OH YEAH?
YEAH! CHECK THIS OUT.
BMO
BMO
MAN, I REALLY LIKE HANGIN' OUT WITH YOU.
ME TOO!
YET...I HAVEN'T BEEN FULLY **HONEST** WITH YOU.
REMEMBER AT OUR LAST SHOW...WHEN YOU FOUND OUT I WAS A WEREWOLF?
YYYES...?

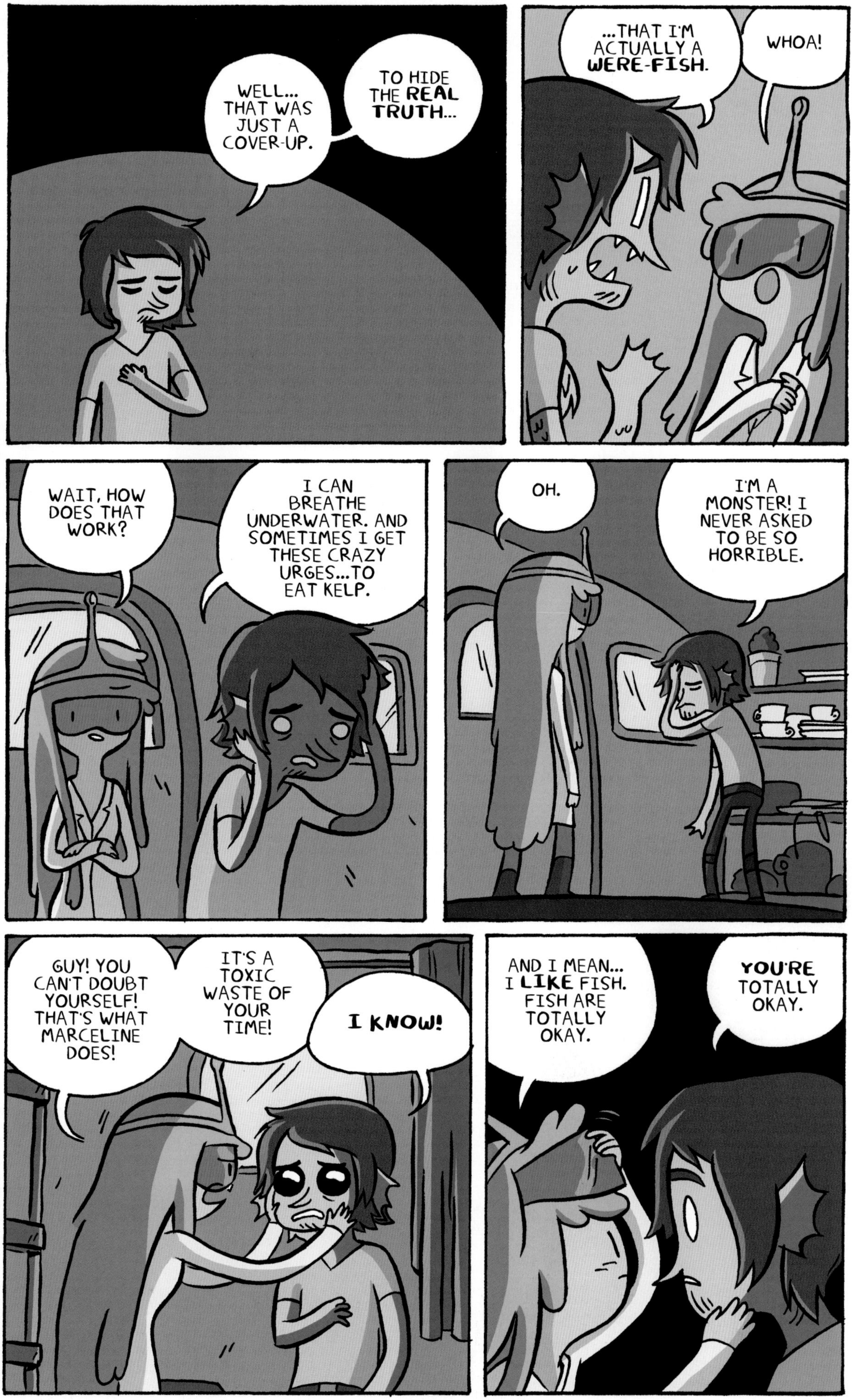
WELL... THAT WAS JUST A COVER-UP.
TO HIDE THE **REAL TRUTH**...
...THAT I'M ACTUALLY A **WERE-FISH**.
WHOA!
WAIT, HOW DOES THAT WORK?
I CAN BREATHE UNDERWATER. AND SOMETIMES I GET THESE CRAZY URGES...TO EAT KELP.
OH.
I'M A MONSTER! I NEVER ASKED TO BE SO HORRIBLE.
GUY! YOU CAN'T DOUBT YOURSELF! THAT'S WHAT MARCELINE DOES!
IT'S A TOXIC WASTE OF YOUR TIME!
I KNOW!
AND I MEAN... I **LIKE** FISH. FISH ARE TOTALLY OKAY.
YOU'RE TOTALLY OKAY.

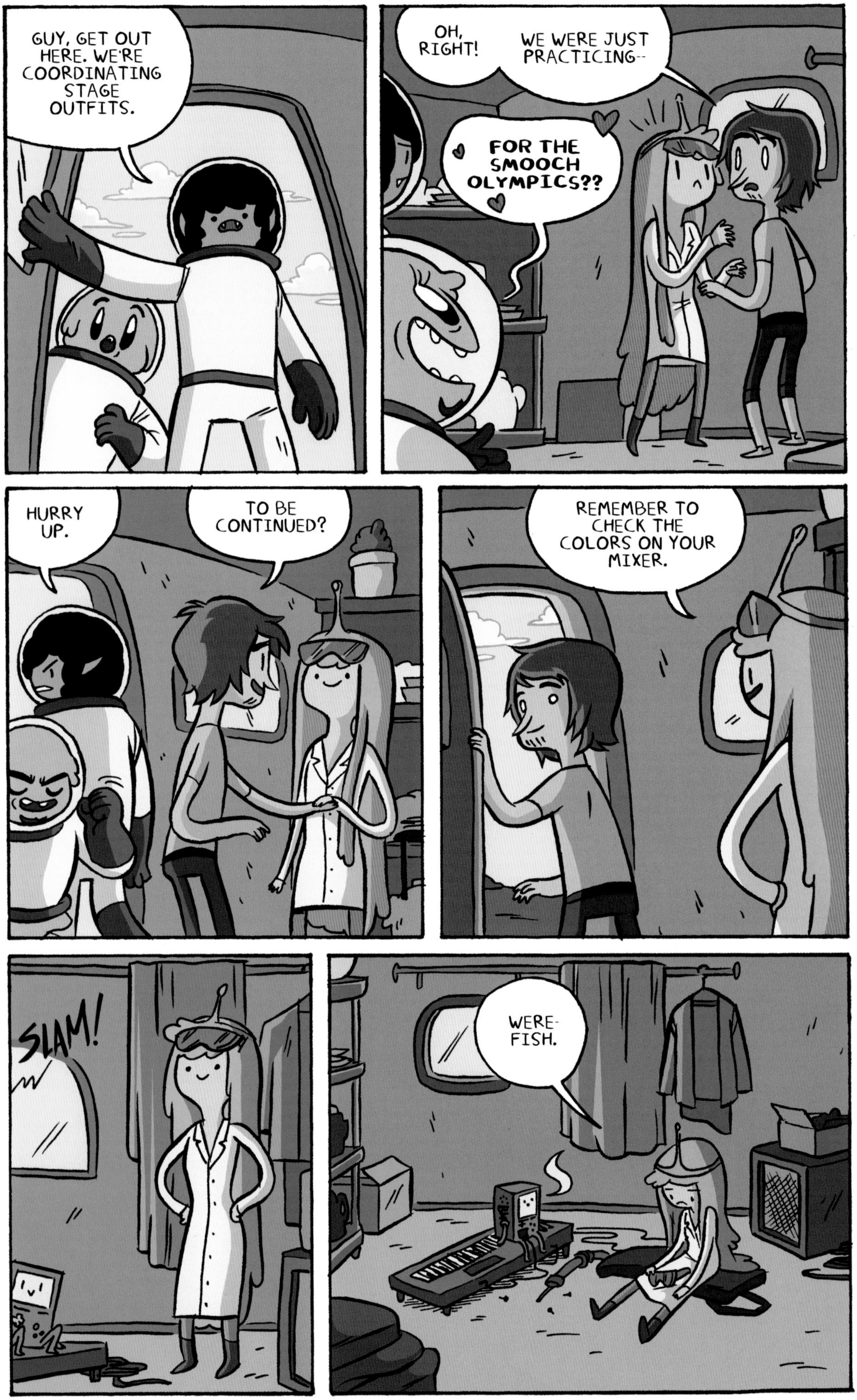
GUY, GET OUT HERE. WE'RE COORDINATING STAGE OUTFITS.
OH, RIGHT!
WE WERE JUST PRACTICING--
FOR THE SMOOCH OLYMPICS??
HURRY UP.
TO BE CONTINUED?
REMEMBER TO CHECK THE COLORS ON YOUR MIXER.
SLAM!
WERE-FISH.

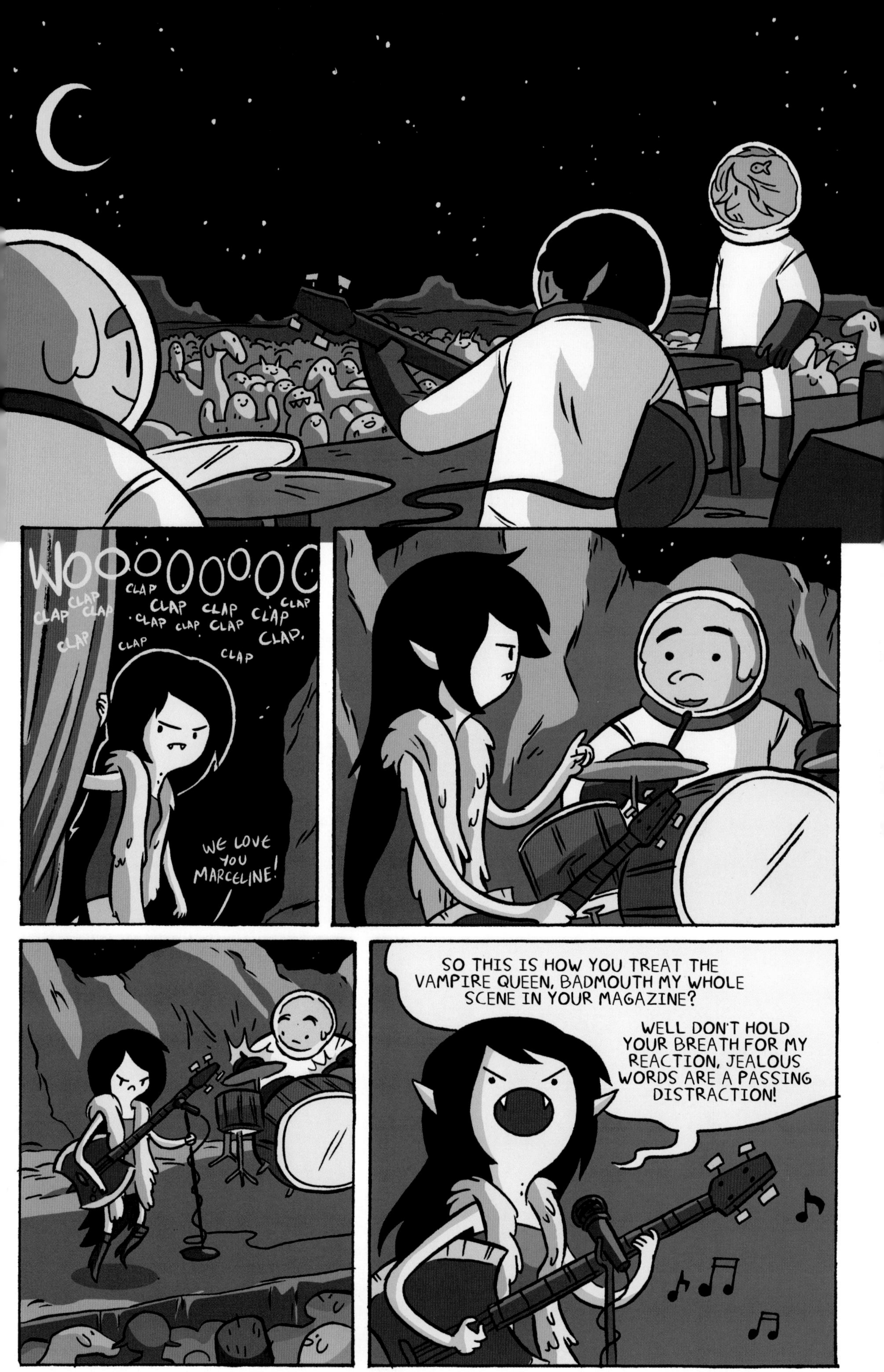
WOOOOOOOOO
CLAP CLAP CLAP CLAP CLAP CLAP CLAP CLAP CLAP CLAP CLAP CLAP CLAP CLAP CLAP
WE LOVE YOU MARCELINE!
SO THIS IS HOW YOU TREAT THE VAMPIRE QUEEN, BADMOUTH MY WHOLE SCENE IN YOUR MAGAZINE?
WELL DON'T HOLD YOUR BREATH FOR MY REACTION, JEALOUS WORDS ARE A PASSING DISTRACTION!

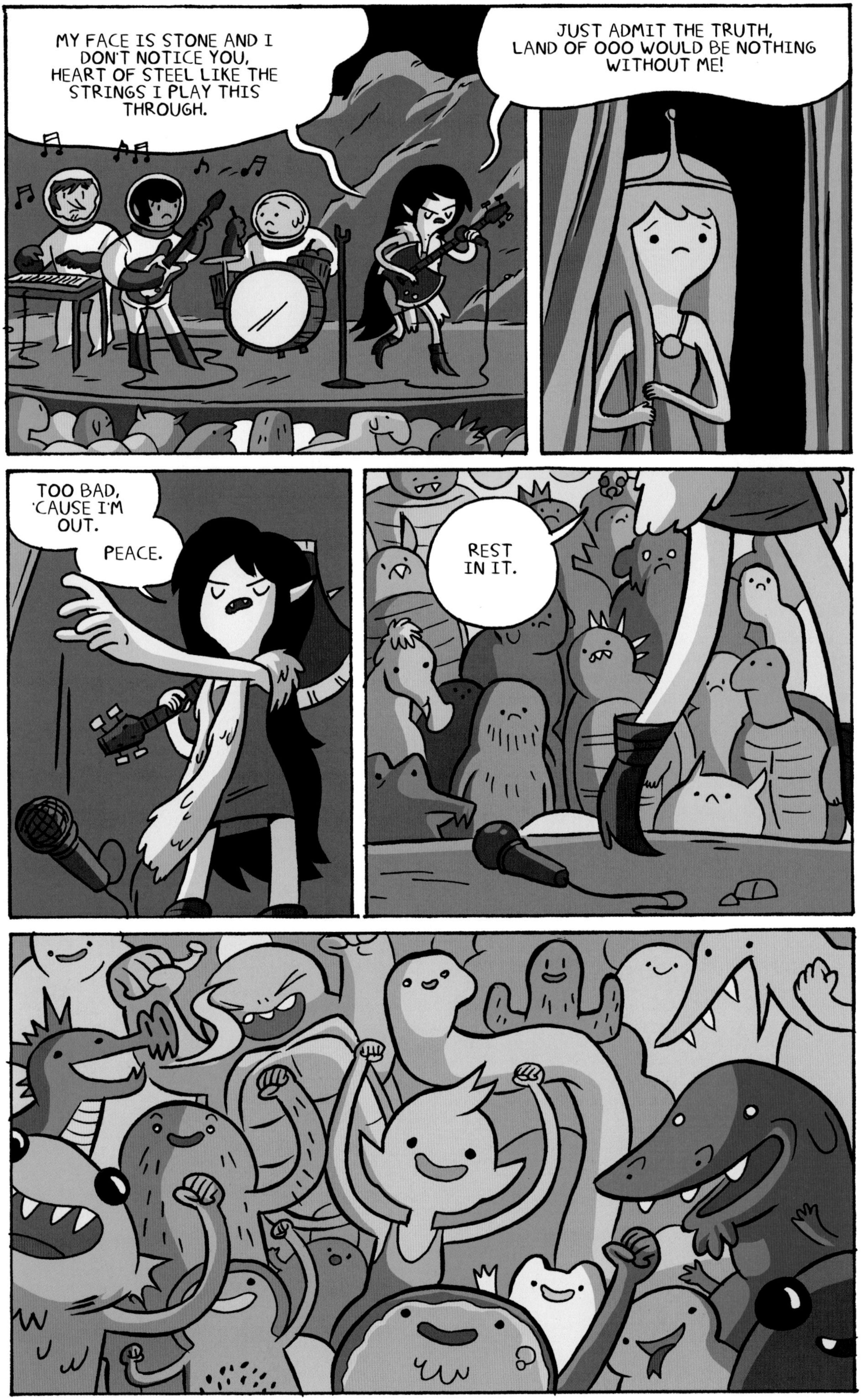
MY FACE IS STONE AND I DON'T NOTICE YOU, HEART OF STEEL LIKE THE STRINGS I PLAY THIS THROUGH.
JUST ADMIT THE TRUTH, LAND OF OOO WOULD BE NOTHING WITHOUT ME!
TOO BAD, 'CAUSE I'M OUT.
PEACE.
REST IN IT.

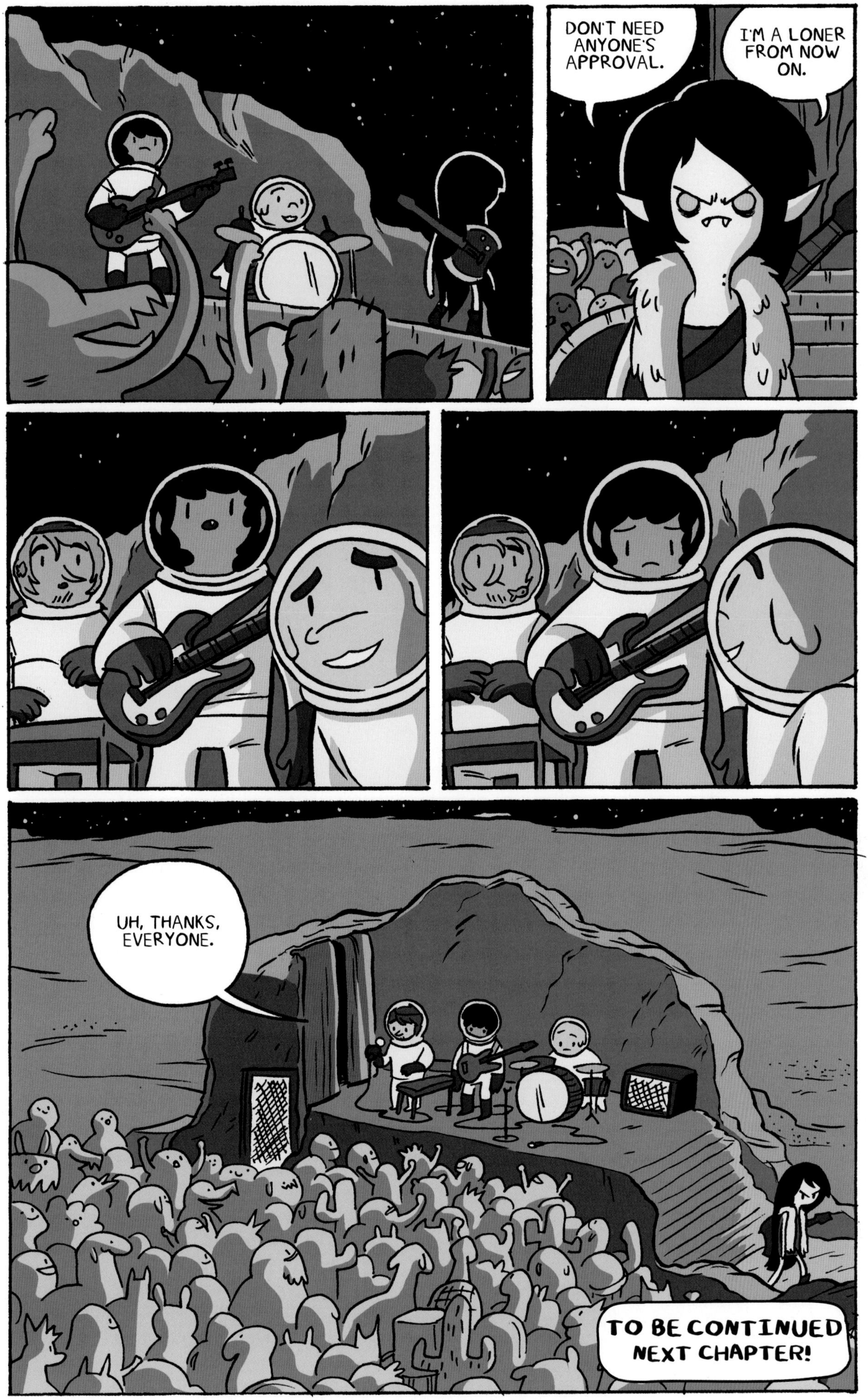
DON'T NEED ANYONE'S APPROVAL.
I'M A LONER FROM NOW ON.
UH, THANKS, EVERYONE.
TO BE CONTINUED NEXT CHAPTER!

CHAPTER FOUR

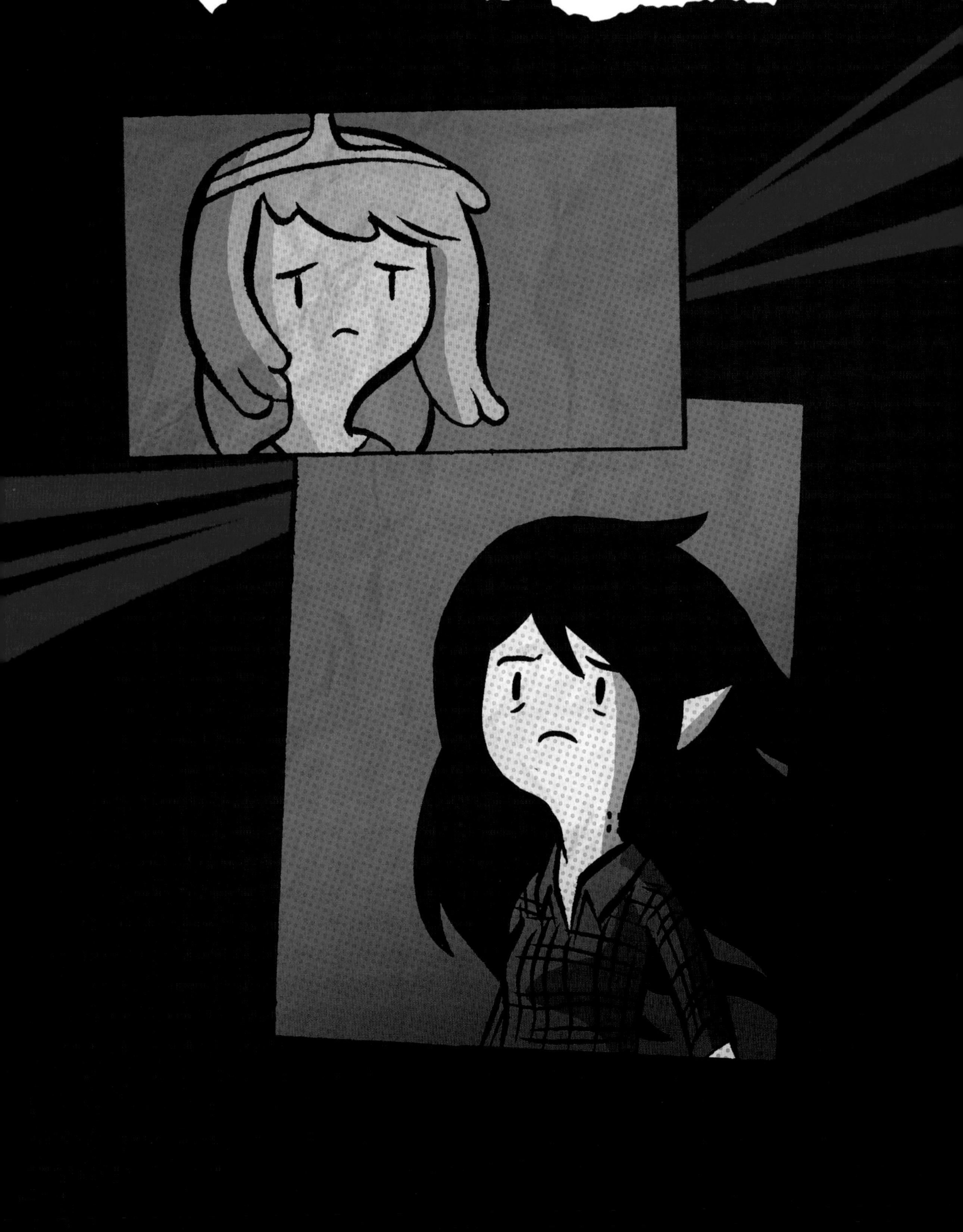

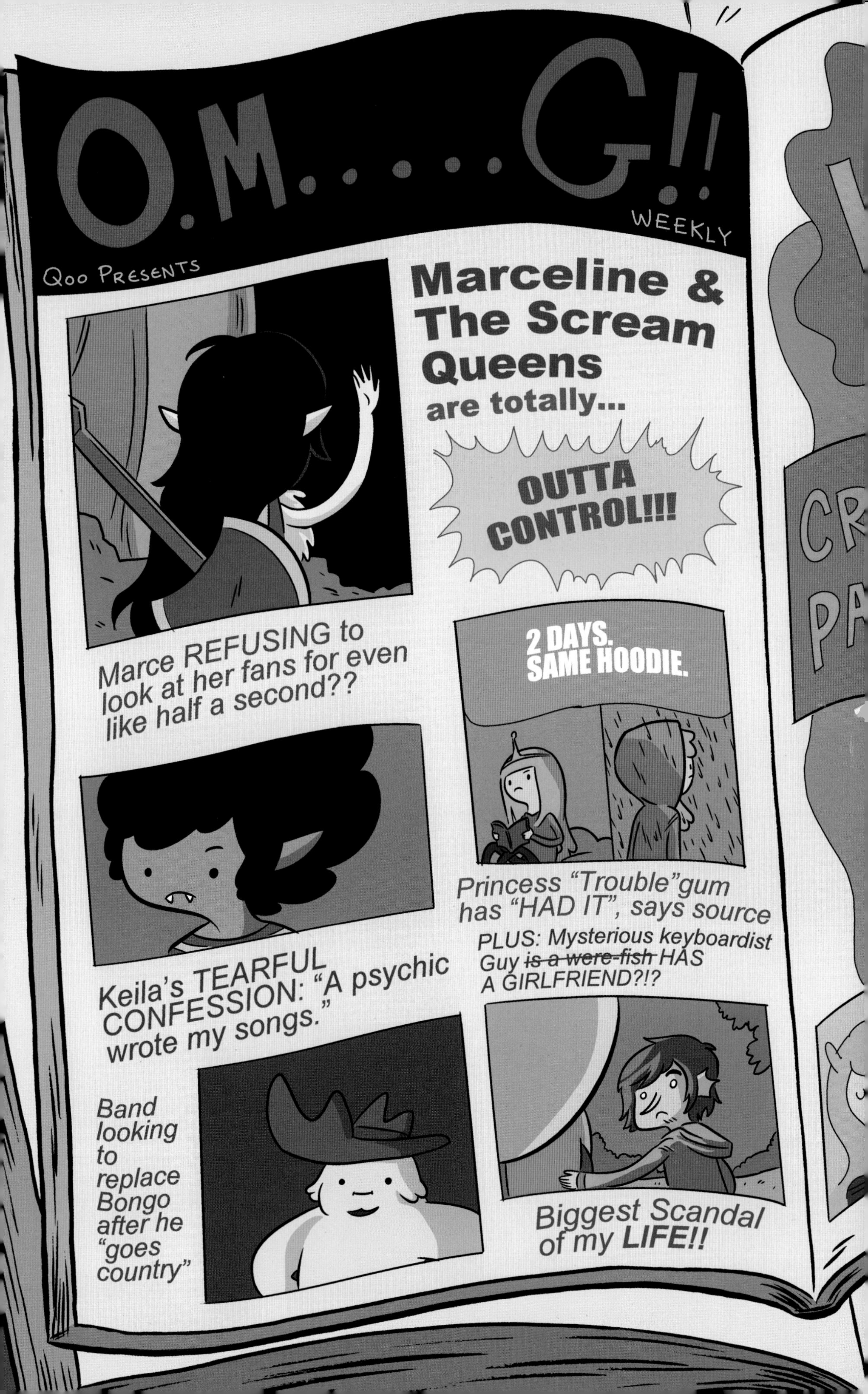
O.M...G!!
WEEKLY
Qoo PRESENTS
Marceline & The Scream Queens
are totally...
OUTTA CONTROL!!!
Marce REFUSING to look at her fans for even like half a second??
2 DAYS. SAME HOODIE.
Princess "Trouble"gum has "HAD IT", says source
PLUS: Mysterious keyboardist Guy ~~is a were-fish~~ HAS A GIRLFRIEND?!?
Keila's TEARFUL CONFESSION: "A psychic wrote my songs."
Band looking to replace Bongo after he "goes country"
Biggest Scandal of my LIFE!!

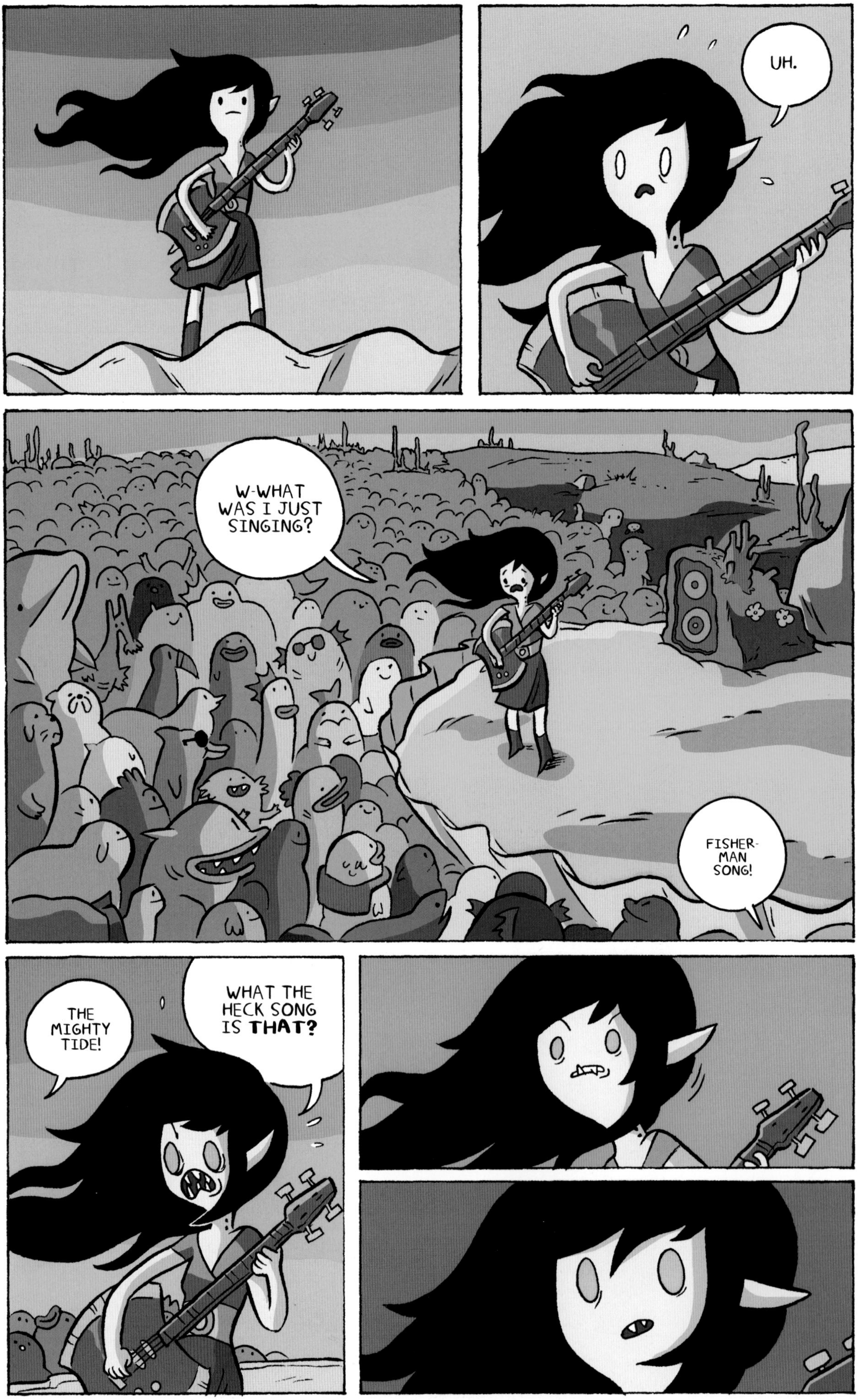
UH.
W-WHAT WAS I JUST SINGING?
FISHER-MAN SONG!
THE MIGHTY TIDE!
WHAT THE HECK SONG IS THAT?

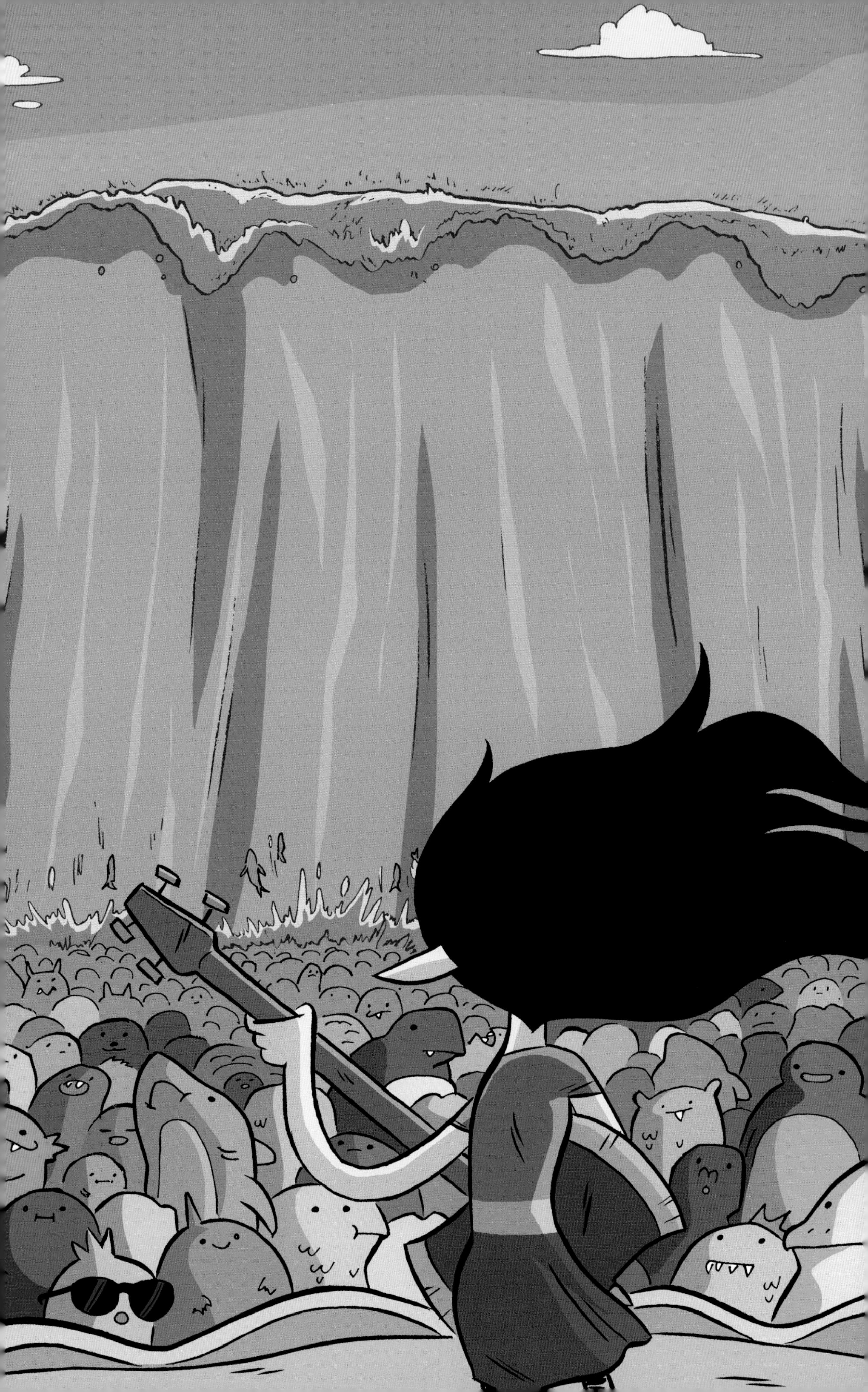

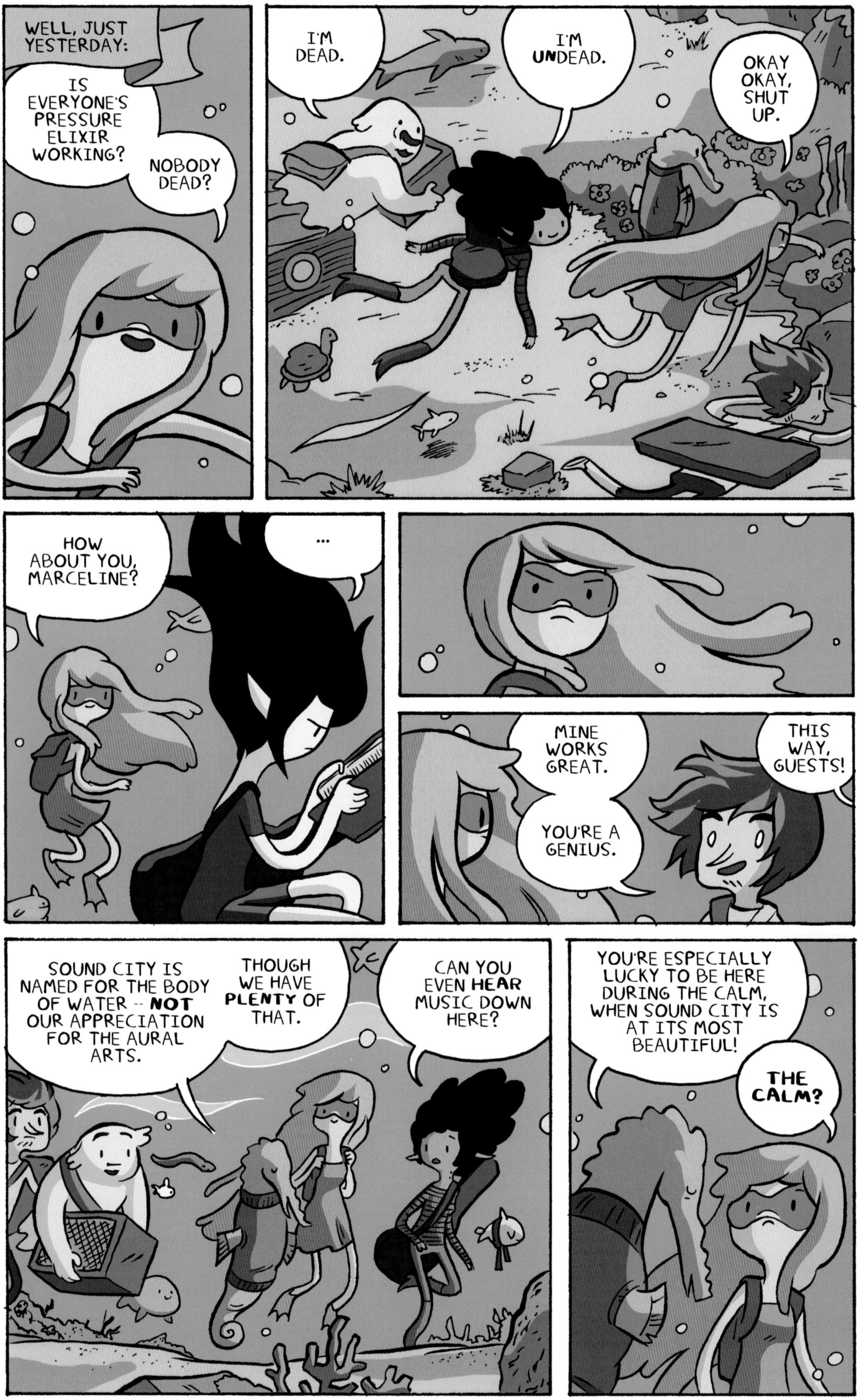
WELL, JUST YESTERDAY:
IS EVERYONE'S PRESSURE ELIXIR WORKING?
NOBODY DEAD?
I'M DEAD.
I'M UNDEAD.
OKAY OKAY, SHUT UP.
HOW ABOUT YOU, MARCELINE?
...
MINE WORKS GREAT.
YOU'RE A GENIUS.
THIS WAY, GUESTS!
SOUND CITY IS NAMED FOR THE BODY OF WATER -- NOT OUR APPRECIATION FOR THE AURAL ARTS.
THOUGH WE HAVE PLENTY OF THAT.
CAN YOU EVEN HEAR MUSIC DOWN HERE?
YOU'RE ESPECIALLY LUCKY TO BE HERE DURING THE CALM, WHEN SOUND CITY IS AT ITS MOST BEAUTIFUL!
THE CALM?

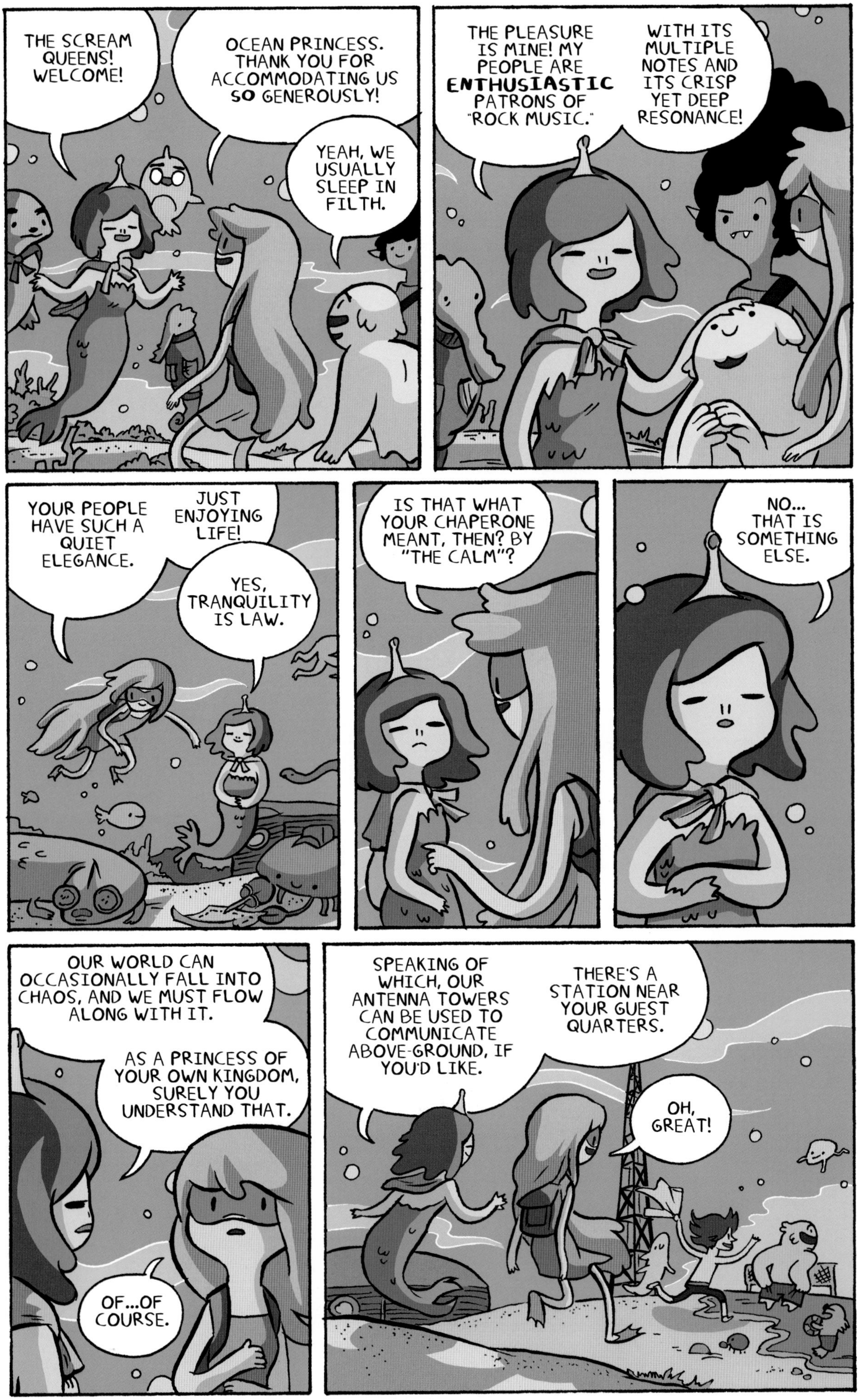
THE SCREAM QUEENS! WELCOME!
OCEAN PRINCESS. THANK YOU FOR ACCOMMODATING US SO GENEROUSLY!
YEAH, WE USUALLY SLEEP IN FILTH.
THE PLEASURE IS MINE! MY PEOPLE ARE ENTHUSIASTIC PATRONS OF "ROCK MUSIC."
WITH ITS MULTIPLE NOTES AND ITS CRISP YET DEEP RESONANCE!
YOUR PEOPLE HAVE SUCH A QUIET ELEGANCE.
JUST ENJOYING LIFE!
YES, TRANQUILITY IS LAW.
IS THAT WHAT YOUR CHAPERONE MEANT, THEN? BY "THE CALM"?
NO... THAT IS SOMETHING ELSE.
OUR WORLD CAN OCCASIONALLY FALL INTO CHAOS, AND WE MUST FLOW ALONG WITH IT.
AS A PRINCESS OF YOUR OWN KINGDOM, SURELY YOU UNDERSTAND THAT.
OF...OF COURSE.
SPEAKING OF WHICH, OUR ANTENNA TOWERS CAN BE USED TO COMMUNICATE ABOVE-GROUND, IF YOU'D LIKE.
THERE'S A STATION NEAR YOUR GUEST QUARTERS.
OH, GREAT!

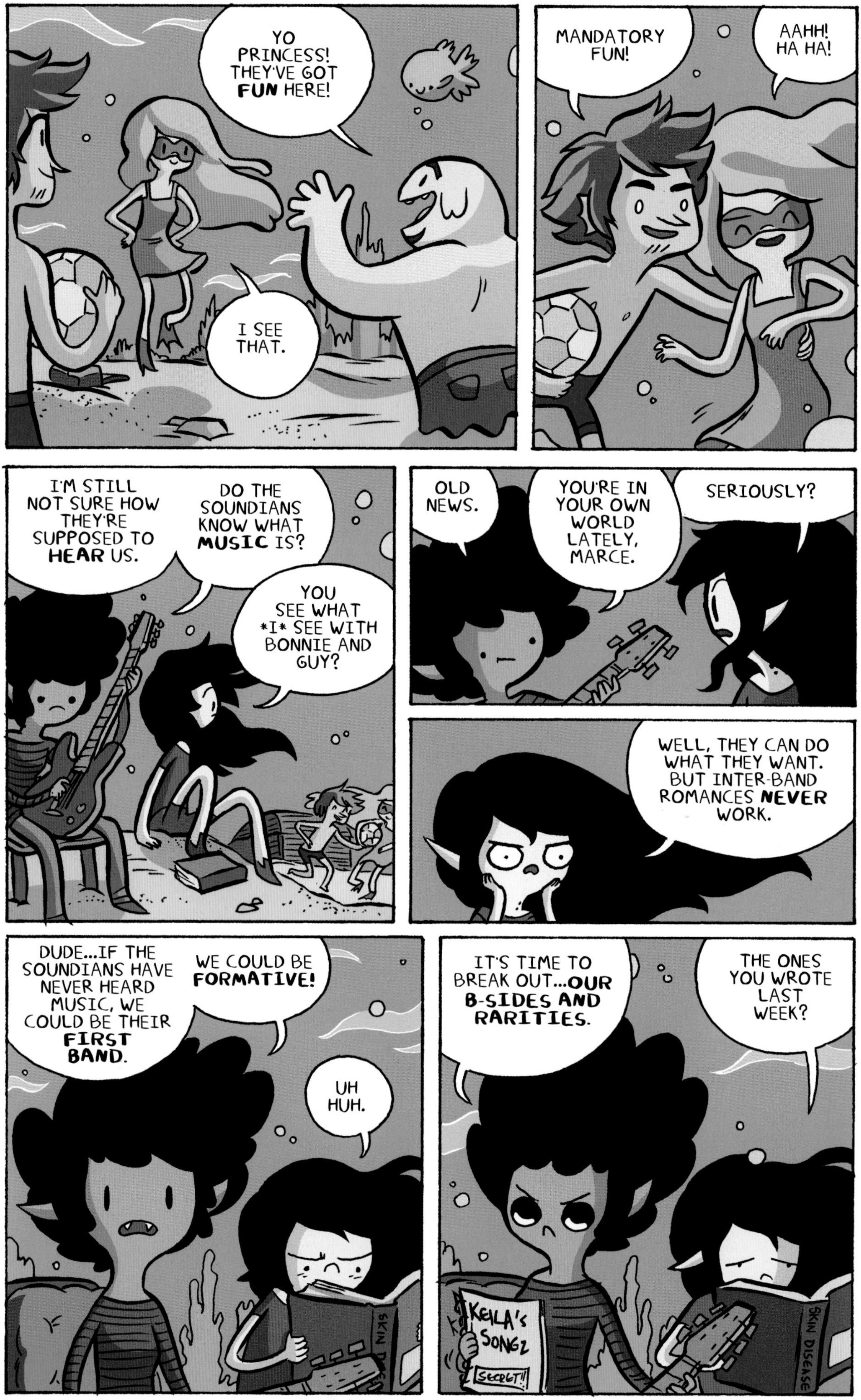
YO PRINCESS! THEY'VE GOT **FUN** HERE!
I SEE THAT.
MANDATORY FUN!
AAHH! HA HA!
I'M STILL NOT SURE HOW THEY'RE SUPPOSED TO **HEAR** US.
DO THE SOUNDIANS KNOW WHAT **MUSIC** IS?
YOU SEE WHAT *I* SEE WITH BONNIE AND GUY?
OLD NEWS.
YOU'RE IN YOUR OWN WORLD LATELY, MARCE.
SERIOUSLY?
WELL, THEY CAN DO WHAT THEY WANT. BUT INTER-BAND ROMANCES **NEVER** WORK.
DUDE...IF THE SOUNDIANS HAVE NEVER HEARD MUSIC, WE COULD BE THEIR **FIRST BAND**.
WE COULD BE **FORMATIVE!**
UH HUH.
SKIN DISEASE
IT'S TIME TO BREAK OUT...**OUR B-SIDES AND RARITIES**.
THE ONES YOU WROTE LAST WEEK?
KEILA'S SONGZ
SECRET!!
SKIN DISEASE

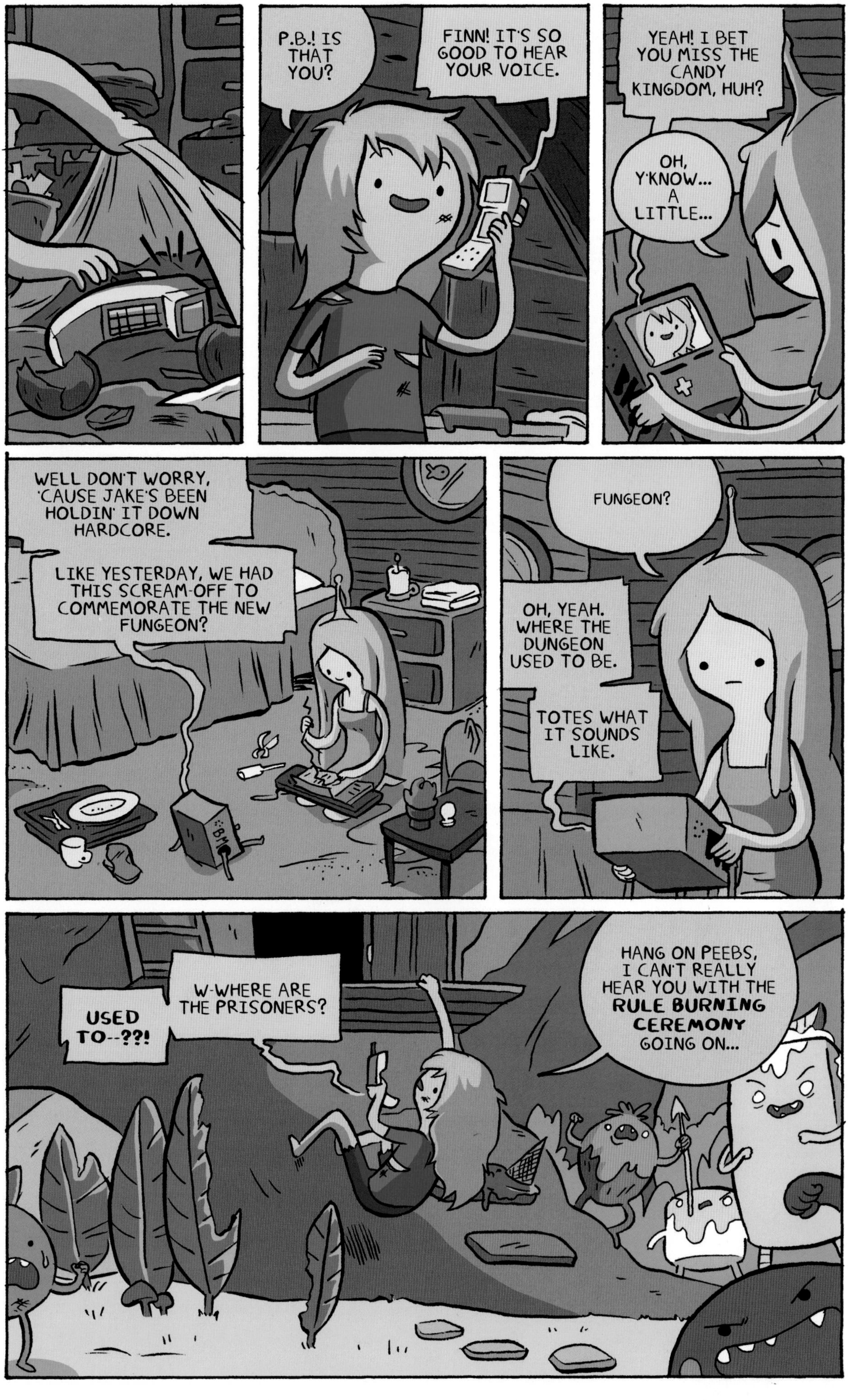
P.B.! IS THAT YOU?
FINN! IT'S SO GOOD TO HEAR YOUR VOICE.
YEAH! I BET YOU MISS THE CANDY KINGDOM, HUH?
OH, Y'KNOW... A LITTLE...
WELL DON'T WORRY, 'CAUSE JAKE'S BEEN HOLDIN' IT DOWN HARDCORE.
LIKE YESTERDAY, WE HAD THIS SCREAM-OFF TO COMMEMORATE THE NEW FUNGEON?
FUNGEON?
OH, YEAH. WHERE THE DUNGEON USED TO BE.
TOTES WHAT IT SOUNDS LIKE.
USED TO--??!
W-WHERE ARE THE PRISONERS?
HANG ON PEEBS, I CAN'T REALLY HEAR YOU WITH THE **RULE BURNING CEREMONY** GOING ON...

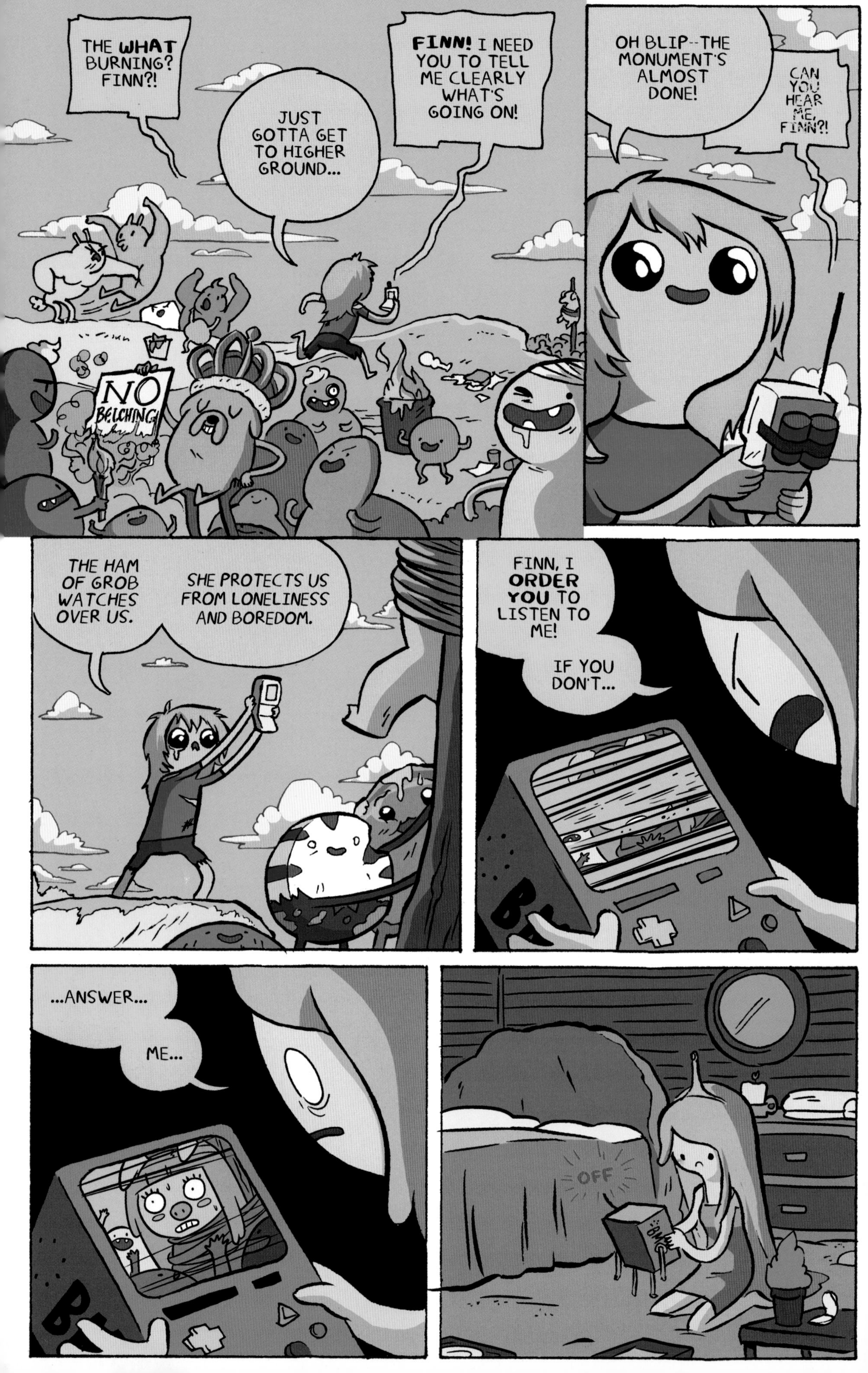
THE WHAT BURNING? FINN?!
JUST GOTTA GET TO HIGHER GROUND...
FINN! I NEED YOU TO TELL ME CLEARLY WHAT'S GOING ON!
NO BELCHING
OH BLIP--THE MONUMENT'S ALMOST DONE!
CAN YOU HEAR ME, FINN?!
THE HAM OF GROB WATCHES OVER US.
SHE PROTECTS US FROM LONELINESS AND BOREDOM.
FINN, I ORDER YOU TO LISTEN TO ME!
IF YOU DON'T...
...ANSWER...
ME...
OFF

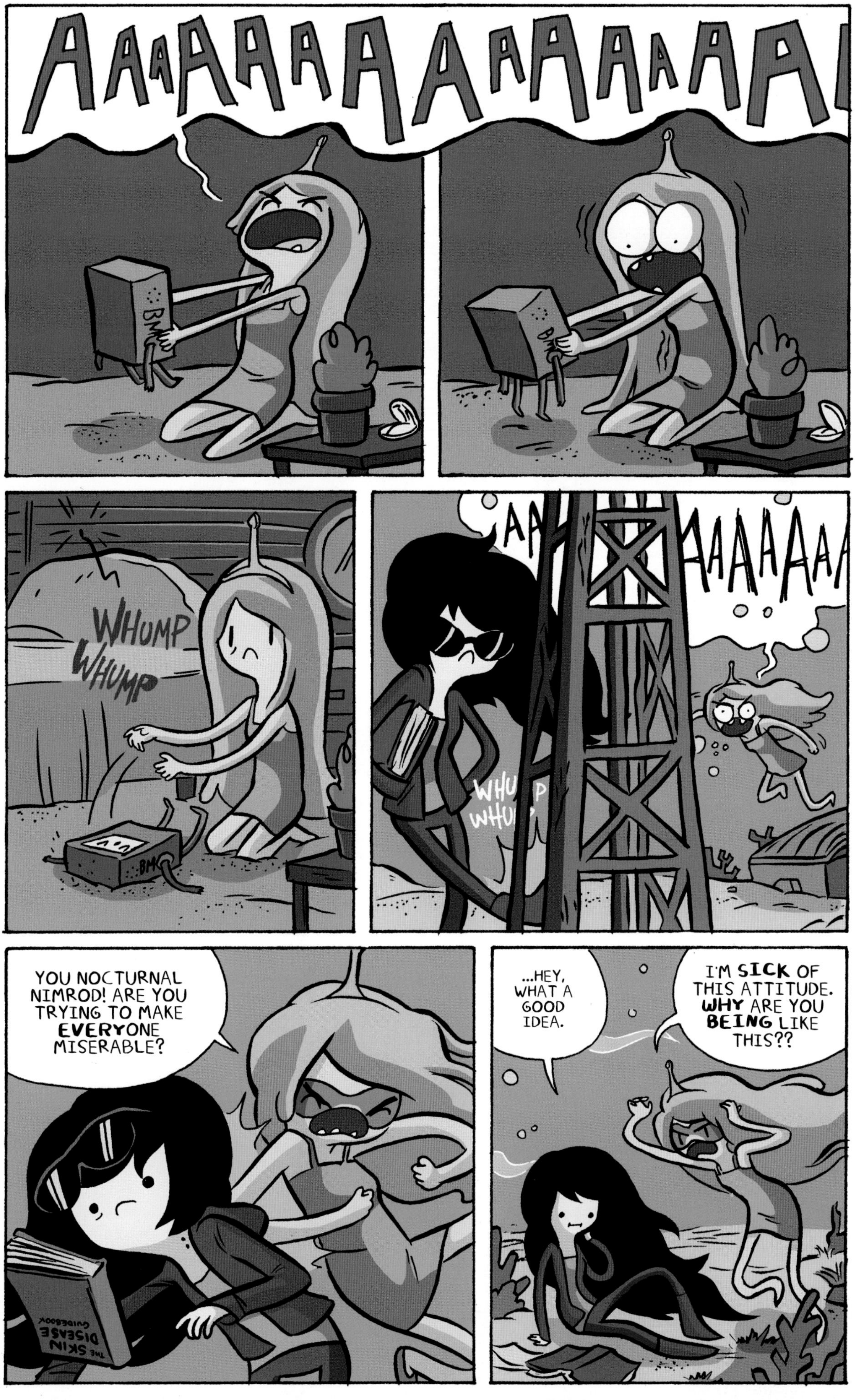
AAAAAAAAAAAAAAA
WHUMP
WHUMP
AAAAAAAAAA
WHUMP
YOU NOCTURNAL NIMROD! ARE YOU TRYING TO MAKE EVERYONE MISERABLE?
THE SKIN DISEASE GUIDEBOOK
...HEY, WHAT A GOOD IDEA.
I'M SICK OF THIS ATTITUDE. WHY ARE YOU BEING LIKE THIS??

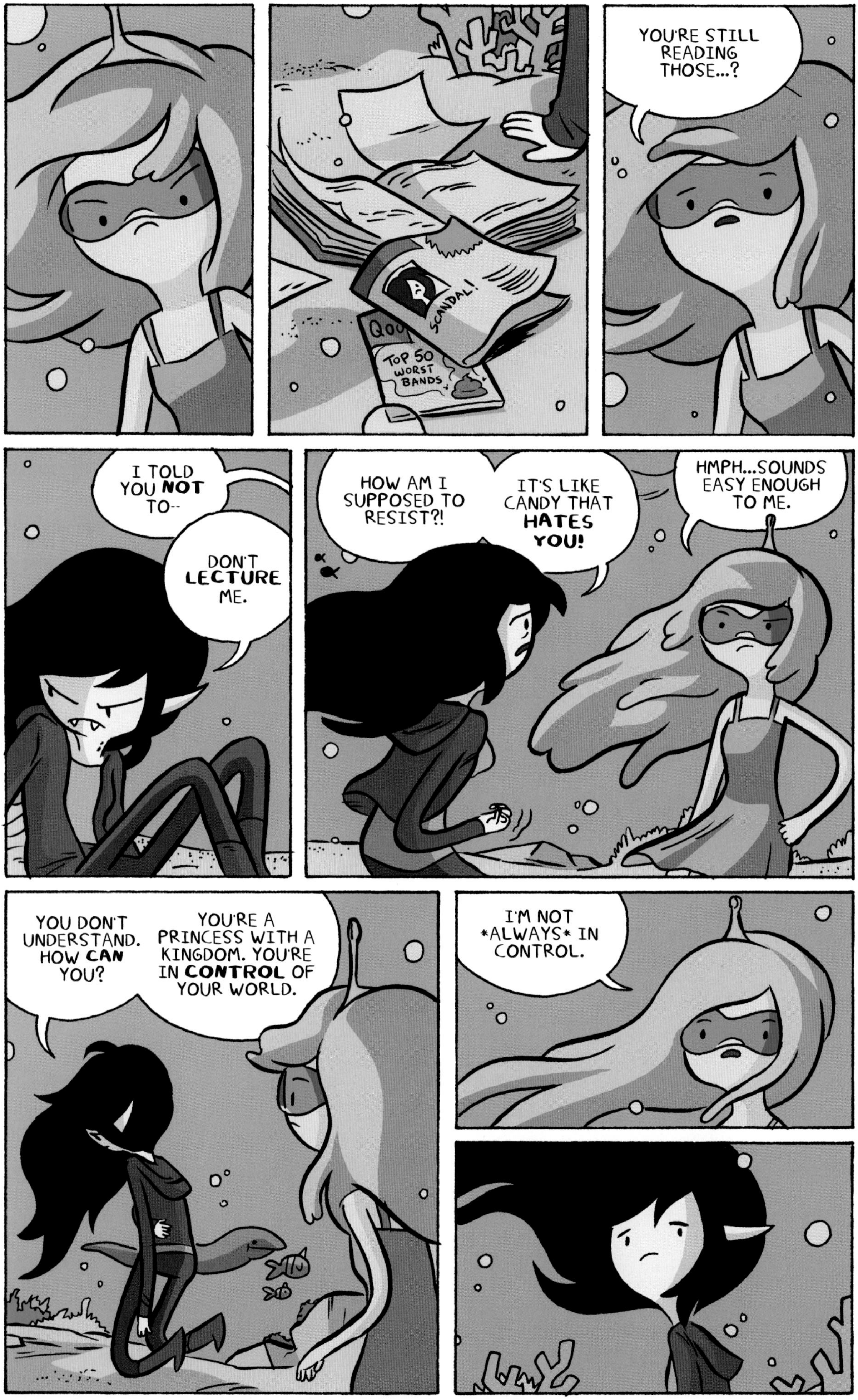
SCANDAL!
TOP 50 WORST BANDS
YOU'RE STILL READING THOSE...?
I TOLD YOU NOT TO--
DON'T LECTURE ME.
HOW AM I SUPPOSED TO RESIST?!
IT'S LIKE CANDY THAT HATES YOU!
HMPH...SOUNDS EASY ENOUGH TO ME.
YOU DON'T UNDERSTAND. HOW CAN YOU?
YOU'RE A PRINCESS WITH A KINGDOM. YOU'RE IN CONTROL OF YOUR WORLD.
I'M NOT *ALWAYS* IN CONTROL.

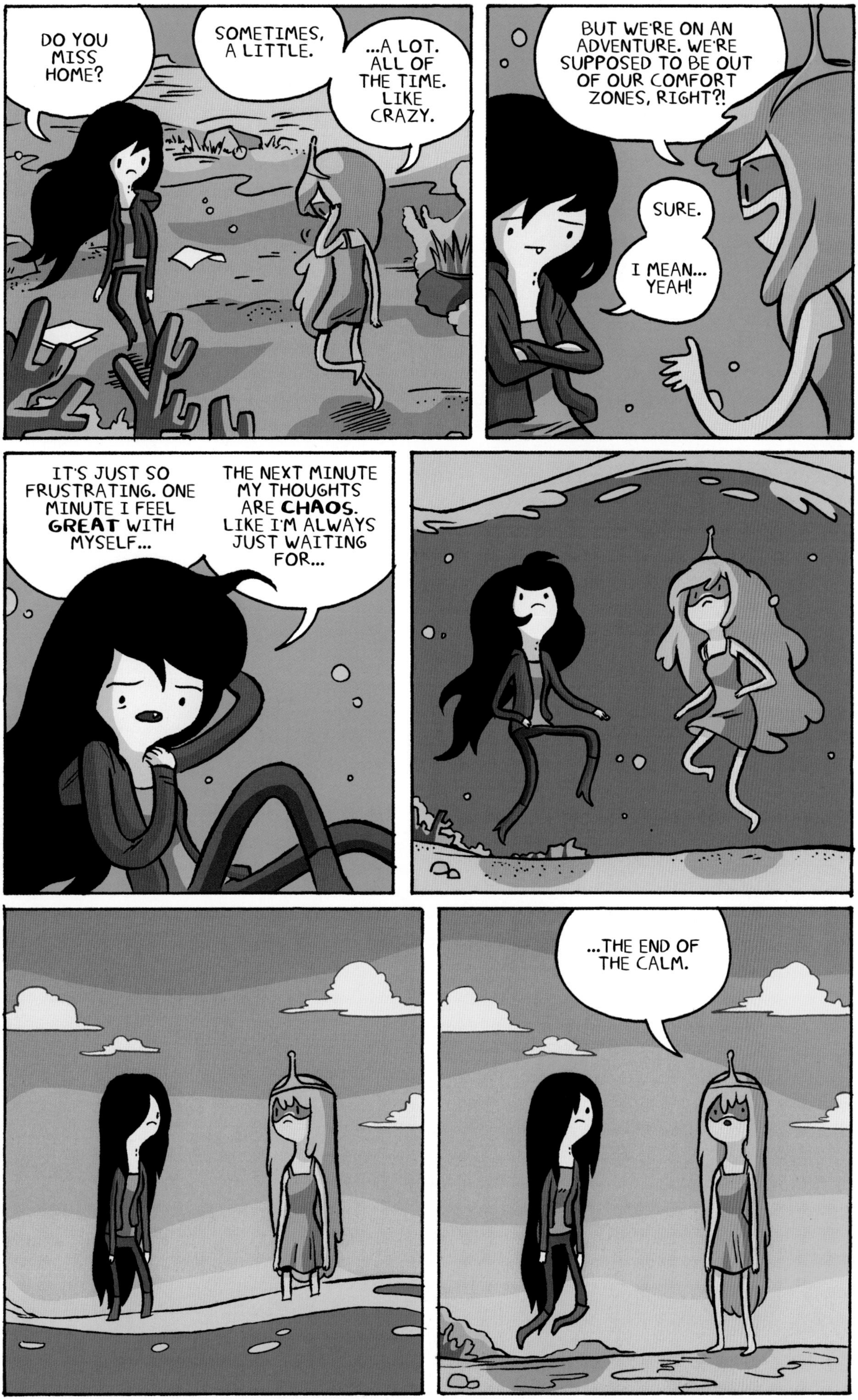
DO YOU MISS HOME?
SOMETIMES, A LITTLE.
...A LOT. ALL OF THE TIME. LIKE CRAZY.
BUT WE'RE ON AN ADVENTURE. WE'RE SUPPOSED TO BE OUT OF OUR COMFORT ZONES, RIGHT?!
SURE.
I MEAN... YEAH!
IT'S JUST SO FRUSTRATING. ONE MINUTE I FEEL GREAT WITH MYSELF...
THE NEXT MINUTE MY THOUGHTS ARE CHAOS. LIKE I'M ALWAYS JUST WAITING FOR...
...THE END OF THE CALM.

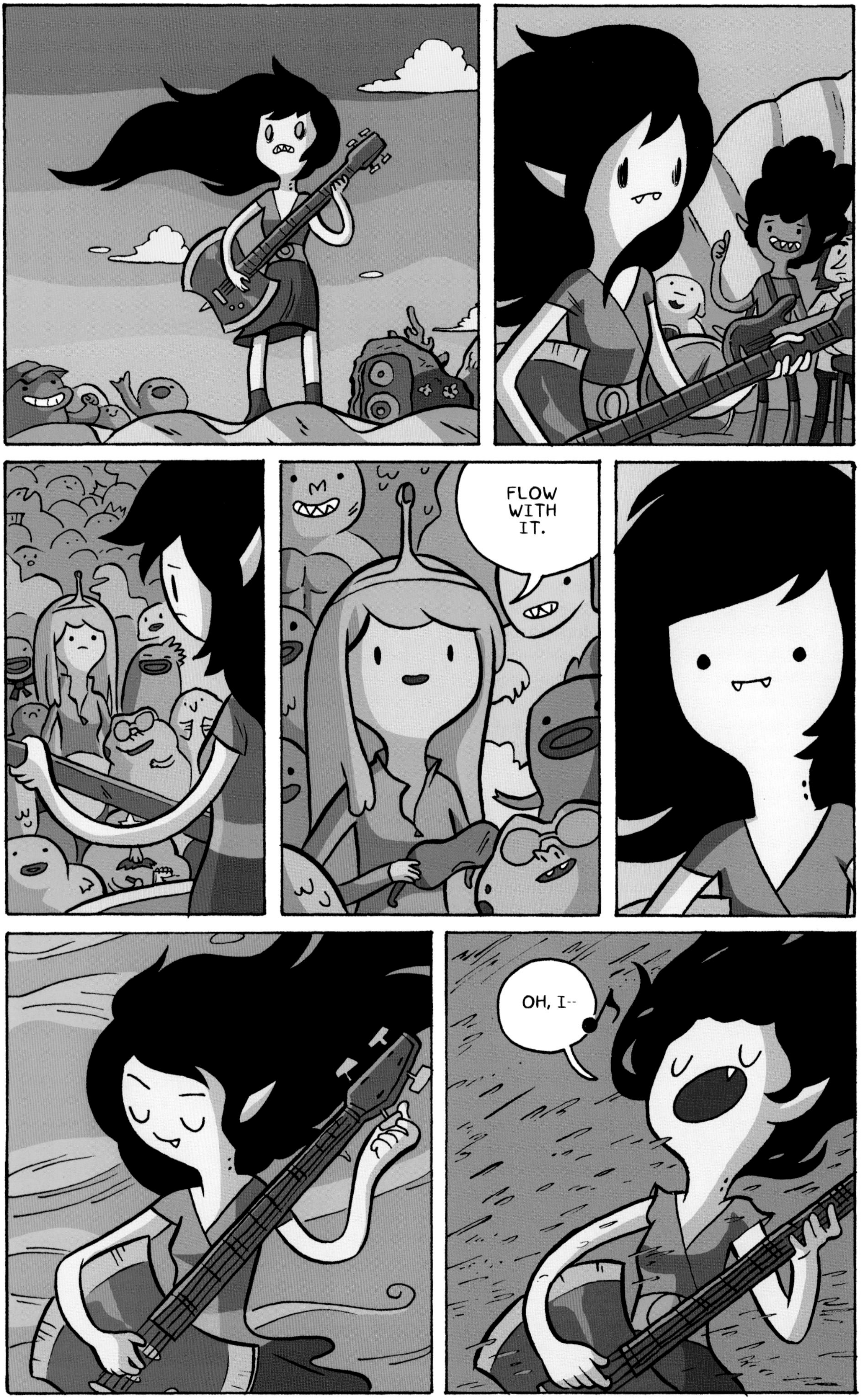
FLOW WITH IT.
OH, I--

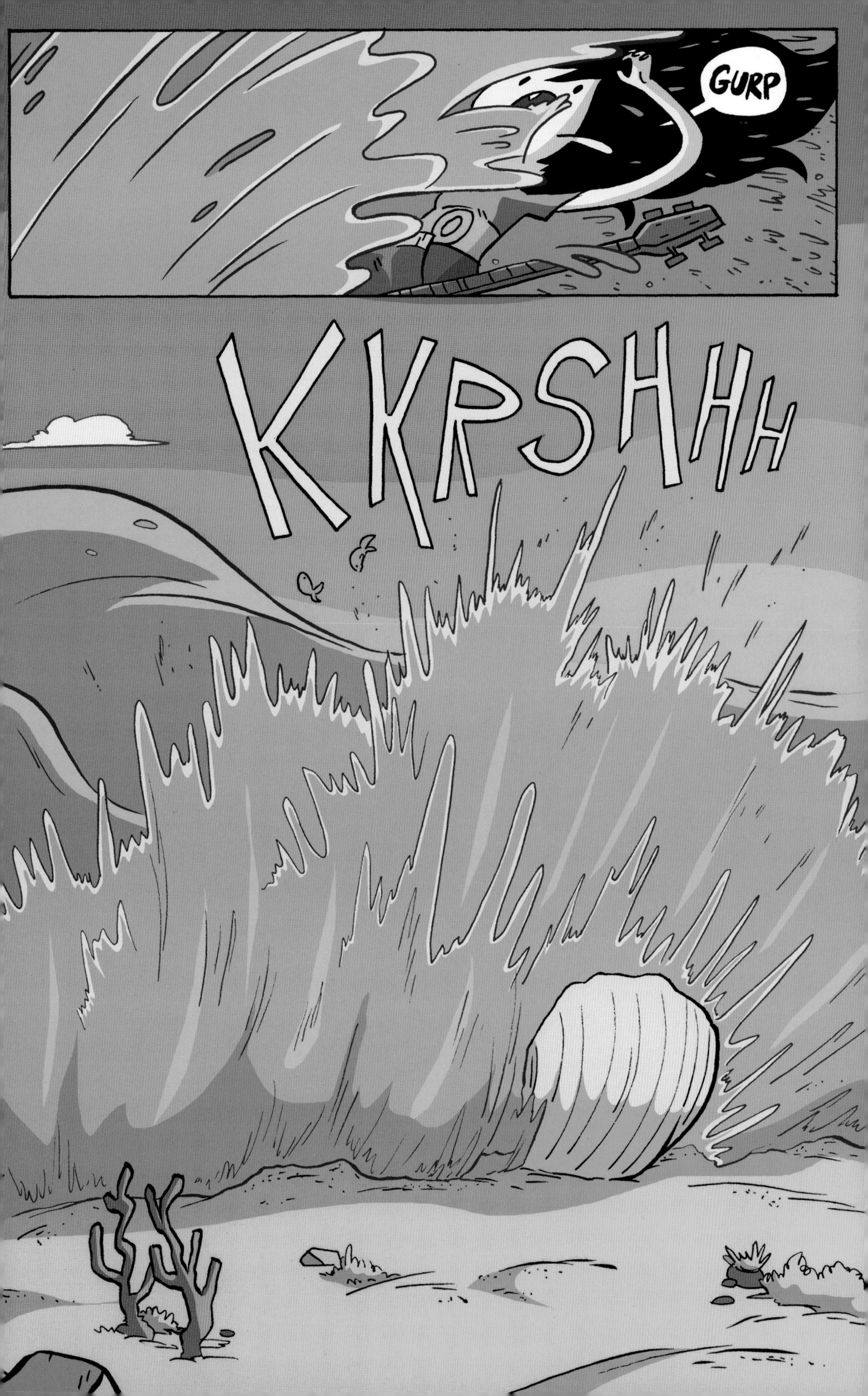
GURP
KKRSHHH

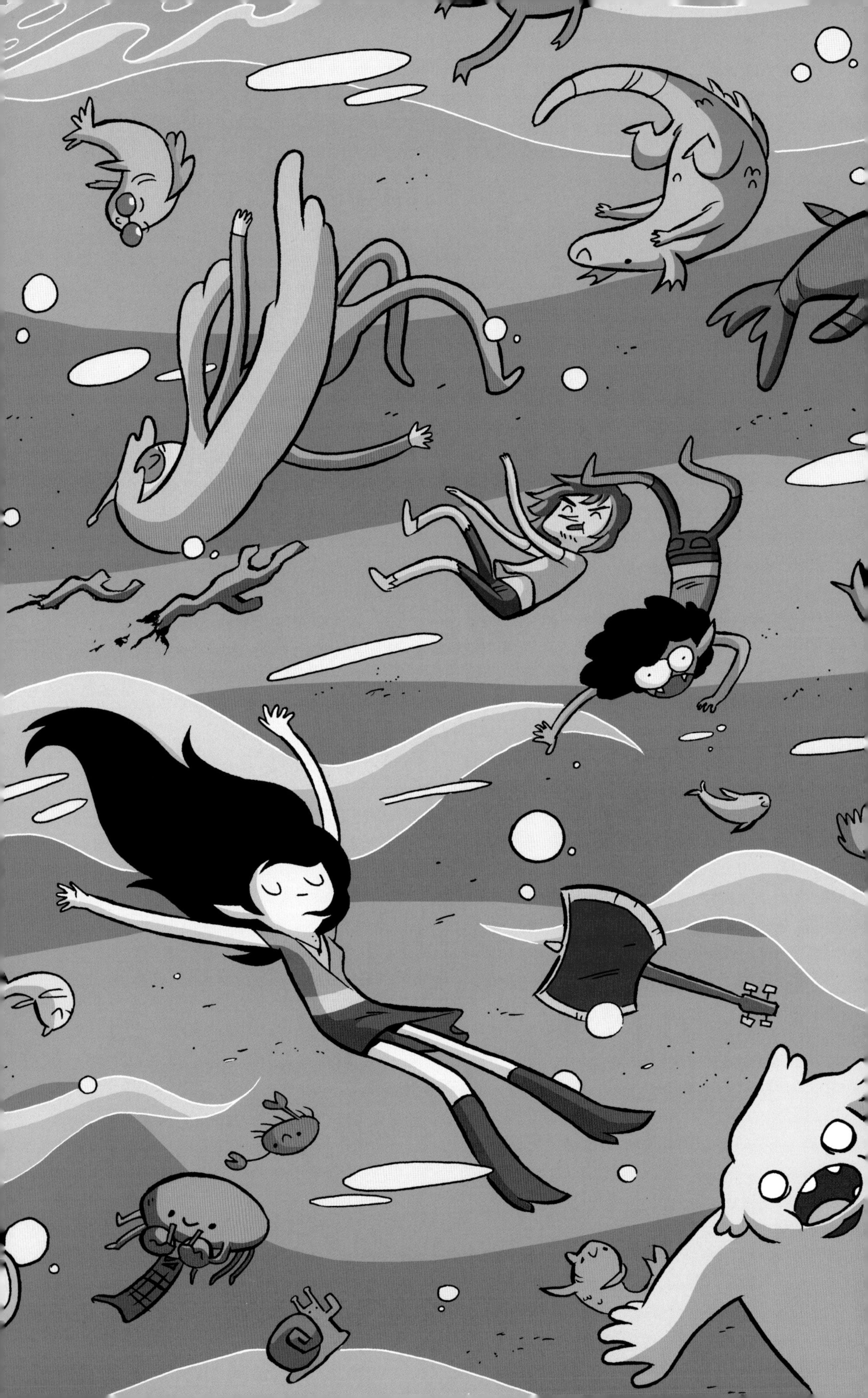

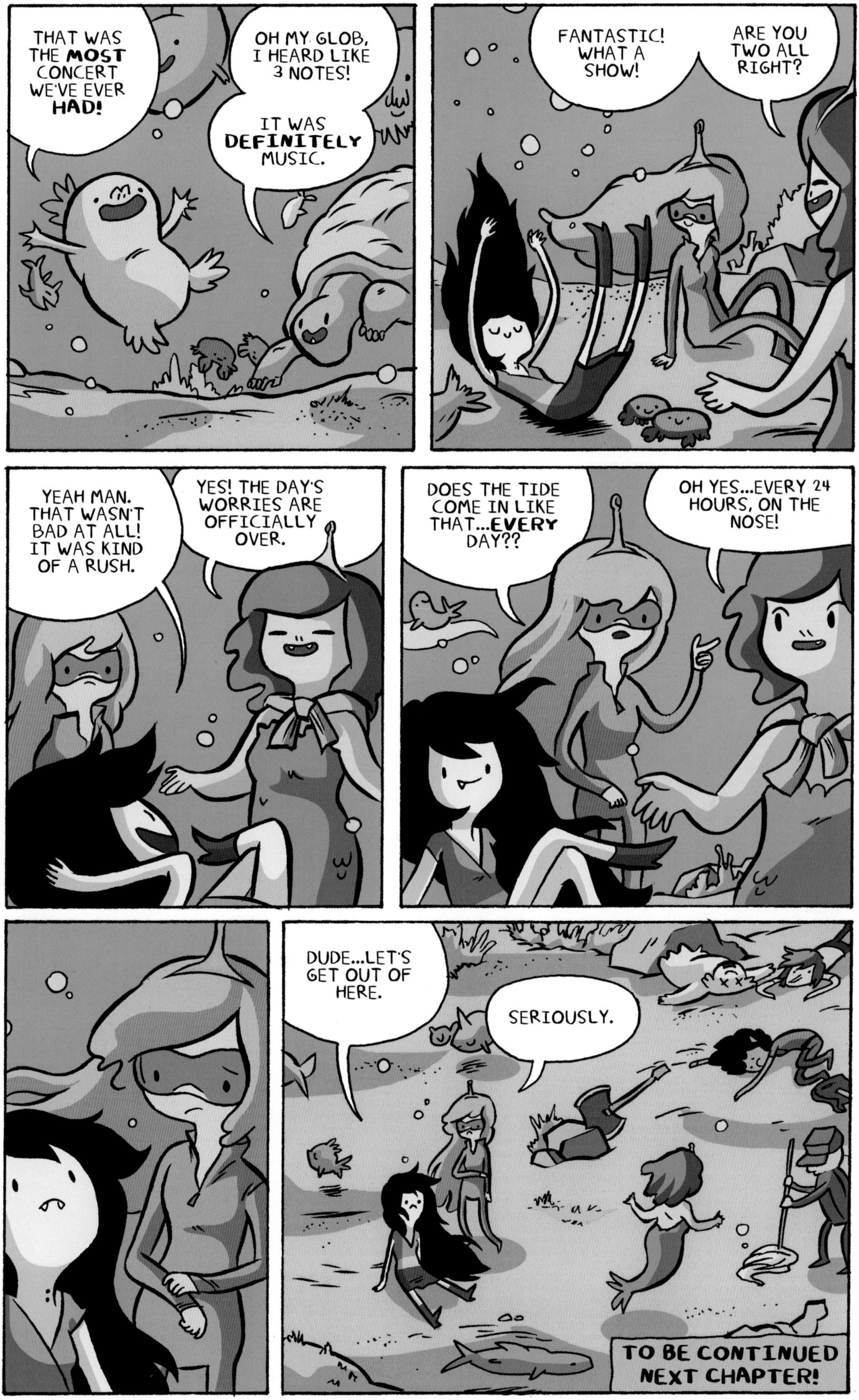
THAT WAS THE **MOST** CONCERT WE'VE EVER **HAD!**
OH MY GLOB, I HEARD LIKE 3 NOTES!
IT WAS **DEFINITELY** MUSIC.
FANTASTIC! WHAT A SHOW!
ARE YOU TWO ALL RIGHT?
YEAH MAN. THAT WASN'T BAD AT ALL! IT WAS KIND OF A RUSH.
YES! THE DAY'S WORRIES ARE OFFICIALLY OVER.
DOES THE TIDE COME IN LIKE THAT...**EVERY** DAY??
OH YES...EVERY 24 HOURS, ON THE NOSE!
DUDE...LET'S GET OUT OF HERE.
SERIOUSLY.
TO BE CONTINUED NEXT CHAPTER!

CHAPTER FIVE

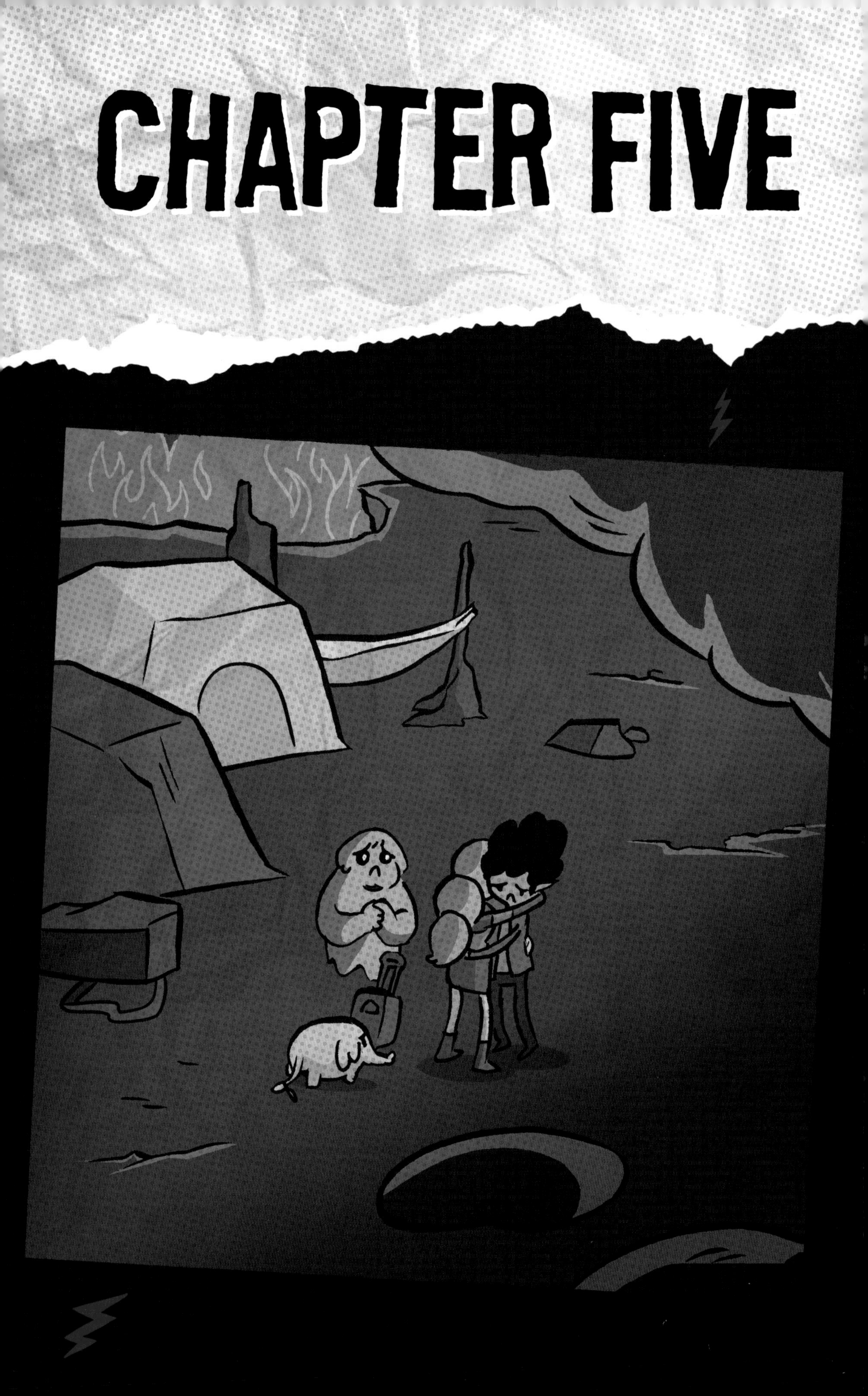

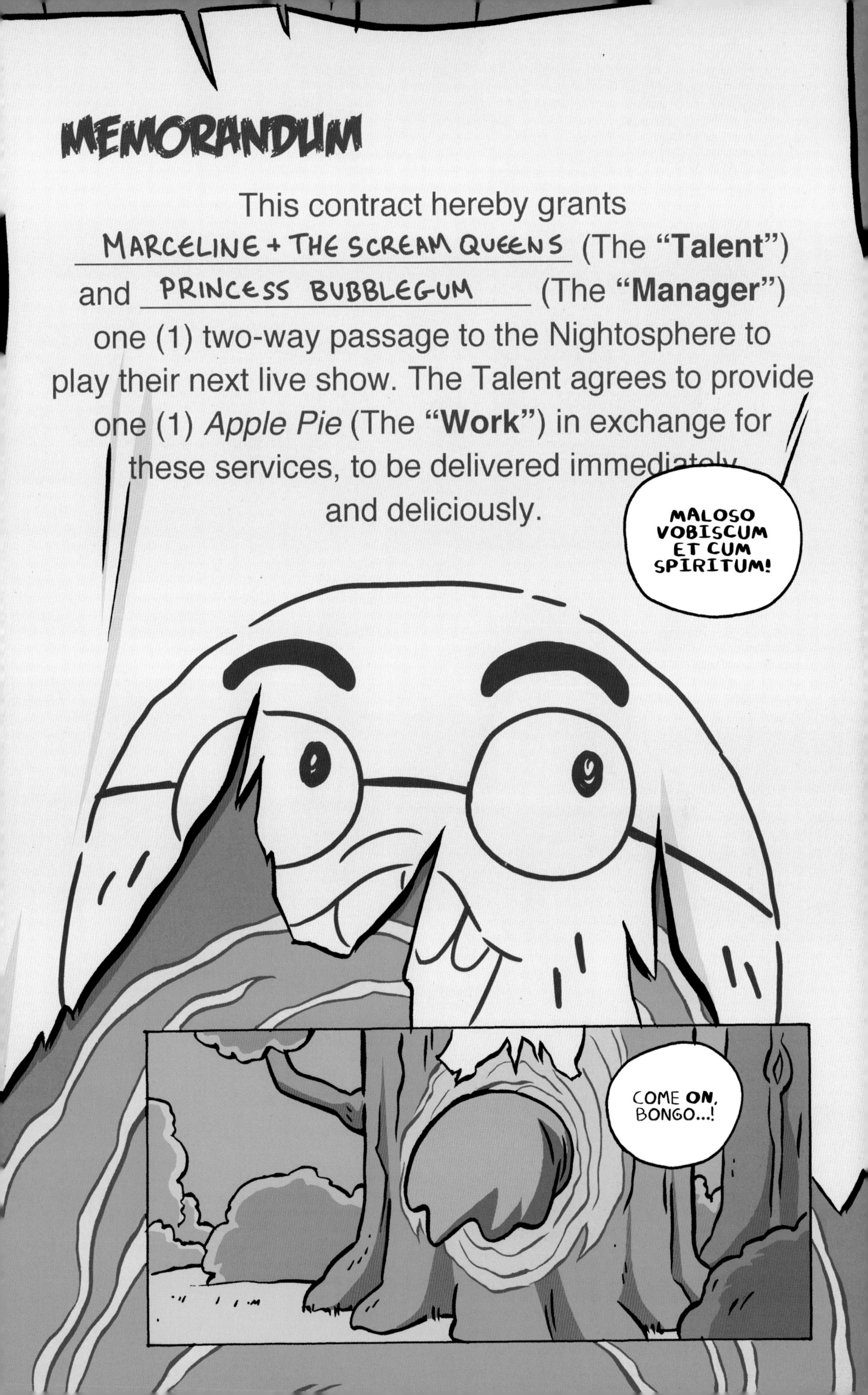
MEMORANDUM
This contract hereby grants
MARCELINE + THE SCREAM QUEENS (The "Talent")
and PRINCESS BUBBLEGUM (The "Manager")
one (1) two-way passage to the Nightosphere to play their next live show. The Talent agrees to provide one (1) Apple Pie (The "Work") in exchange for these services, to be delivered immediately and deliciously.
MALOSO VOBISCUM ET CUM SPIRITUM!
COME ON, BONGO...!

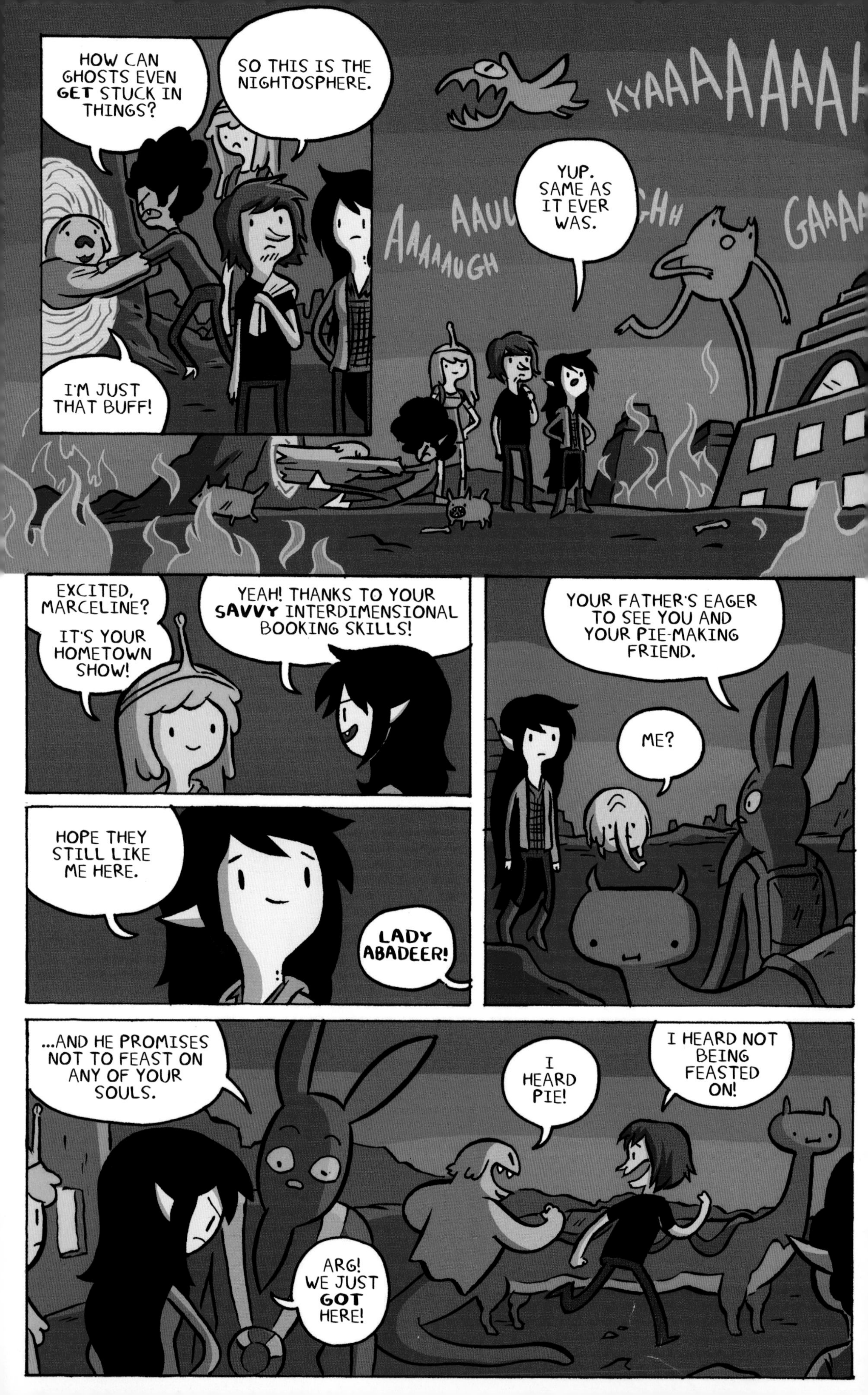
HOW CAN GHOSTS EVEN GET STUCK IN THINGS?
SO THIS IS THE NIGHTOSPHERE.
I'M JUST THAT BUFF!
KYAAAAAAAAH
YUP. SAME AS IT EVER WAS.
AAAAAAUGH
AAUGHH
GAAA
EXCITED, MARCELINE?
IT'S YOUR HOMETOWN SHOW!
YEAH! THANKS TO YOUR SAVVY INTERDIMENSIONAL BOOKING SKILLS!
HOPE THEY STILL LIKE ME HERE.
LADY ABADEER!
YOUR FATHER'S EAGER TO SEE YOU AND YOUR PIE-MAKING FRIEND.
ME?
...AND HE PROMISES NOT TO FEAST ON ANY OF YOUR SOULS.
ARG! WE JUST GOT HERE!
I HEARD PIE!
I HEARD NOT BEING FEASTED ON!

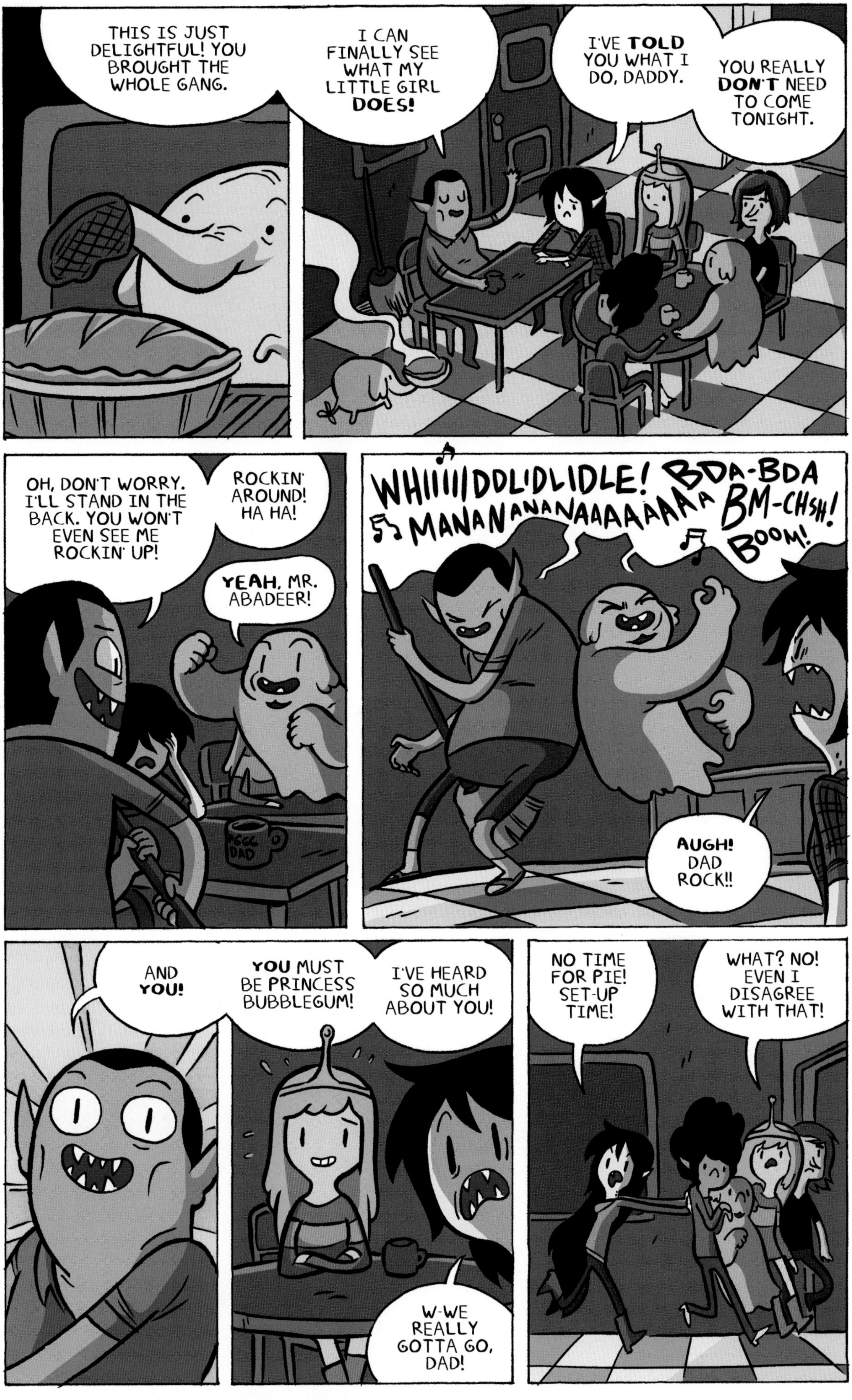
THIS IS JUST DELIGHTFUL! YOU BROUGHT THE WHOLE GANG.
I CAN FINALLY SEE WHAT MY LITTLE GIRL DOES!
I'VE TOLD YOU WHAT I DO, DADDY.
YOU REALLY DON'T NEED TO COME TONIGHT.
OH, DON'T WORRY. I'LL STAND IN THE BACK. YOU WON'T EVEN SEE ME ROCKIN' UP!
ROCKIN' AROUND! HA HA!
YEAH, MR. ABADEER!
#666 DAD
WHIIIIIIDDLIDLIDLE! BDA-BDA MANANANANAAAAAAAAA BM-CHSH! BOOM!
AUGH! DAD ROCK!!
AND YOU!
YOU MUST BE PRINCESS BUBBLEGUM!
I'VE HEARD SO MUCH ABOUT YOU!
W-WE REALLY GOTTA GO, DAD!
NO TIME FOR PIE! SET-UP TIME!
WHAT? NO! EVEN I DISAGREE WITH THAT!

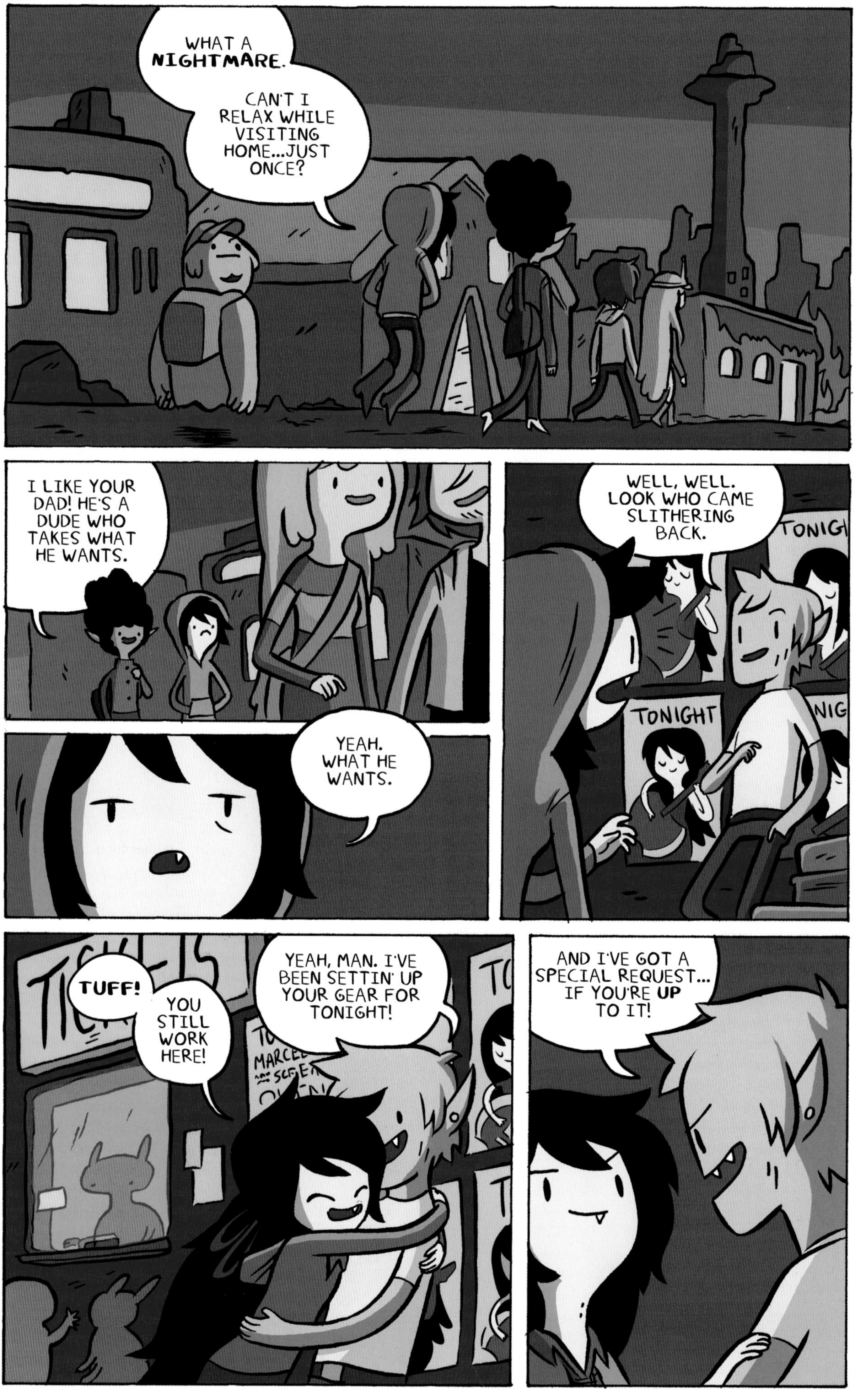
WHAT A NIGHTMARE.
CAN'T I RELAX WHILE VISITING HOME...JUST ONCE?
I LIKE YOUR DAD! HE'S A DUDE WHO TAKES WHAT HE WANTS.
YEAH. WHAT HE WANTS.
WELL, WELL. LOOK WHO CAME SLITHERING BACK.
TONIGHT
TUFF!
YOU STILL WORK HERE!
YEAH, MAN. I'VE BEEN SETTIN' UP YOUR GEAR FOR TONIGHT!
AND I'VE GOT A SPECIAL REQUEST... IF YOU'RE UP TO IT!

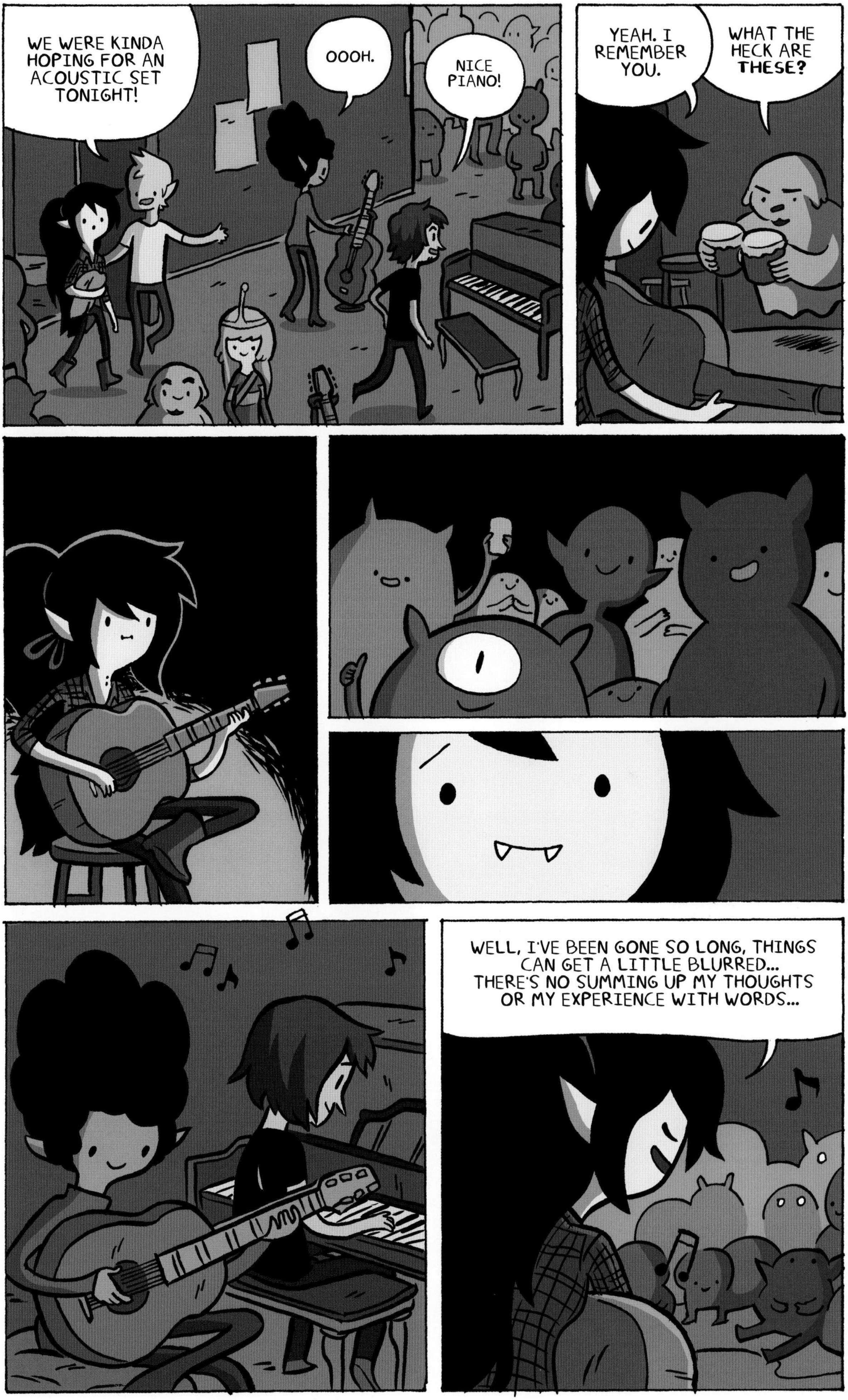
WE WERE KINDA HOPING FOR AN ACOUSTIC SET TONIGHT!
OOOH.
NICE PIANO!
YEAH. I REMEMBER YOU.
WHAT THE HECK ARE THESE?
WELL, I'VE BEEN GONE SO LONG, THINGS CAN GET A LITTLE BLURRED... THERE'S NO SUMMING UP MY THOUGHTS OR MY EXPERIENCE WITH WORDS...

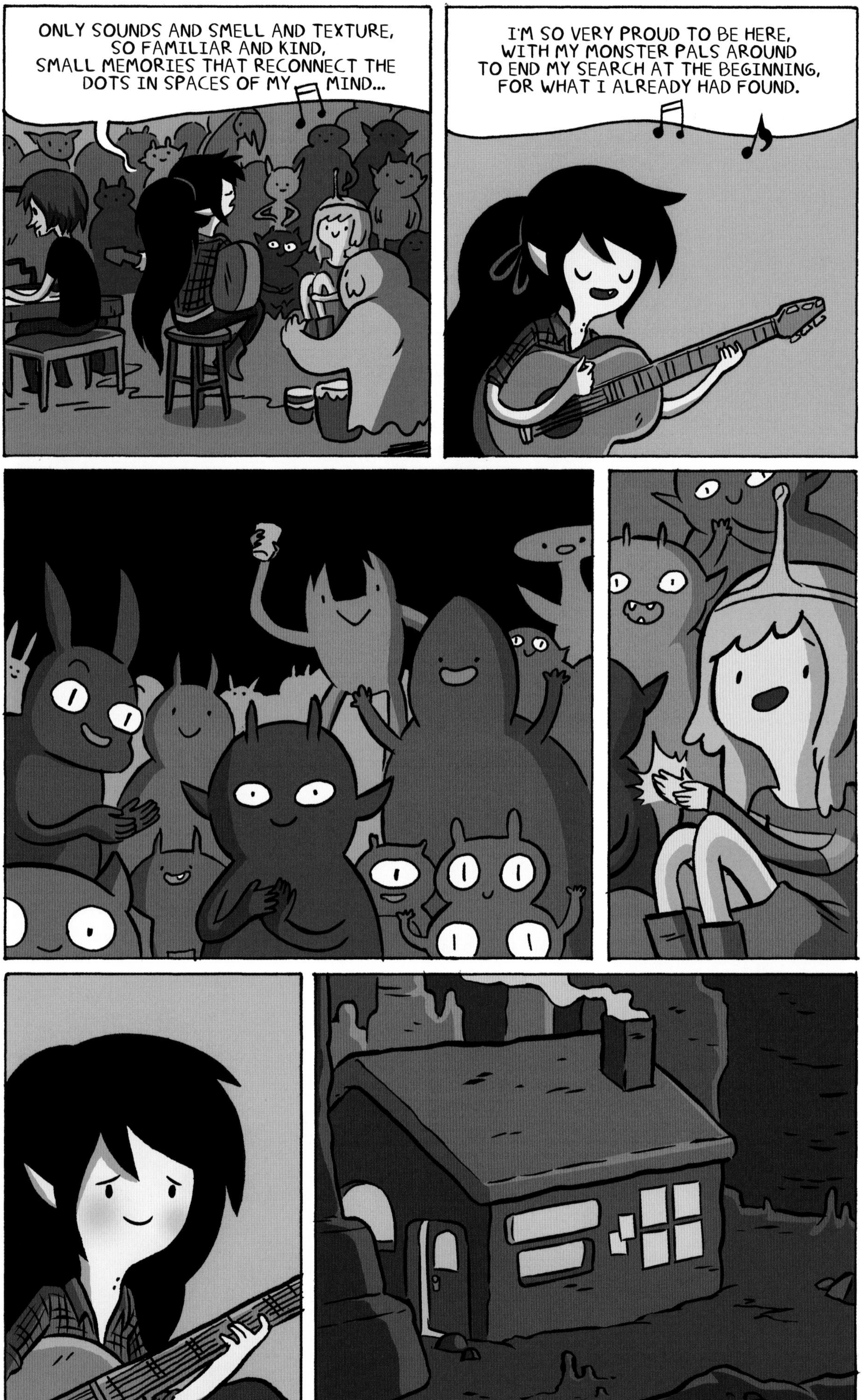
ONLY SOUNDS AND SMELL AND TEXTURE, SO FAMILIAR AND KIND, SMALL MEMORIES THAT RECONNECT THE DOTS IN SPACES OF MY MIND...
I'M SO VERY PROUD TO BE HERE, WITH MY MONSTER PALS AROUND TO END MY SEARCH AT THE BEGINNING, FOR WHAT I ALREADY HAD FOUND.

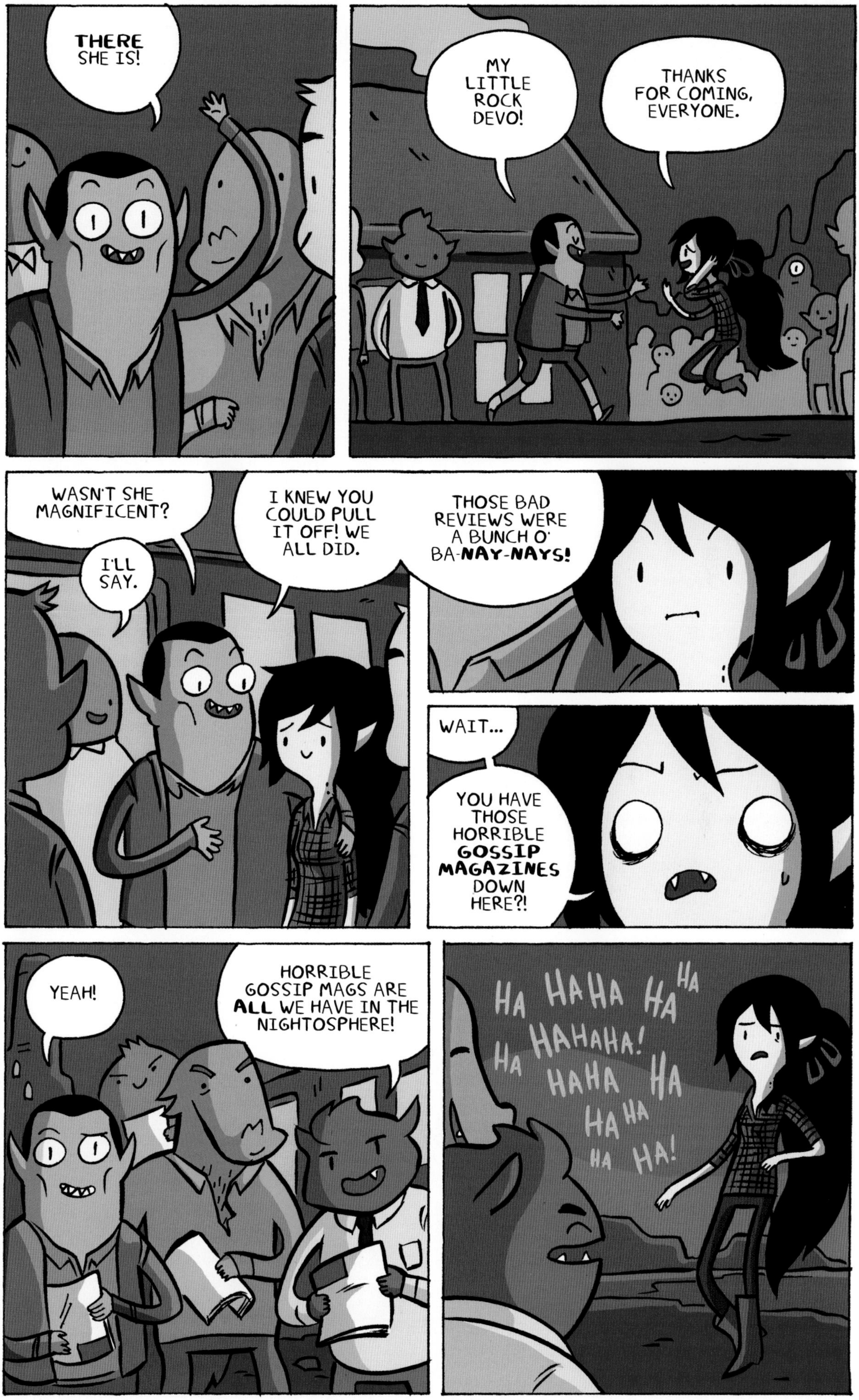
THERE SHE IS!
MY LITTLE ROCK DEVO!
THANKS FOR COMING, EVERYONE.
WASN'T SHE MAGNIFICENT?
I'LL SAY.
I KNEW YOU COULD PULL IT OFF! WE ALL DID.
THOSE BAD REVIEWS WERE A BUNCH O' BA-NAY-NAYS!
WAIT...
YOU HAVE THOSE HORRIBLE GOSSIP MAGAZINES DOWN HERE?!
YEAH!
HORRIBLE GOSSIP MAGS ARE ALL WE HAVE IN THE NIGHTOSPHERE!
HA HAHA HA HA
HA HAHAHA!
HA HAHA HA
HA HA
HA HA!

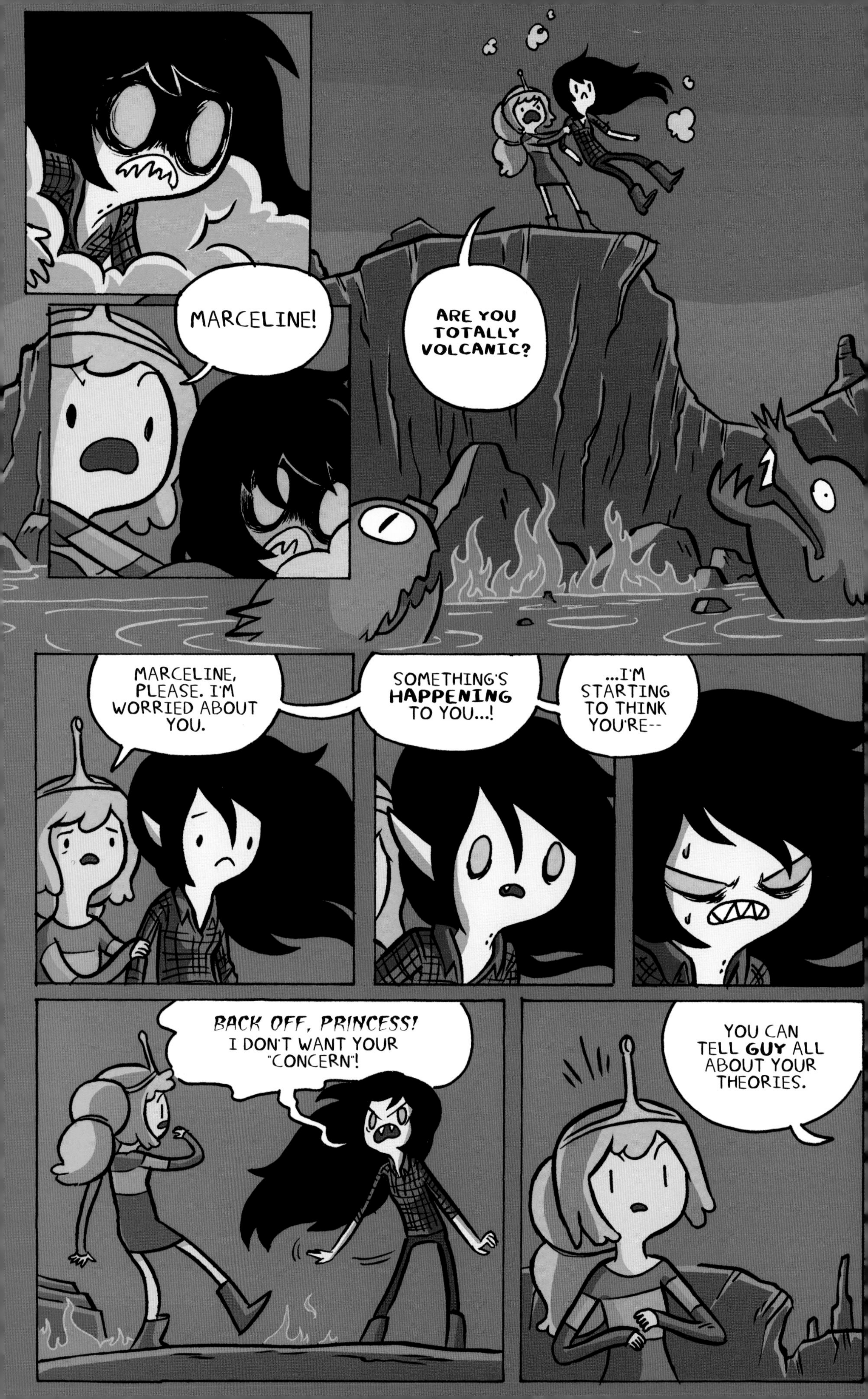
MARCELINE!
ARE YOU TOTALLY VOLCANIC?
MARCELINE, PLEASE. I'M WORRIED ABOUT YOU.
SOMETHING'S **HAPPENING** TO YOU...!
...I'M STARTING TO THINK YOU'RE--
BACK OFF, PRINCESS! I DON'T WANT YOUR "CONCERN"!
YOU CAN TELL **GUY** ALL ABOUT YOUR THEORIES.

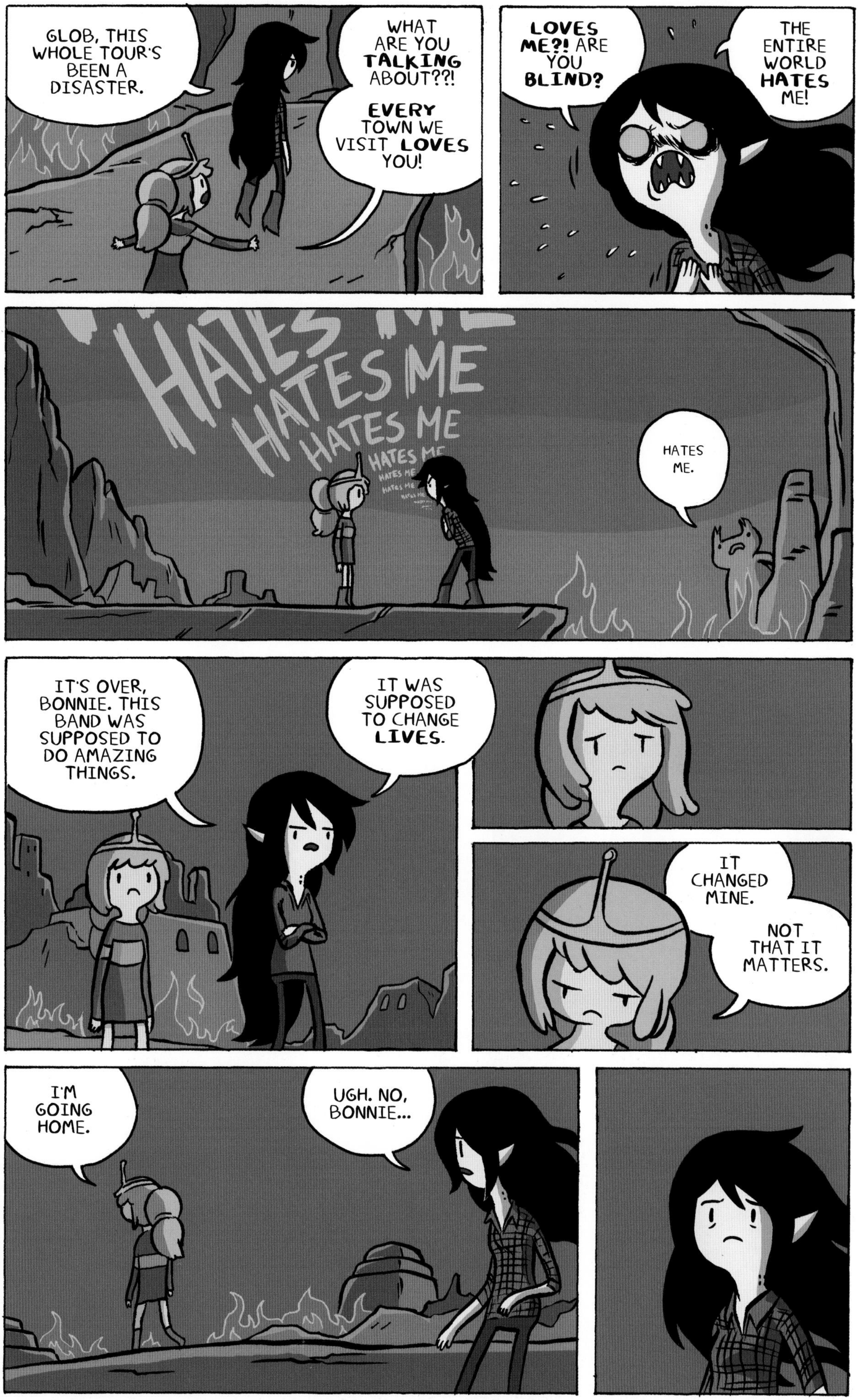
GLOB, THIS WHOLE TOUR'S BEEN A DISASTER.
WHAT ARE YOU **TALKING** ABOUT??!
EVERY TOWN WE VISIT **LOVES** YOU!
LOVES ME?! ARE YOU **BLIND?**
THE ENTIRE WORLD **HATES** ME!
HATES ME
HATES ME
HATES ME
HATES ME
HATES ME
HATES ME
HATES ME
HATES ME.
IT'S OVER, BONNIE. THIS BAND WAS SUPPOSED TO DO AMAZING THINGS.
IT WAS SUPPOSED TO CHANGE **LIVES**.
IT CHANGED MINE.
NOT THAT IT MATTERS.
I'M GOING HOME.
UGH. NO, BONNIE...

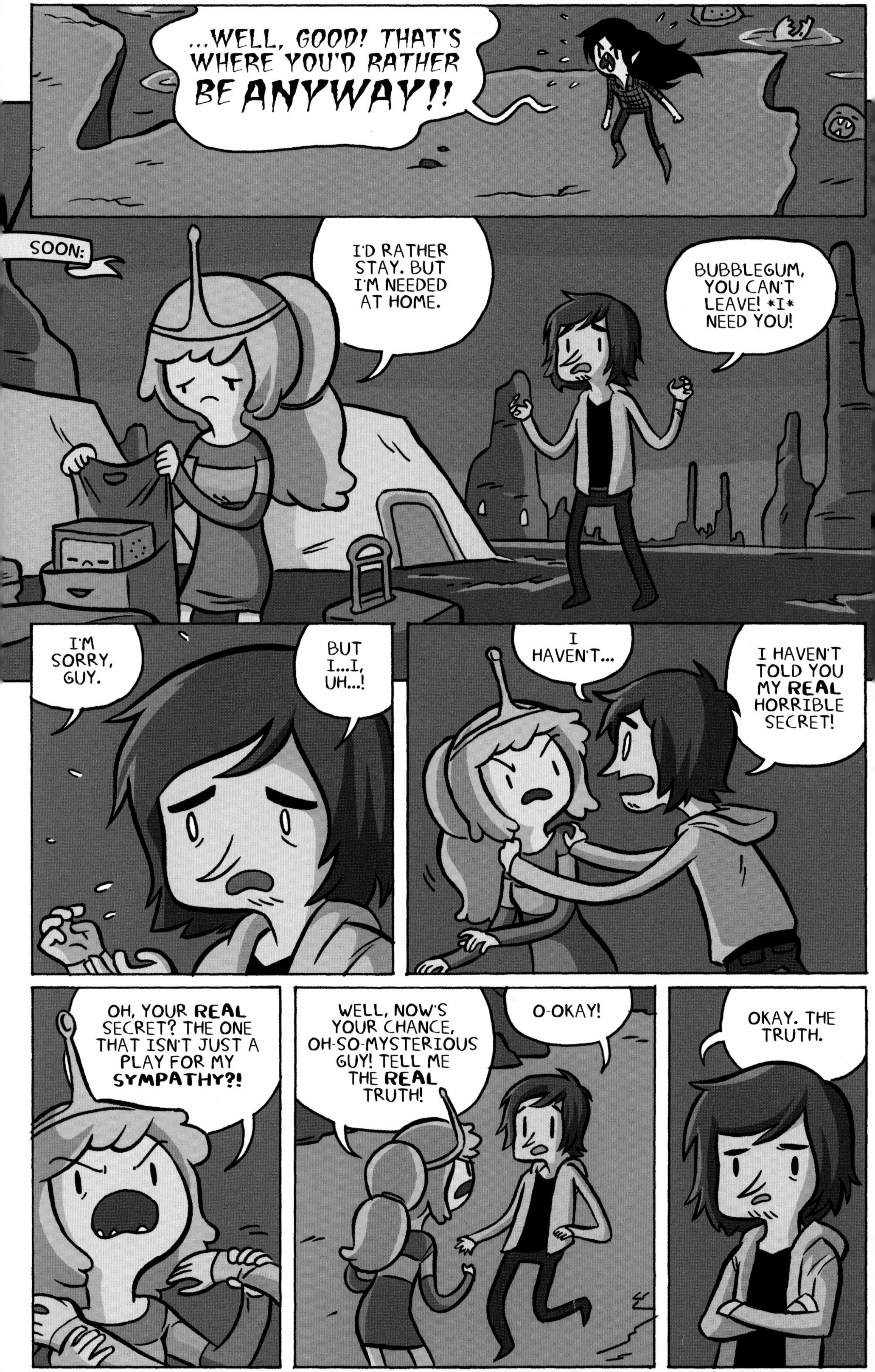
...WELL, GOOD! THAT'S WHERE YOU'D RATHER BE ANYWAY!!
SOON:
I'D RATHER STAY. BUT I'M NEEDED AT HOME.
BUBBLEGUM, YOU CAN'T LEAVE! *I* NEED YOU!
I'M SORRY, GUY.
BUT I...I, UH...!
I HAVEN'T...
I HAVEN'T TOLD YOU MY REAL HORRIBLE SECRET!
OH, YOUR REAL SECRET? THE ONE THAT ISN'T JUST A PLAY FOR MY SYMPATHY?!
WELL, NOW'S YOUR CHANCE, OH-SO-MYSTERIOUS GUY! TELL ME THE REAL TRUTH!
O-OKAY!
OKAY. THE TRUTH.

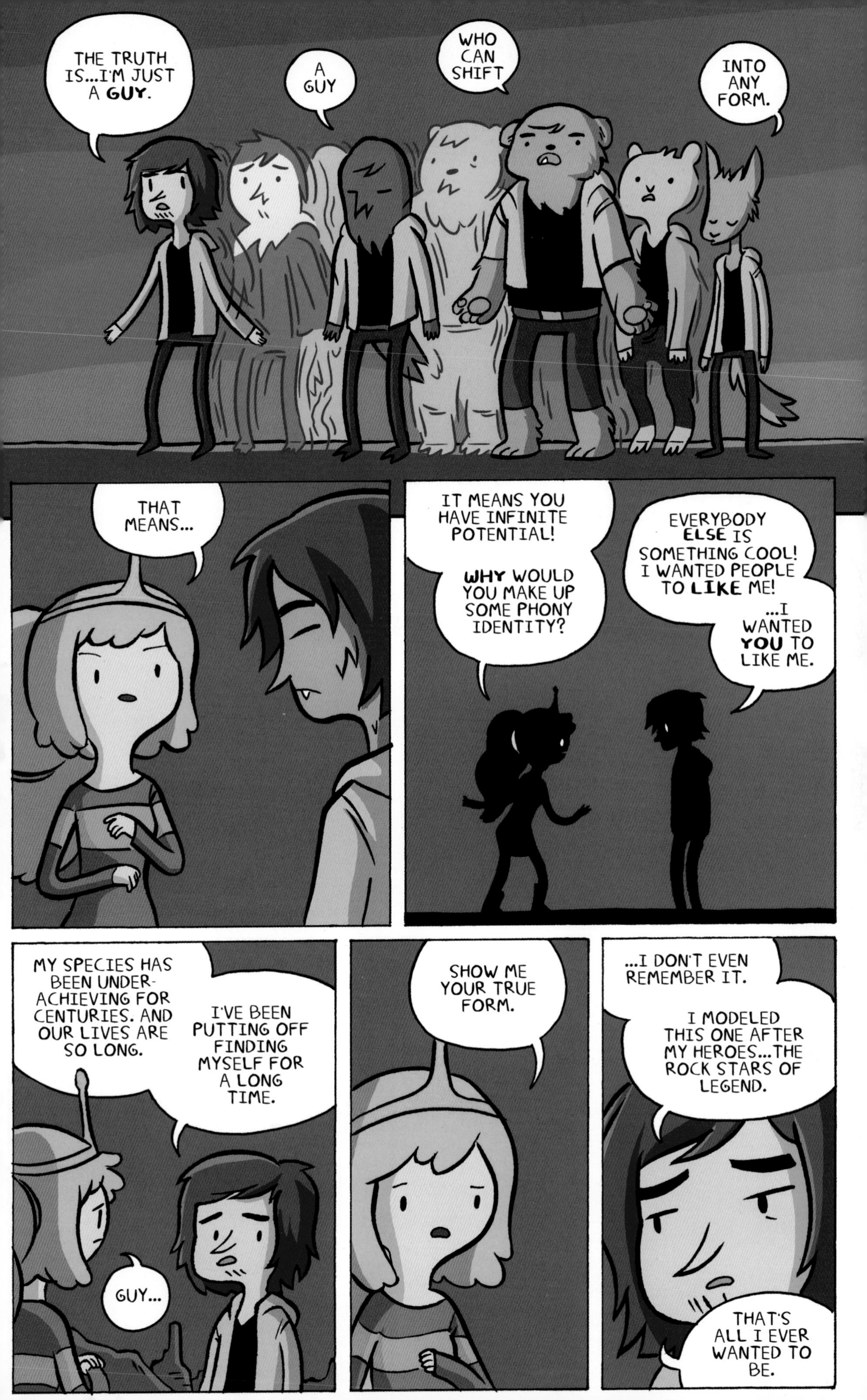
THE TRUTH IS...I'M JUST A **GUY**.
A GUY
WHO CAN SHIFT
INTO ANY FORM.
THAT MEANS...
IT MEANS YOU HAVE INFINITE POTENTIAL!
WHY WOULD YOU MAKE UP SOME PHONY IDENTITY?
EVERYBODY **ELSE** IS SOMETHING COOL! I WANTED PEOPLE TO **LIKE** ME!
...I WANTED **YOU** TO LIKE ME.
MY SPECIES HAS BEEN UNDER-ACHIEVING FOR CENTURIES. AND OUR LIVES ARE SO LONG.
I'VE BEEN PUTTING OFF FINDING MYSELF FOR A LONG TIME.
GUY...
SHOW ME YOUR TRUE FORM.
...I DON'T EVEN REMEMBER IT.
I MODELED THIS ONE AFTER MY HEROES...THE ROCK STARS OF LEGEND.
THAT'S ALL I EVER WANTED TO BE.

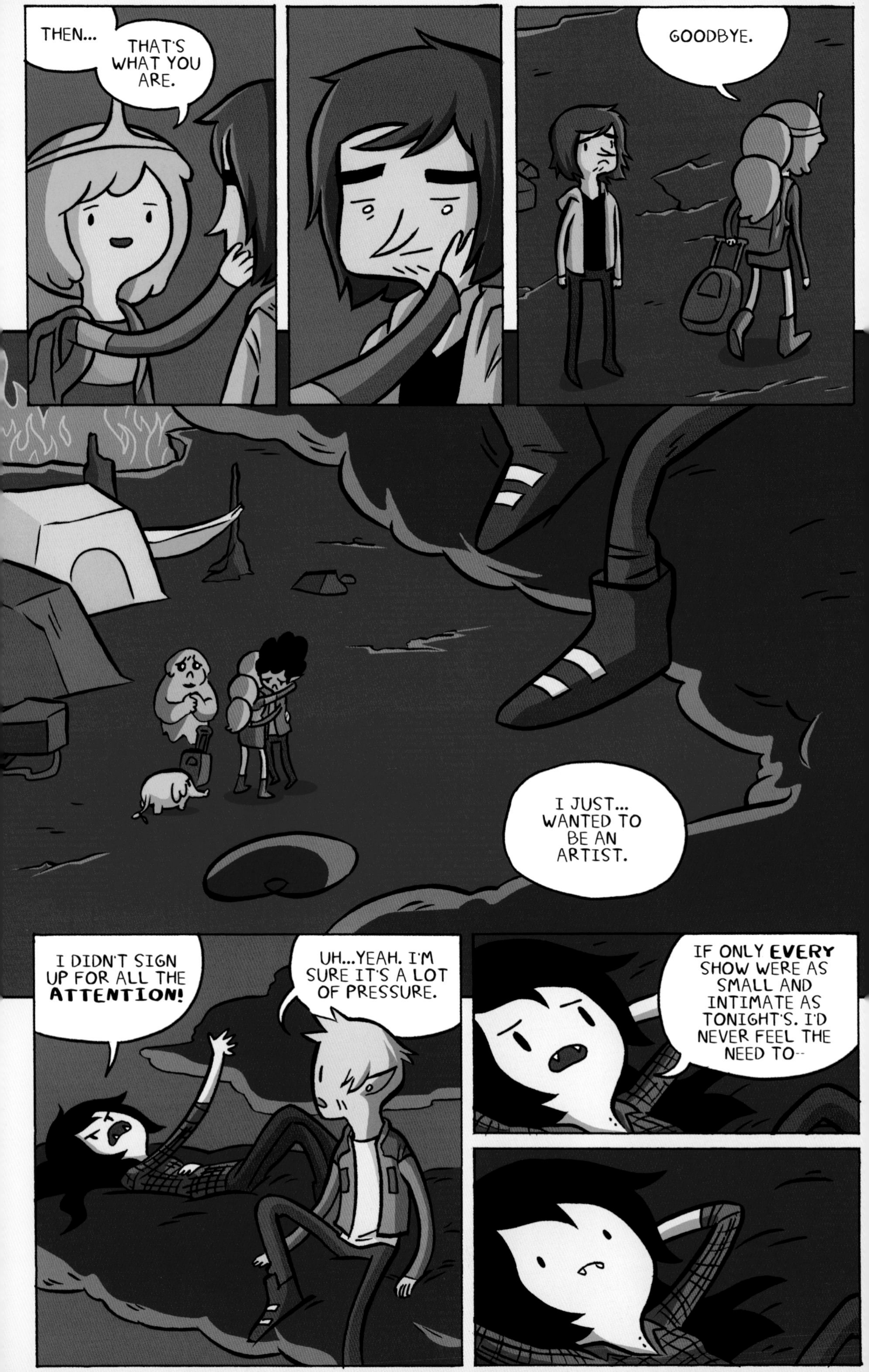
THEN...
THAT'S WHAT YOU ARE.
GOODBYE.
I JUST... WANTED TO BE AN ARTIST.
I DIDN'T SIGN UP FOR ALL THE **ATTENTION!**
UH...YEAH. I'M SURE IT'S A LOT OF PRESSURE.
IF ONLY **EVERY** SHOW WERE AS SMALL AND INTIMATE AS TONIGHT'S. I'D NEVER FEEL THE NEED TO--

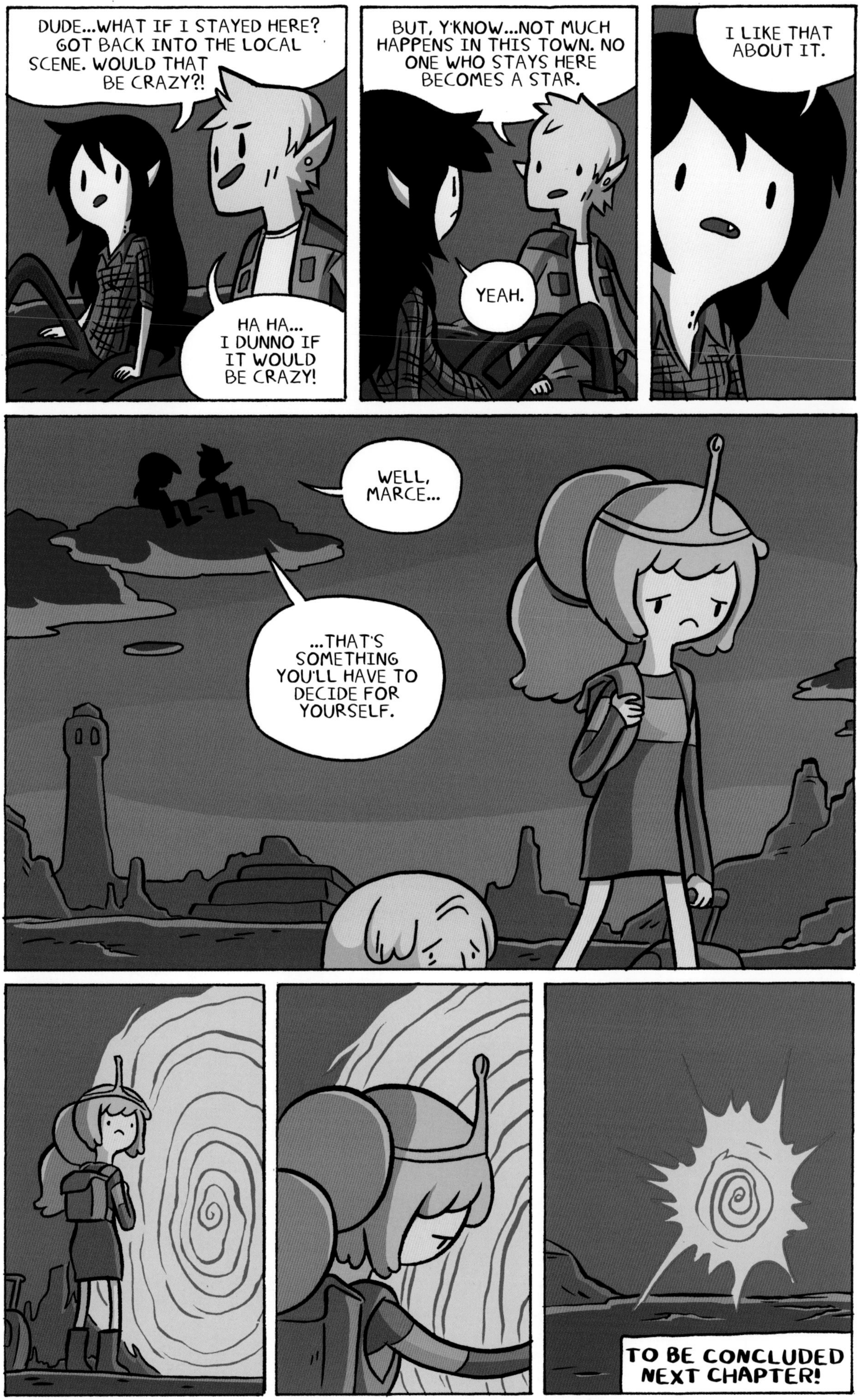
DUDE...WHAT IF I STAYED HERE? GOT BACK INTO THE LOCAL SCENE. WOULD THAT BE CRAZY?!
HA HA... I DUNNO IF IT WOULD BE CRAZY!
BUT, Y'KNOW...NOT MUCH HAPPENS IN THIS TOWN. NO ONE WHO STAYS HERE BECOMES A STAR.
YEAH.
I LIKE THAT ABOUT IT.
WELL, MARCE...
...THAT'S SOMETHING YOU'LL HAVE TO DECIDE FOR YOURSELF.
TO BE CONCLUDED NEXT CHAPTER!

CHAPTER SIX

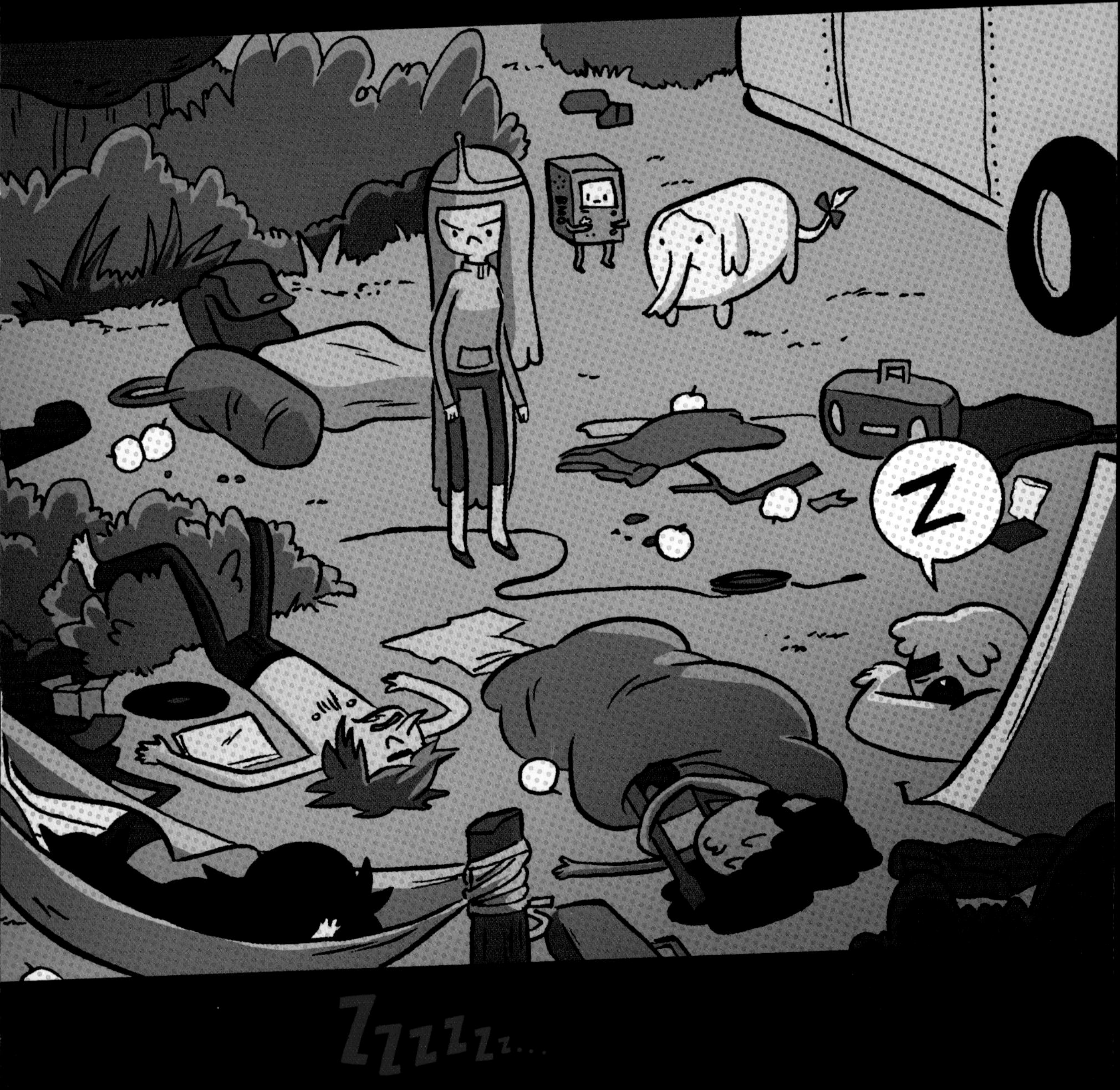

Z
ZZZZZZz...

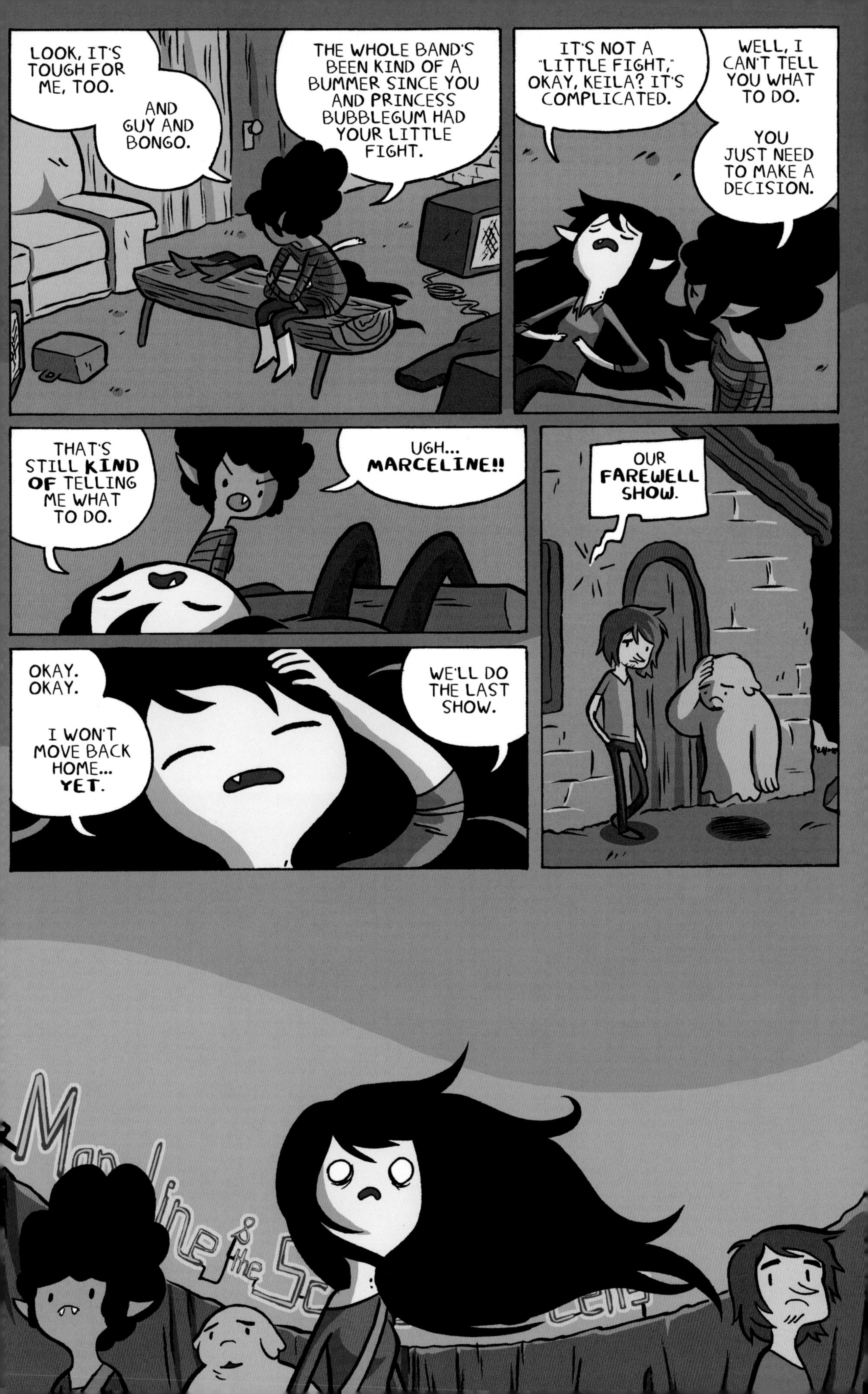
LOOK, IT'S TOUGH FOR ME, TOO.
AND GUY AND BONGO.
THE WHOLE BAND'S BEEN KIND OF A BUMMER SINCE YOU AND PRINCESS BUBBLEGUM HAD YOUR LITTLE FIGHT.
IT'S NOT A "LITTLE FIGHT," OKAY, KEILA? IT'S COMPLICATED.
WELL, I CAN'T TELL YOU WHAT TO DO.
YOU JUST NEED TO MAKE A DECISION.
THAT'S STILL KIND OF TELLING ME WHAT TO DO.
UGH... MARCELINE!!
OUR FAREWELL SHOW.
OKAY. OKAY.
I WON'T MOVE BACK HOME... YET.
WE'LL DO THE LAST SHOW.

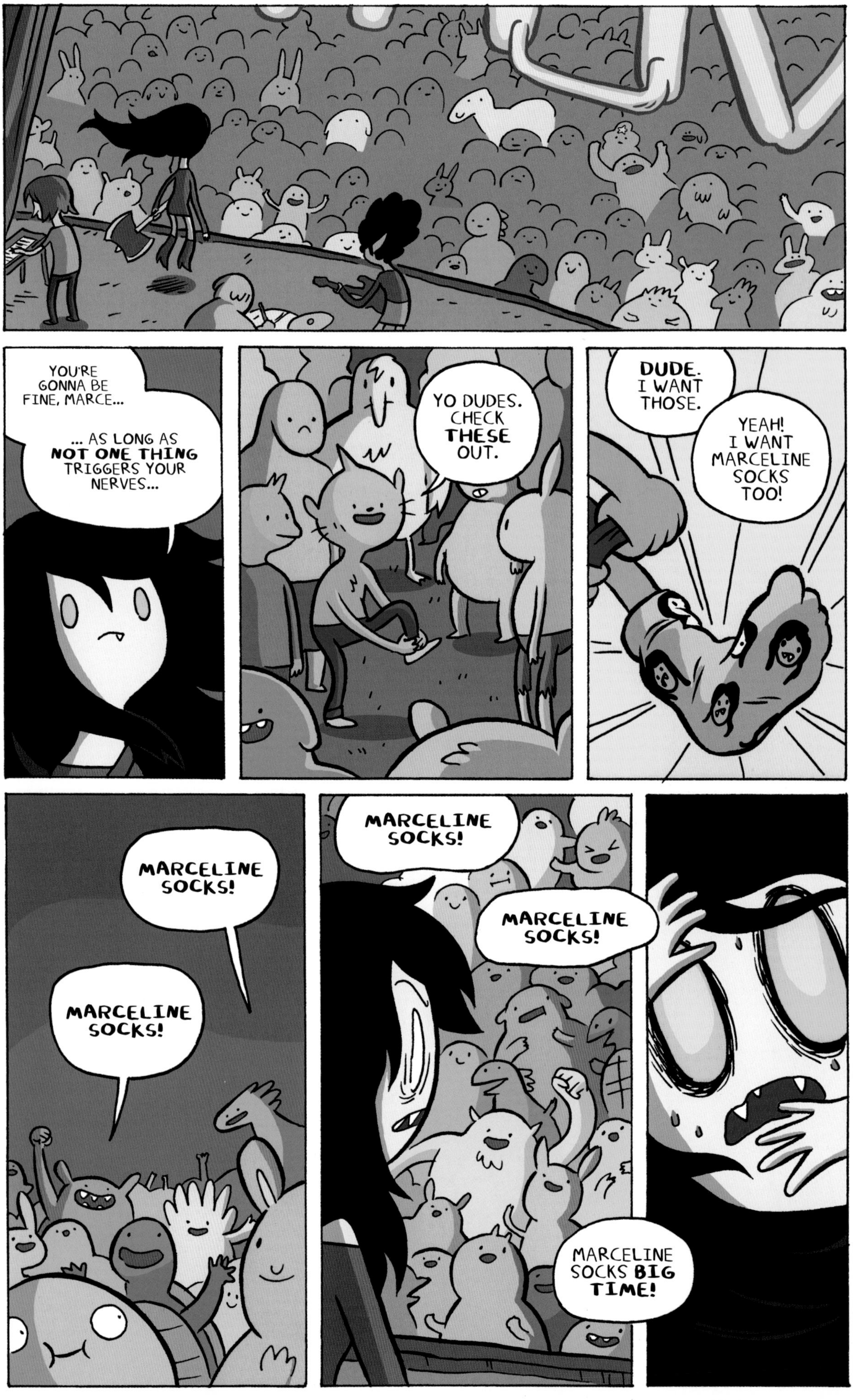

YOU'RE GONNA BE FINE, MARCE...
... AS LONG AS NOT ONE THING TRIGGERS YOUR NERVES...
YO DUDES. CHECK THESE OUT.
DUDE. I WANT THOSE.
YEAH! I WANT MARCELINE SOCKS TOO!
MARCELINE SOCKS!
MARCELINE SOCKS!
MARCELINE SOCKS!
MARCELINE SOCKS!
MARCELINE SOCKS BIG TIME!

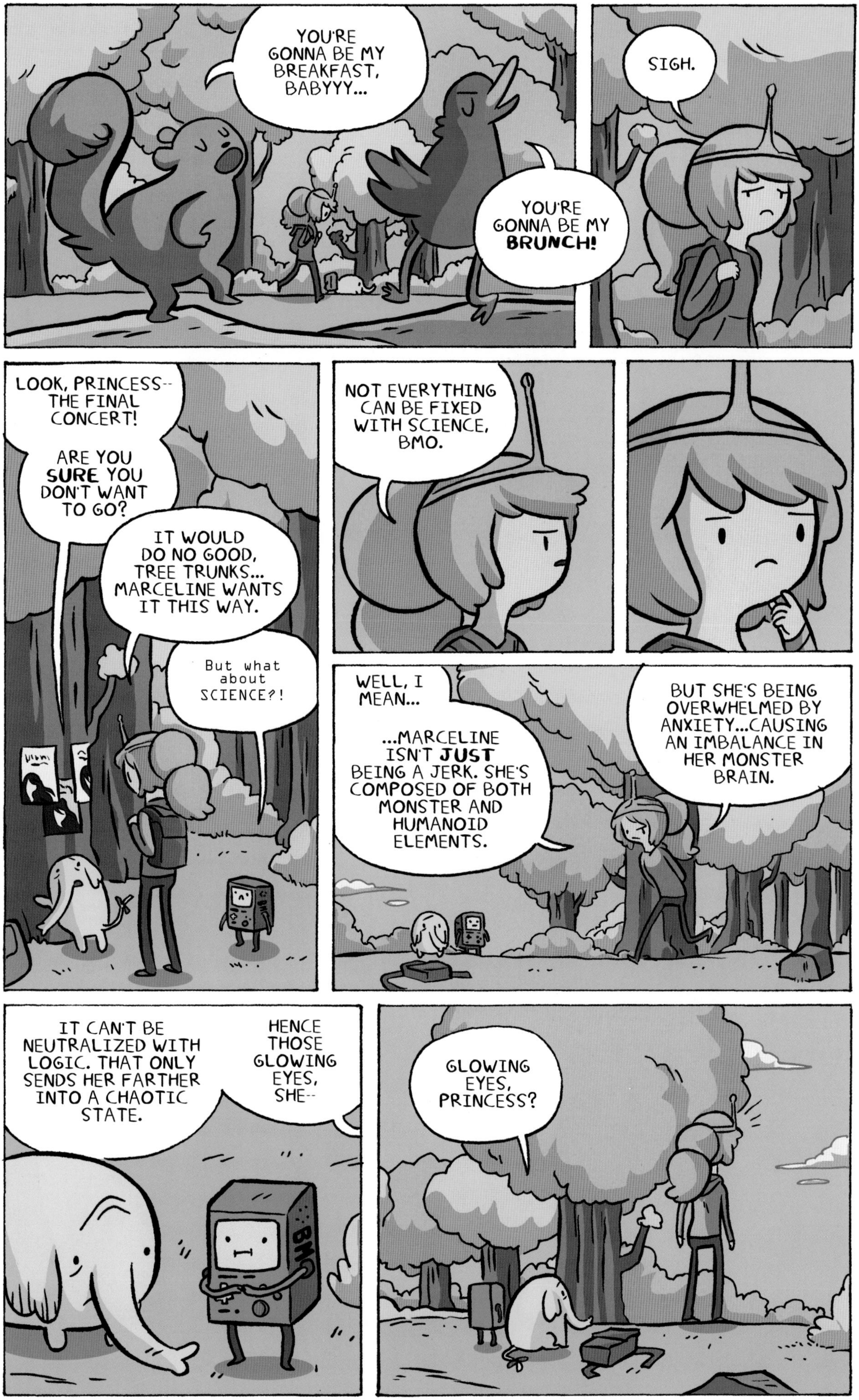
YOU'RE GONNA BE MY BREAKFAST, BABYYY...
YOU'RE GONNA BE MY **BRUNCH!**
SIGH.
LOOK, PRINCESS-- THE FINAL CONCERT!
ARE YOU **SURE** YOU DON'T WANT TO GO?
IT WOULD DO NO GOOD, TREE TRUNKS... MARCELINE WANTS IT THIS WAY.
But what about SCIENCE?!
NOT EVERYTHING CAN BE FIXED WITH SCIENCE, BMO.
WELL, I MEAN...
...MARCELINE ISN'T **JUST** BEING A JERK. SHE'S COMPOSED OF BOTH MONSTER AND HUMANOID ELEMENTS.
BUT SHE'S BEING OVERWHELMED BY ANXIETY...CAUSING AN IMBALANCE IN HER MONSTER BRAIN.
IT CAN'T BE NEUTRALIZED WITH LOGIC. THAT ONLY SENDS HER FARTHER INTO A CHAOTIC STATE.
HENCE THOSE GLOWING EYES, SHE--
GLOWING EYES, PRINCESS?

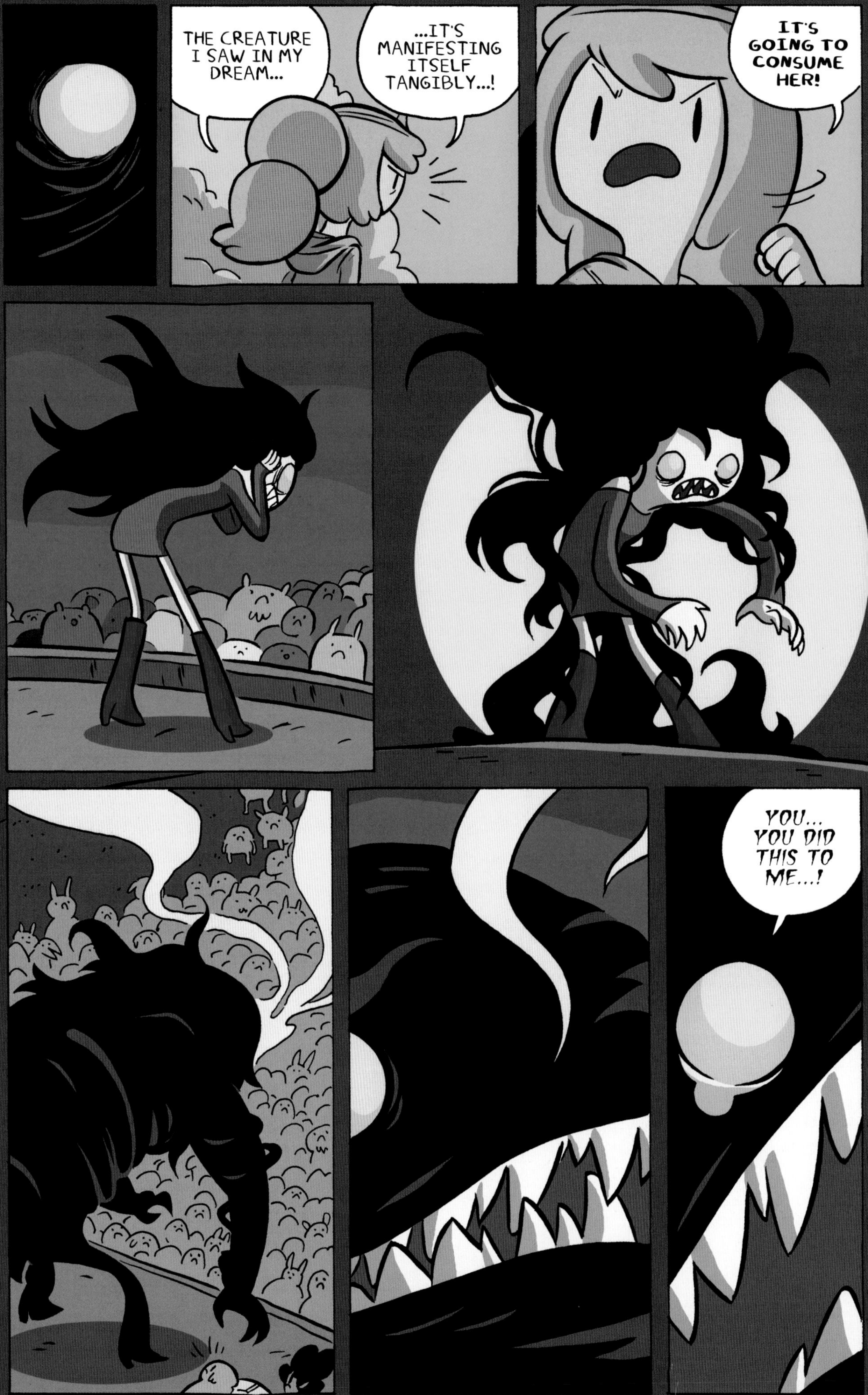
THE CREATURE I SAW IN MY DREAM...
...IT'S MANIFESTING ITSELF TANGIBLY...!
IT'S GOING TO CONSUME HER!
YOU... YOU DID THIS TO ME...!

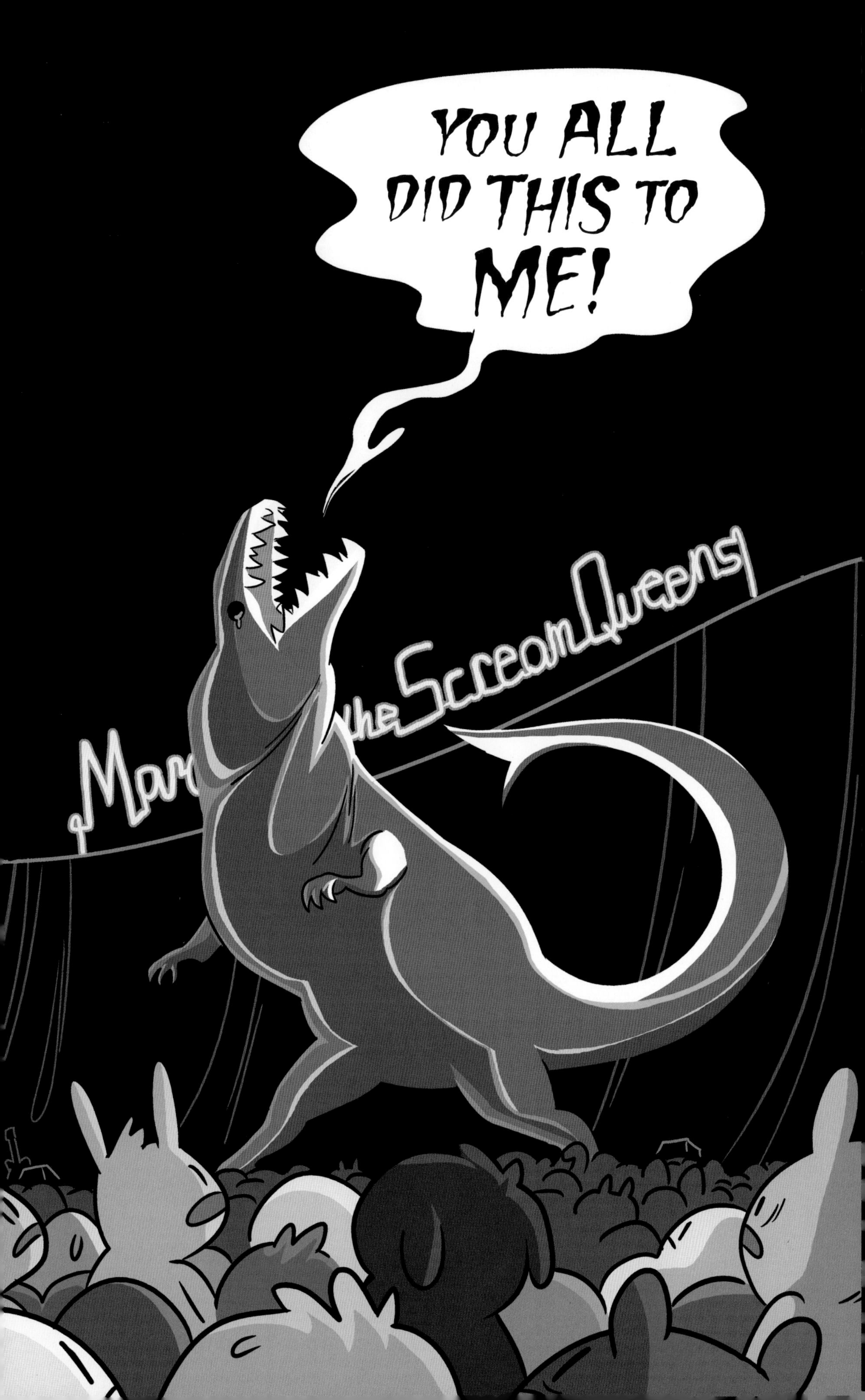
YOU ALL DID THIS TO ME!
the Scream Queens

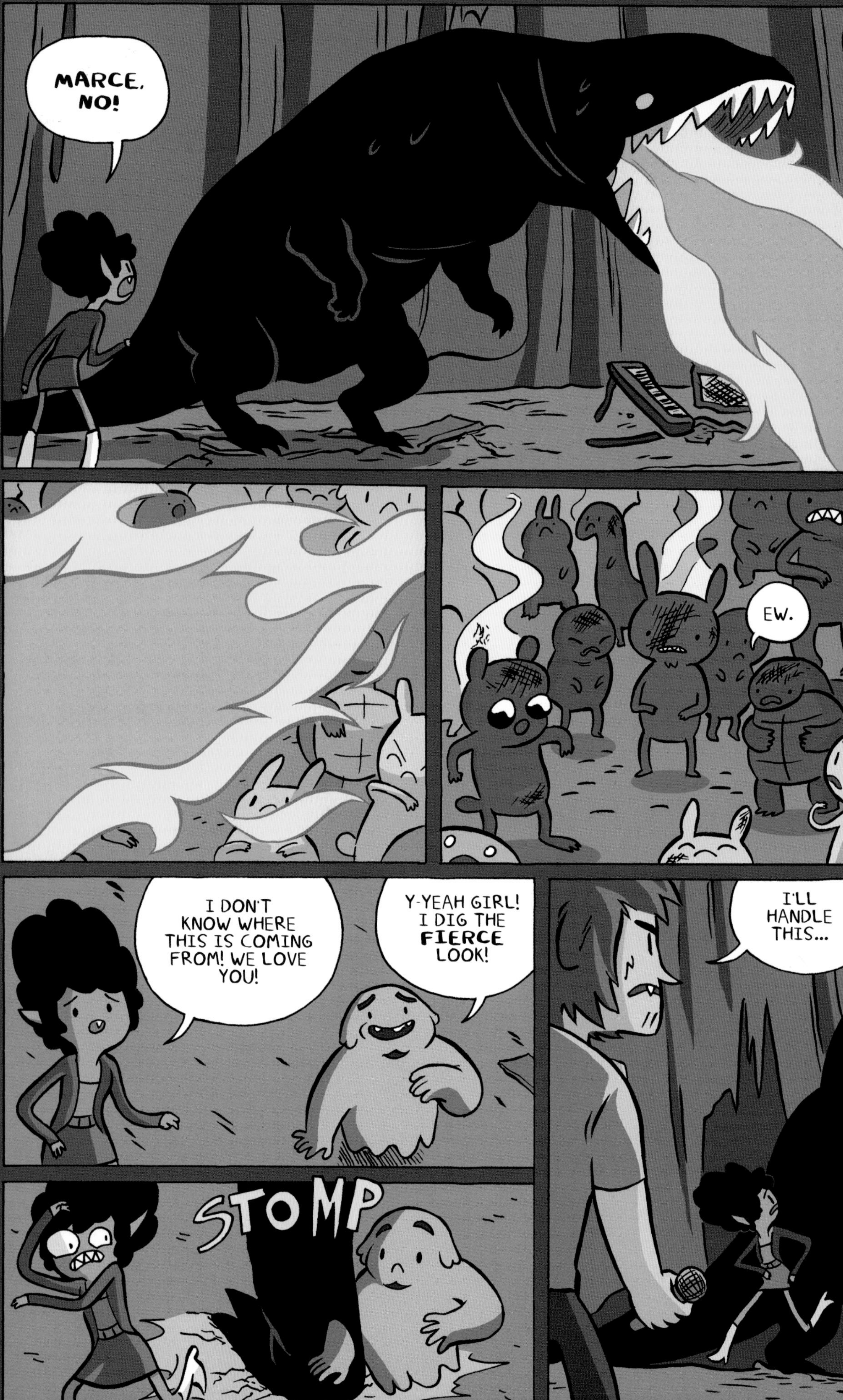
MARCE, NO!
EW.
I DON'T KNOW WHERE THIS IS COMING FROM! WE LOVE YOU!
Y-YEAH GIRL! I DIG THE **FIERCE** LOOK!
STOMP
I'LL HANDLE THIS...

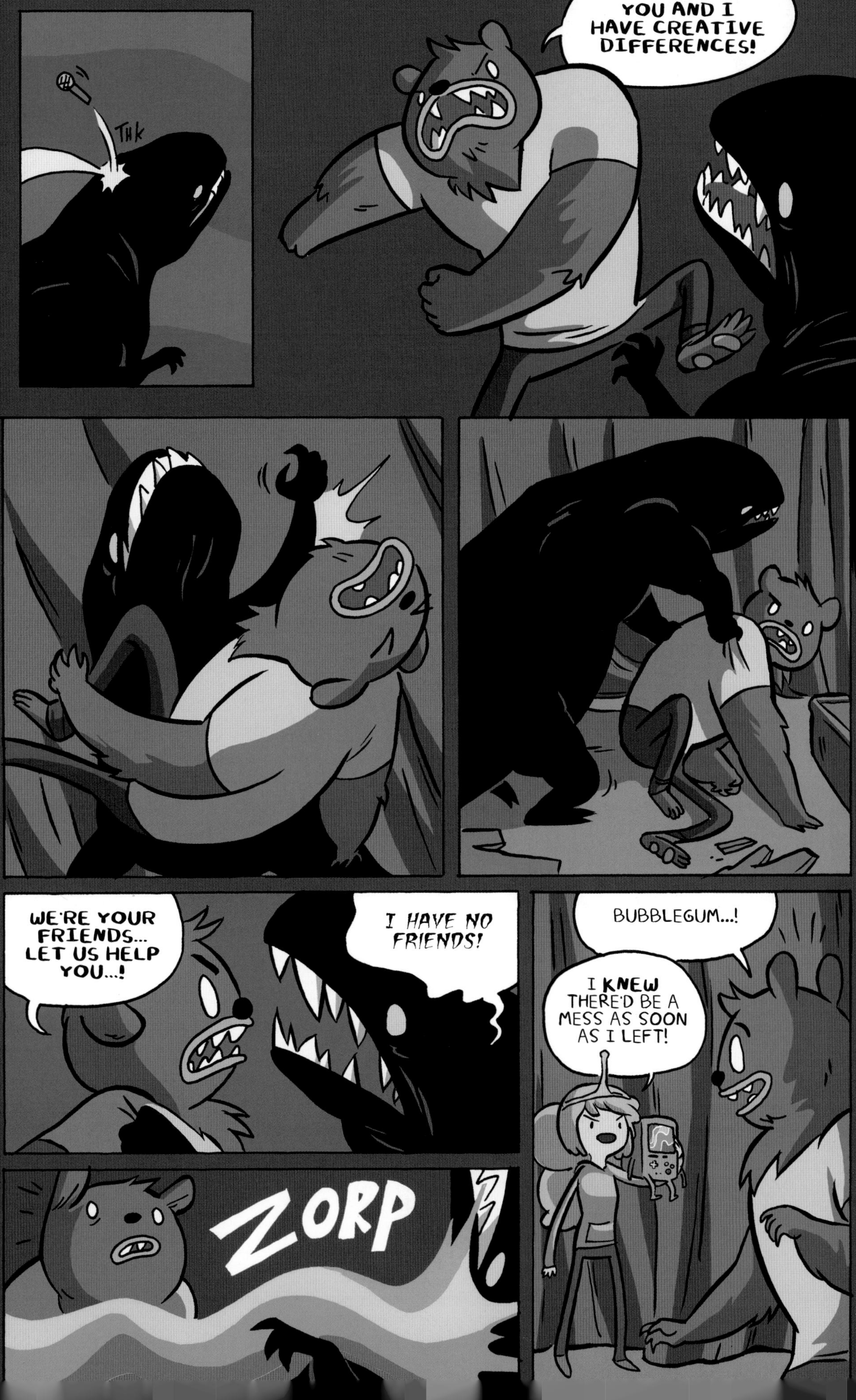
THK
YOU AND I HAVE CREATIVE DIFFERENCES!
WE'RE YOUR FRIENDS... LET US HELP YOU...!
I HAVE NO FRIENDS!
ZORP
BUBBLEGUM...!
I KNEW THERE'D BE A MESS AS SOON AS I LEFT!

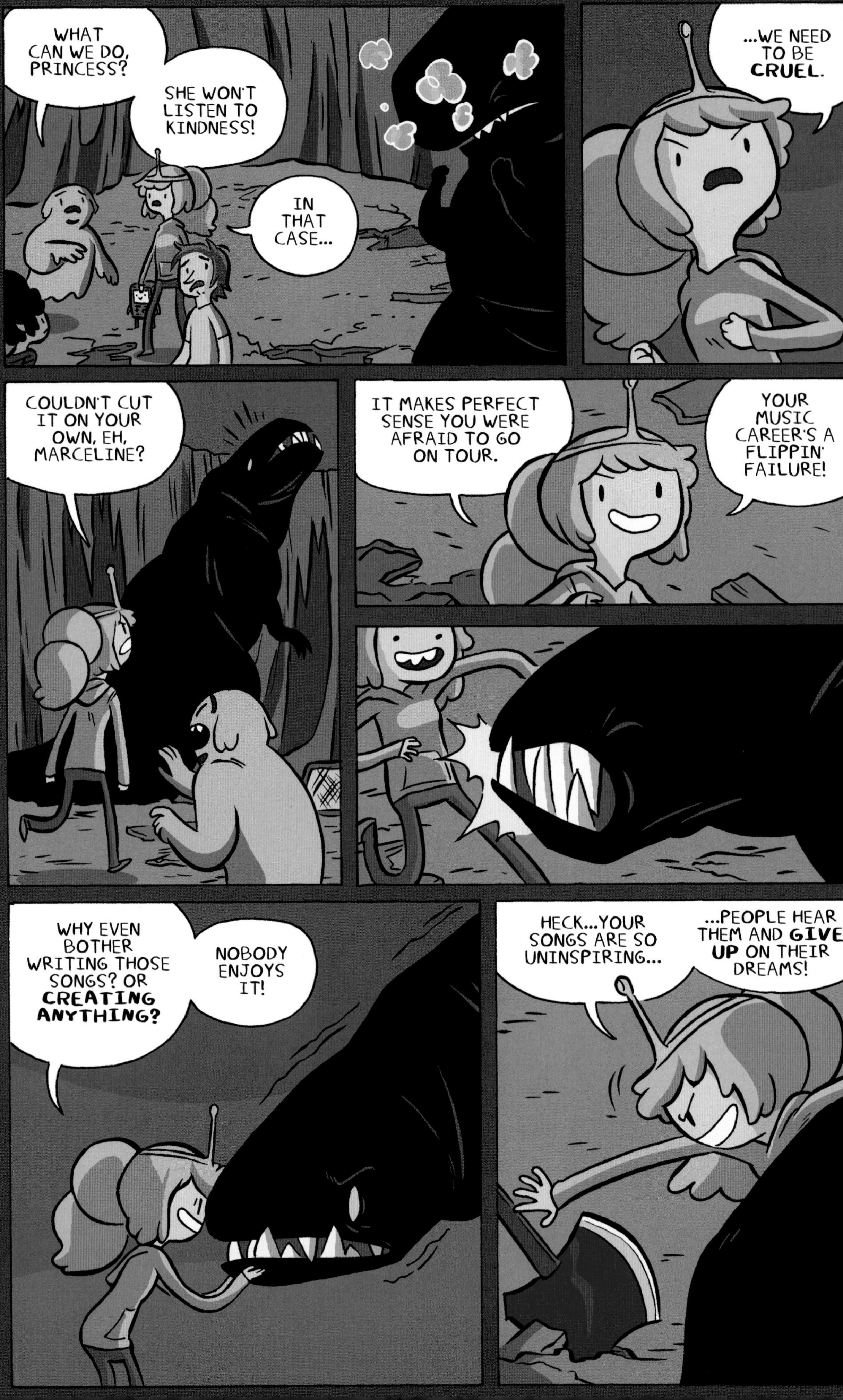
WHAT CAN WE DO, PRINCESS?
SHE WON'T LISTEN TO KINDNESS!
IN THAT CASE...
...WE NEED TO BE **CRUEL**.
COULDN'T CUT IT ON YOUR OWN, EH, MARCELINE?
IT MAKES PERFECT SENSE YOU WERE AFRAID TO GO ON TOUR.
YOUR MUSIC CAREER'S A FLIPPIN' FAILURE!
WHY EVEN BOTHER WRITING THOSE SONGS? OR **CREATING ANYTHING?**
NOBODY ENJOYS IT!
HECK...YOUR SONGS ARE SO UNINSPIRING...
...PEOPLE HEAR THEM AND **GIVE UP** ON THEIR DREAMS!

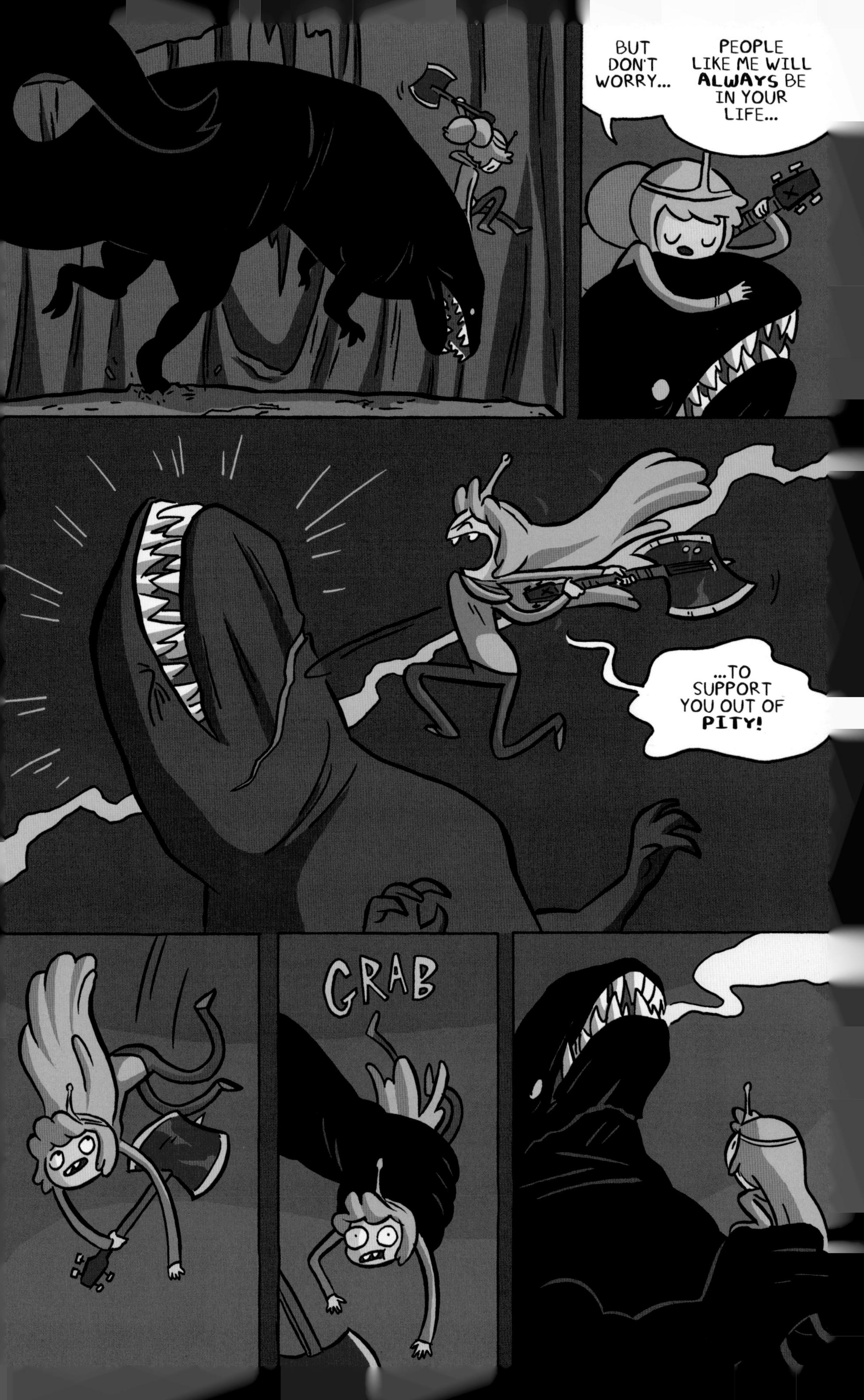
BUT DON'T WORRY...
PEOPLE LIKE ME WILL **ALWAYS** BE IN YOUR LIFE...
...TO SUPPORT YOU OUT OF **PITY!**
GRAB

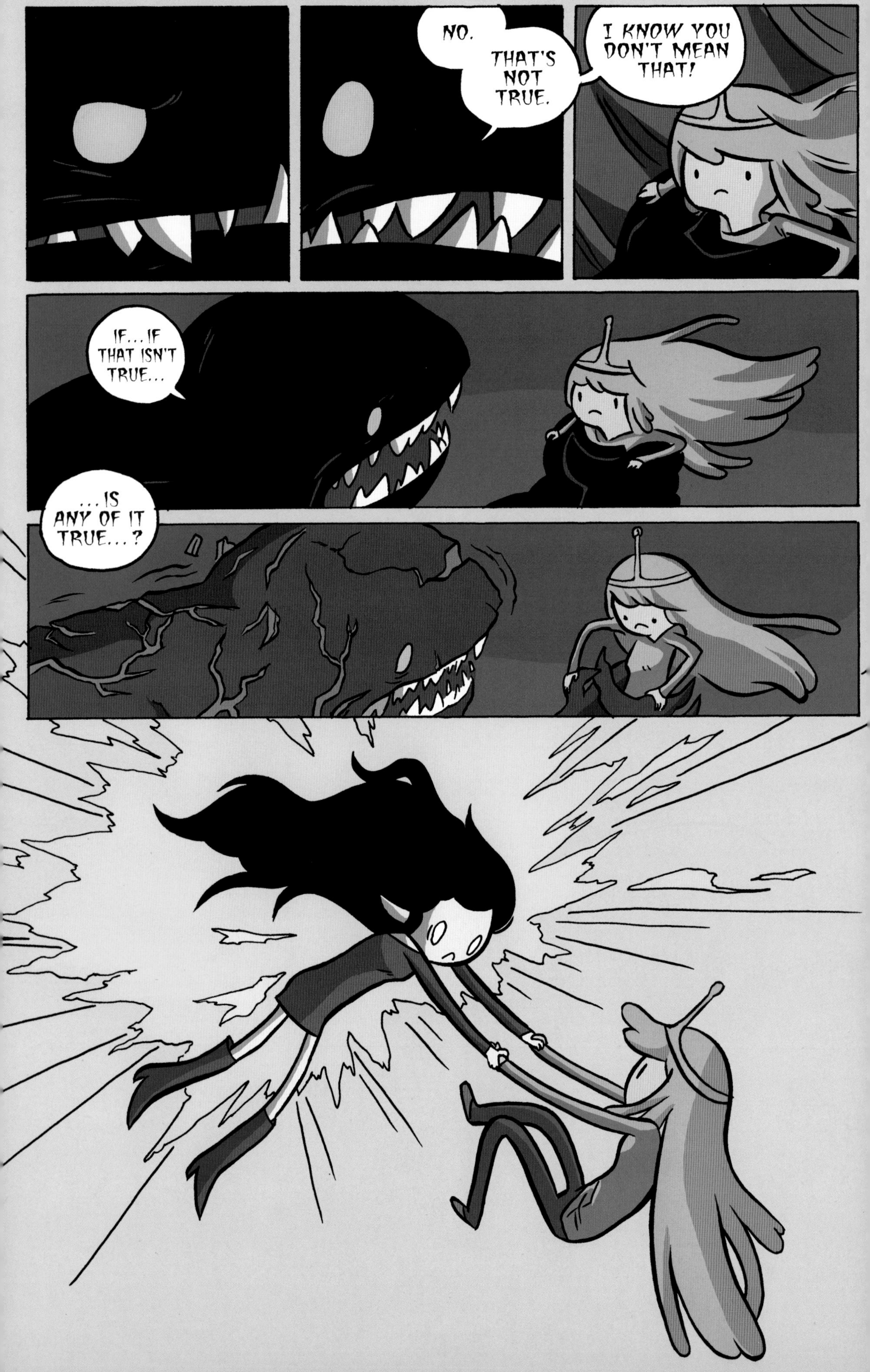
NO.
THAT'S NOT TRUE.
I KNOW YOU DON'T MEAN THAT!
IF...IF THAT ISN'T TRUE...
...IS ANY OF IT TRUE...?

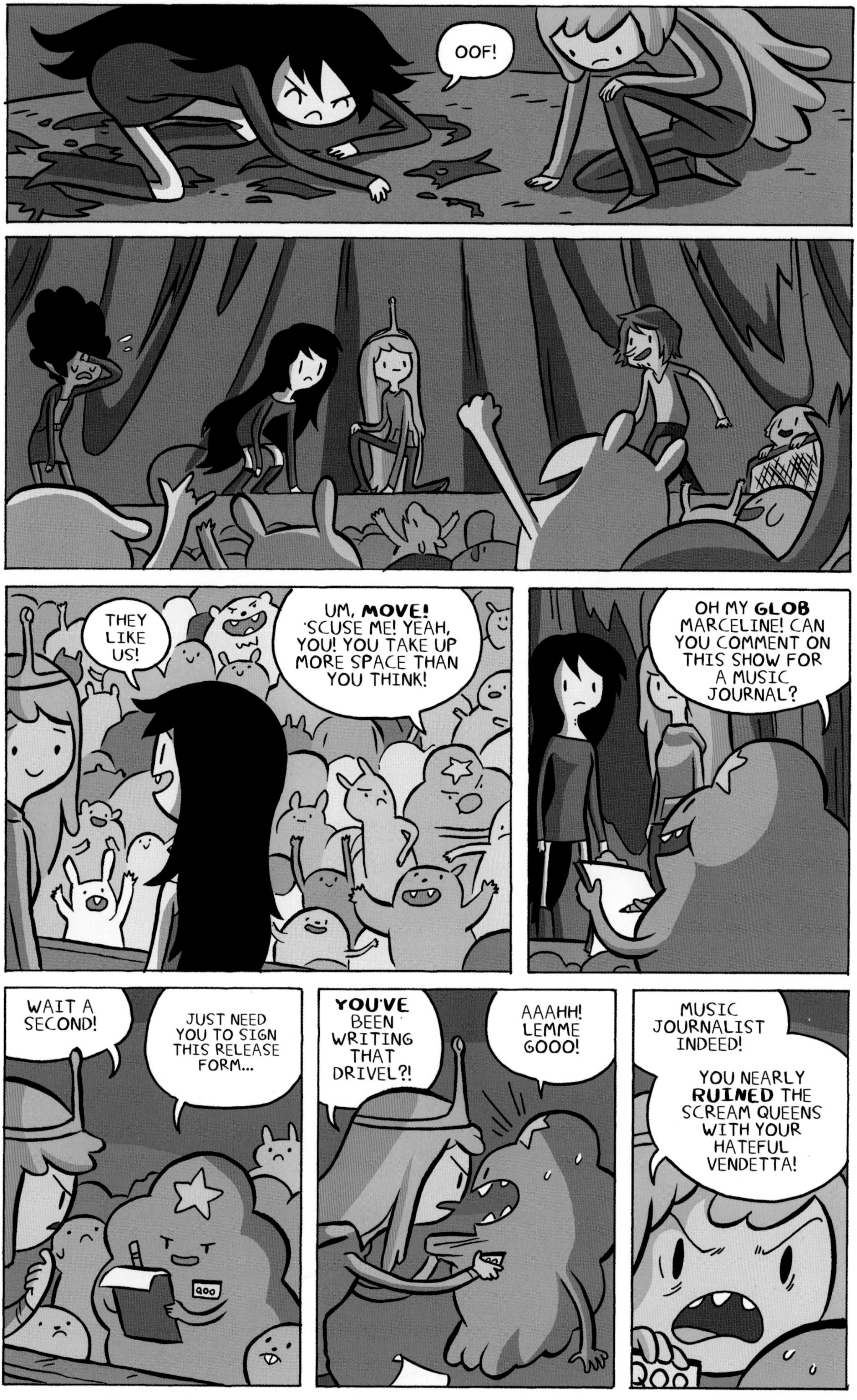
OOF!
THEY LIKE US!
UM, **MOVE!** 'SCUSE ME! YEAH, YOU! YOU TAKE UP MORE SPACE THAN YOU THINK!
OH MY **GLOB** MARCELINE! CAN YOU COMMENT ON THIS SHOW FOR A MUSIC JOURNAL?
WAIT A SECOND!
JUST NEED YOU TO SIGN THIS RELEASE FORM...
YOU'VE BEEN WRITING THAT DRIVEL?!
AAAHH! LEMME GOOO!
MUSIC JOURNALIST INDEED!
YOU NEARLY **RUINED** THE SCREAM QUEENS WITH YOUR HATEFUL VENDETTA!

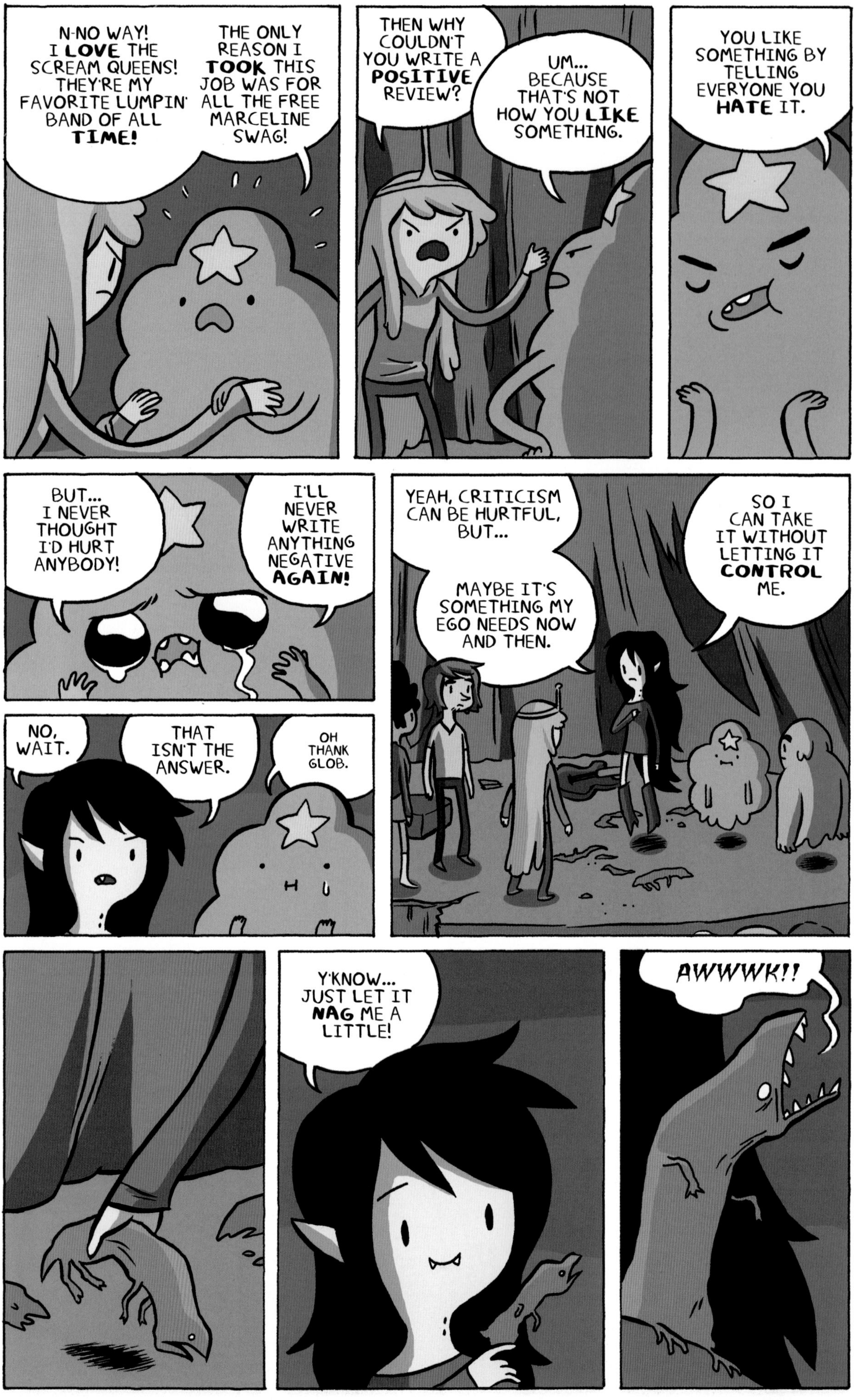
N-NO WAY! I **LOVE** THE SCREAM QUEENS! THEY'RE MY FAVORITE LUMPIN' BAND OF ALL **TIME!**
THE ONLY REASON I **TOOK** THIS JOB WAS FOR ALL THE FREE MARCELINE SWAG!
THEN WHY COULDN'T YOU WRITE A **POSITIVE** REVIEW?
UM... BECAUSE THAT'S NOT HOW YOU **LIKE** SOMETHING.
YOU LIKE SOMETHING BY TELLING EVERYONE YOU **HATE** IT.
BUT... I NEVER THOUGHT I'D HURT ANYBODY!
I'LL NEVER WRITE ANYTHING NEGATIVE **AGAIN!**
YEAH, CRITICISM CAN BE HURTFUL, BUT...
MAYBE IT'S SOMETHING MY EGO NEEDS NOW AND THEN.
SO I CAN TAKE IT WITHOUT LETTING IT **CONTROL** ME.
NO, WAIT.
THAT ISN'T THE ANSWER.
OH THANK GLOB.
Y'KNOW... JUST LET IT **NAG** ME A LITTLE!
AWWWK!!

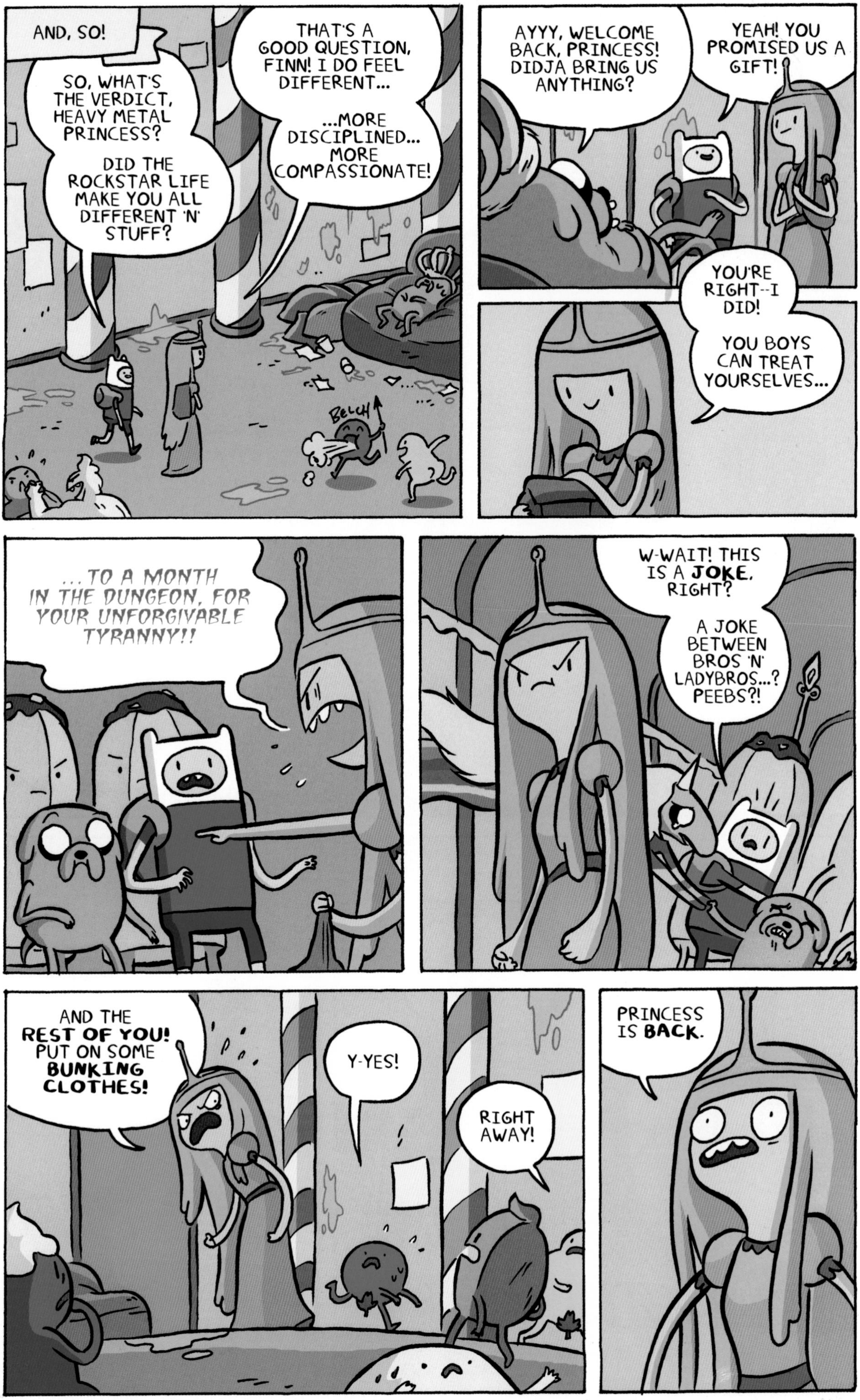

AND, SO!
SO, WHAT'S THE VERDICT, HEAVY METAL PRINCESS?
DID THE ROCKSTAR LIFE MAKE YOU ALL DIFFERENT 'N' STUFF?
THAT'S A GOOD QUESTION, FINN! I DO FEEL DIFFERENT...
...MORE DISCIPLINED... MORE COMPASSIONATE!
BELCH
AYYY, WELCOME BACK, PRINCESS! DIDJA BRING US ANYTHING?
YEAH! YOU PROMISED US A GIFT!
YOU'RE RIGHT--I DID!
YOU BOYS CAN TREAT YOURSELVES...
...TO A MONTH IN THE DUNGEON, FOR YOUR UNFORGIVABLE TYRANNY!!
W-WAIT! THIS IS A JOKE, RIGHT?
A JOKE BETWEEN BROS 'N' LADYBROS...? PEEBS?!
AND THE REST OF YOU! PUT ON SOME BUNKING CLOTHES!
Y-YES!
RIGHT AWAY!
PRINCESS IS BACK.

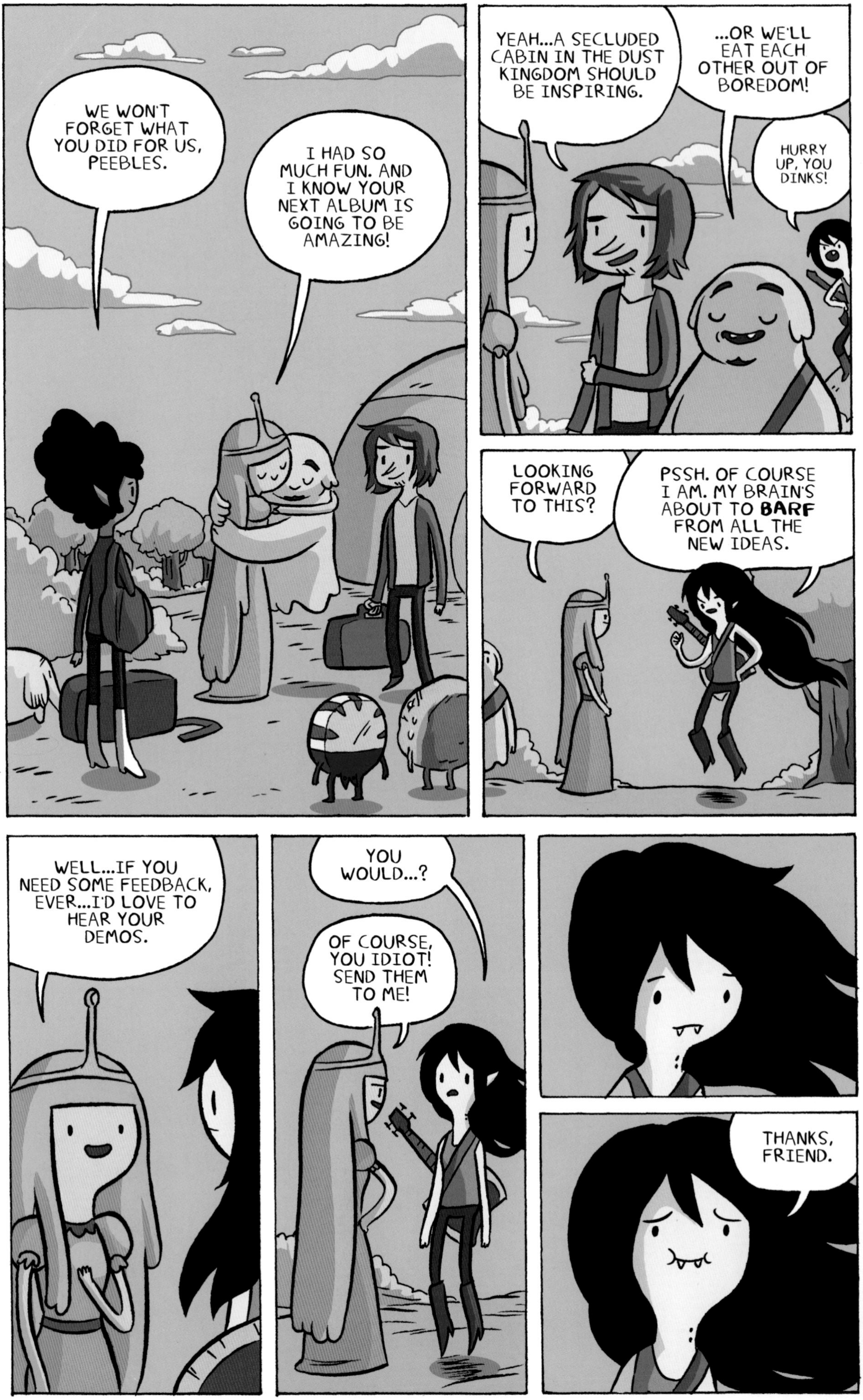

WE WON'T FORGET WHAT YOU DID FOR US, PEEBLES.
I HAD SO MUCH FUN. AND I KNOW YOUR NEXT ALBUM IS GOING TO BE AMAZING!
YEAH...A SECLUDED CABIN IN THE DUST KINGDOM SHOULD BE INSPIRING.
...OR WE'LL EAT EACH OTHER OUT OF BOREDOM!
HURRY UP, YOU DINKS!
LOOKING FORWARD TO THIS?
PSSH. OF COURSE I AM. MY BRAIN'S ABOUT TO **BARF** FROM ALL THE NEW IDEAS.
WELL...IF YOU NEED SOME FEEDBACK, EVER...I'D LOVE TO HEAR YOUR DEMOS.
YOU WOULD...?
OF COURSE, YOU IDIOT! SEND THEM TO ME!
THANKS, FRIEND.

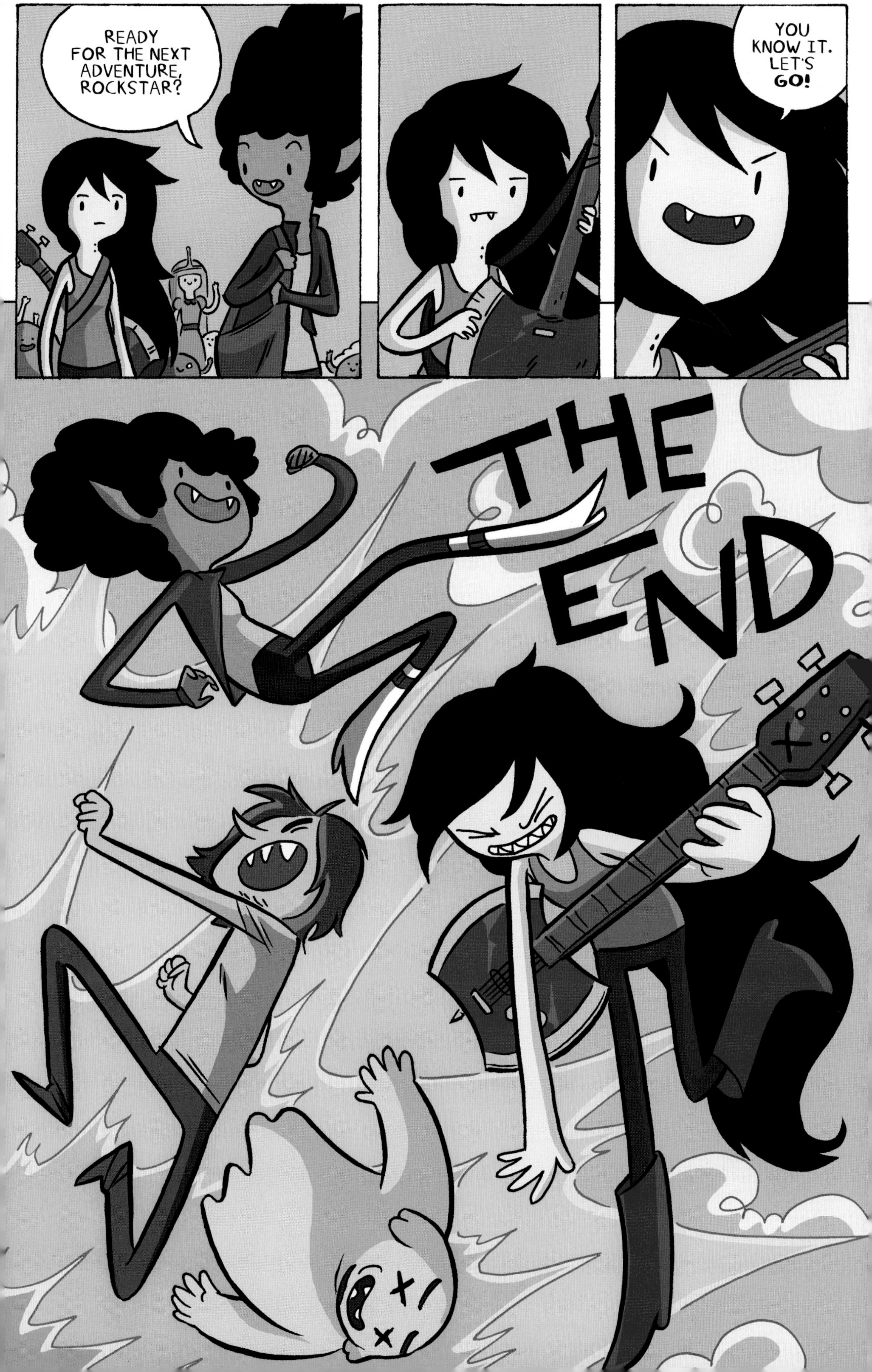
READY FOR THE NEXT ADVENTURE, ROCKSTAR?
YOU KNOW IT. LET'S GO!
THE END

COVER BANDS

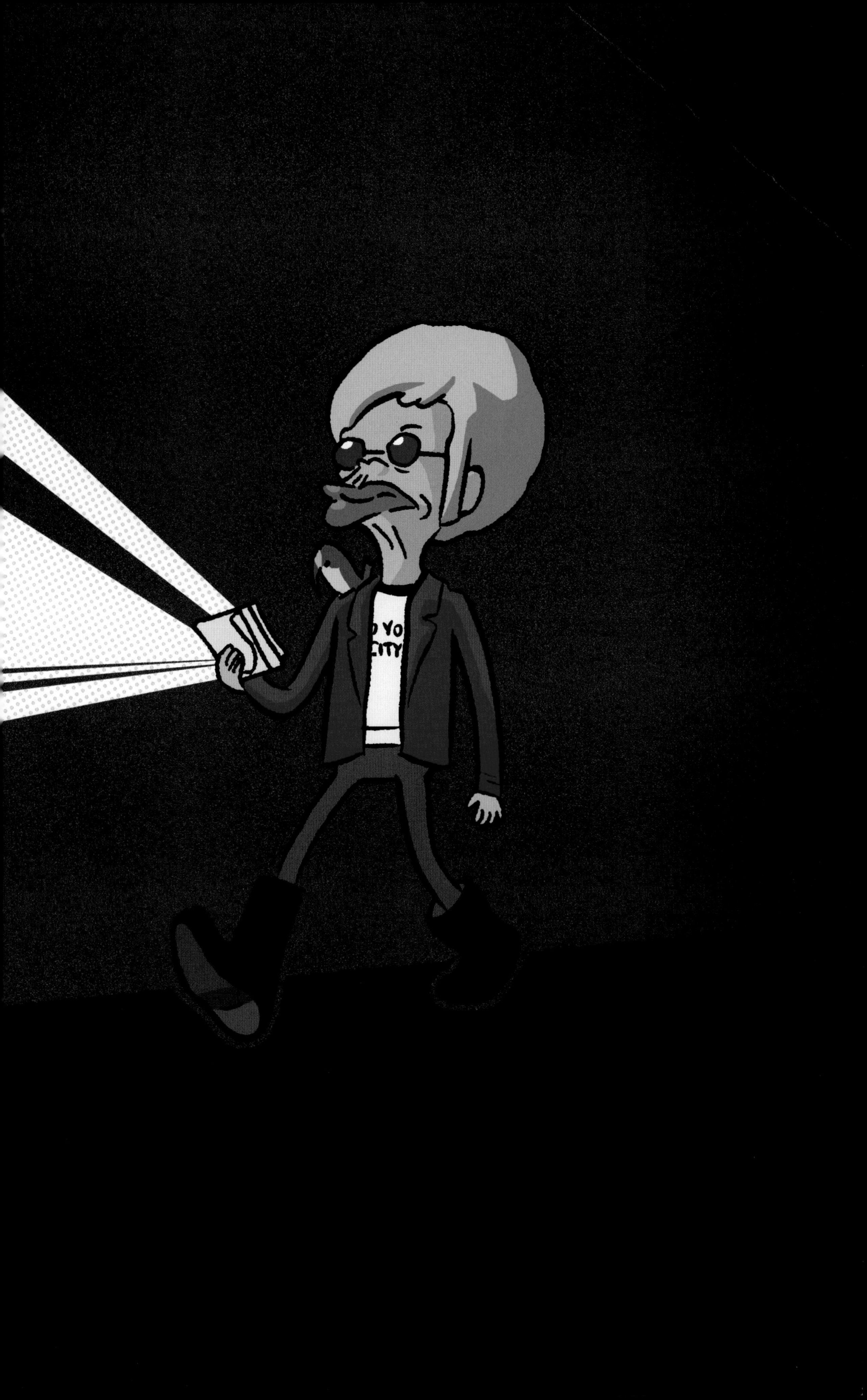

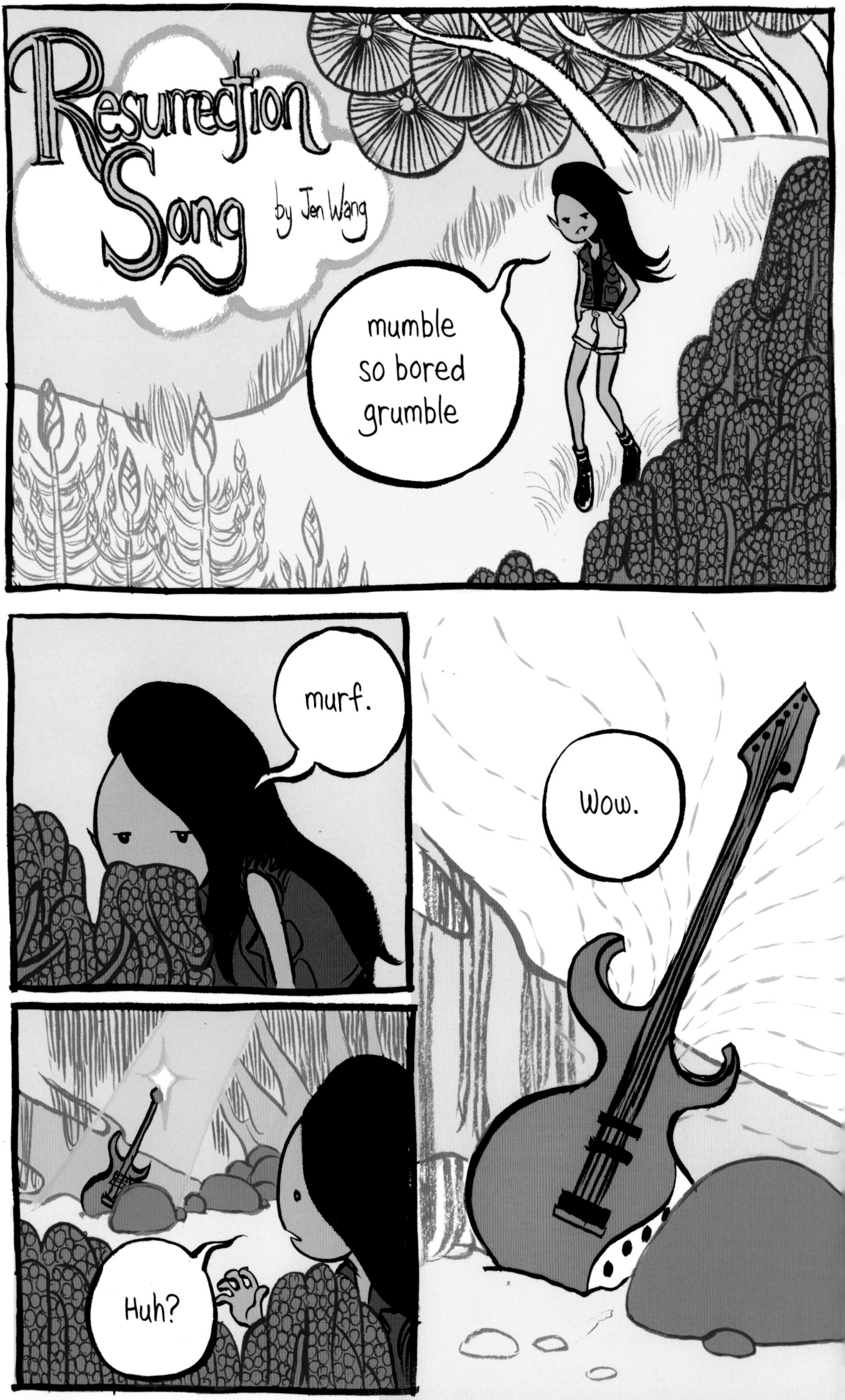
Resurrection Song
by Jen Wang
mumble so bored grumble
murf.
Huh?
Wow.

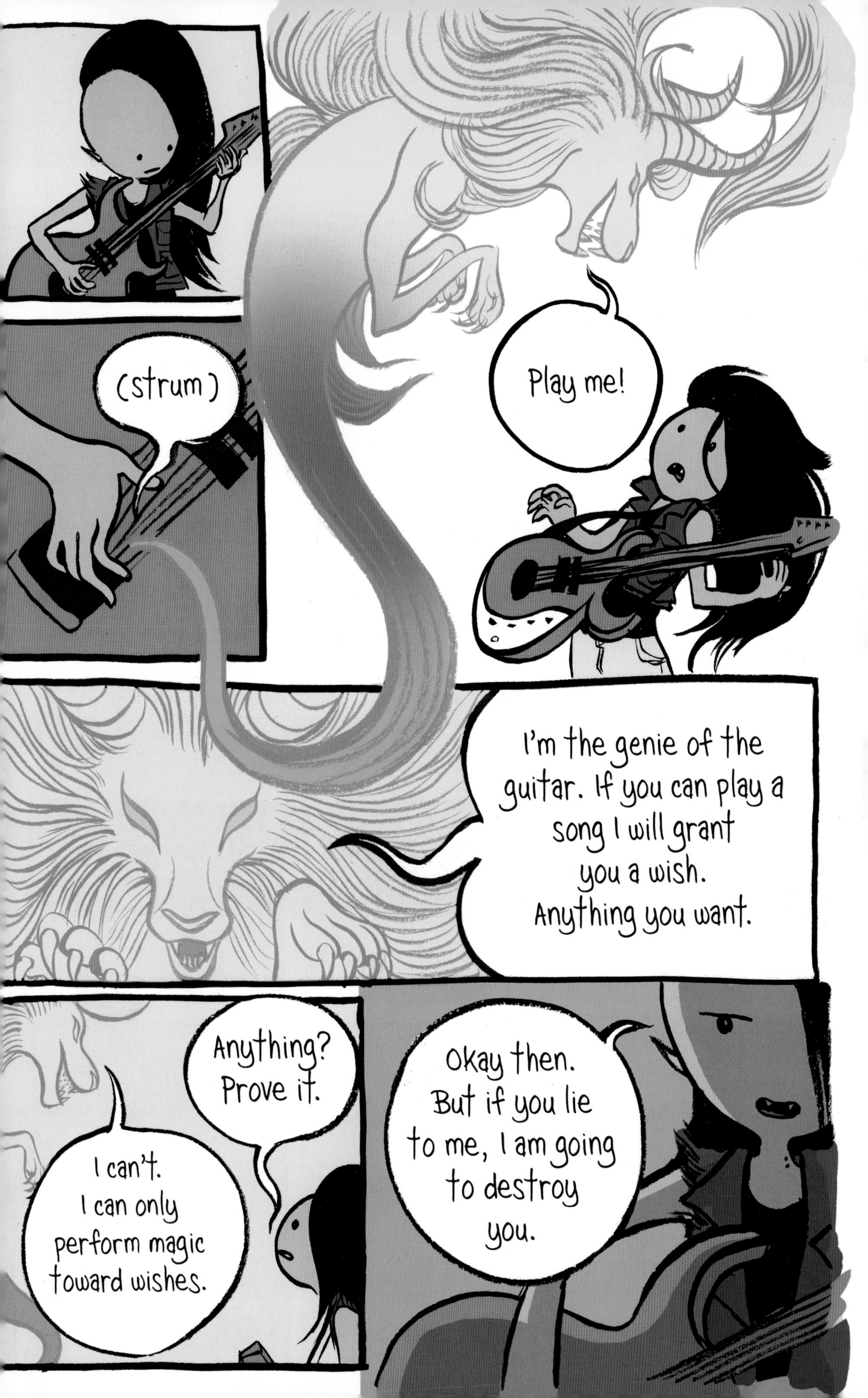
(strum)
Play me!
I'm the genie of the guitar. If you can play a song I will grant you a wish. Anything you want.
Anything? Prove it.
I can't. I can only perform magic toward wishes.
Okay then. But if you lie to me, I am going to destroy you.

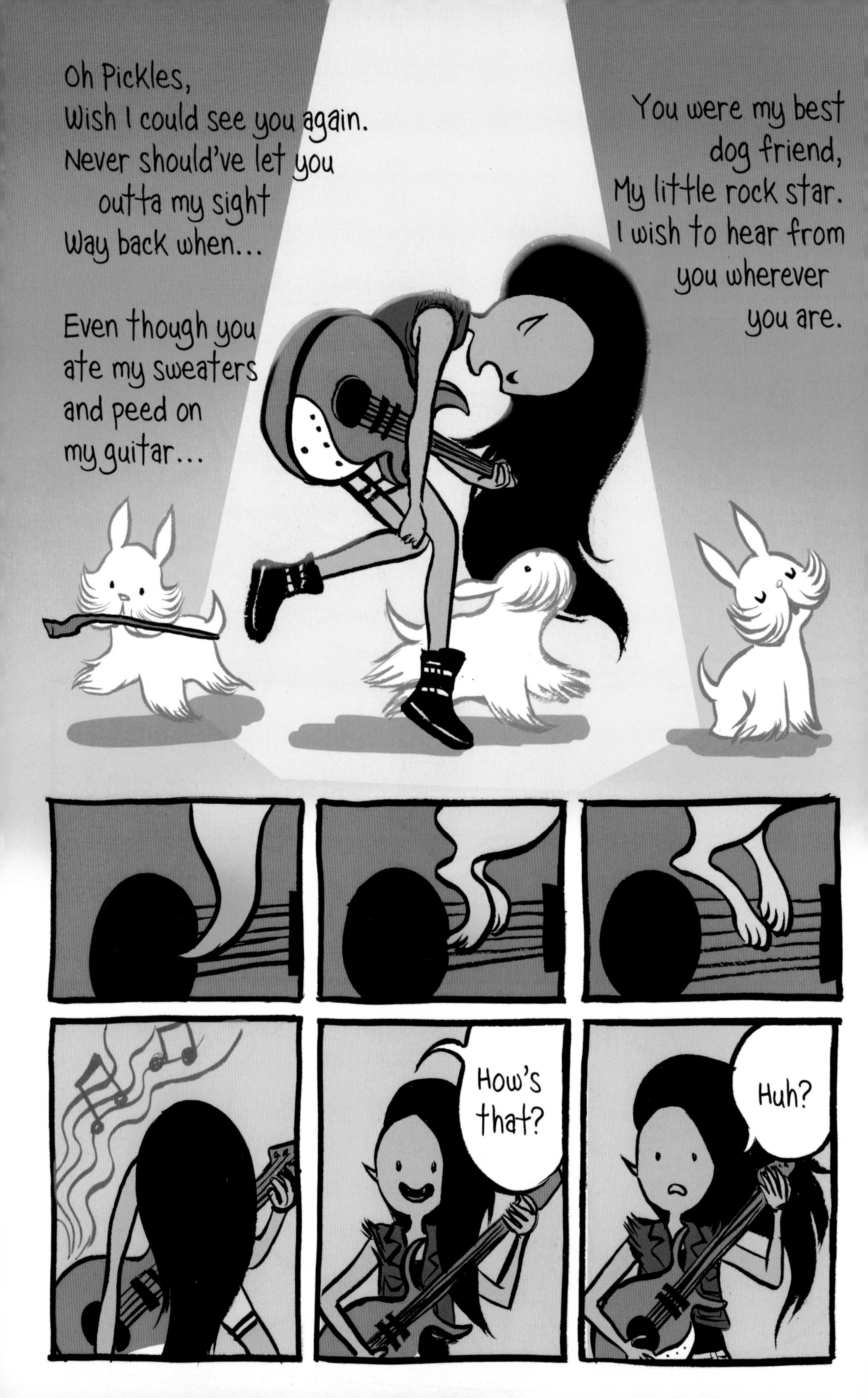
Oh Pickles,
Wish I could see you again.
Never should've let you
outta my sight
Way back when...
Even though you
ate my sweaters
and peed on
my guitar...
You were my best
dog friend,
My little rock star.
I wish to hear from
you wherever
you are.
How's that?
Huh?

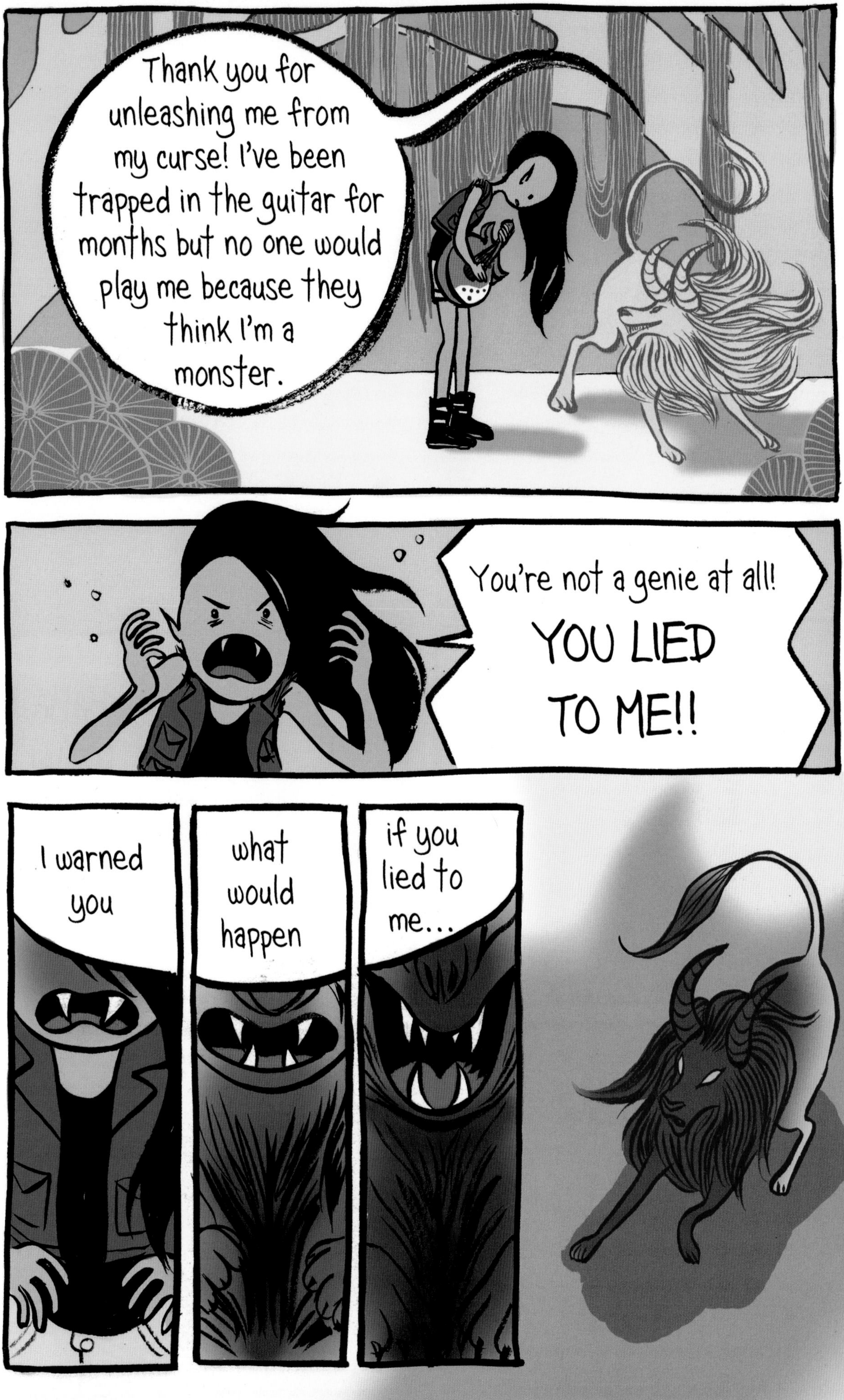
Thank you for unleashing me from my curse! I've been trapped in the guitar for months but no one would play me because they think I'm a monster.
You're not a genie at all!
YOU LIED TO ME!!
I warned you
what would happen
if you lied to me...

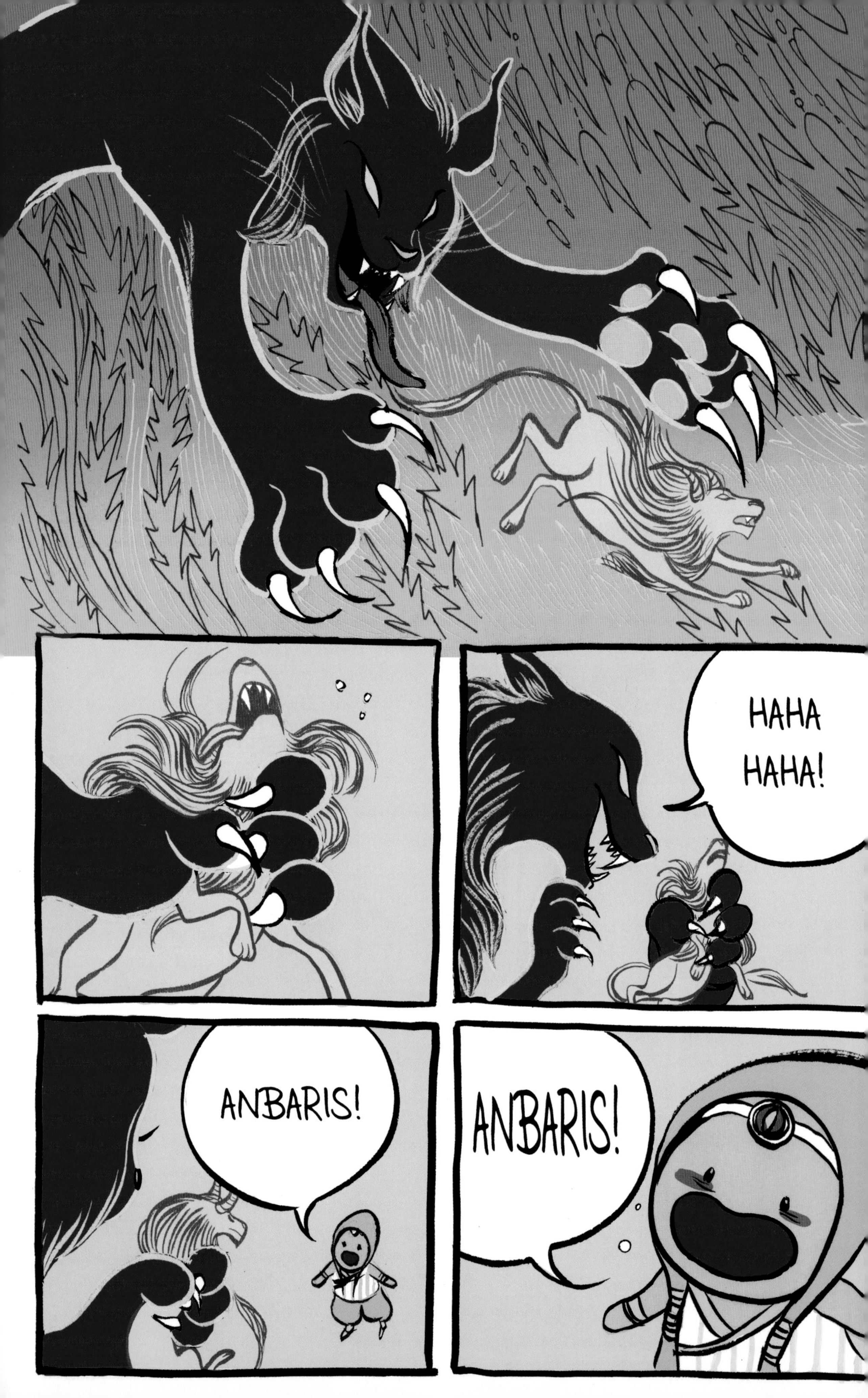
HAHA HAHA!
ANBARIS!
ANBARIS!

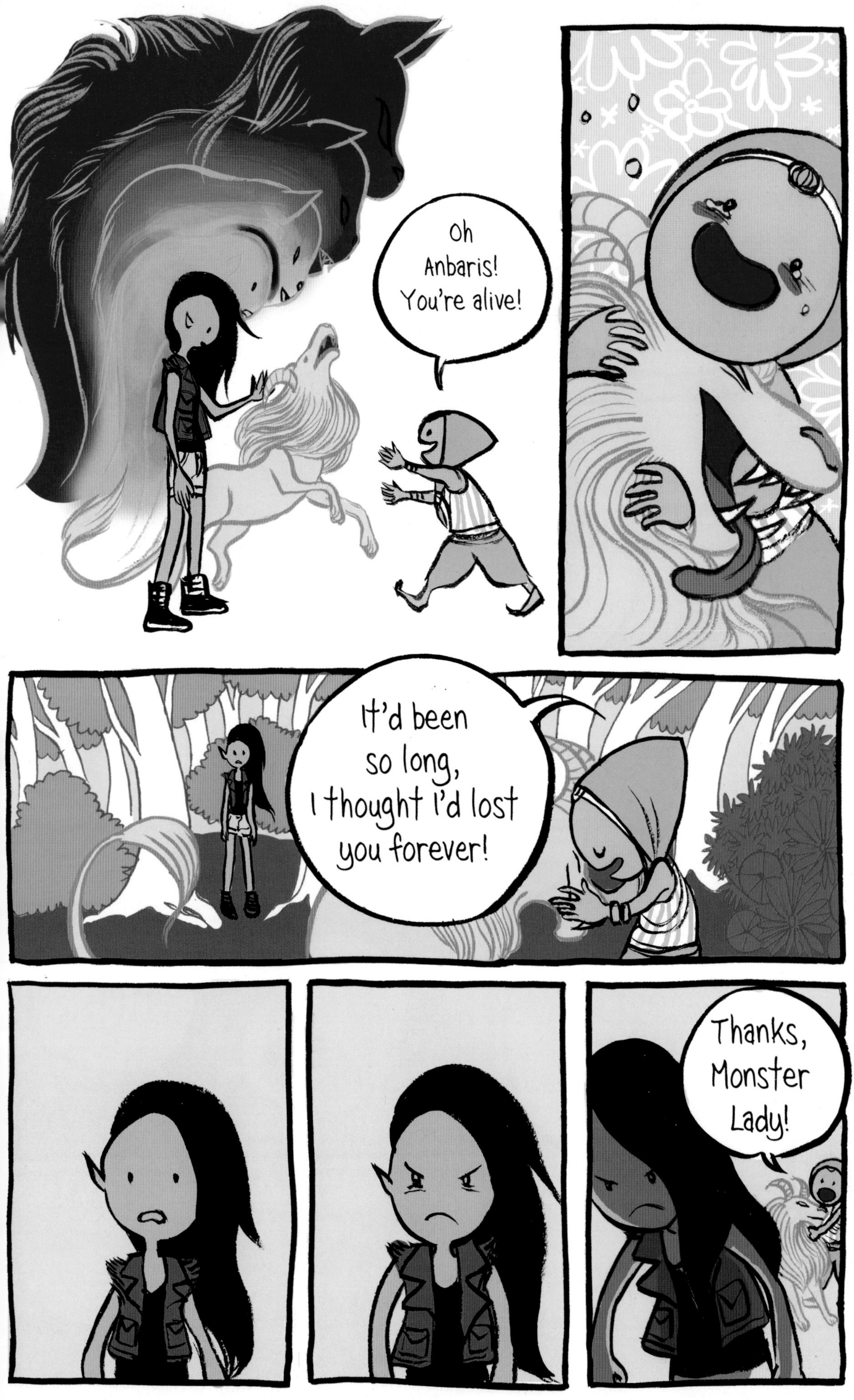
Oh Anbaris! You're alive!
It'd been so long, I thought I'd lost you forever!
Thanks, Monster Lady!

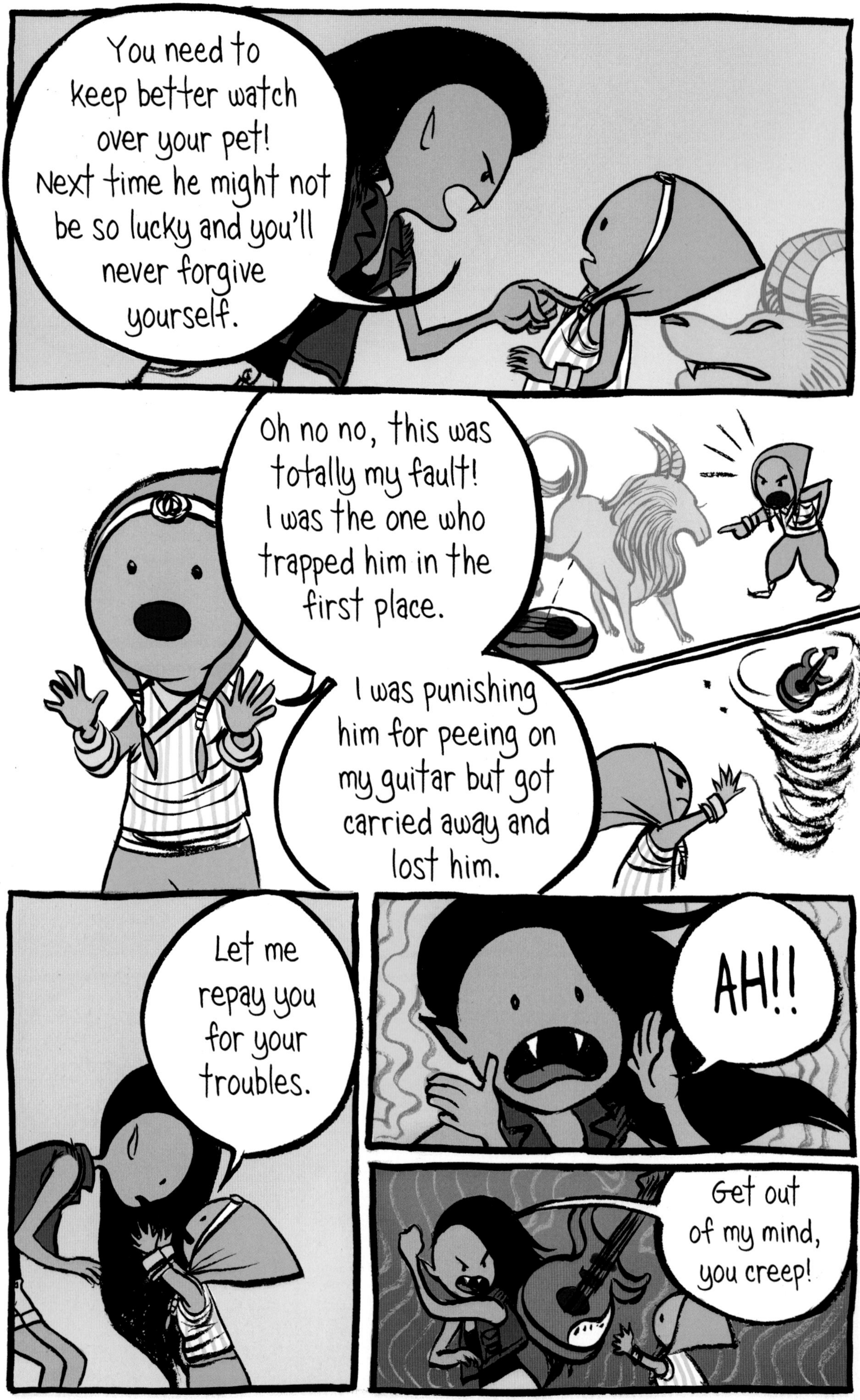
You need to keep better watch over your pet! Next time he might not be so lucky and you'll never forgive yourself.
Oh no no, this was totally my fault! I was the one who trapped him in the first place.
I was punishing him for peeing on my guitar but got carried away and lost him.
Let me repay you for your troubles.
AH!!
Get out of my mind, you creep!

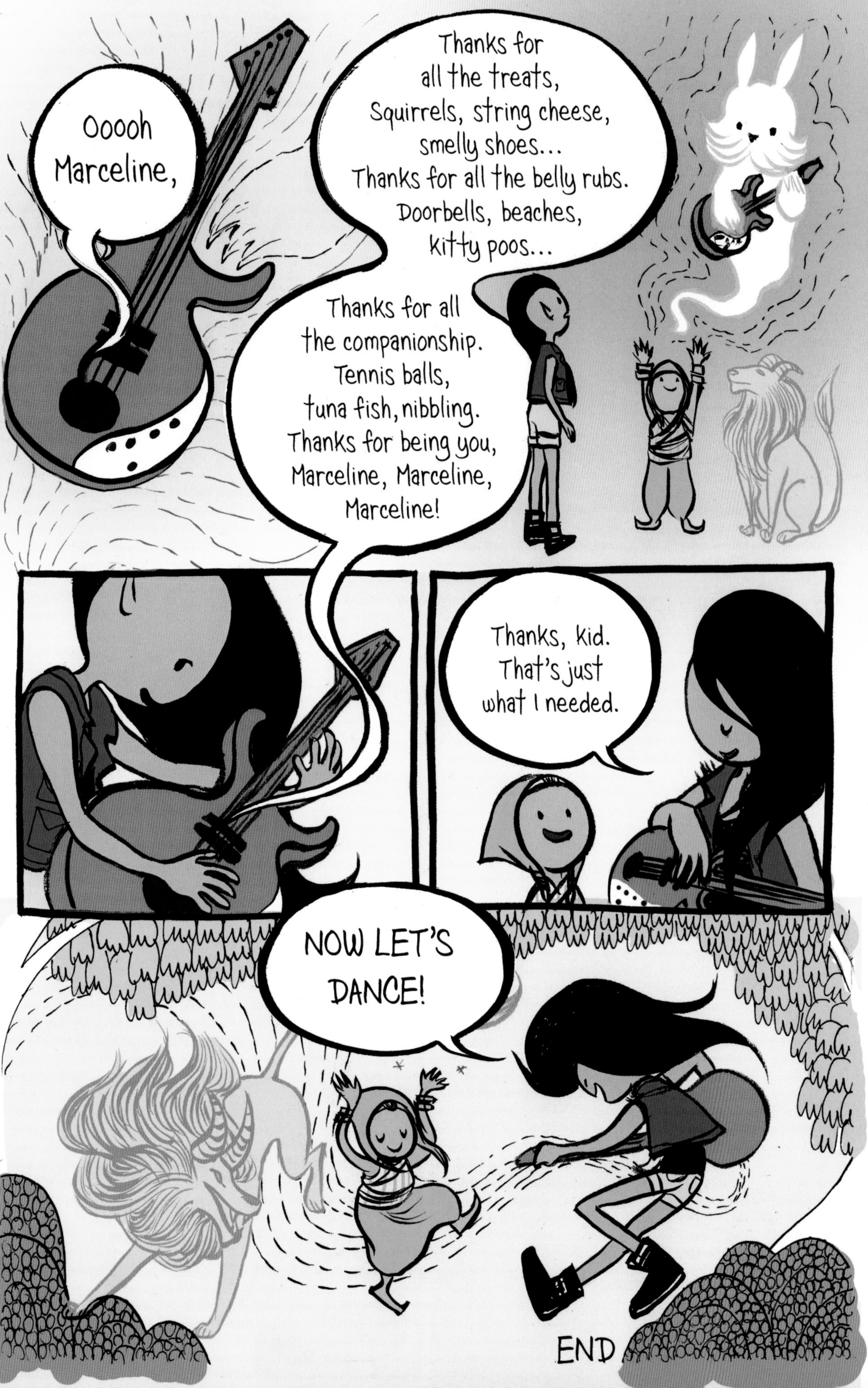
Ooooh Marceline,
Thanks for all the treats, Squirrels, string cheese, smelly shoes... Thanks for all the belly rubs. Doorbells, beaches, kitty poos...
Thanks for all the companionship. Tennis balls, tuna fish, nibbling. Thanks for being you, Marceline, Marceline, Marceline!
Thanks, kid. That's just what I needed.
NOW LET'S DANCE!
END

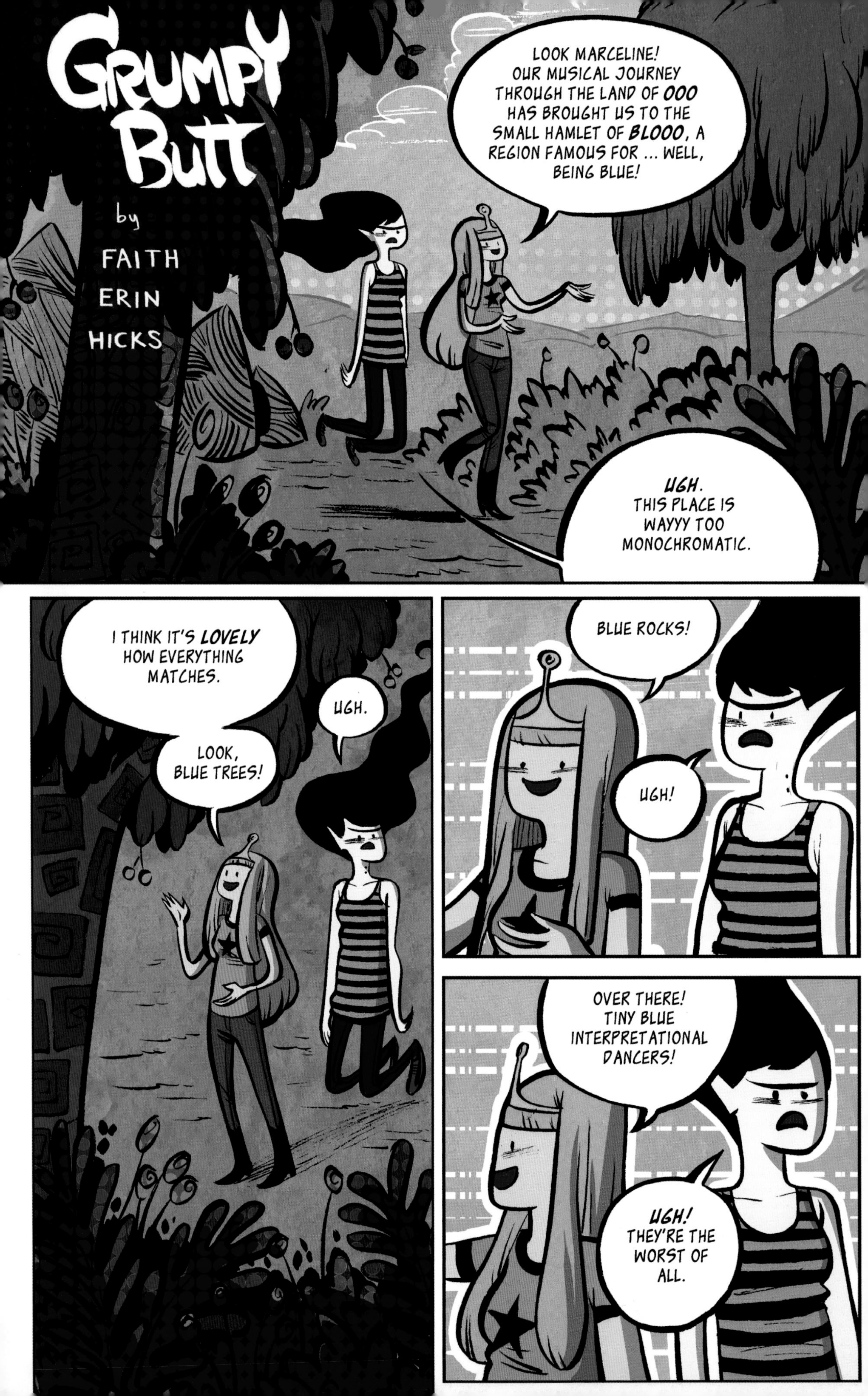
GRUMPY BUTT
by FAITH ERIN HICKS
LOOK MARCELINE! OUR MUSICAL JOURNEY THROUGH THE LAND OF OOO HAS BROUGHT US TO THE SMALL HAMLET OF BLOOO, A REGION FAMOUS FOR ... WELL, BEING BLUE!
UGH. THIS PLACE IS WAYYY TOO MONOCHROMATIC.
I THINK IT'S LOVELY HOW EVERYTHING MATCHES.
UGH.
LOOK, BLUE TREES!
BLUE ROCKS!
UGH!
OVER THERE! TINY BLUE INTERPRETATIONAL DANCERS!
UGH! THEY'RE THE WORST OF ALL.

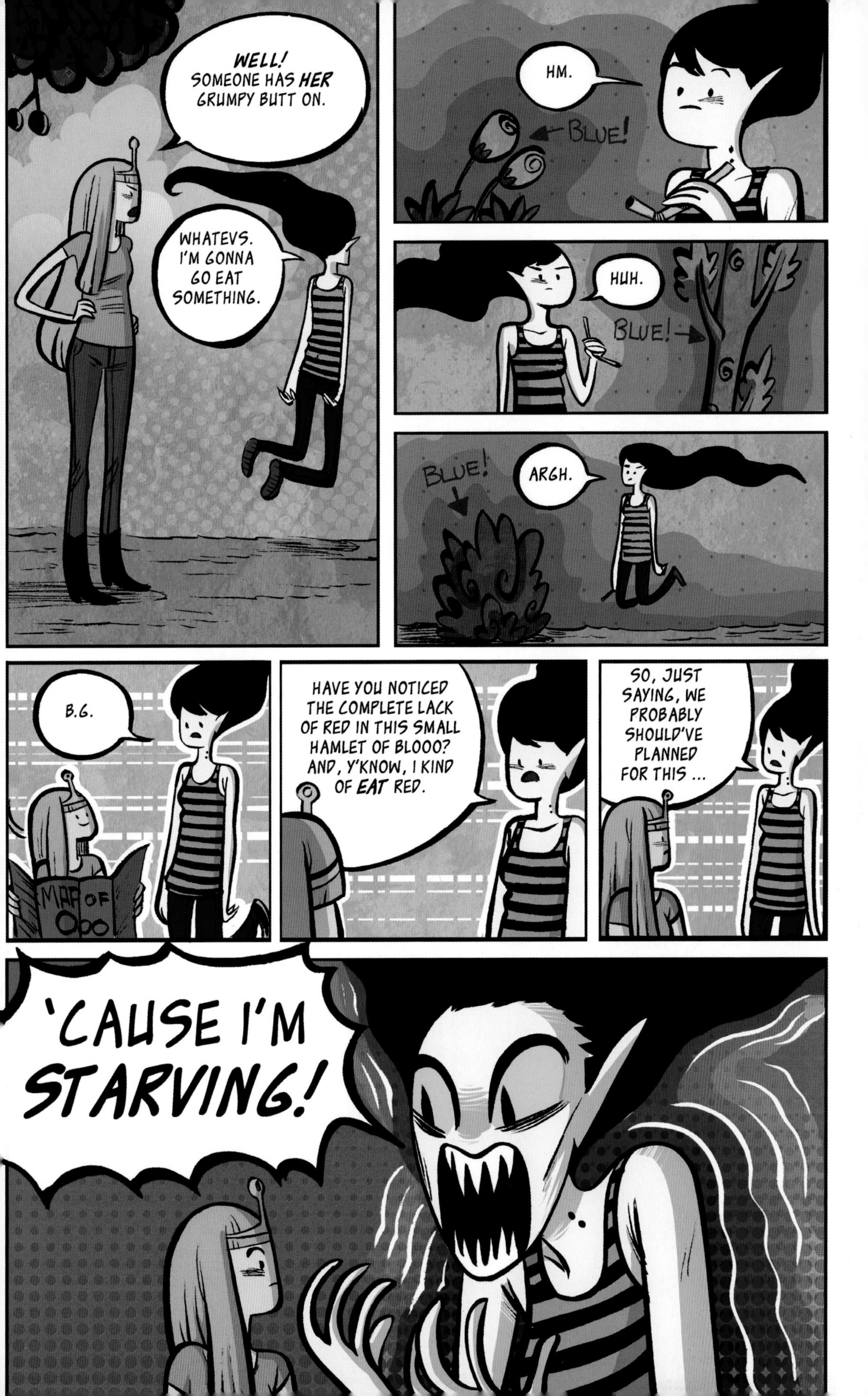
WELL! SOMEONE HAS HER GRUMPY BUTT ON.
WHATEVS. I'M GONNA GO EAT SOMETHING.
HM.
BLUE!
HUH.
BLUE!
BLUE!
ARGH.
B.G.
MAP OF OOO
HAVE YOU NOTICED THE COMPLETE LACK OF RED IN THIS SMALL HAMLET OF BLOOO? AND, Y'KNOW, I KIND OF EAT RED.
SO, JUST SAYING, WE PROBABLY SHOULD'VE PLANNED FOR THIS ...
'CAUSE I'M STARVING!

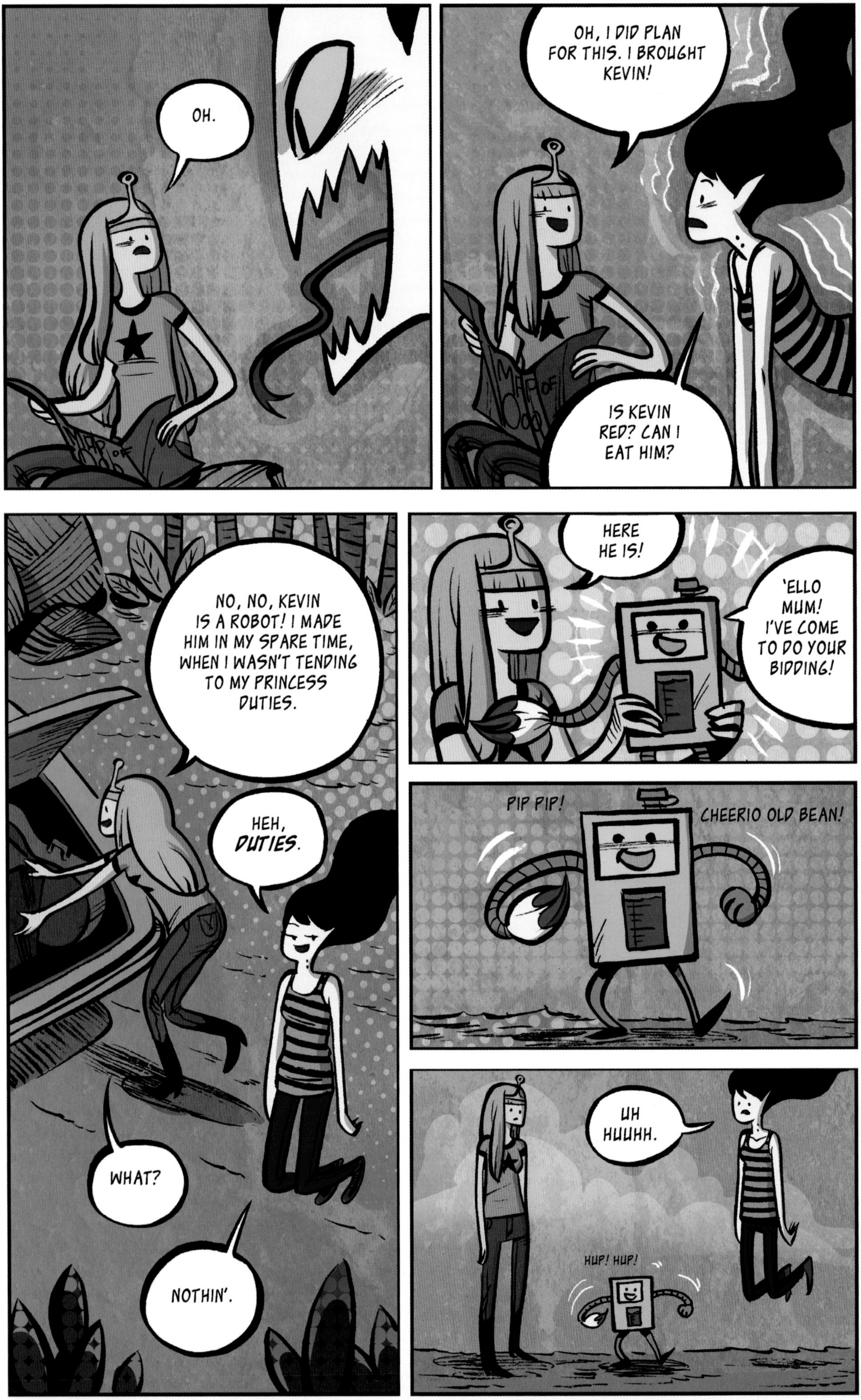
OH.
OH, I DID PLAN FOR THIS. I BROUGHT KEVIN!
IS KEVIN RED? CAN I EAT HIM?
NO, NO, KEVIN IS A ROBOT! I MADE HIM IN MY SPARE TIME, WHEN I WASN'T TENDING TO MY PRINCESS DUTIES.
HEH, *DUTIES*.
WHAT?
NOTHIN'.
HERE HE IS!
'ELLO MUM! I'VE COME TO DO YOUR BIDDING!
PIP PIP!
CHEERIO OLD BEAN!
UH HUUHH.
HUP! HUP!

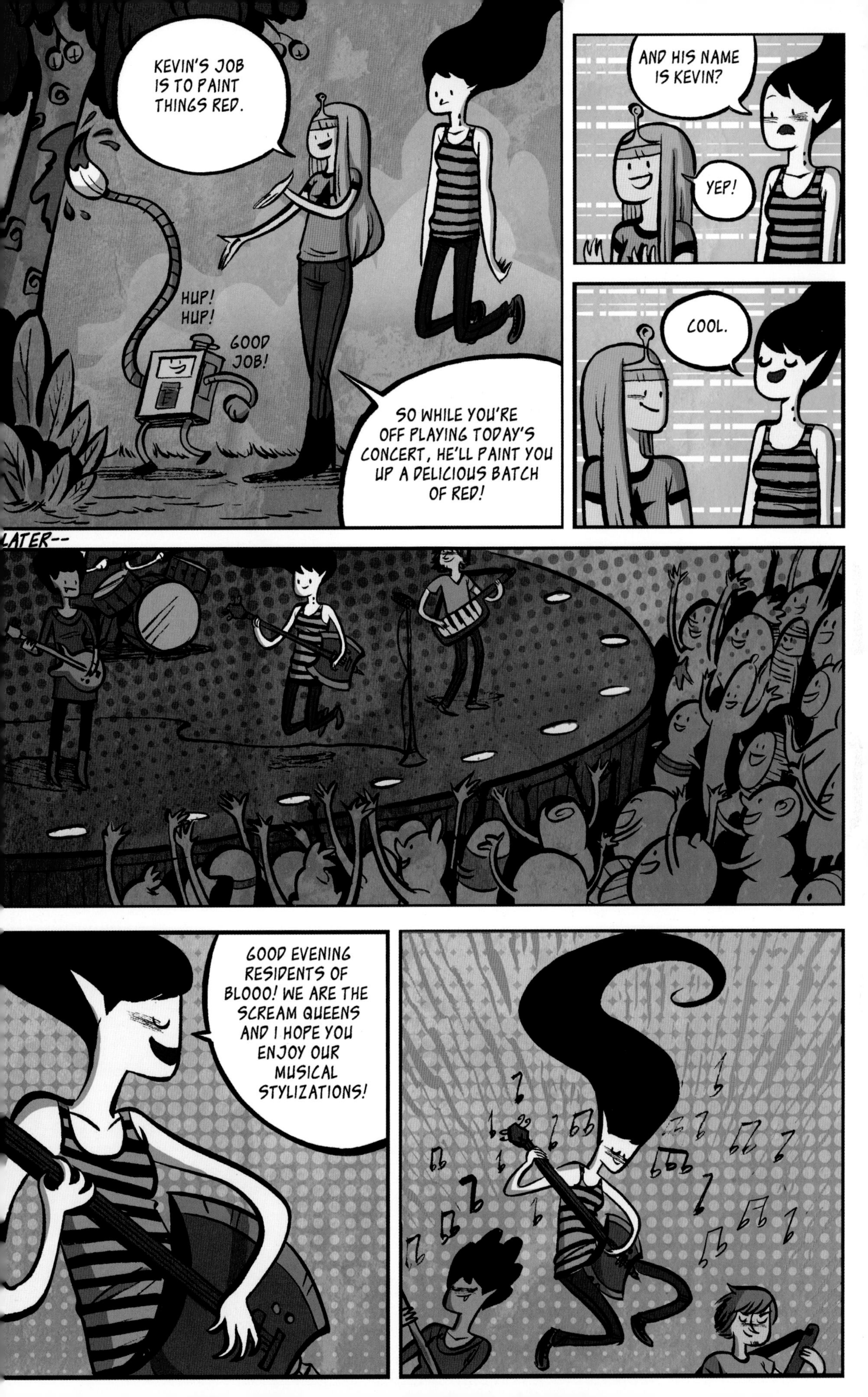
KEVIN'S JOB IS TO PAINT THINGS RED.
HUP! HUP!
GOOD JOB!
SO WHILE YOU'RE OFF PLAYING TODAY'S CONCERT, HE'LL PAINT YOU UP A DELICIOUS BATCH OF RED!
AND HIS NAME IS KEVIN?
YEP!
COOL.
LATER--
GOOD EVENING RESIDENTS OF BLOOO! WE ARE THE SCREAM QUEENS AND I HOPE YOU ENJOY OUR MUSICAL STYLIZATIONS!

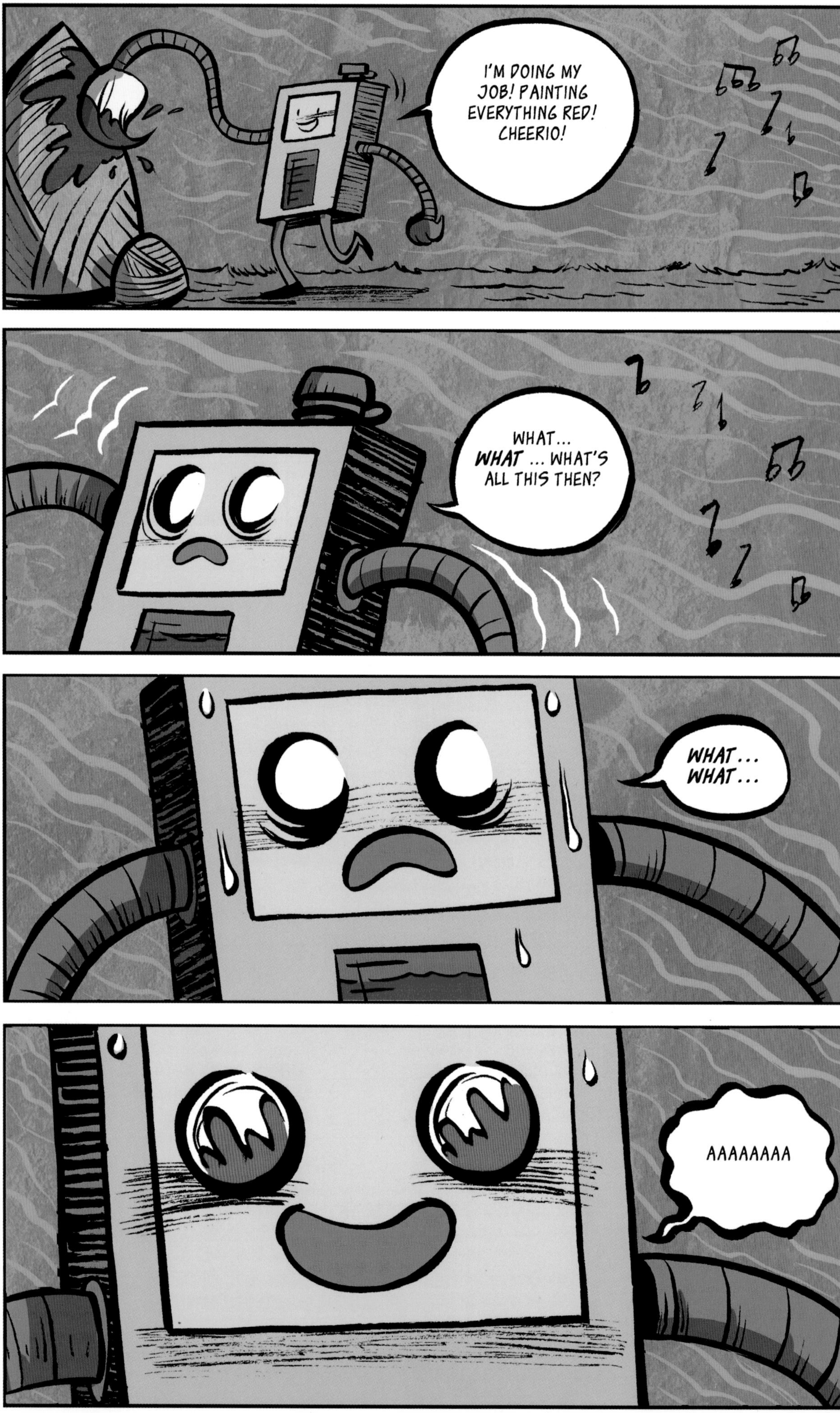
I'M DOING MY JOB! PAINTING EVERYTHING RED! CHEERIO!
WHAT... WHAT ... WHAT'S ALL THIS THEN?
WHAT... WHAT...
AAAAAAAA

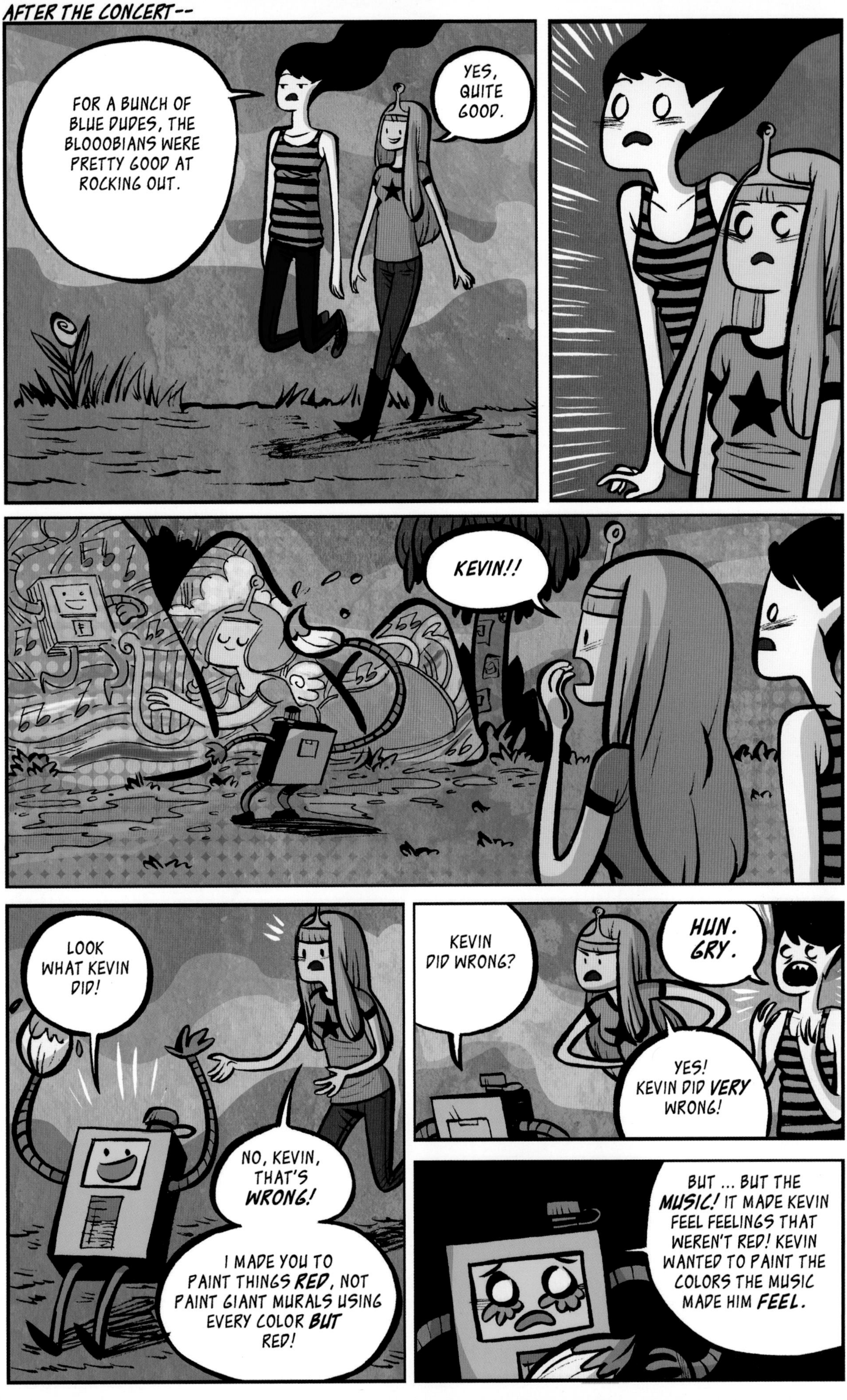
AFTER THE CONCERT--
FOR A BUNCH OF BLUE DUDES, THE BLOOOBIANS WERE PRETTY GOOD AT ROCKING OUT.
YES, QUITE GOOD.
KEVIN!!
LOOK WHAT KEVIN DID!
NO, KEVIN, THAT'S WRONG!
I MADE YOU TO PAINT THINGS RED, NOT PAINT GIANT MURALS USING EVERY COLOR BUT RED!
KEVIN DID WRONG?
HUN. GRY.
YES! KEVIN DID VERY WRONG!
BUT ... BUT THE MUSIC! IT MADE KEVIN FEEL FEELINGS THAT WEREN'T RED! KEVIN WANTED TO PAINT THE COLORS THE MUSIC MADE HIM FEEL.

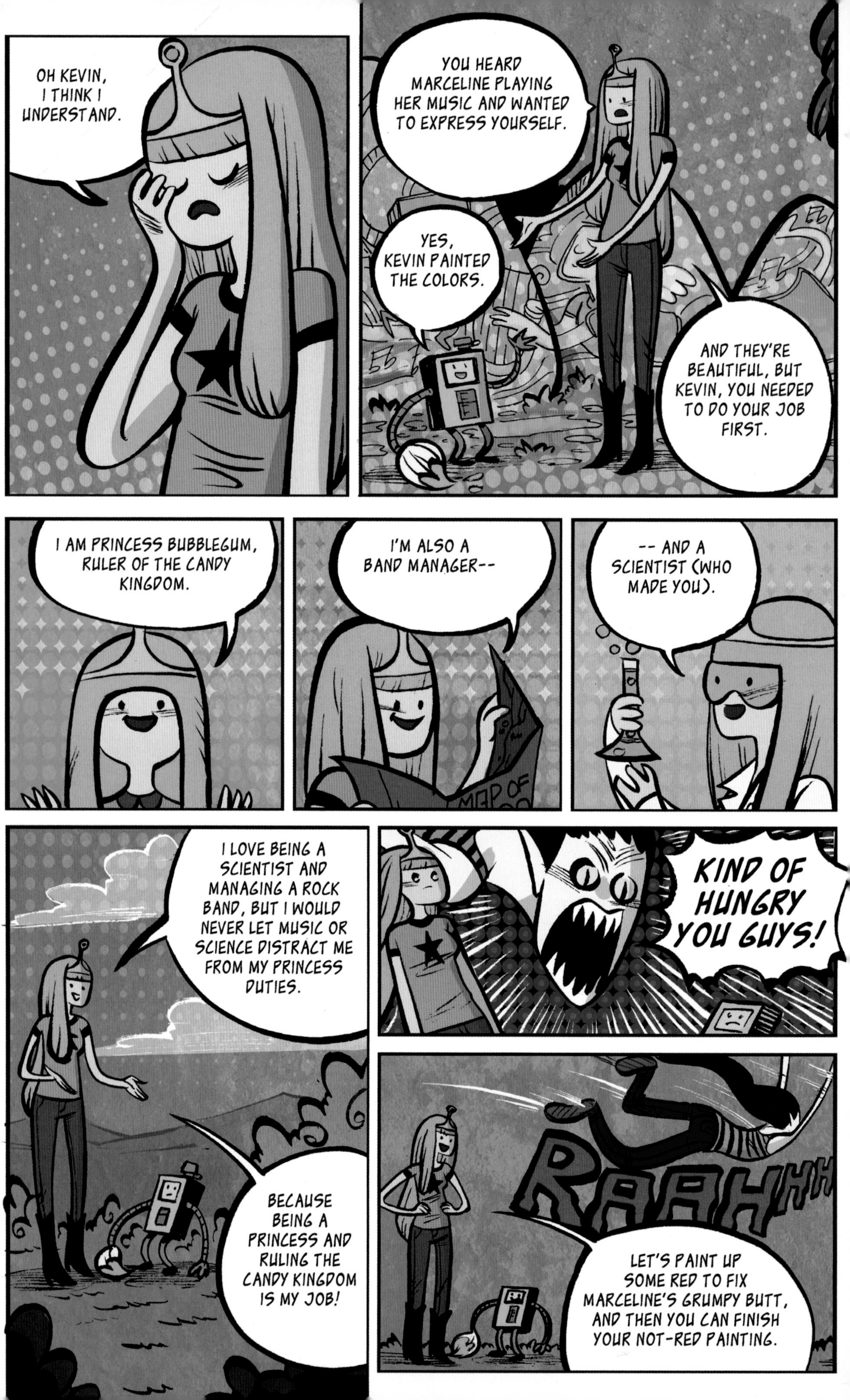
OH KEVIN, I THINK I UNDERSTAND.
YOU HEARD MARCELINE PLAYING HER MUSIC AND WANTED TO EXPRESS YOURSELF.
YES, KEVIN PAINTED THE COLORS.
AND THEY'RE BEAUTIFUL, BUT KEVIN, YOU NEEDED TO DO YOUR JOB FIRST.
I AM PRINCESS BUBBLEGUM, RULER OF THE CANDY KINGDOM.
I'M ALSO A BAND MANAGER--
-- AND A SCIENTIST (WHO MADE YOU).
I LOVE BEING A SCIENTIST AND MANAGING A ROCK BAND, BUT I WOULD NEVER LET MUSIC OR SCIENCE DISTRACT ME FROM MY PRINCESS DUTIES.
BECAUSE BEING A PRINCESS AND RULING THE CANDY KINGDOM IS MY JOB!
KIND OF HUNGRY YOU GUYS!
RAAAHHH
LET'S PAINT UP SOME RED TO FIX MARCELINE'S GRUMPY BUTT, AND THEN YOU CAN FINISH YOUR NOT-RED PAINTING.

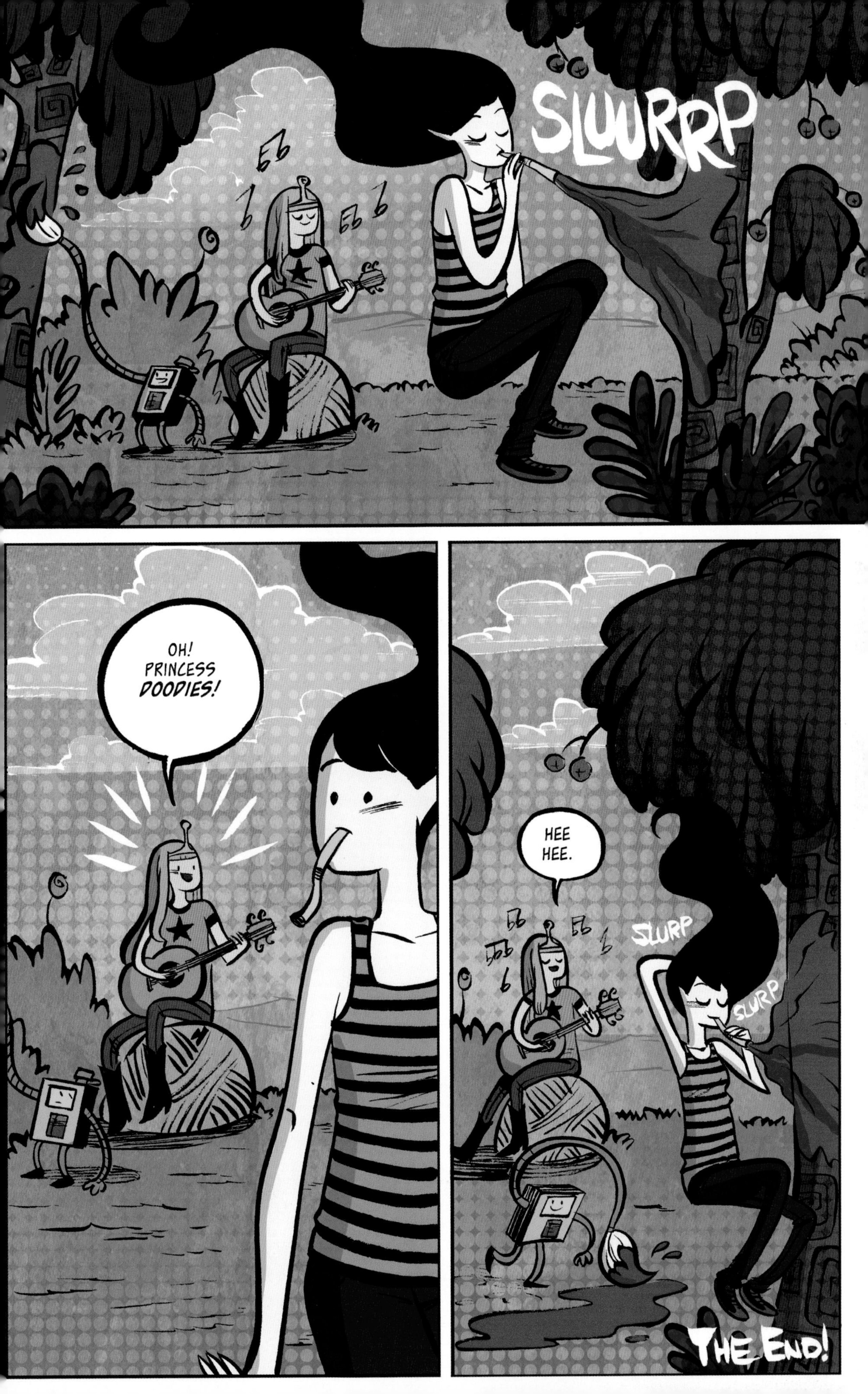
SLUURRP
OH! PRINCESS DOODIES!
HEE HEE.
SLURP
SLURP
THE END!

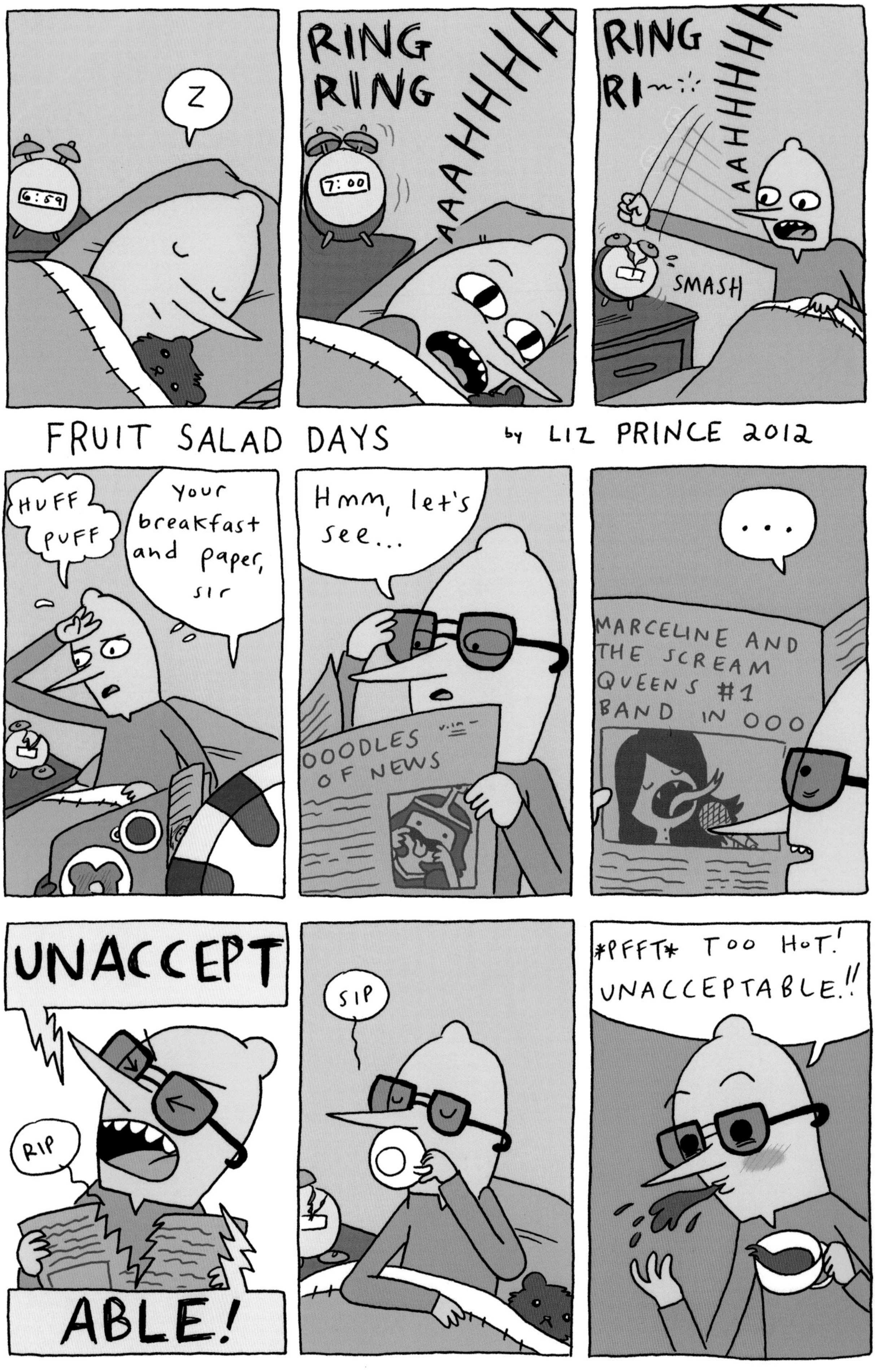

Z
6:59
RING
RING
AAAHHHHHH
7:00
RING
RI~
AAAHHHHHH
SMASH
FRUIT SALAD DAYS
by LIZ PRINCE 2012
HUFF PUFF
Your breakfast and paper, sir
Hmm, let's see...
OOODLES OF NEWS
...
MARCELINE AND THE SCREAM QUEENS #1 BAND IN OOO
UNACCEPT
RIP
ABLE!
SIP
PFFT TOO HOT! UNACCEPTABLE!!

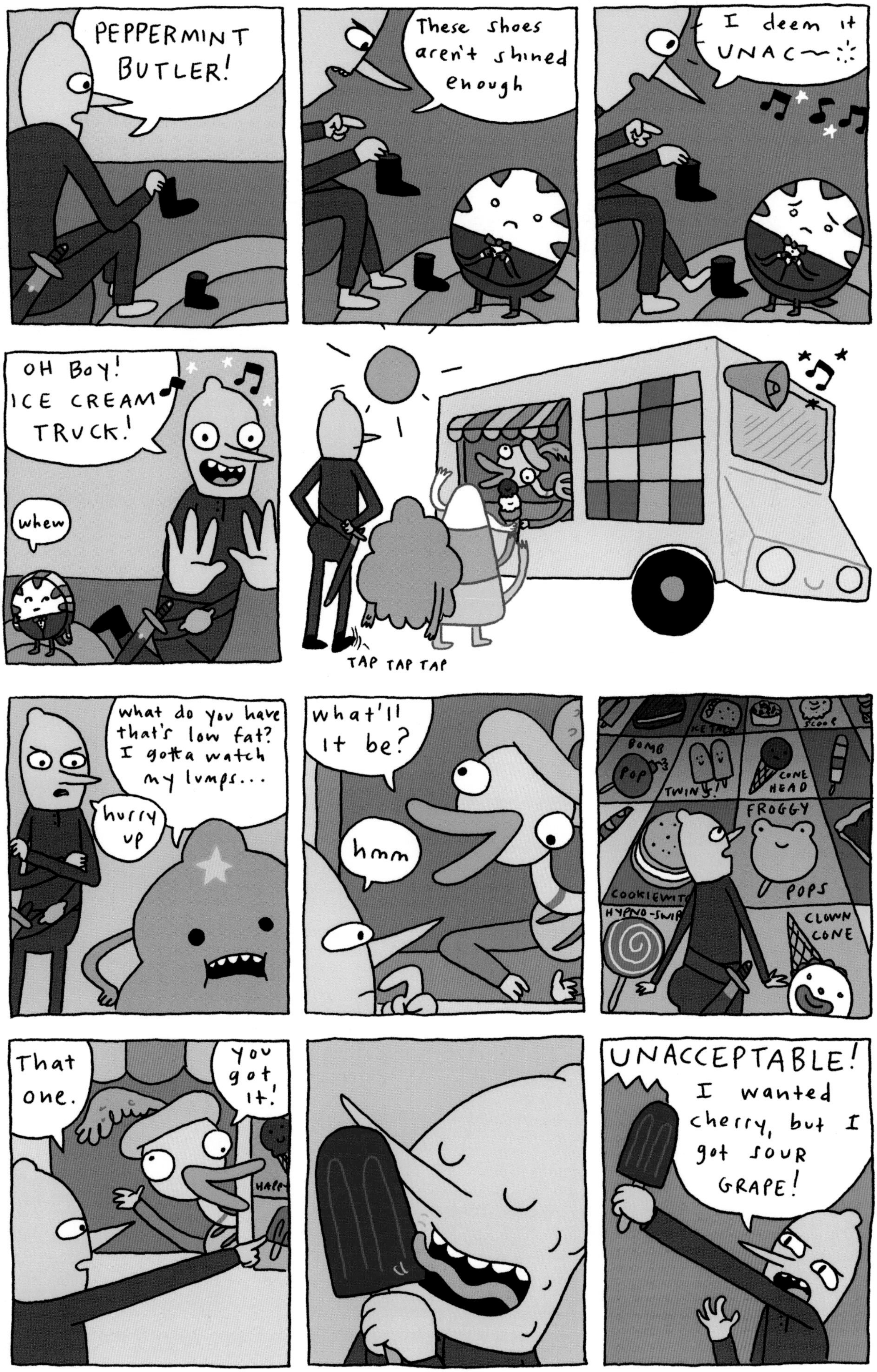
PEPPERMINT BUTLER!
These shoes aren't shined enough
I deem it UNAC~
OH BOY! ICE CREAM TRUCK!
whew
TAP TAP TAP
what do you have that's low fat? I gotta watch my lumps...
hurry up
what'll it be?
hmm
BOMB POP
TWINS!
CONE HEAD
FROGGY POPS
CLOWN CONE
That one.
You got it!
UNACCEPTABLE! I wanted cherry, but I got SOUR GRAPE!

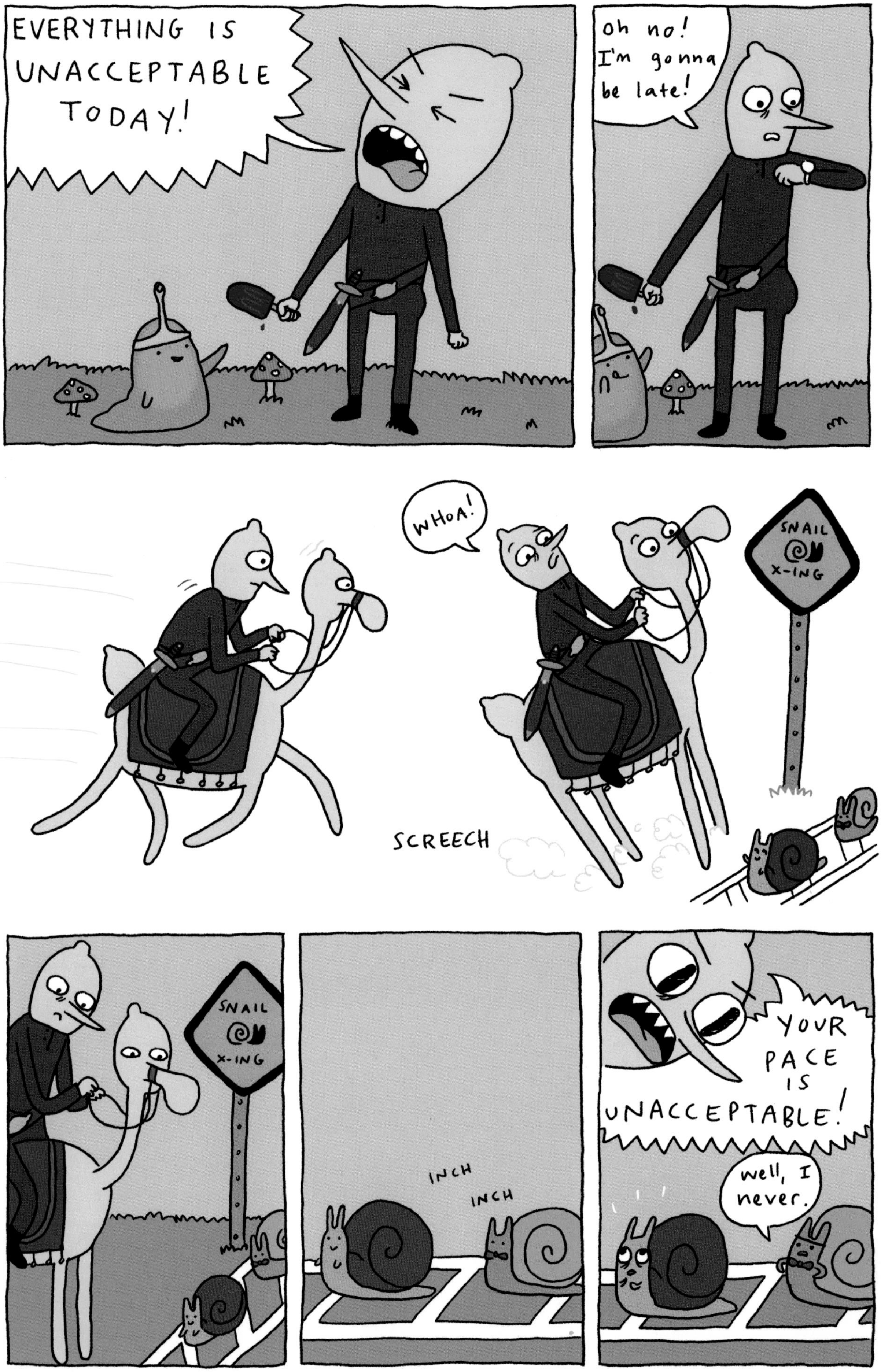
EVERYTHING IS UNACCEPTABLE TODAY!
oh no! I'm gonna be late!
WHOA!
SNAIL X-ING
SCREECH
SNAIL X-ING
INCH
INCH
YOUR PACE IS UNACCEPTABLE!
well, I never.

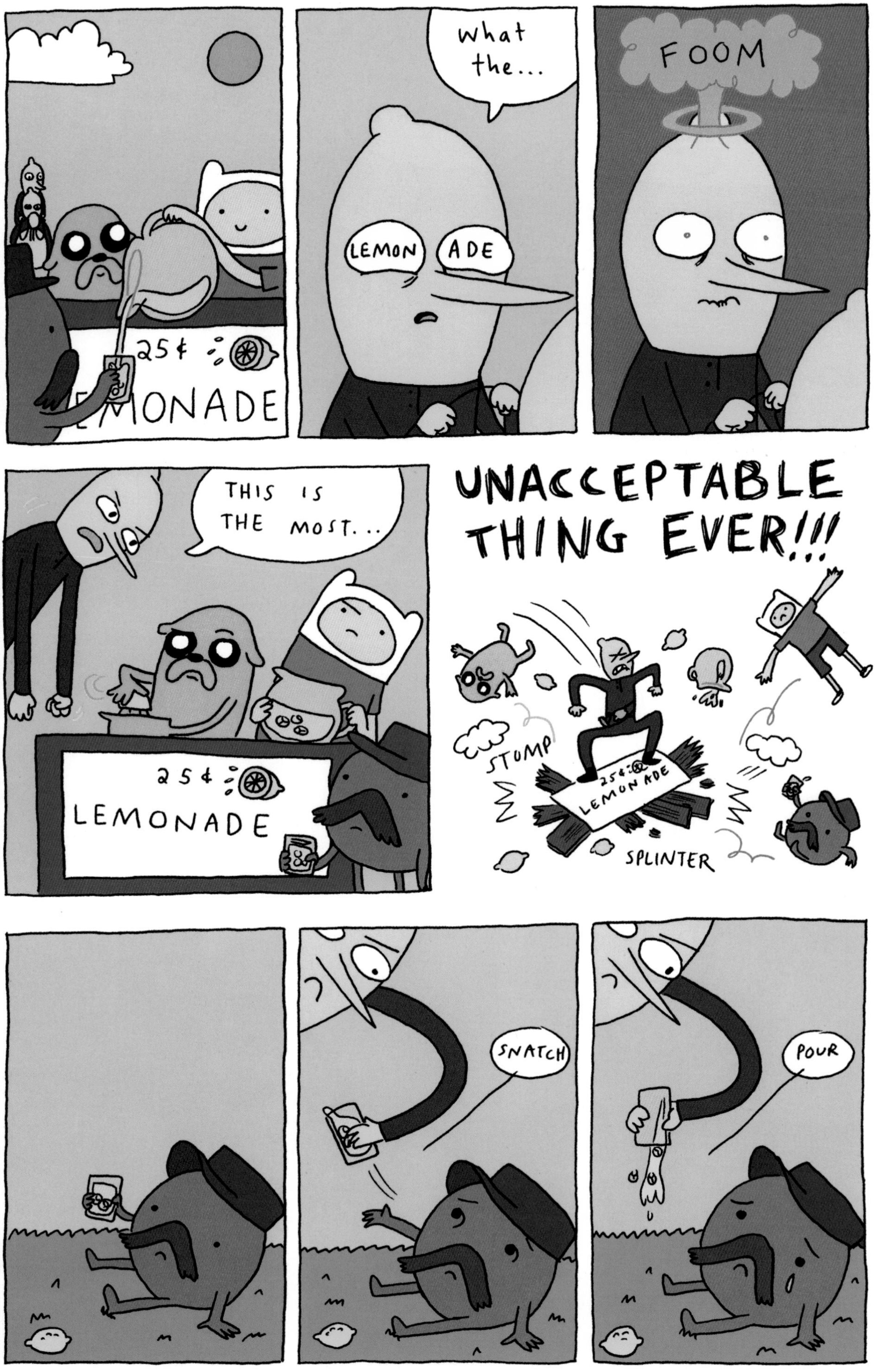

25¢
LEMONADE
what the...
LEMON ADE
FOOM
THIS IS THE MOST...
25¢
LEMONADE
UNACCEPTABLE THING EVER!!!
STOMP
25¢ LEMONADE
SPLINTER
SNATCH
POUR

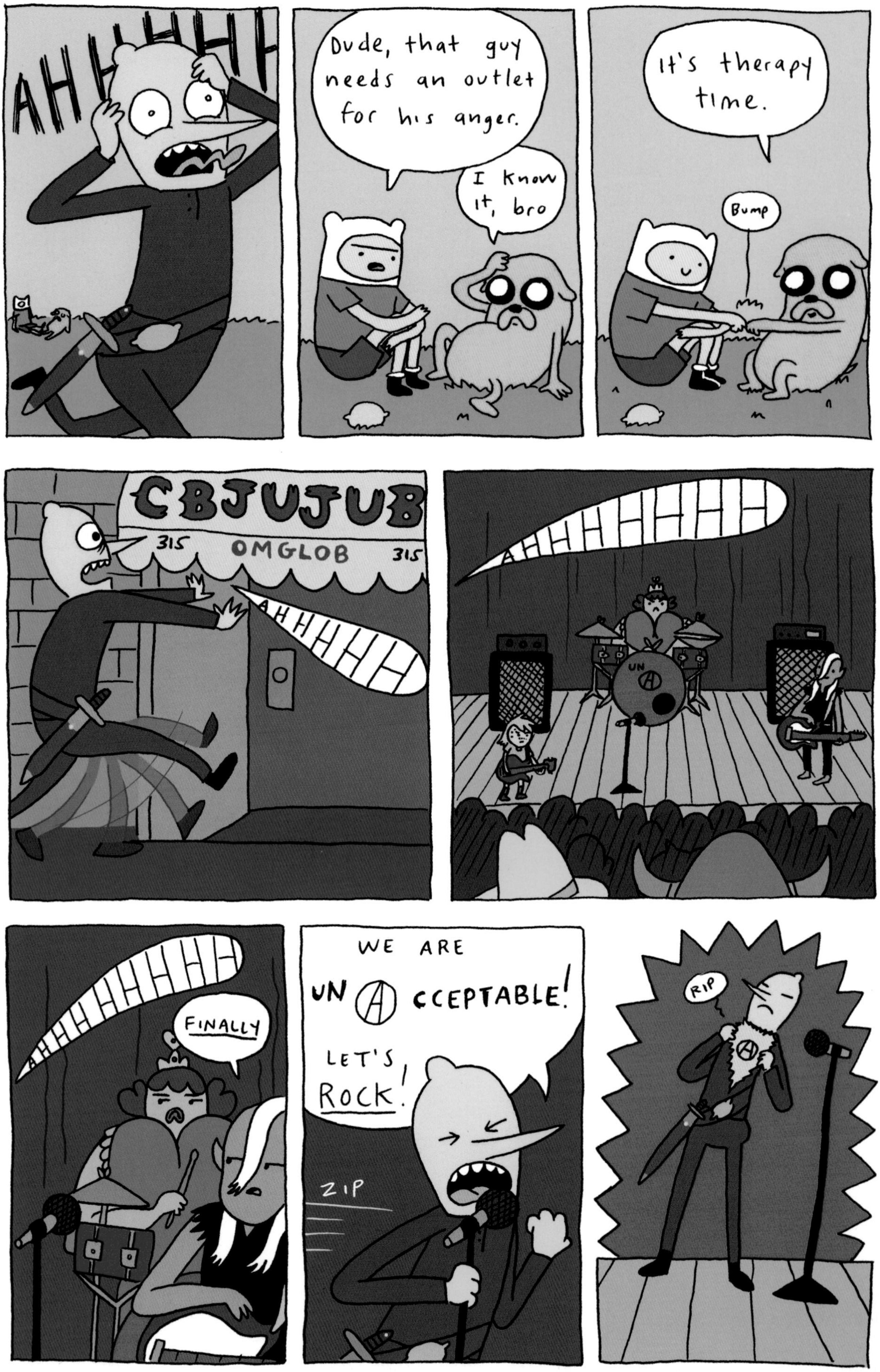
AHHHHHH
Dude, that guy needs an outlet for his anger.
I know it, bro
It's therapy time.
Bump
CBJUJUB
315
OMGLOB
315
AHHHHHH
AHHHHHHHH
AHHHHHHHHHH
FINALLY
WE ARE UN Ⓐ CCEPTABLE!
LET'S ROCK!
ZIP
RIP

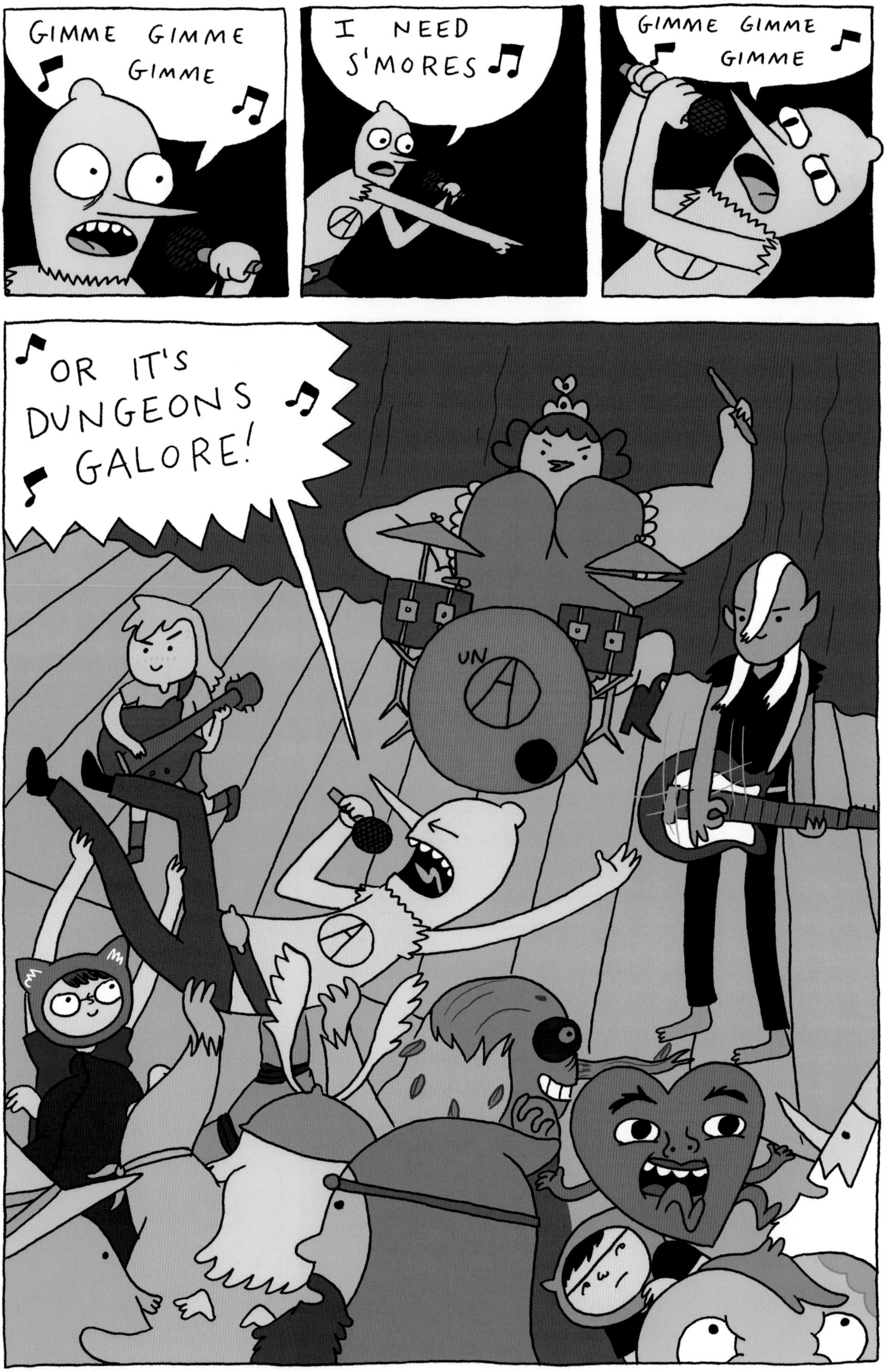
GIMME GIMME GIMME
I NEED S'MORES
GIMME GIMME GIMME
OR IT'S DUNGEONS GALORE!

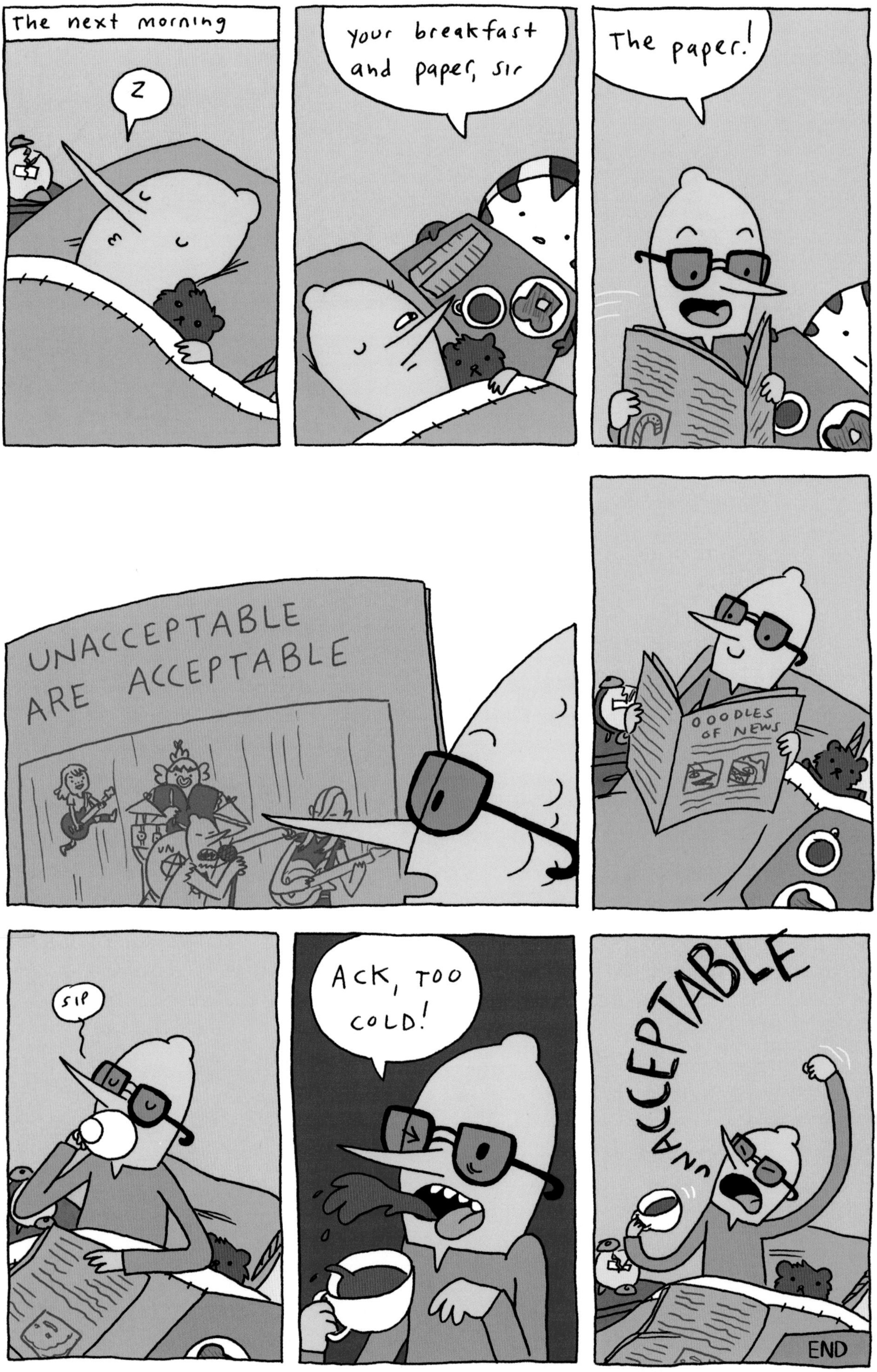
the next morning
Z
your breakfast and paper, sir
The paper!
UNACCEPTABLE ARE ACCEPTABLE
UN
OODLES OF NEWS
SIP
ACK, TOO COLD!
UNACCEPTABLE
END

ANANTH PANAGARIYA & YUKO OTA

THE BOOTLEGGER

TONIGHT ONLY

MARCELINE & the scream queens

Ol' Starchy's ready for the show!

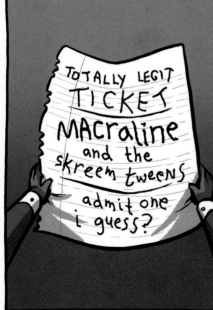

TOTALLY LEGIT TICKET MACraline and the skreem tweens admit one i guess?

Starchy, I have bad news ...

... your ticket is a FAKE!

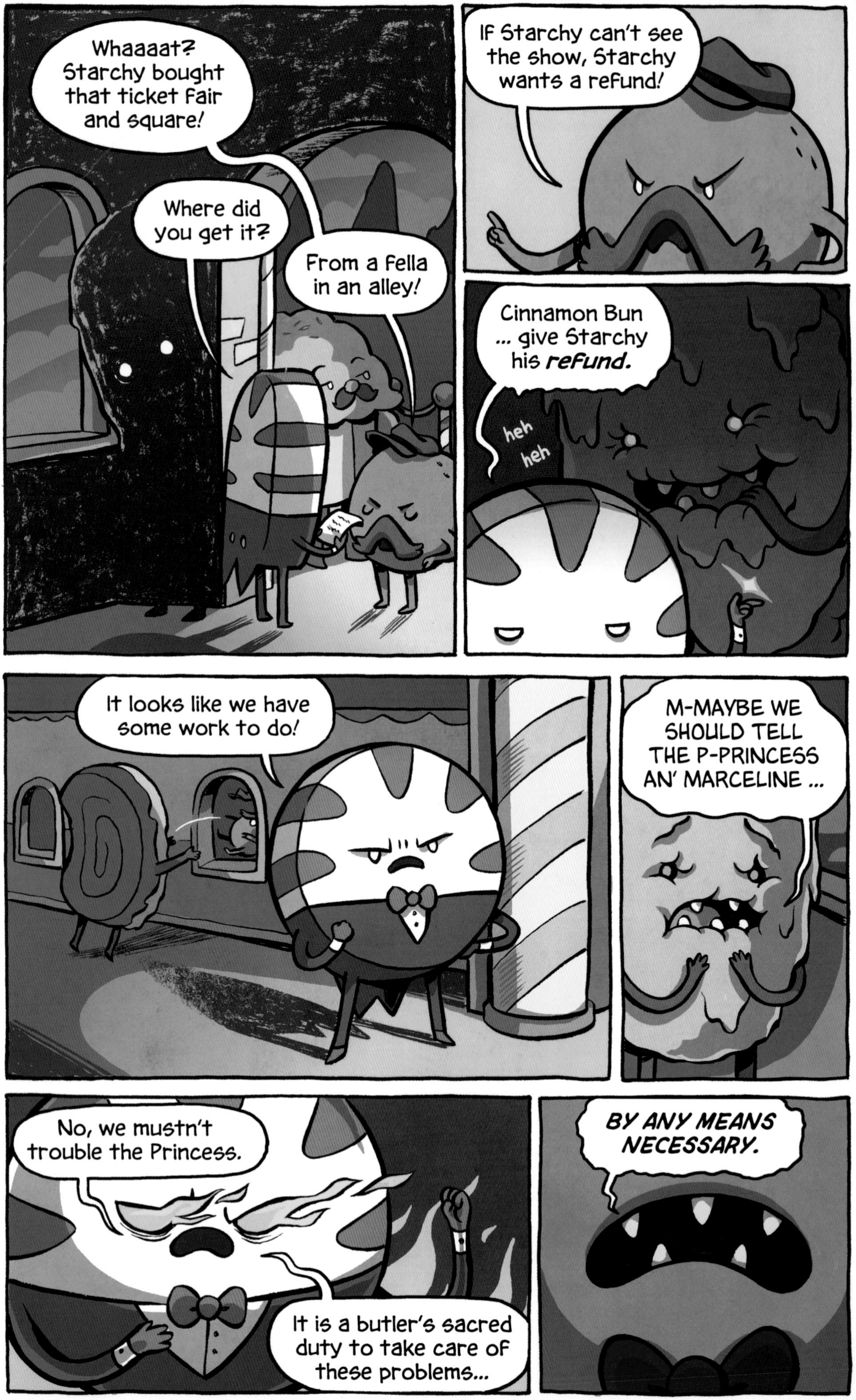
Whaaaat? Starchy bought that ticket fair and square!
Where did you get it?
From a fella in an alley!
If Starchy can't see the show, Starchy wants a refund!
Cinnamon Bun ... give Starchy his *refund.*
heh heh
It looks like we have some work to do!
M-MAYBE WE SHOULD TELL THE P-PRINCESS AN' MARCELINE ...
No, we mustn't trouble the Princess.
It is a butler's sacred duty to take care of these problems...
BY ANY MEANS NECESSARY.

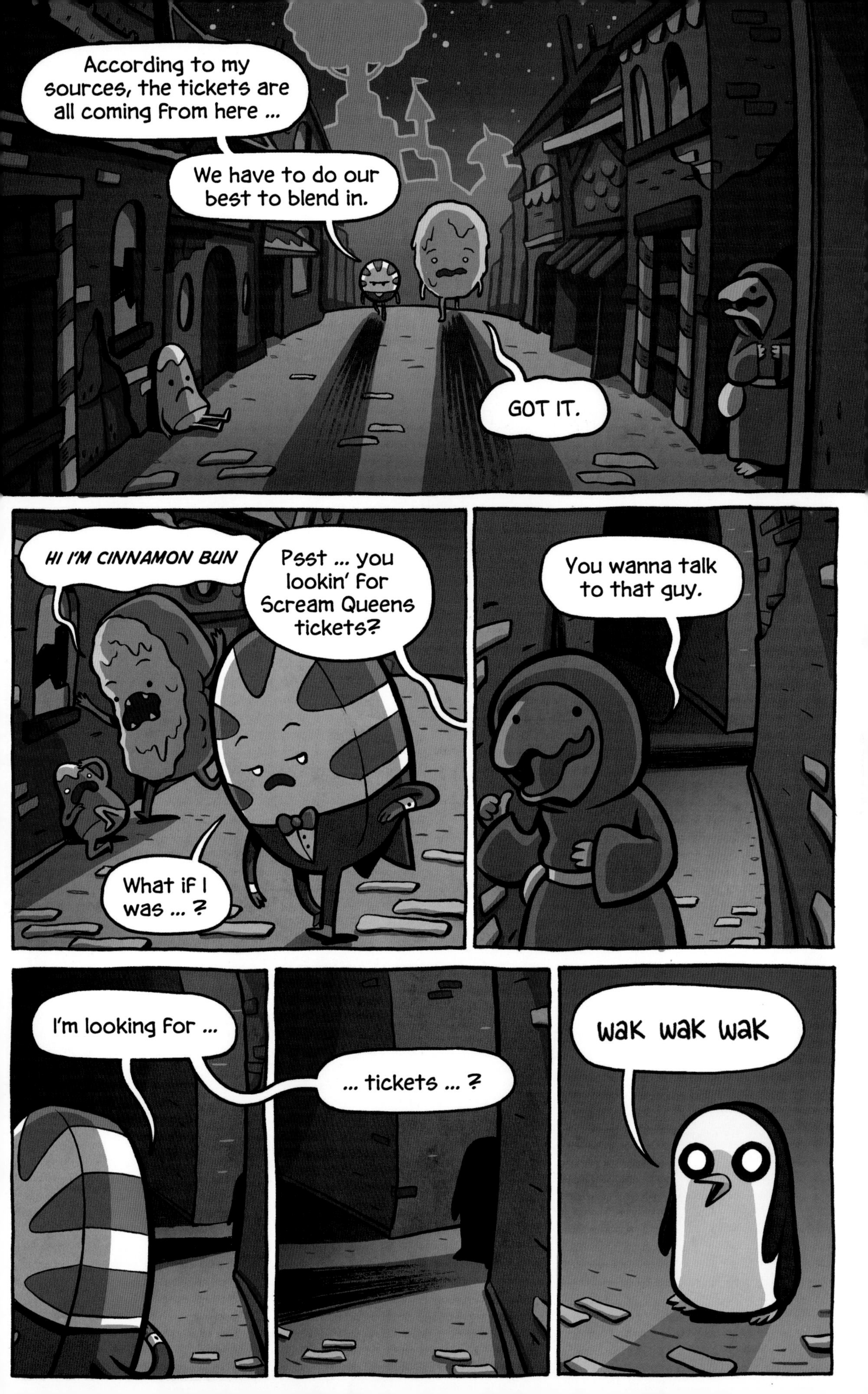
According to my sources, the tickets are all coming from here ...
We have to do our best to blend in.
GOT IT.
HI I'M CINNAMON BUN
Psst ... you lookin' for Scream Queens tickets?
What if I was ... ?
You wanna talk to that guy.
I'm looking for ...
... tickets ... ?
wak wak wak

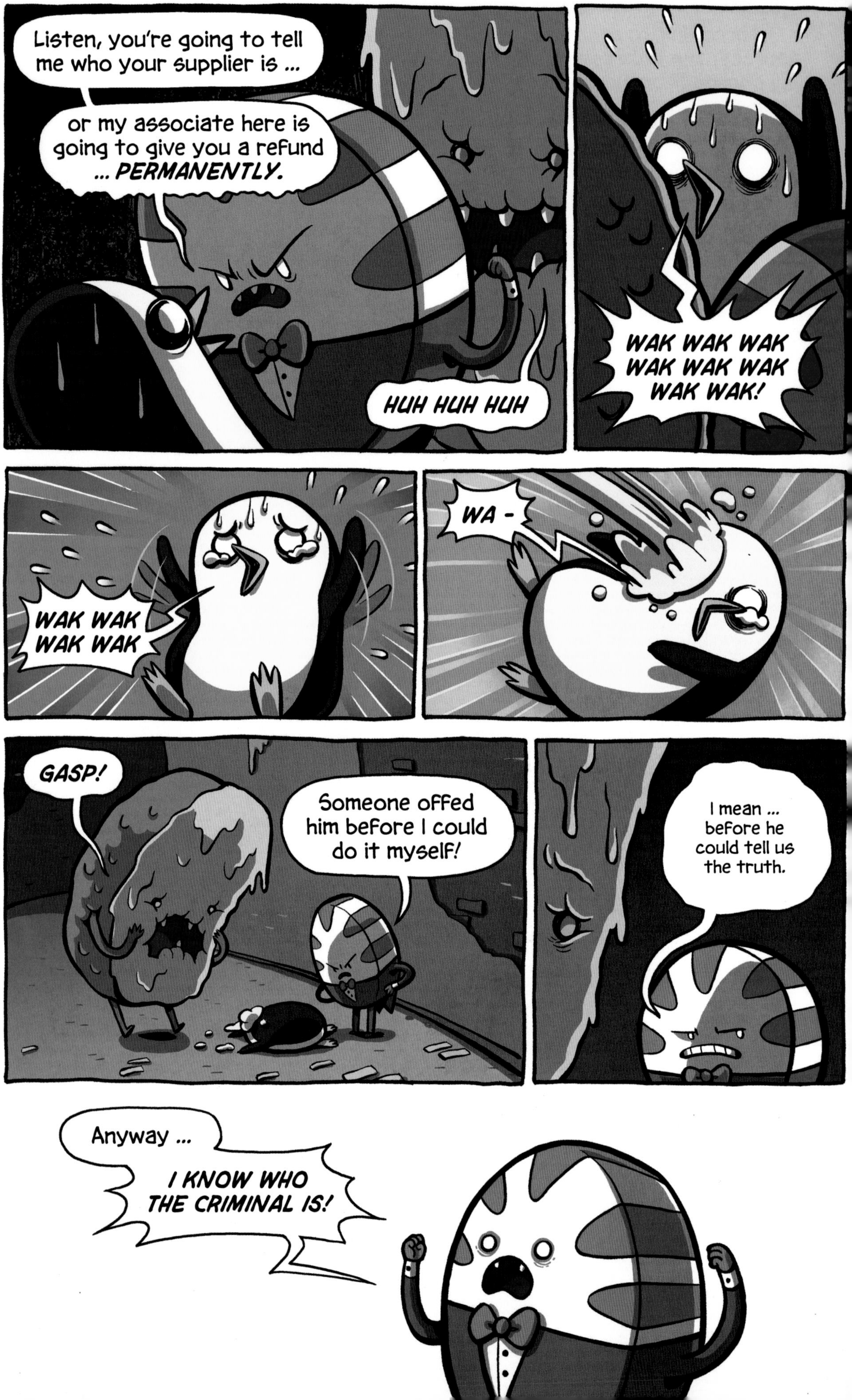
Listen, you're going to tell me who your supplier is ...
or my associate here is going to give you a refund ... PERMANENTLY.
HUH HUH HUH
WAK WAK WAK WAK WAK WAK WAK WAK!
WAK WAK WAK WAK
WA -
GASP!
Someone offed him before I could do it myself!
I mean ... before he could tell us the truth.
Anyway ...
I KNOW WHO THE CRIMINAL IS!

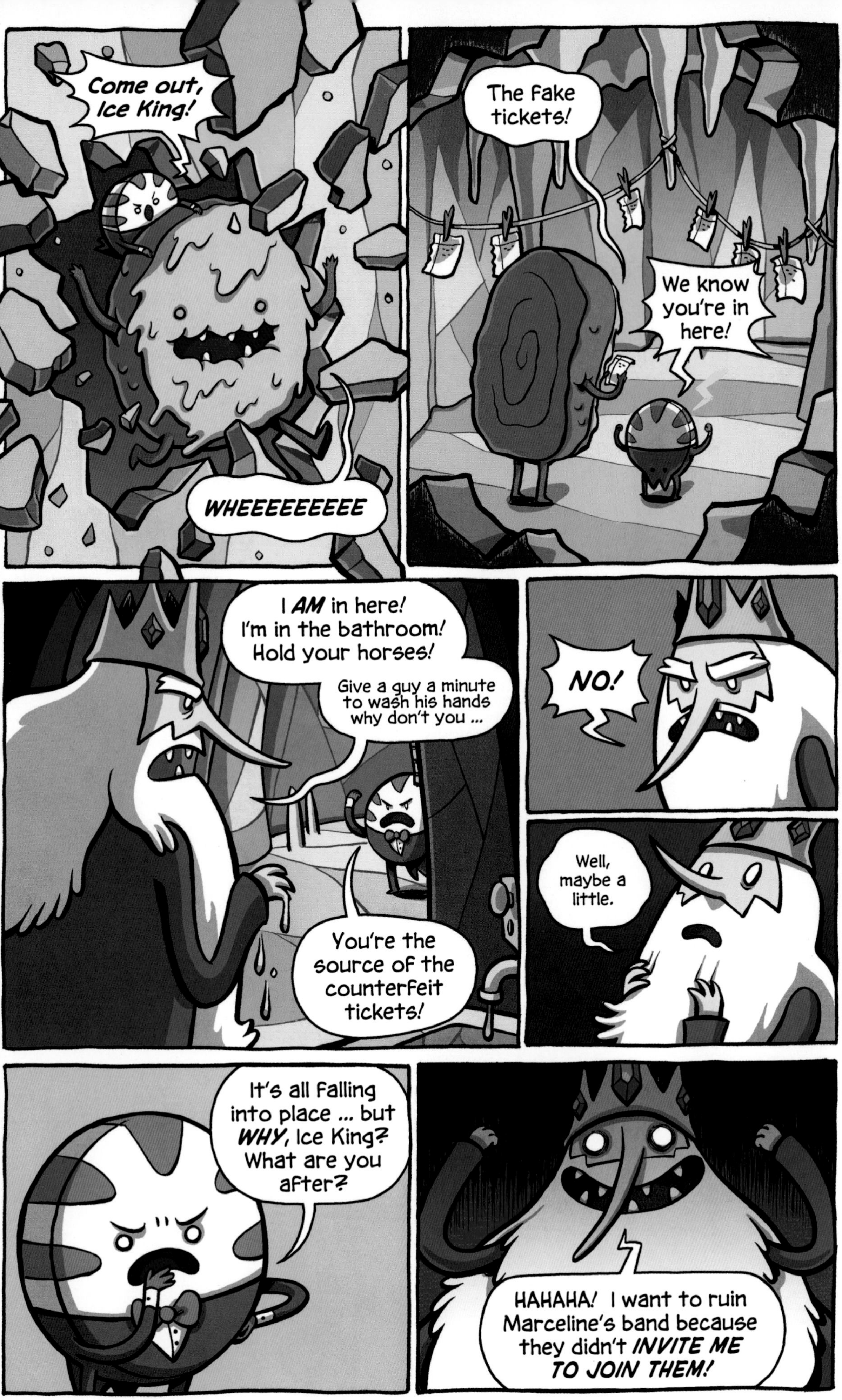

Come out, Ice King!
WHEEEEEEEEE
The fake tickets!
We know you're in here!
I AM in here! I'm in the bathroom! Hold your horses!
Give a guy a minute to wash his hands why don't you ...
You're the source of the counterfeit tickets!
NO!
Well, maybe a little.
It's all falling into place ... but WHY, Ice King? What are you after?
HAHAHA! I want to ruin Marceline's band because they didn't INVITE ME TO JOIN THEM!

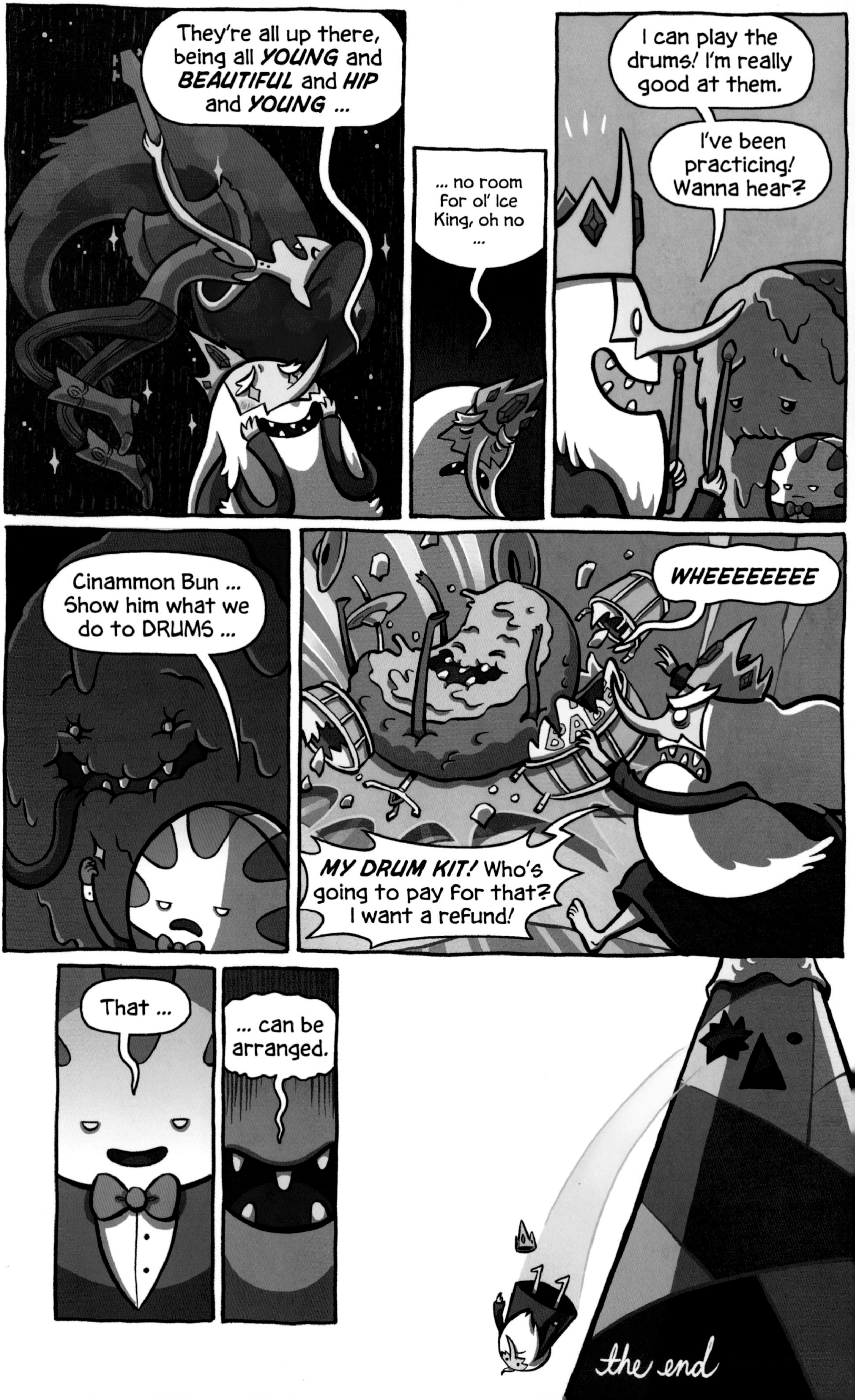

They're all up there, being all *YOUNG* and *BEAUTIFUL* and *HIP* and *YOUNG* ...
... no room for ol' Ice King, oh no ...
I can play the drums! I'm really good at them.
I've been practicing! Wanna hear?
Cinammon Bun ... Show him what we do to DRUMS ...
WHEEEEEEEE
MY DRUM KIT! Who's going to pay for that? I want a refund!
That ...
... can be arranged.
the end

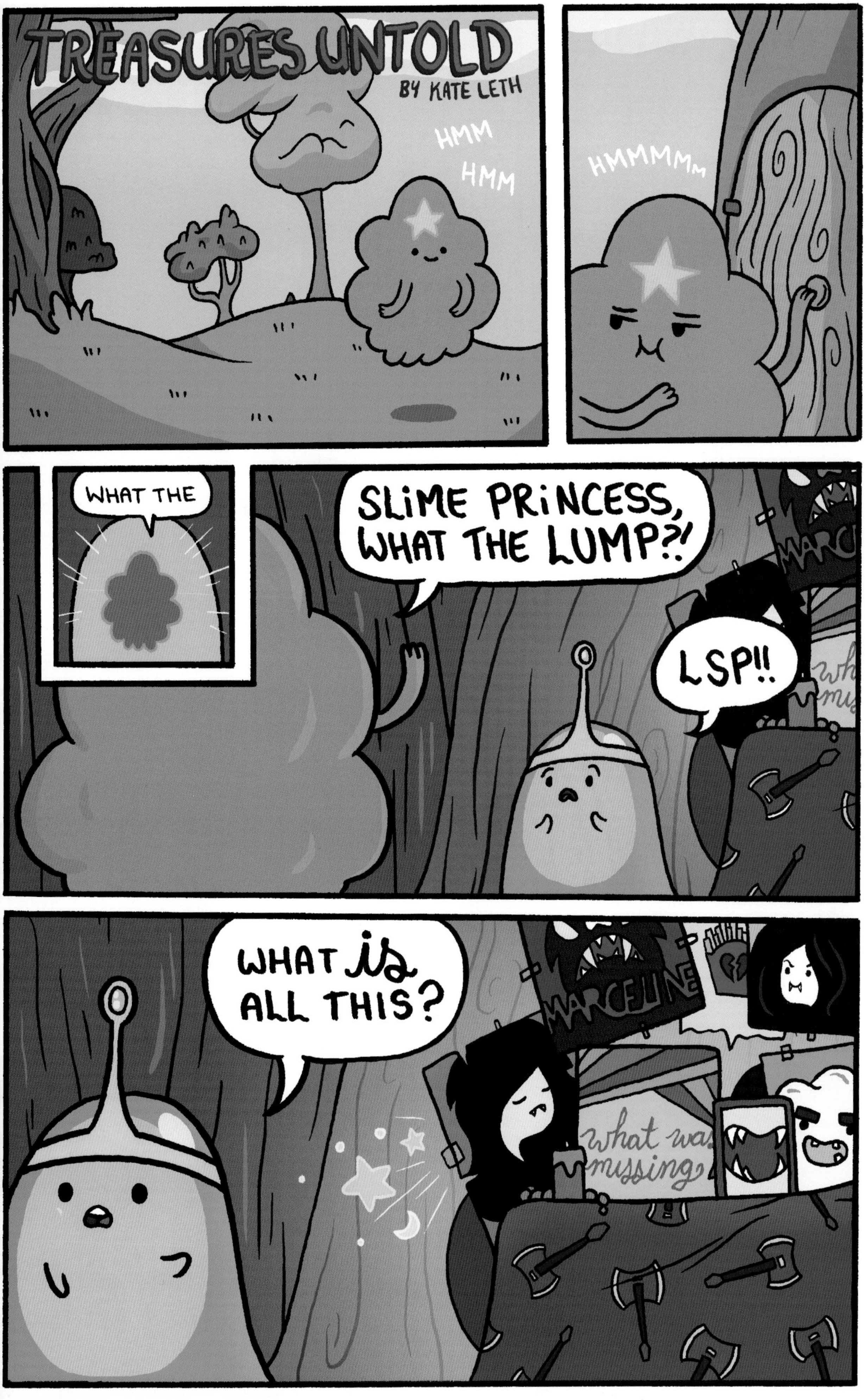
TREASURES UNTOLD
BY KATE LETH
HMM
HMM
HMMMMmm
WHAT THE
SLIME PRINCESS, WHAT THE LUMP?!
LSP!!
WHAT is ALL THIS?
MARCELINE
what was missing

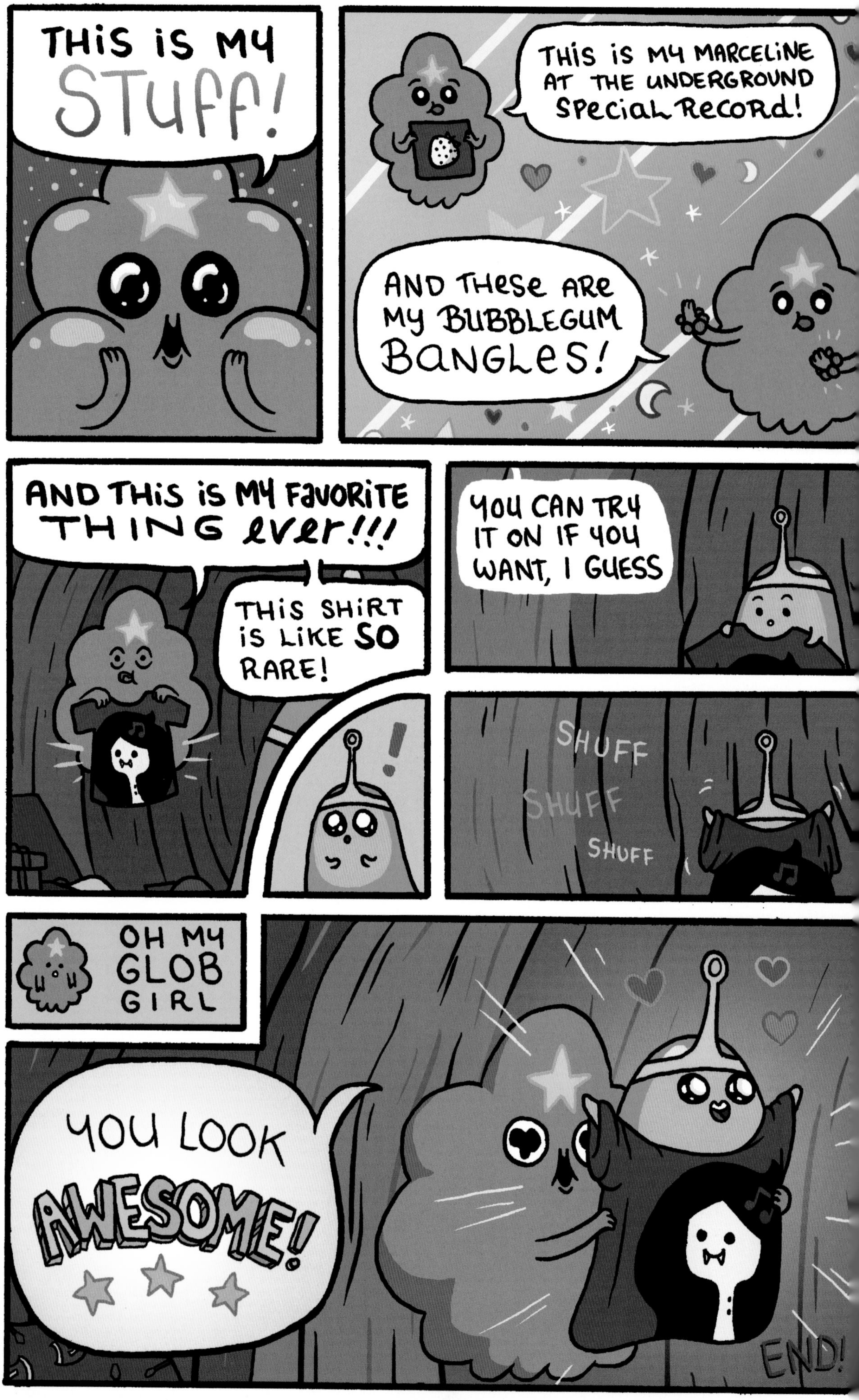

THIS IS MY STUFF!
THIS IS MY MARCELINE AT THE UNDERGROUND SPECIAL RECORD!
AND THESE ARE MY BUBBLEGUM BANGLES!
AND THIS IS MY FAVORITE THING ever!!!
THIS SHIRT IS LIKE SO RARE!
!
YOU CAN TRY IT ON IF YOU WANT, I GUESS
SHUFF
SHUFF
SHUFF
OH MY GLOB GIRL
YOU LOOK AWESOME!
END!

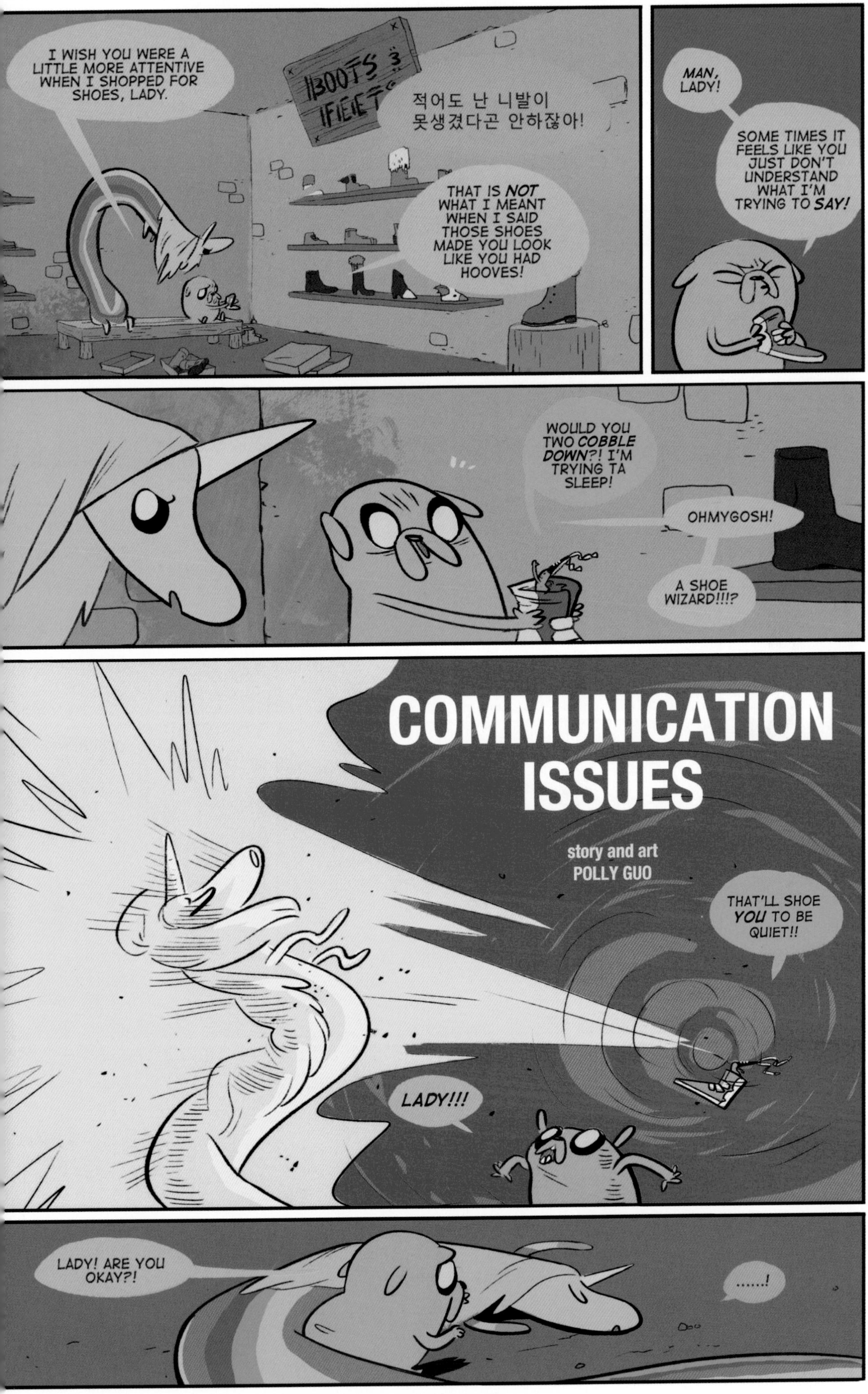

I WISH YOU WERE A LITTLE MORE ATTENTIVE WHEN I SHOPPED FOR SHOES, LADY.
BOOTS 3 FEET
적어도 난 니발이 못생겼다곤 안하잖아!
THAT IS NOT WHAT I MEANT WHEN I SAID THOSE SHOES MADE YOU LOOK LIKE YOU HAD HOOVES!
MAN, LADY!
SOME TIMES IT FEELS LIKE YOU JUST DON'T UNDERSTAND WHAT I'M TRYING TO SAY!
WOULD YOU TWO COBBLE DOWN?! I'M TRYING TA SLEEP!
OHMYGOSH!
A SHOE WIZARD!!!?
COMMUNICATION ISSUES
story and art POLLY GUO
THAT'LL SHOE YOU TO BE QUIET!!
LADY!!!
LADY! ARE YOU OKAY?!
......!

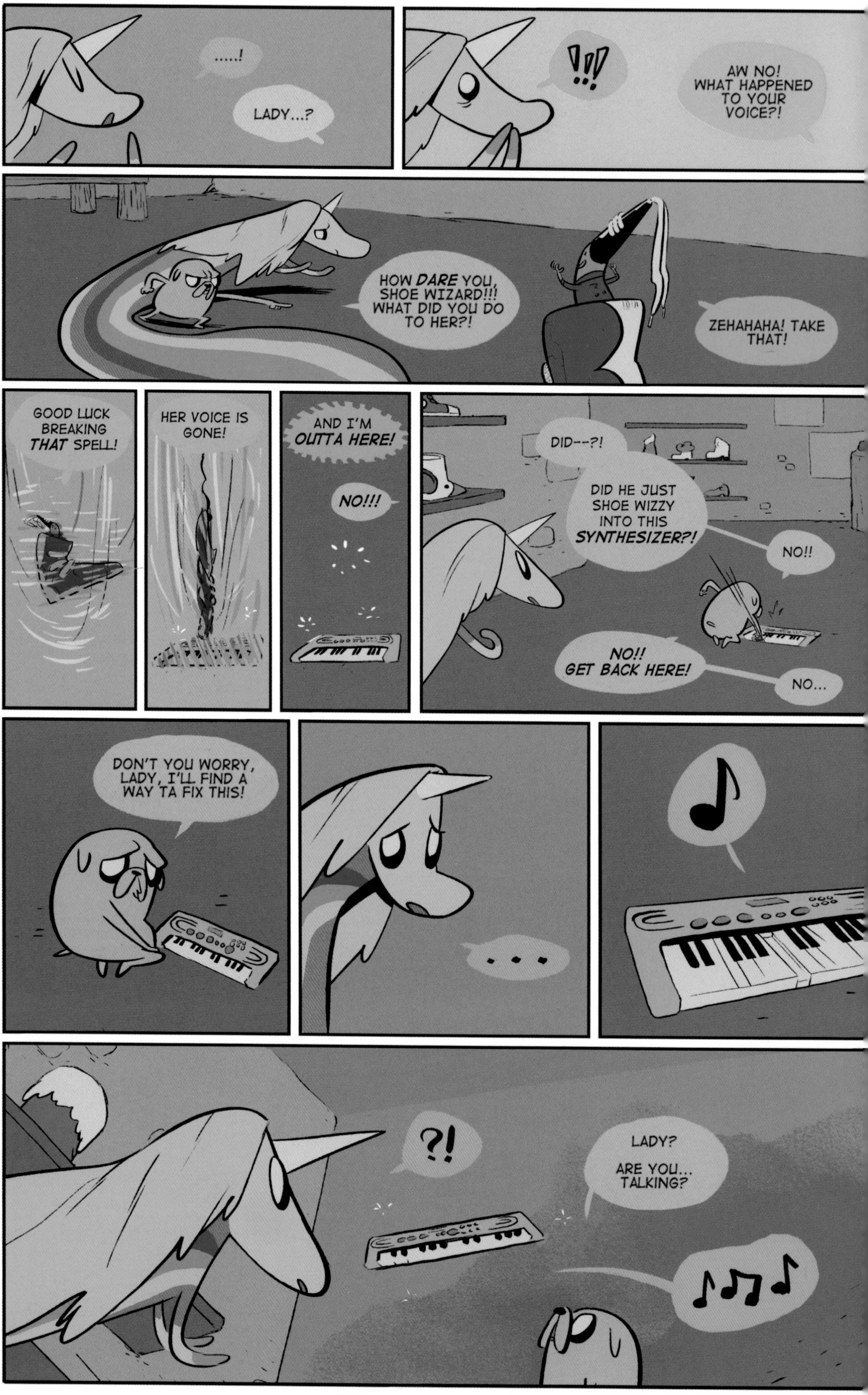
.....!
LADY...?
!!!
AW NO! WHAT HAPPENED TO YOUR VOICE?!
HOW DARE YOU, SHOE WIZARD!!! WHAT DID YOU DO TO HER?!
ZEHAHAHA! TAKE THAT!
GOOD LUCK BREAKING THAT SPELL!
HER VOICE IS GONE!
AND I'M OUTTA HERE!
NO!!!
DID--?!
DID HE JUST SHOE WIZZY INTO THIS SYNTHESIZER?!
NO!!
NO!! GET BACK HERE!
NO...
DON'T YOU WORRY, LADY, I'LL FIND A WAY TA FIX THIS!
...
?!
LADY?
ARE YOU... TALKING?

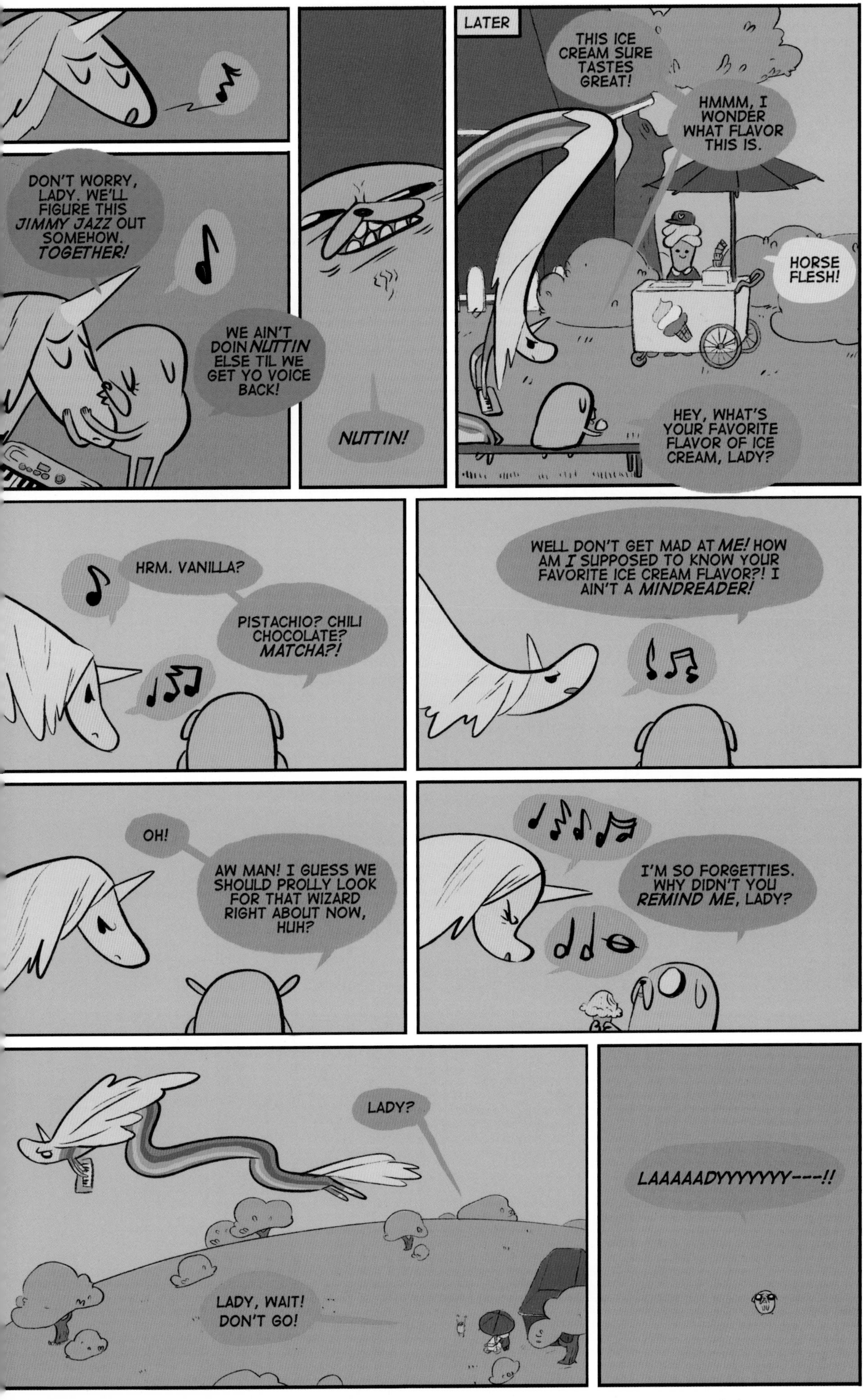
DON'T WORRY, LADY. WE'LL FIGURE THIS JIMMY JAZZ OUT SOMEHOW. TOGETHER!
WE AIN'T DOIN NUTTIN ELSE TIL WE GET YO VOICE BACK!
NUTTIN!
LATER
THIS ICE CREAM SURE TASTES GREAT!
HMMM, I WONDER WHAT FLAVOR THIS IS.
HORSE FLESH!
HEY, WHAT'S YOUR FAVORITE FLAVOR OF ICE CREAM, LADY?
HRM. VANILLA?
PISTACHIO? CHILI CHOCOLATE? MATCHA?!
WELL DON'T GET MAD AT ME! HOW AM I SUPPOSED TO KNOW YOUR FAVORITE ICE CREAM FLAVOR?! I AIN'T A MINDREADER!
OH!
AW MAN! I GUESS WE SHOULD PROLLY LOOK FOR THAT WIZARD RIGHT ABOUT NOW, HUH?
I'M SO FORGETTIES. WHY DIDN'T YOU REMIND ME, LADY?
LADY?
LADY, WAIT! DON'T GO!
LAAAAADYYYYYYY---!!

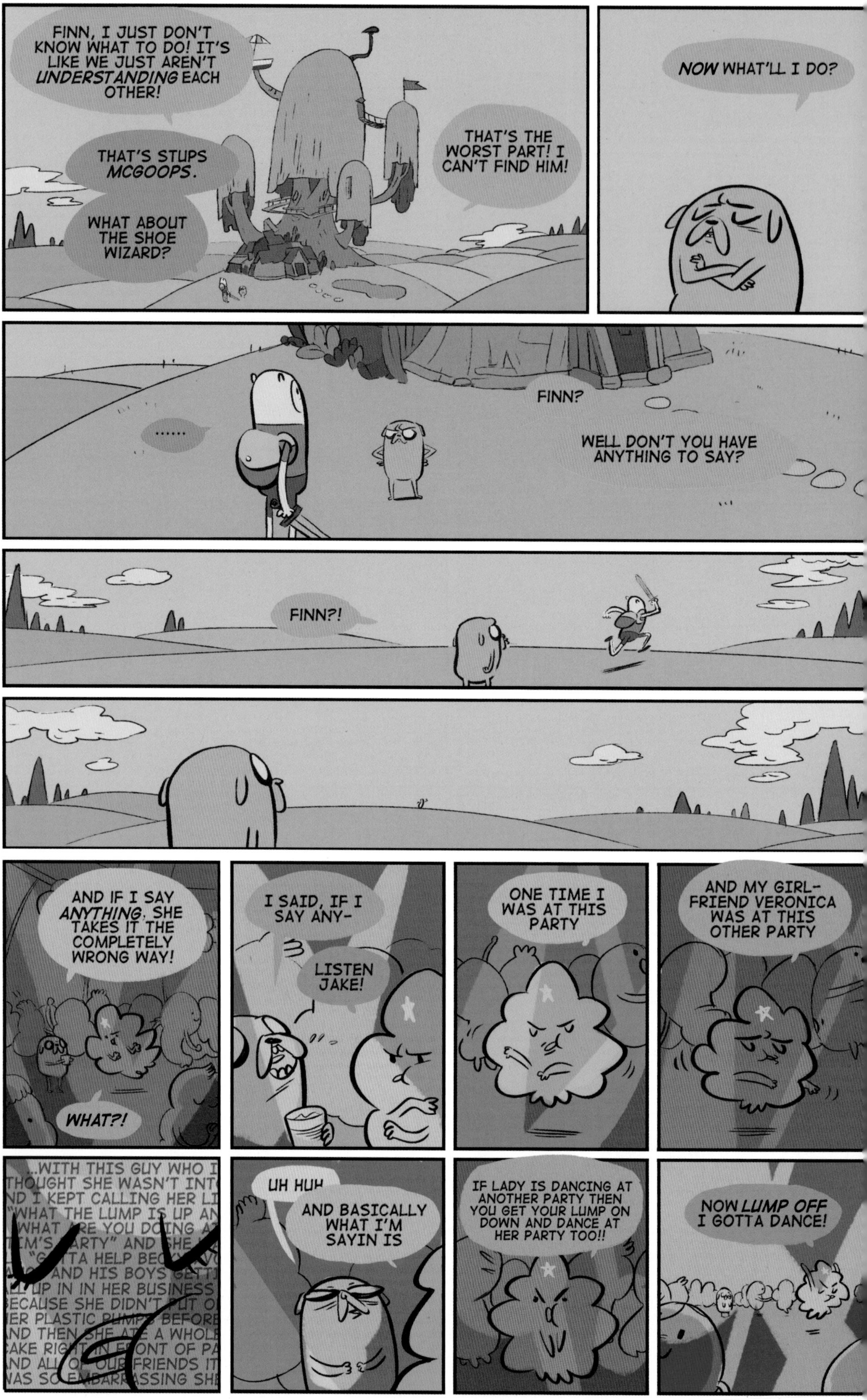
FINN, I JUST DON'T KNOW WHAT TO DO! IT'S LIKE WE JUST AREN'T *UNDERSTANDING* EACH OTHER!
THAT'S STUPS *MCGOOPS*.
WHAT ABOUT THE SHOE WIZARD?
THAT'S THE WORST PART! I CAN'T FIND HIM!
NOW WHAT'LL I DO?
FINN?
......
WELL DON'T YOU HAVE ANYTHING TO SAY?
FINN?!
AND IF I SAY *ANYTHING*, SHE TAKES IT THE COMPLETELY WRONG WAY!
WHAT?!
I SAID, IF I SAY ANY-
LISTEN JAKE!
ONE TIME I WAS AT THIS PARTY
AND MY GIRL-FRIEND VERONICA WAS AT THIS OTHER PARTY
UH HUH
AND BASICALLY WHAT I'M SAYIN IS
IF LADY IS DANCING AT ANOTHER PARTY THEN YOU GET YOUR LUMP ON DOWN AND DANCE AT HER PARTY TOO!!
NOW *LUMP OFF* I GOTTA DANCE!

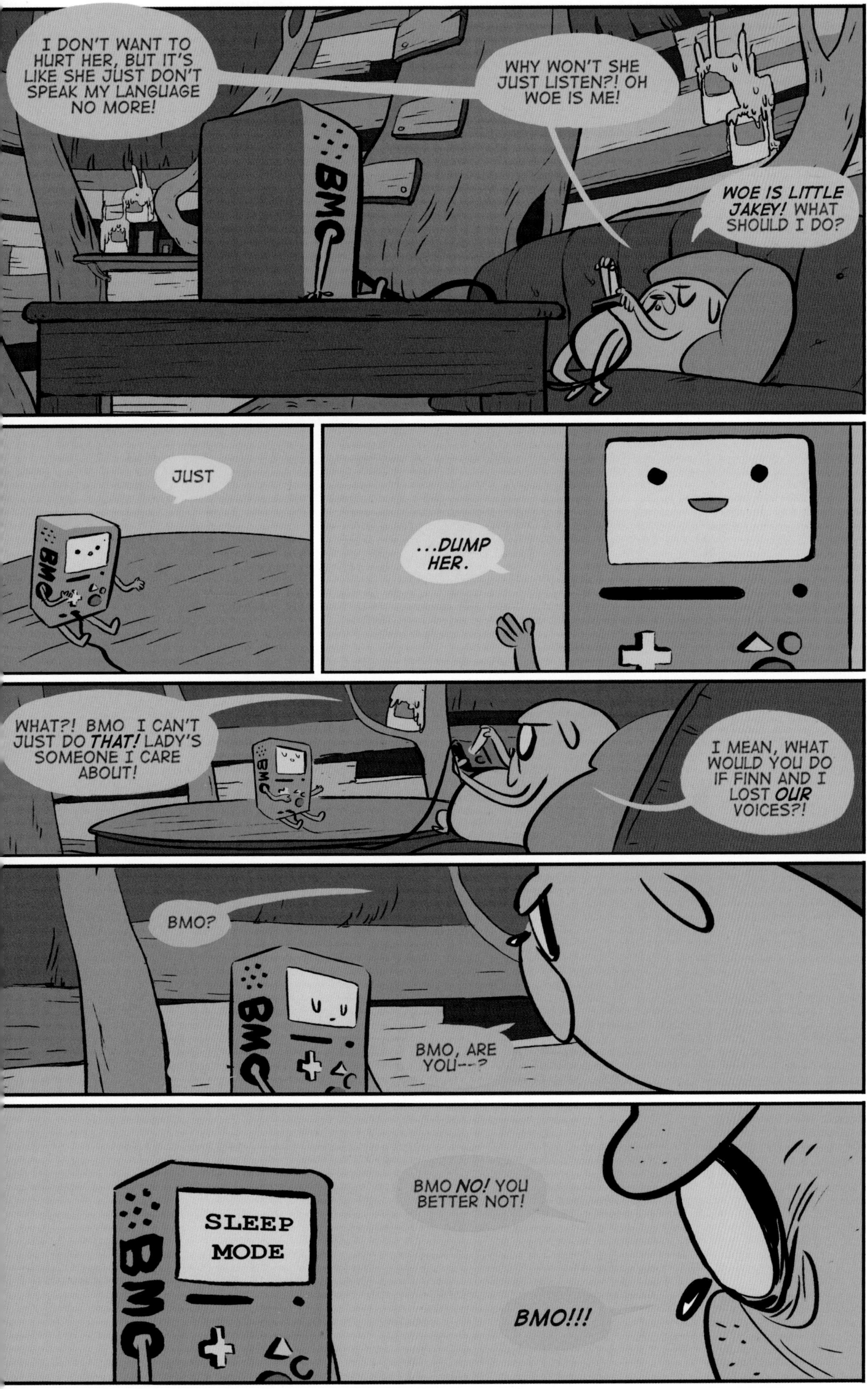
I DON'T WANT TO HURT HER, BUT IT'S LIKE SHE JUST DON'T SPEAK MY LANGUAGE NO MORE!
WHY WON'T SHE JUST LISTEN?! OH WOE IS ME!
WOE IS LITTLE JAKEY! WHAT SHOULD I DO?
BMO
JUST
...DUMP HER.
WHAT?! BMO I CAN'T JUST DO THAT! LADY'S SOMEONE I CARE ABOUT!
I MEAN, WHAT WOULD YOU DO IF FINN AND I LOST OUR VOICES?!
BMO?
BMO, ARE YOU--?
SLEEP MODE
BMO NO! YOU BETTER NOT!
BMO!!!

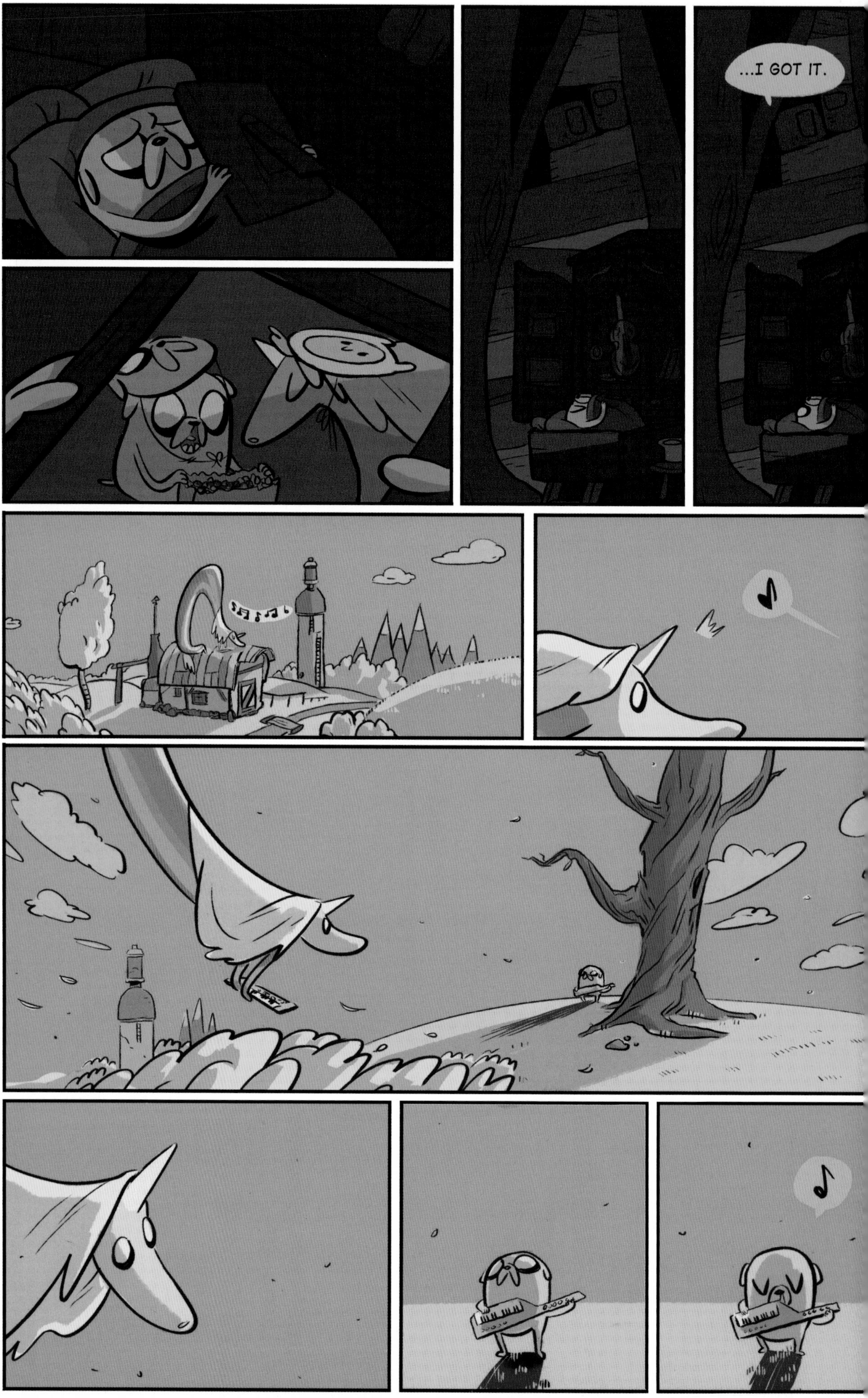
...I GOT IT.

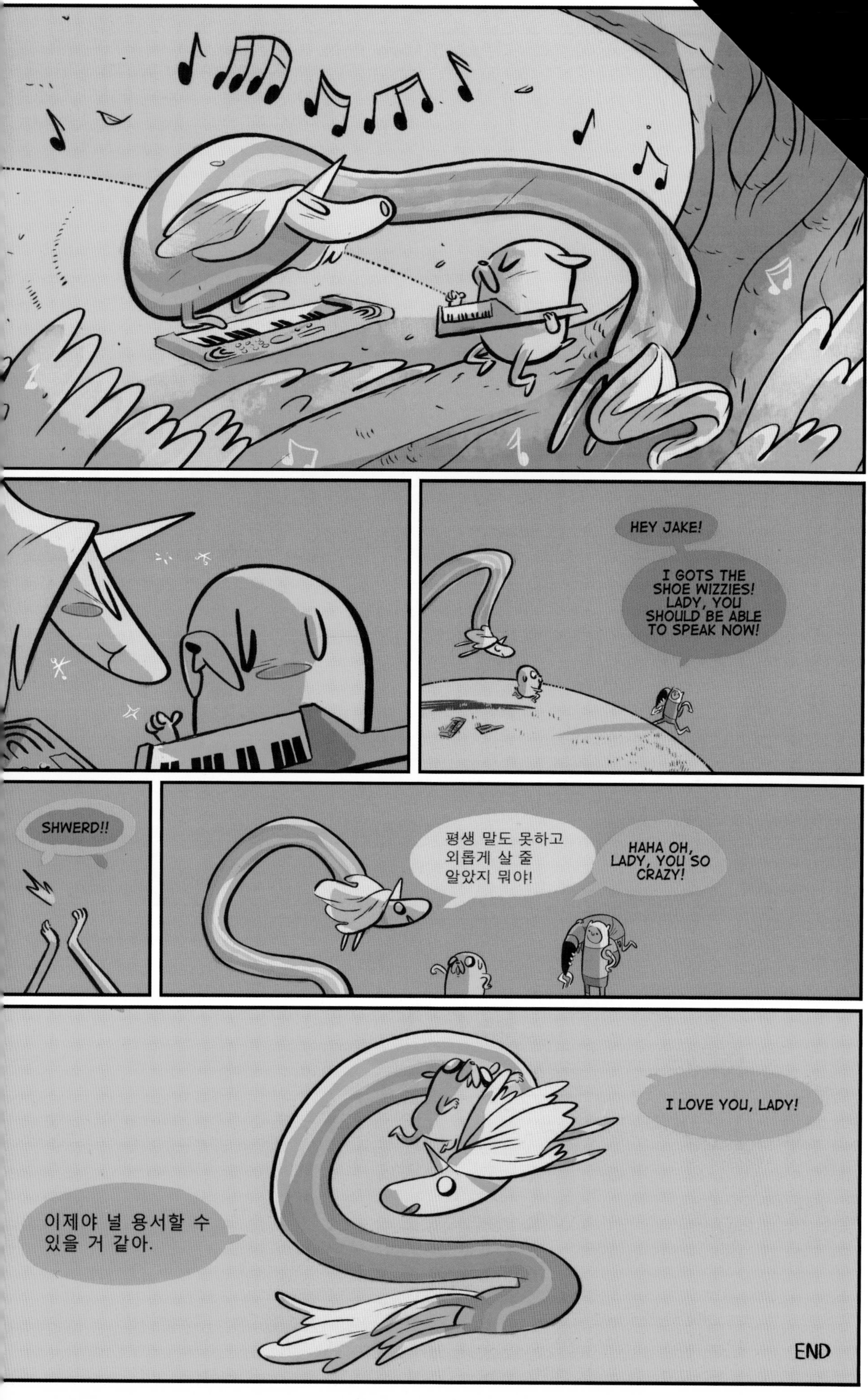
HEY JAKE!
I GOTS THE SHOE WIZZIES! LADY, YOU SHOULD BE ABLE TO SPEAK NOW!
SHWERD!!
평생 말도 못하고 외롭게 살 줄 알았지 뭐야!
HAHA OH, LADY, YOU SO CRAZY!
I LOVE YOU, LADY!
이제야 널 용서할 수 있을 거 같아.
END

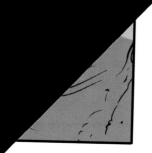

Marceline & The Scream Queens in... ~FFIN BREAK

~ PREPARES THE SCREAM QUEENS FOR THIS YEAR'S BATTLE OF THE BANDS, ~TH ~ A RIVAL ROCKER FROM THE BAND, **VAN HALENSING** (LAST YEAR'S ~ QUEENS) ~ LOOKS ON WITH MALICIOUS INTENT!

COME ON, GUYS! THINK OF HOW COOL IT'D BE IF WE POPPED OUT OF THESE 'COFFINS' AT THE OPENING OF THE BATTLE TONIGHT!

MMM... I LIKE IT!

I DUNNO ~ HOW AM I SUPPOSED TO ROCK-OUT ON GUITAR WHILE I'M STUCK INSIDE THIS THING?

I'M GOING TO GET YOU THIS YEAR, MARCELINE!

AWW, YOU CAN DO IT, KEILA!

EHH, WELL I CAN'T THINK ABOUT ANY OF THIS ANYMORE ~ NOT UNTIL I GET SOMETHIN' TO EAT!

YEAH ~ ME TOO! I NEED ME SOMETHIN' **RED!** I'M SO WEAK I WOULDN'T BE ABLE TO TRANSFORM MYSELF INTO A LITTLE FEROCIOUS KITTEN...

LUNCH BREAK?

SOUNDS GOOD!

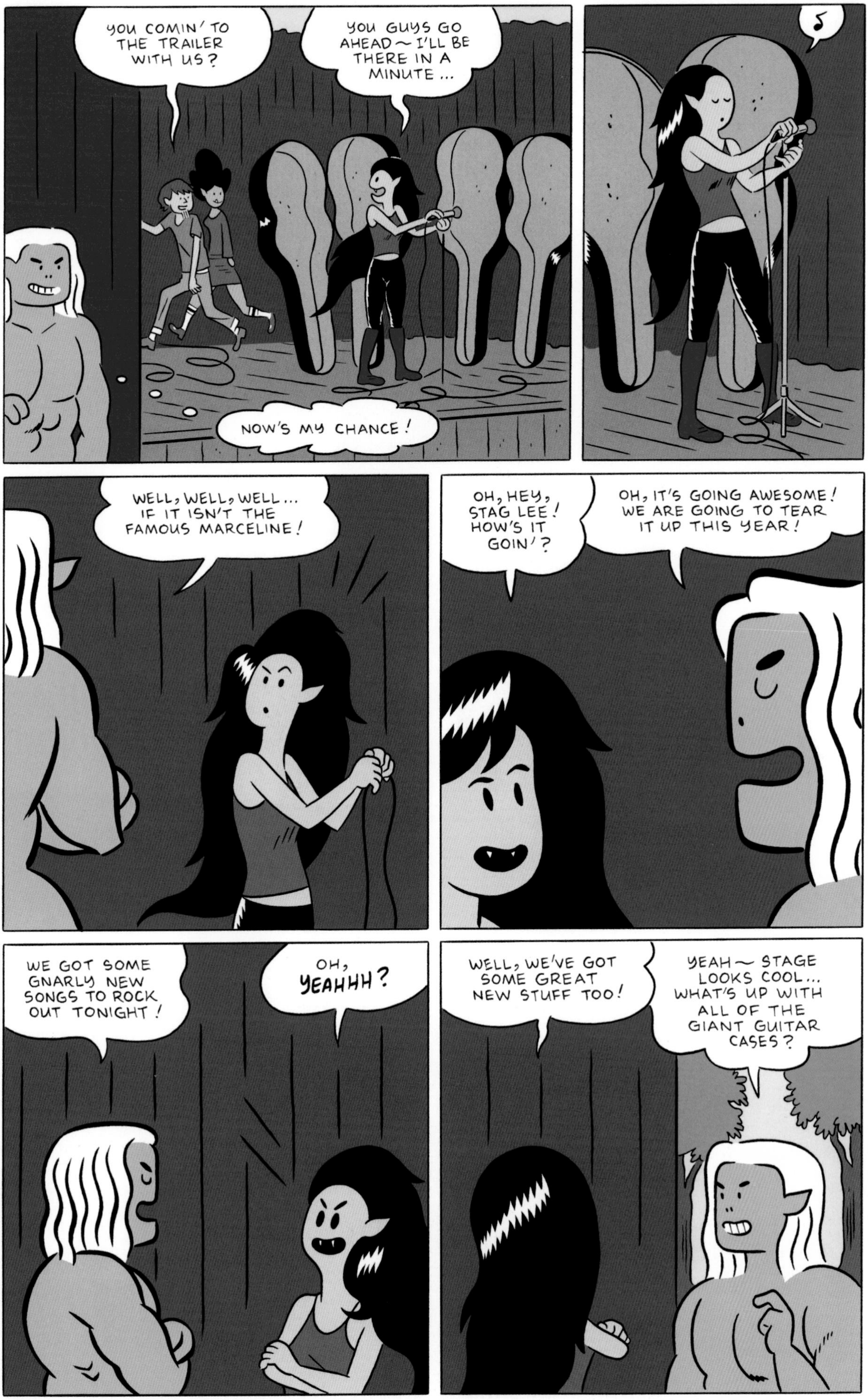
YOU COMIN' TO THE TRAILER WITH US?
YOU GUYS GO AHEAD~ I'LL BE THERE IN A MINUTE...
NOW'S MY CHANCE!
WELL, WELL, WELL... IF IT ISN'T THE FAMOUS MARCELINE!
OH, HEY, STAG LEE! HOW'S IT GOIN'?
OH, IT'S GOING AWESOME! WE ARE GOING TO TEAR IT UP THIS YEAR!
WE GOT SOME GNARLY NEW SONGS TO ROCK OUT TONIGHT!
OH, YEAHHH?
WELL, WE'VE GOT SOME GREAT NEW STUFF TOO!
YEAH~ STAGE LOOKS COOL... WHAT'S UP WITH ALL OF THE GIANT GUITAR CASES?

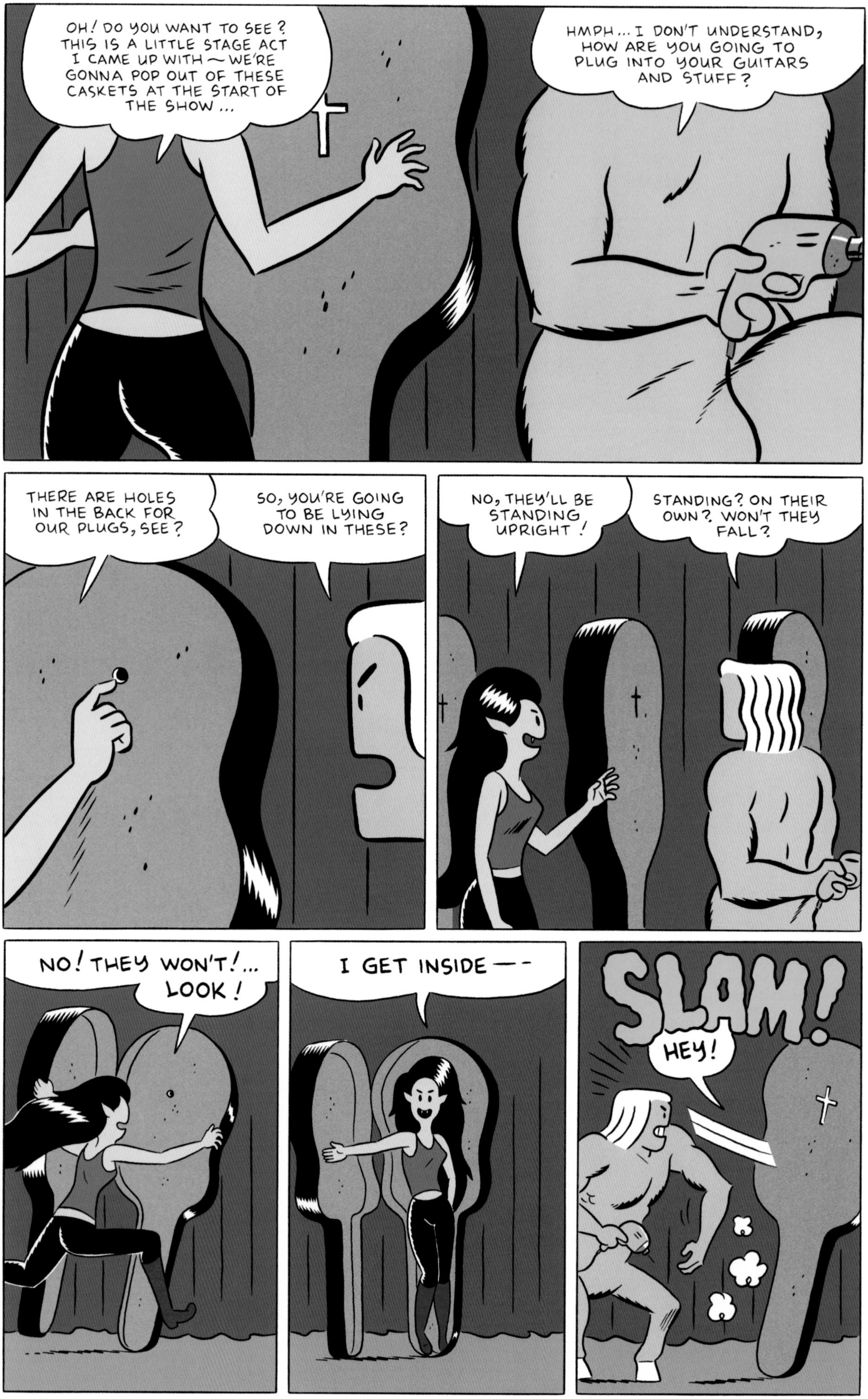
OH! DO YOU WANT TO SEE? THIS IS A LITTLE STAGE ACT I CAME UP WITH ~ WE'RE GONNA POP OUT OF THESE CASKETS AT THE START OF THE SHOW...
HMPH... I DON'T UNDERSTAND, HOW ARE YOU GOING TO PLUG INTO YOUR GUITARS AND STUFF?
THERE ARE HOLES IN THE BACK FOR OUR PLUGS, SEE?
SO, YOU'RE GOING TO BE LYING DOWN IN THESE?
NO, THEY'LL BE STANDING UPRIGHT!
STANDING? ON THEIR OWN? WON'T THEY FALL?
NO! THEY WON'T!... LOOK!
I GET INSIDE --
SLAM!
HEY!

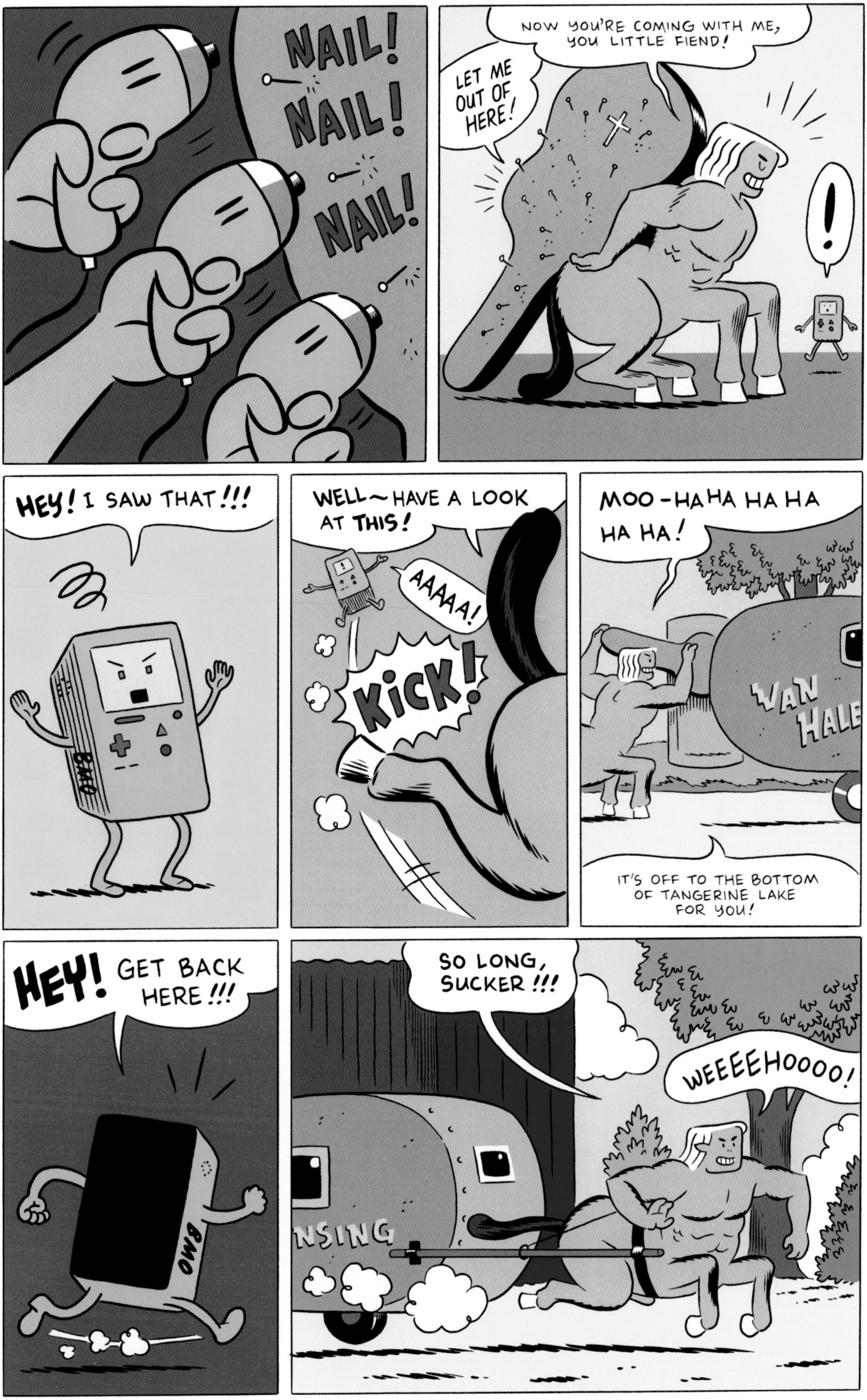
NAIL!
NAIL!
NAIL!
NOW YOU'RE COMING WITH ME, YOU LITTLE FIEND!
LET ME OUT OF HERE!
!
HEY! I SAW THAT!!!
BMO
WELL~ HAVE A LOOK AT THIS!
AAAAA!
KICK!
MOO-HAHA HA HA HA HA HA!
VAN HALE
IT'S OFF TO THE BOTTOM OF TANGERINE LAKE FOR YOU!
HEY! GET BACK HERE!!!
BMO
SO LONG, SUCKER!!!
WEEEEHOOOO!
NSING

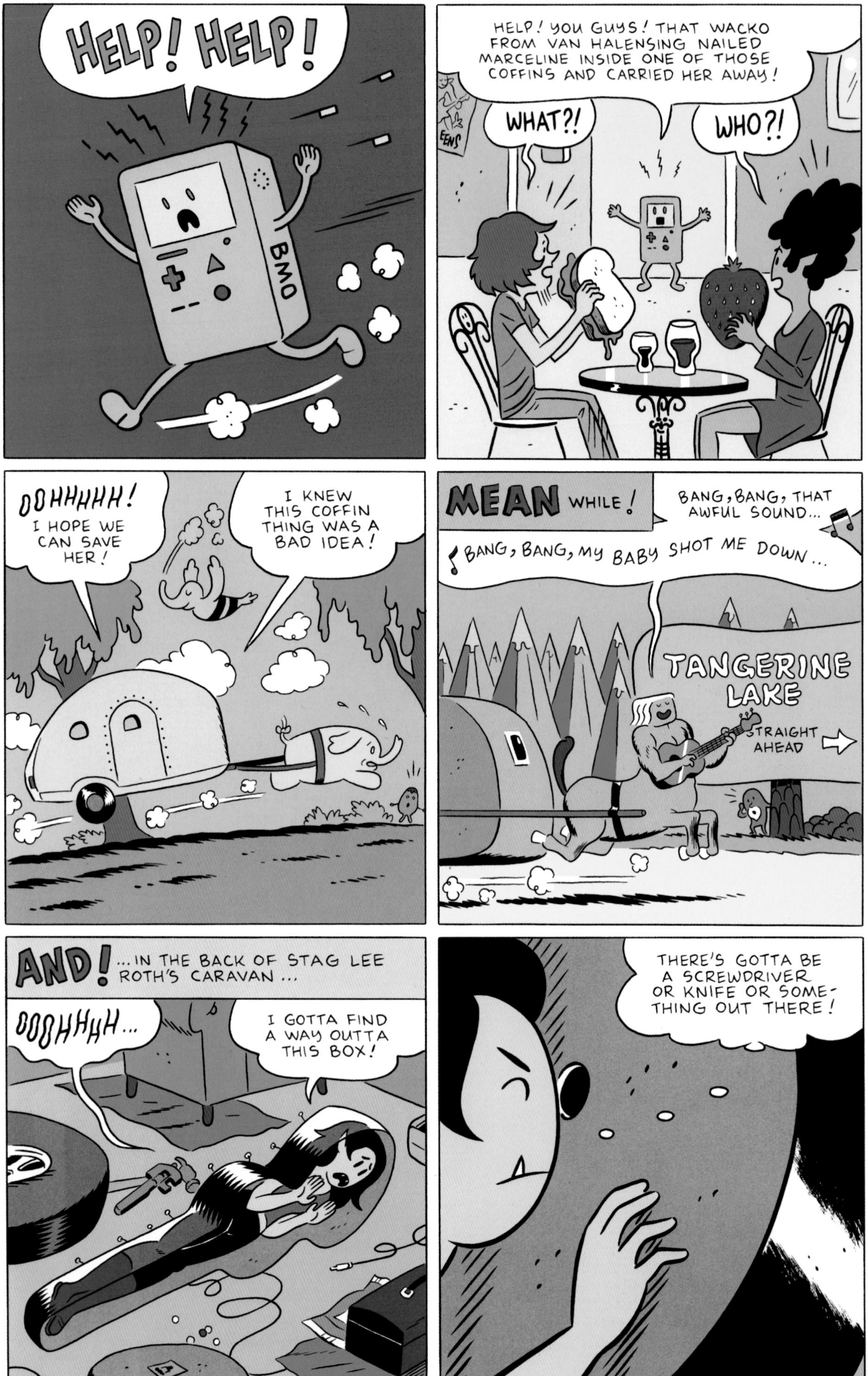
HELP! HELP!
BMO
HELP! YOU GUYS! THAT WACKO FROM VAN HALENSING NAILED MARCELINE INSIDE ONE OF THOSE COFFINS AND CARRIED HER AWAY!
WHAT?!
WHO?!
OOHHHHH! I HOPE WE CAN SAVE HER!
I KNEW THIS COFFIN THING WAS A BAD IDEA!
MEANWHILE!
BANG, BANG, THAT AWFUL SOUND...
BANG, BANG, MY BABY SHOT ME DOWN...
TANGERINE LAKE
STRAIGHT AHEAD
AND! ...IN THE BACK OF STAG LEE ROTH'S CARAVAN...
OOOHHHH...
I GOTTA FIND A WAY OUTTA THIS BOX!
THERE'S GOTTA BE A SCREWDRIVER OR KNIFE OR SOMETHING OUT THERE!

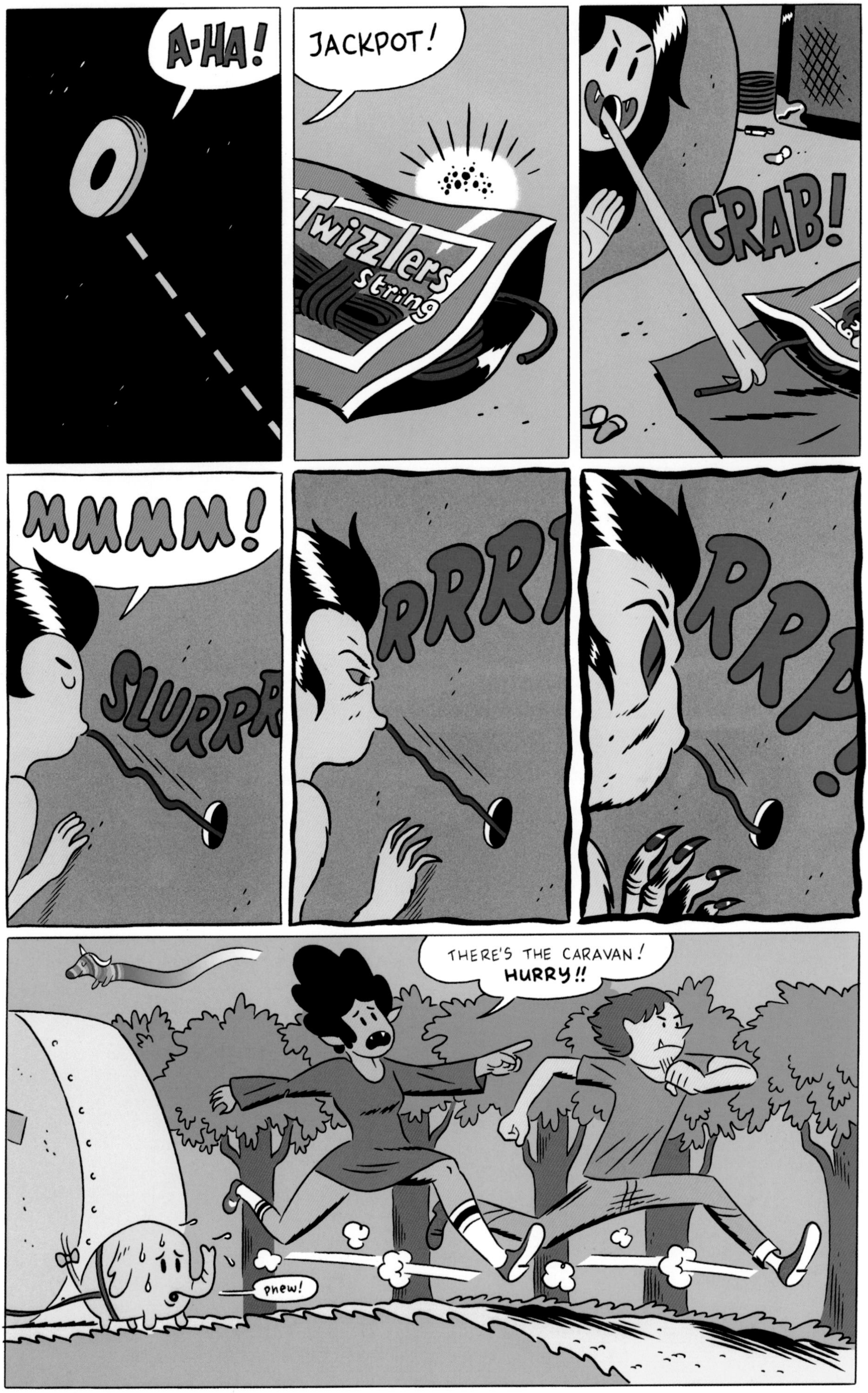
A-HA!
JACKPOT!
Twizzlers string
GRAB!
MMMM!
SLURRR
RRRR
RRRP!
THERE'S THE CARAVAN! HURRY!!
phew!

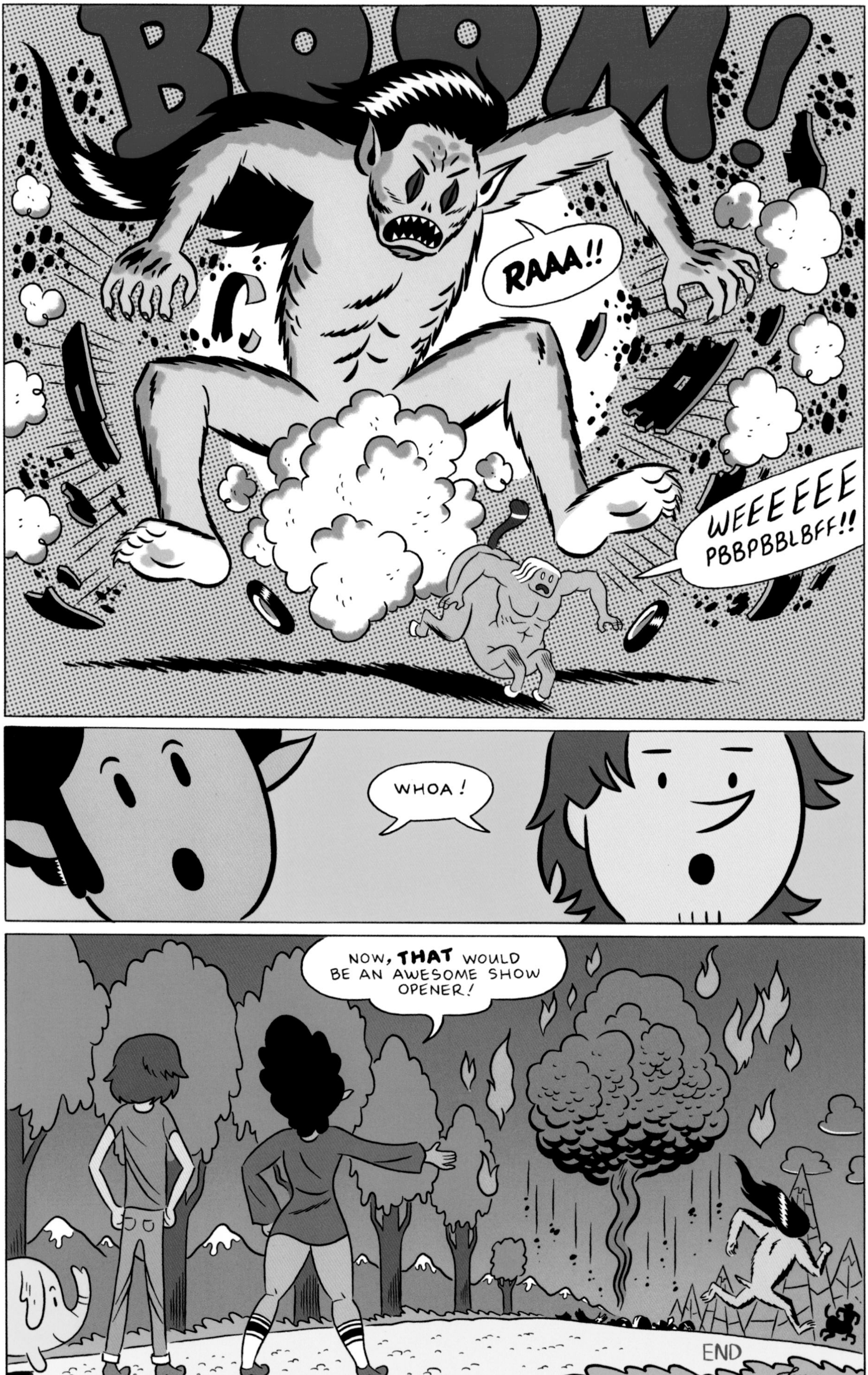
BOOM!
RAAA!!
WEEEEEE PBBPBBLBFF!!
WHOA!
NOW, **THAT** WOULD BE AN AWESOME SHOW OPENER!
END

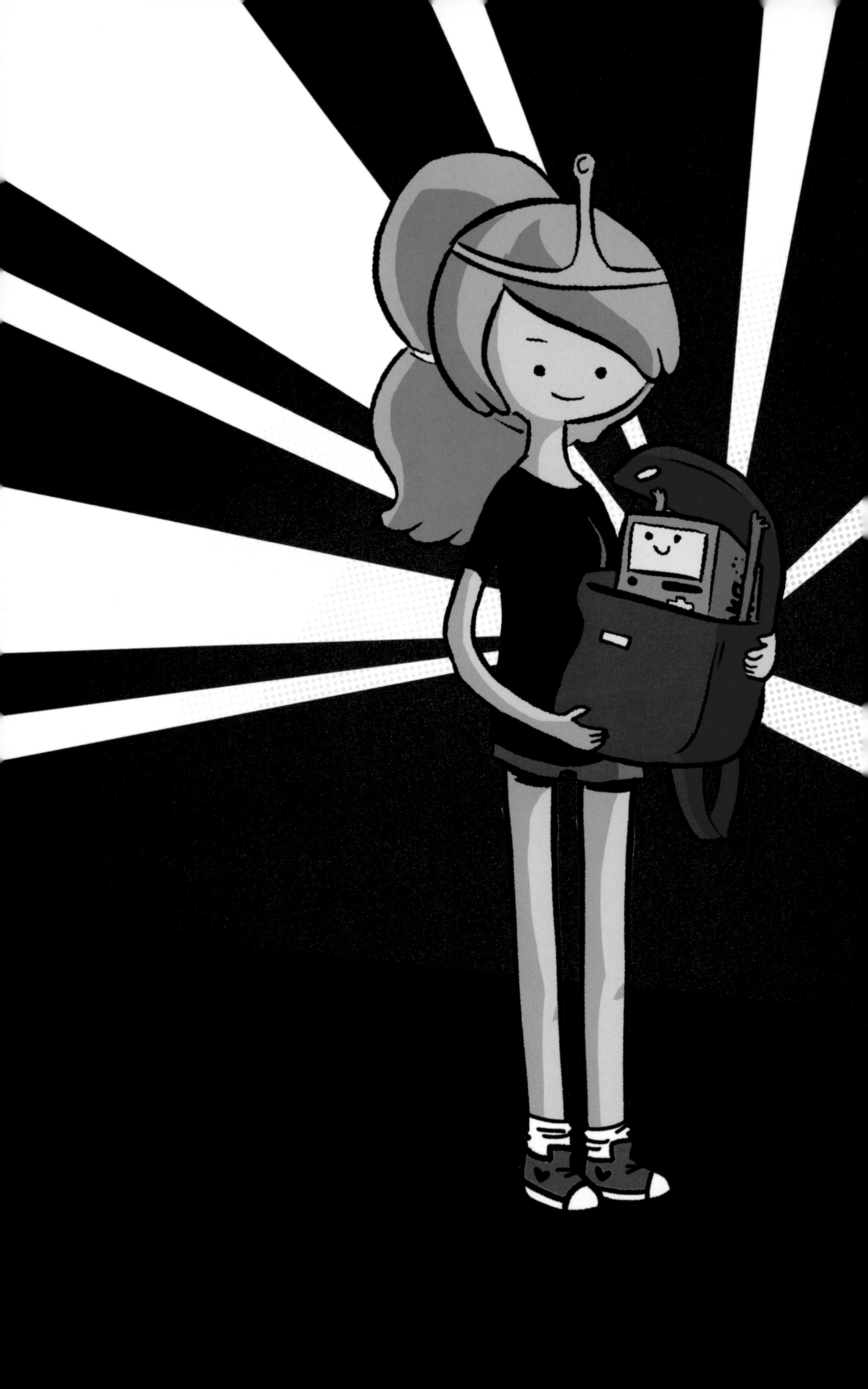

COLLECTOR'S ITEMS

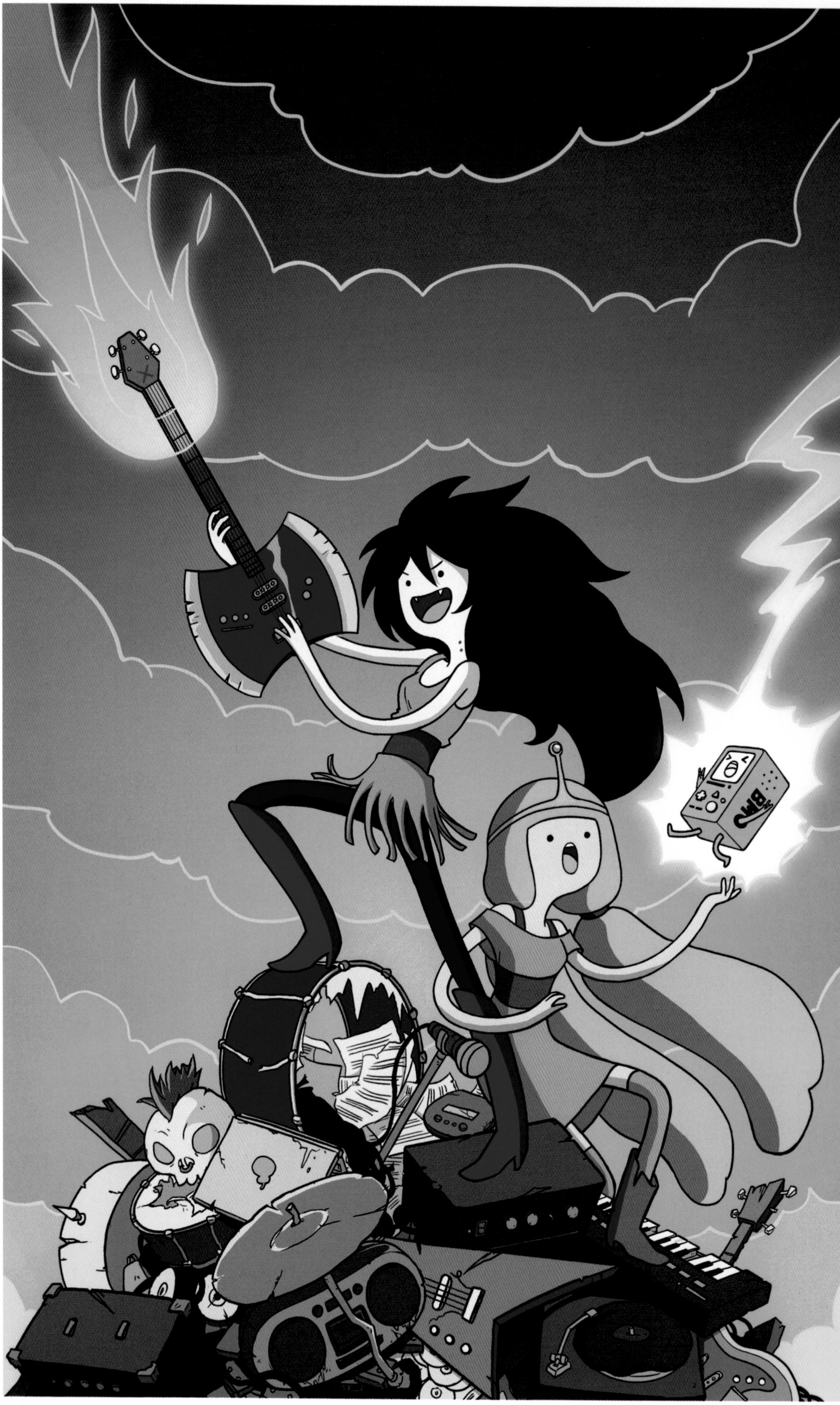

ISSUE ONE | JEN BENNETT WITH COLORS BY LISA MOORE

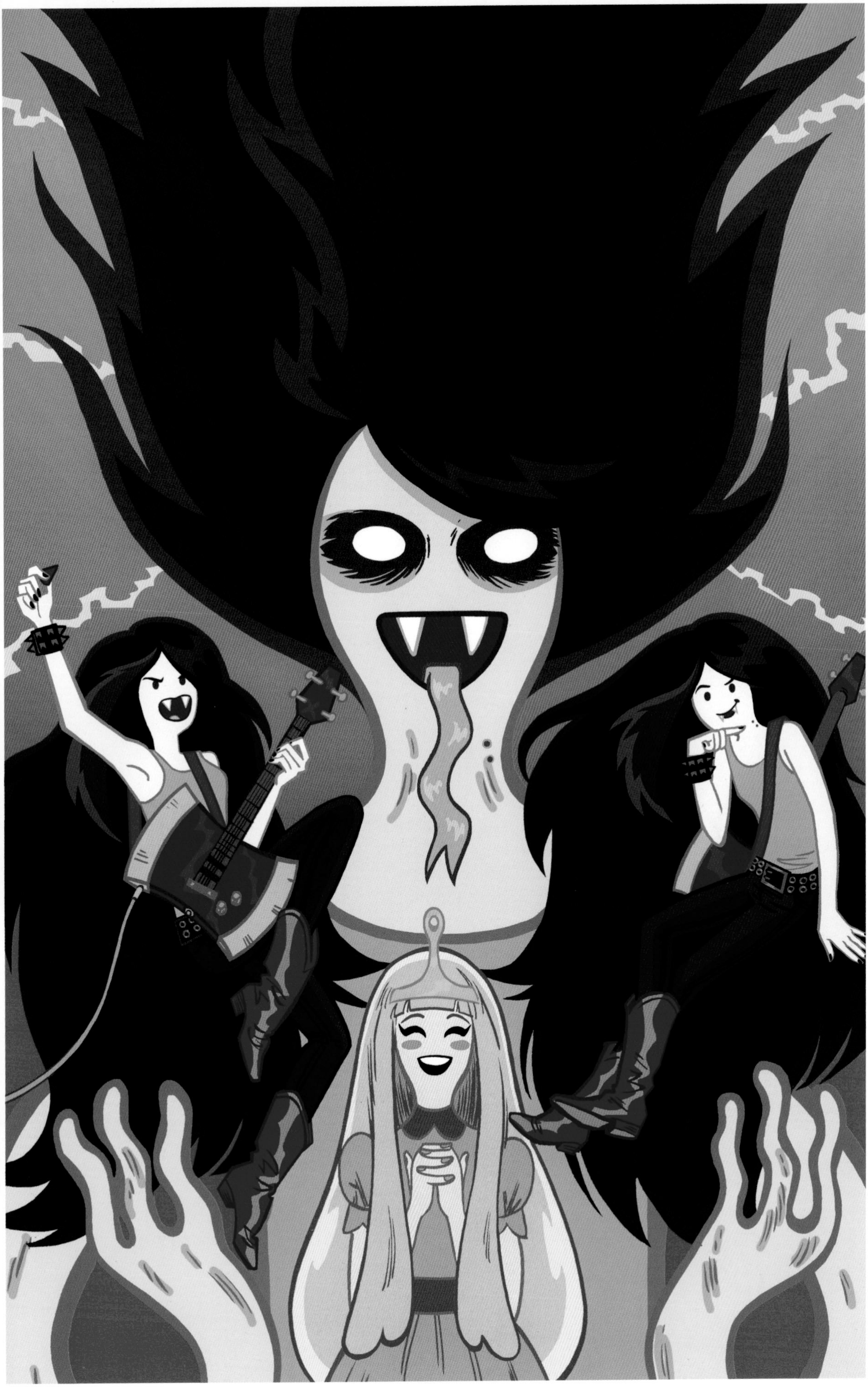

ISSUE ONE | CHYNNA CLUGSTON-FLORES

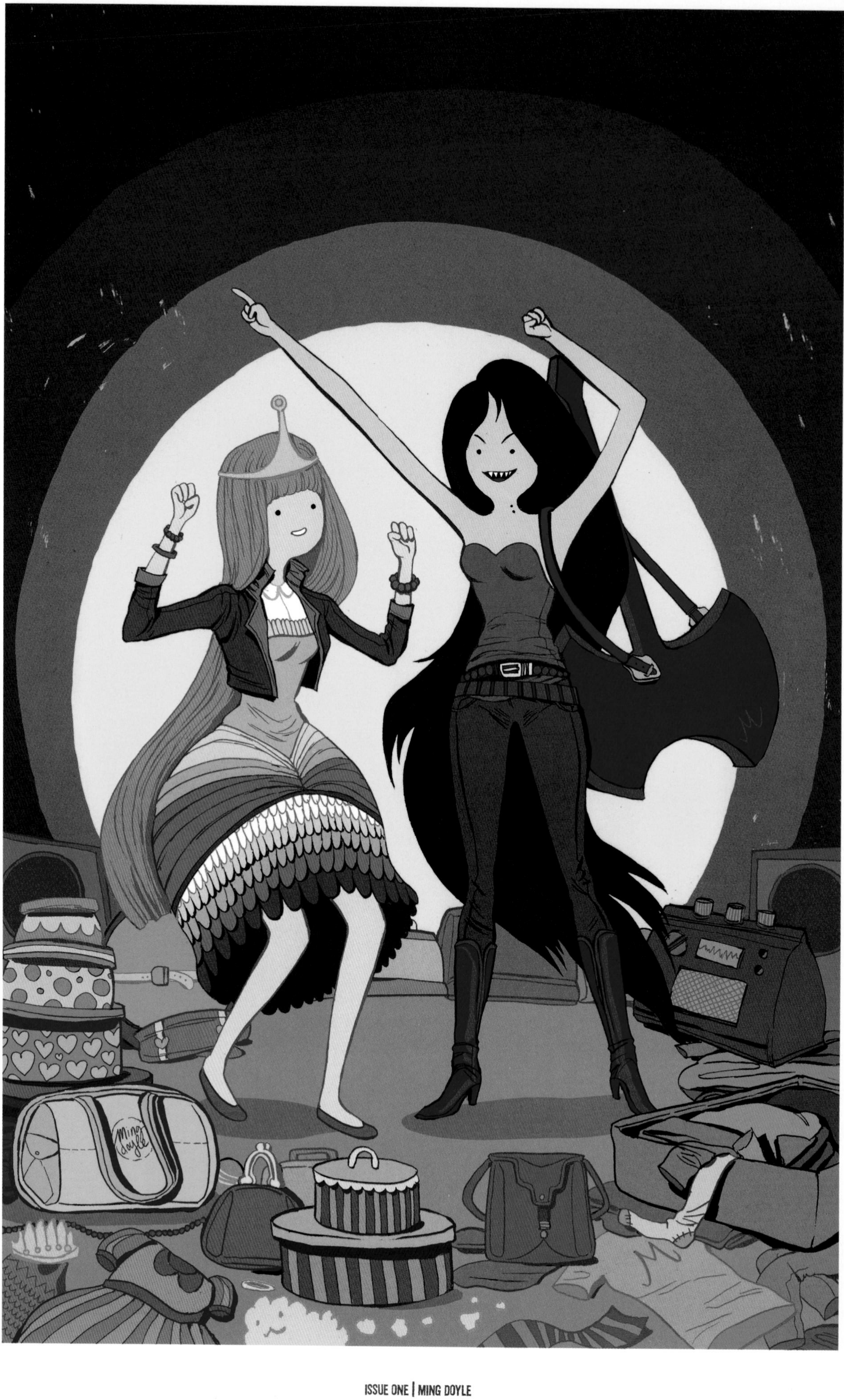
Ming
doyle

ISSUE ONE | MING DOYLE

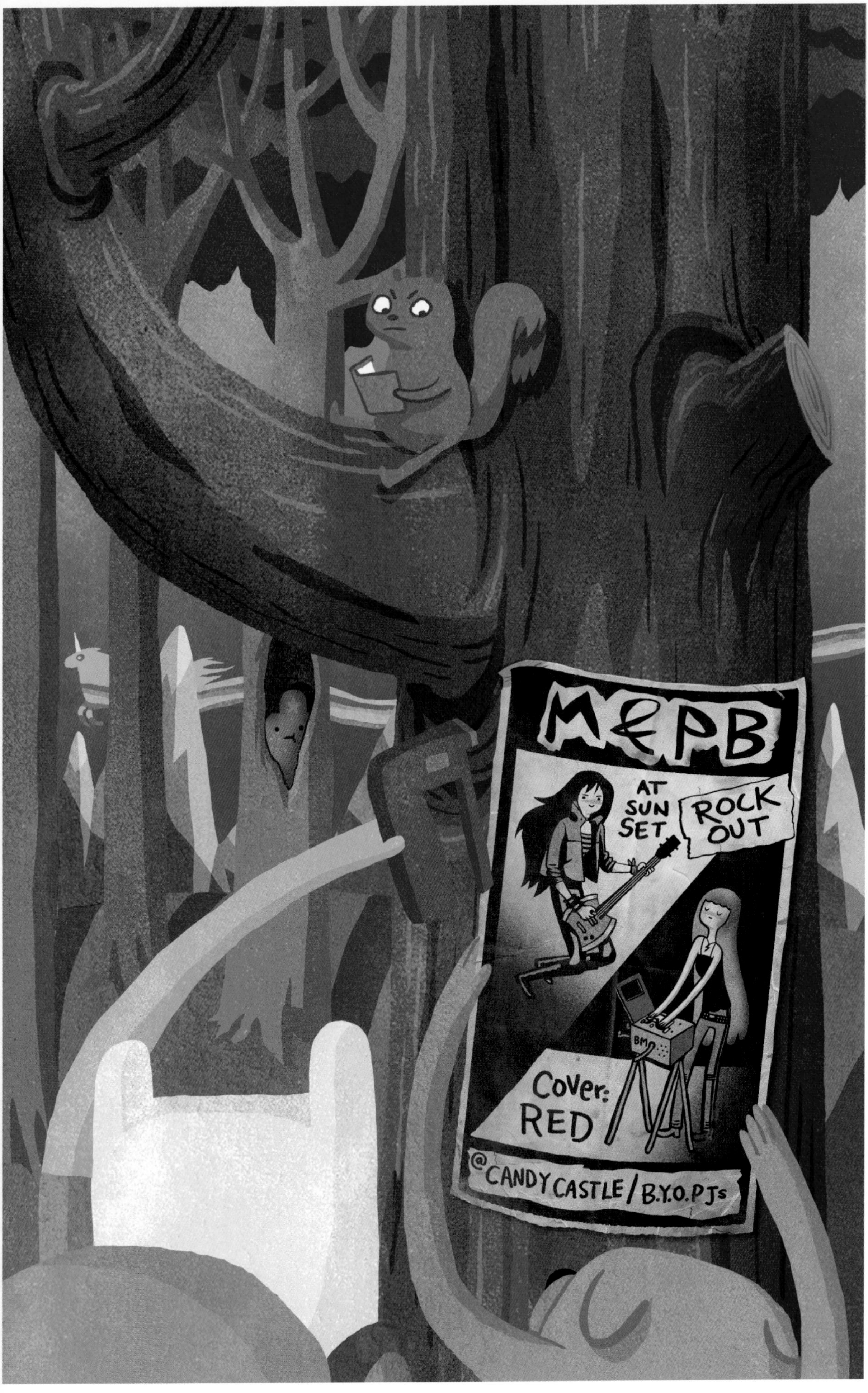
M&PB
AT SUN SET
ROCK OUT
BM
Cover: RED
@CANDY CASTLE / B.Y.O.PJs

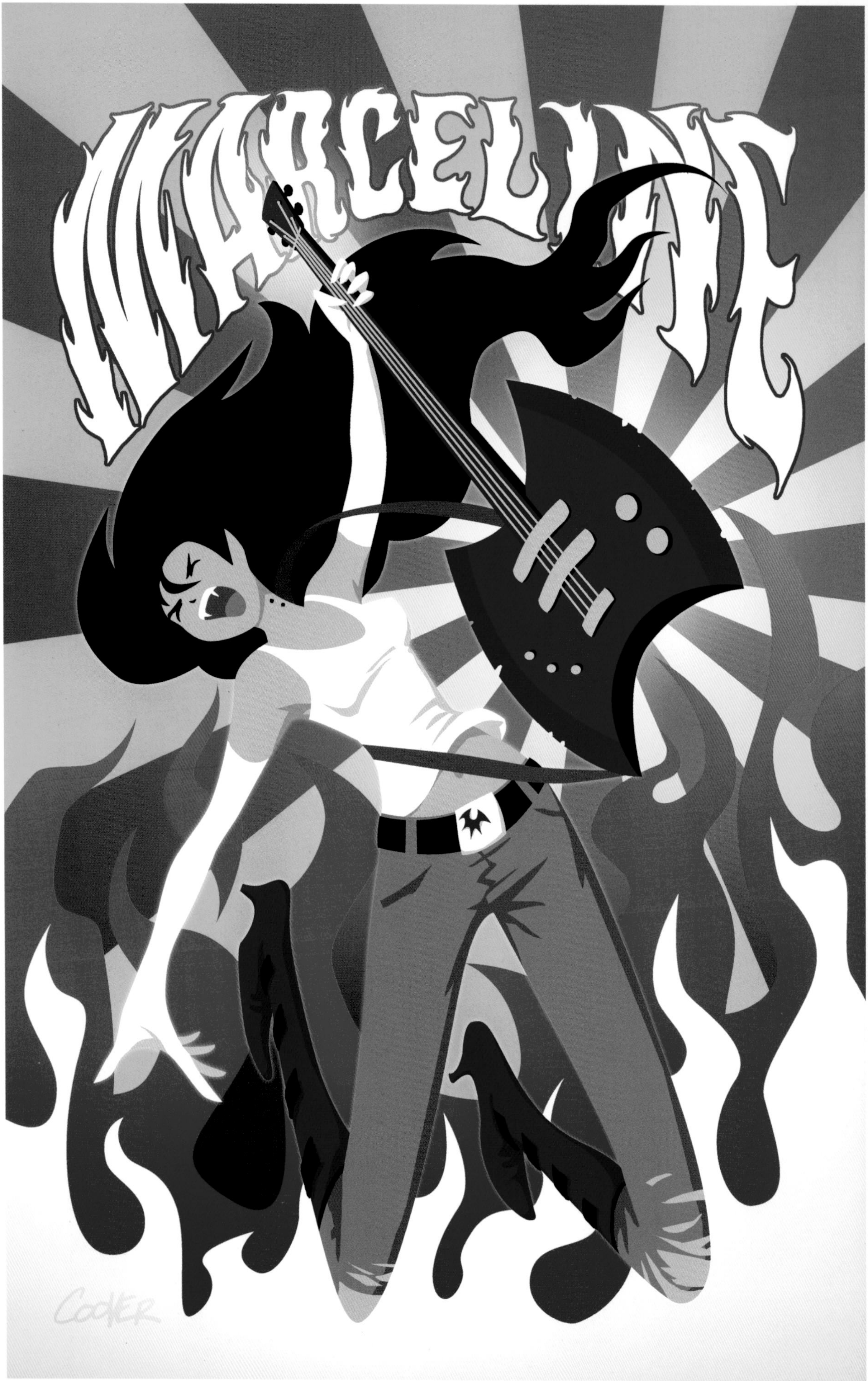
MARCELINE
COOVER

ISSUE ONE | COLLEEN COOVER

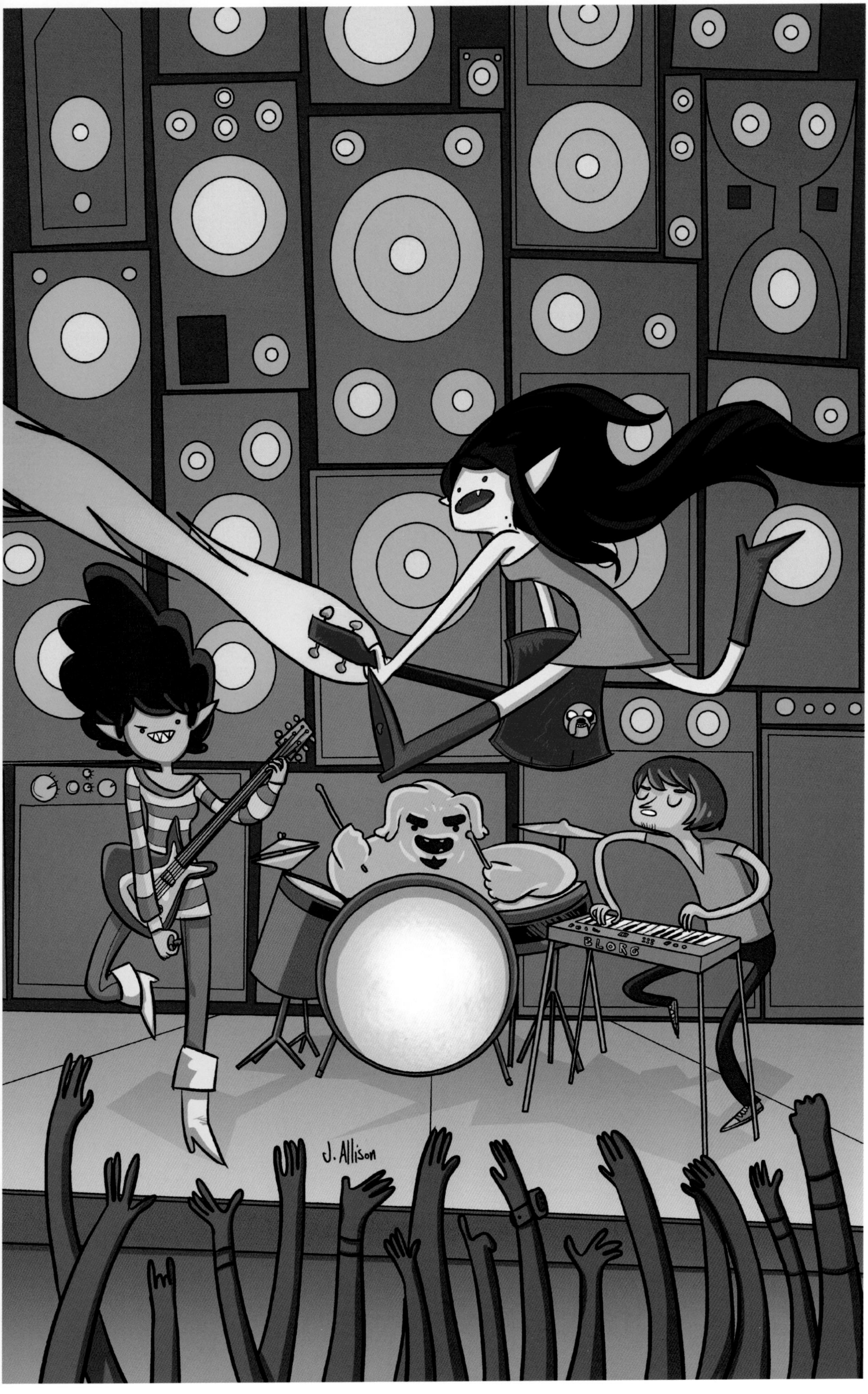
J. Allison
BLORG

ISSUE ONE BOOM! STUDIOS EXCLUSIVE | JOHN ALLISON WITH COLORS BY STEVE WANDS

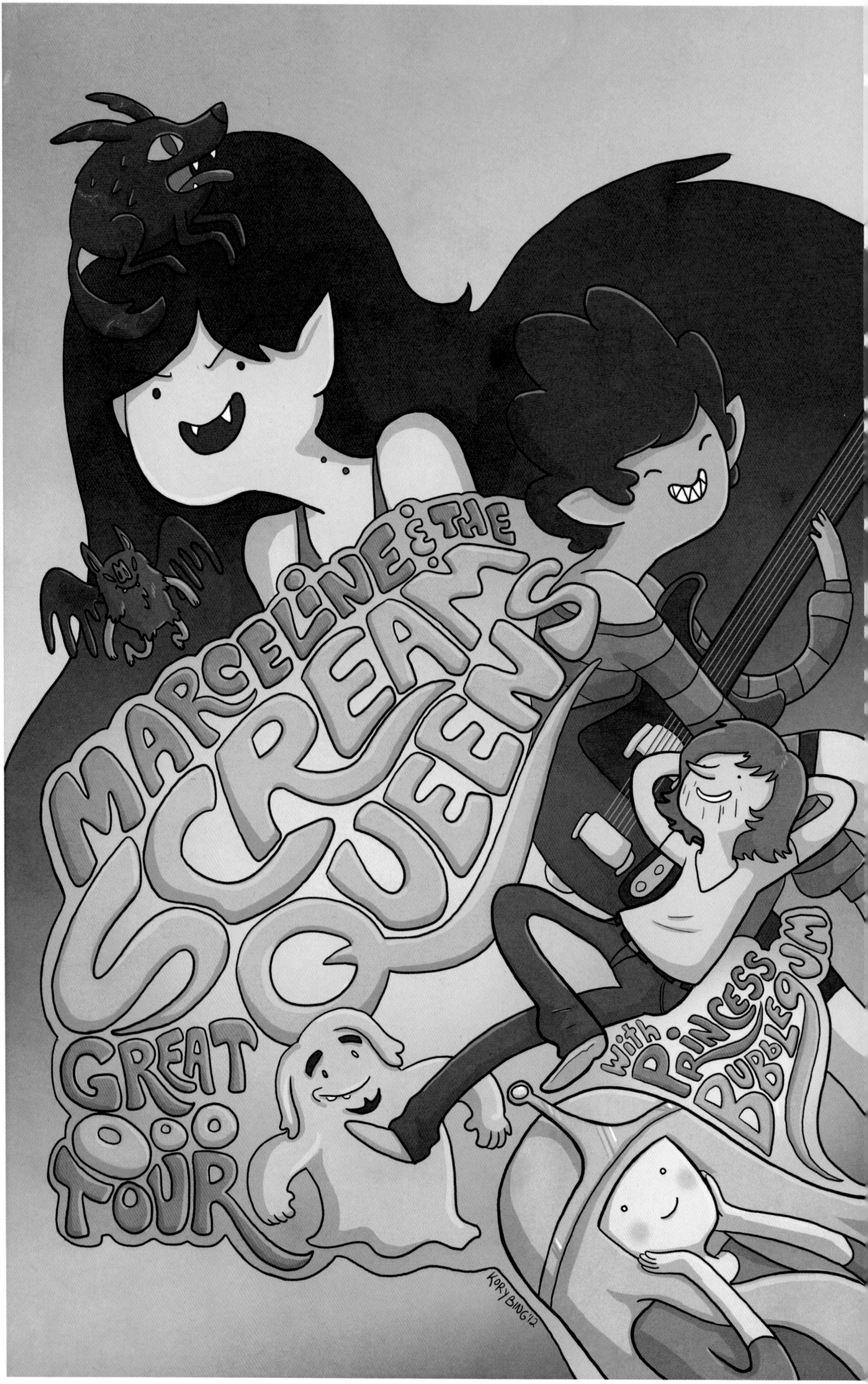
MARCELINE & THE SCREAM QUEENS
GREAT OOO TOUR
with PRINCESS BUBBLEGUM
KORY BING '12

ISSUE ONE SECOND PRINT | KORY BING

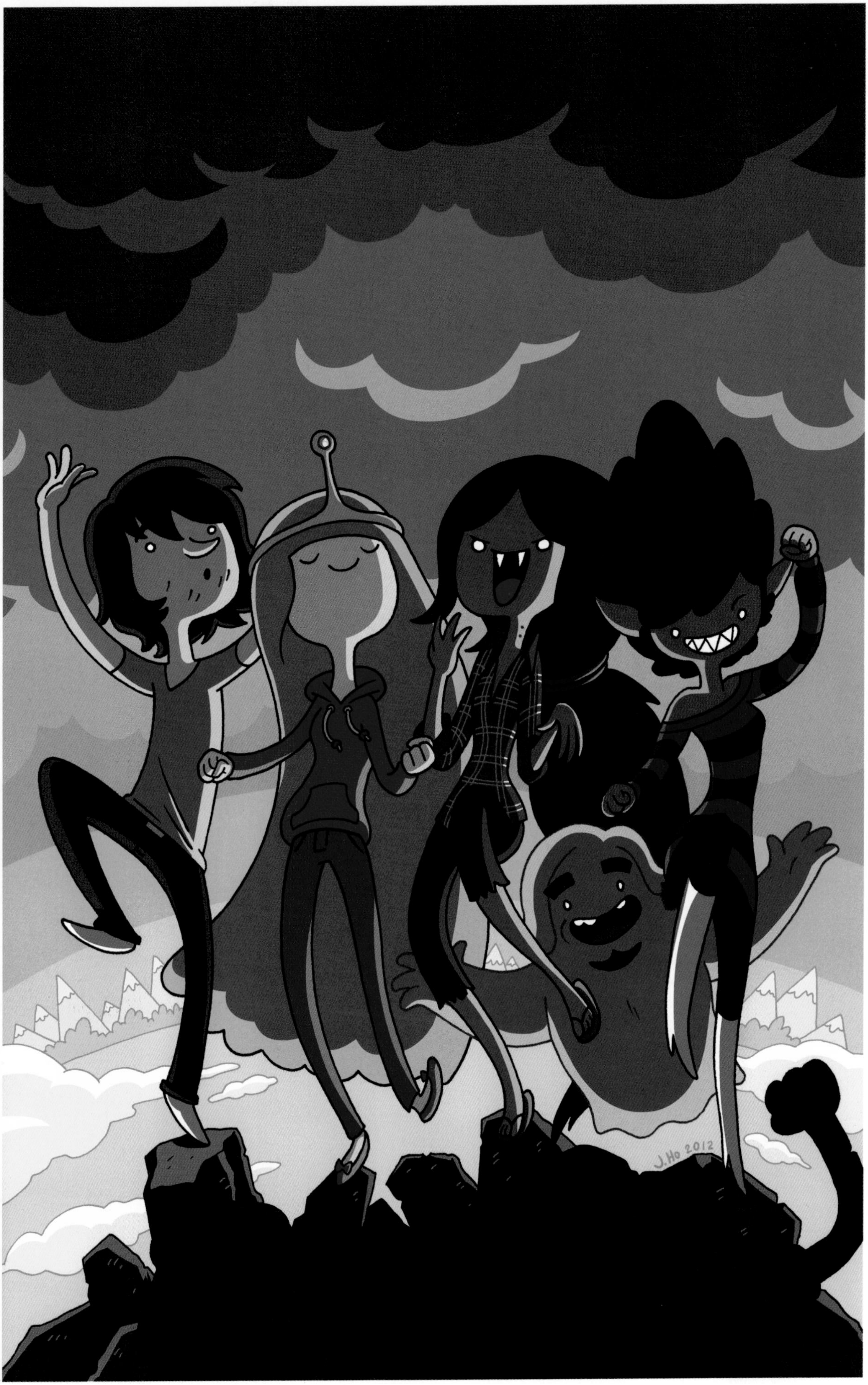
J.Ho 2012

ISSUE ONE AWESOME CONS EXCLUSIVE | JASON HO

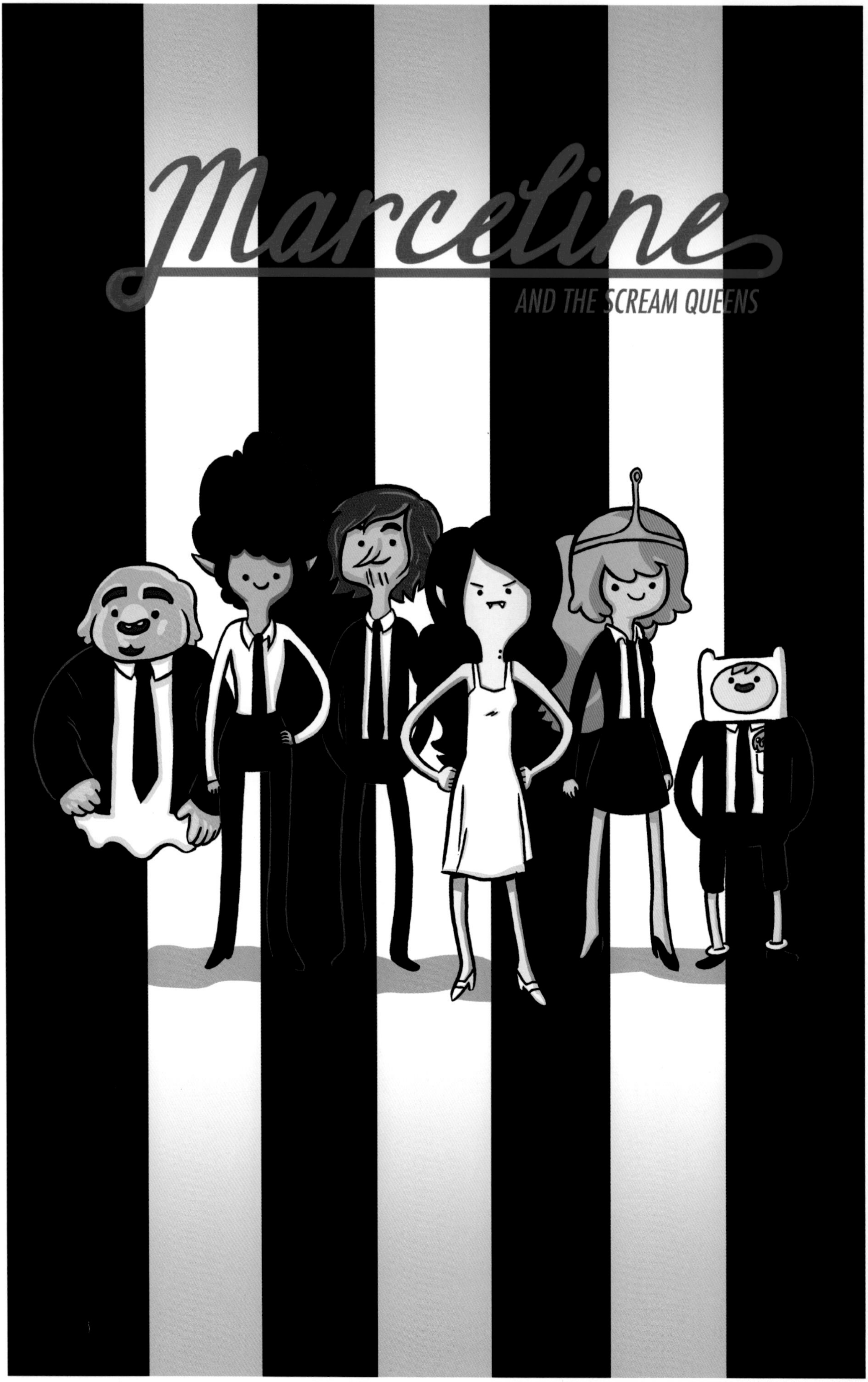
Marceline
AND THE SCREAM QUEENS

ISSUE ONE SAN DIEGO COMIC-CON EXCLUSIVE | MEREDITH GRAN WITH COLORS BY STEVE WANDS

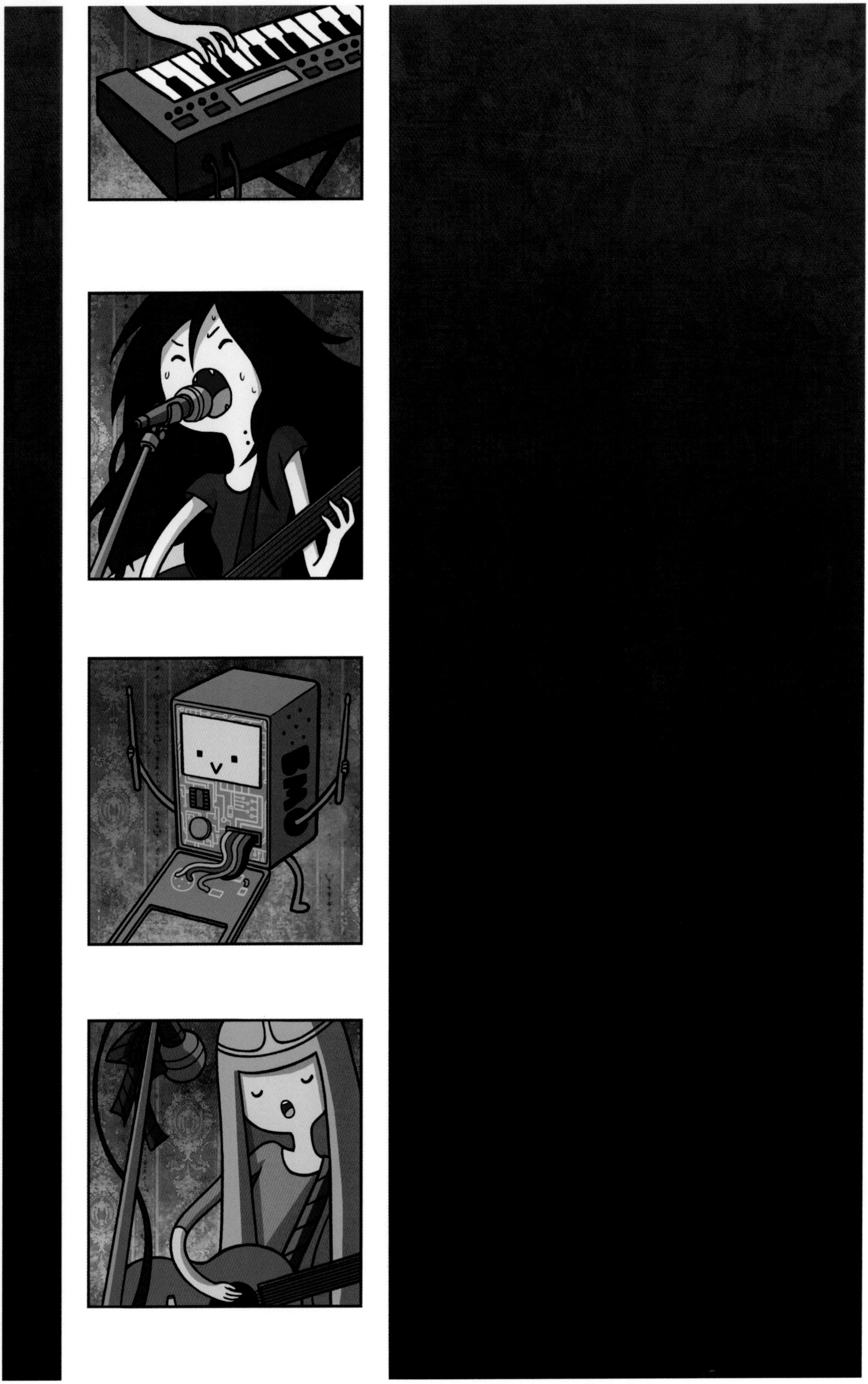
BMO

ISSUE TWO | JEN BENNETT WITH COLORS BY LISA MOORE

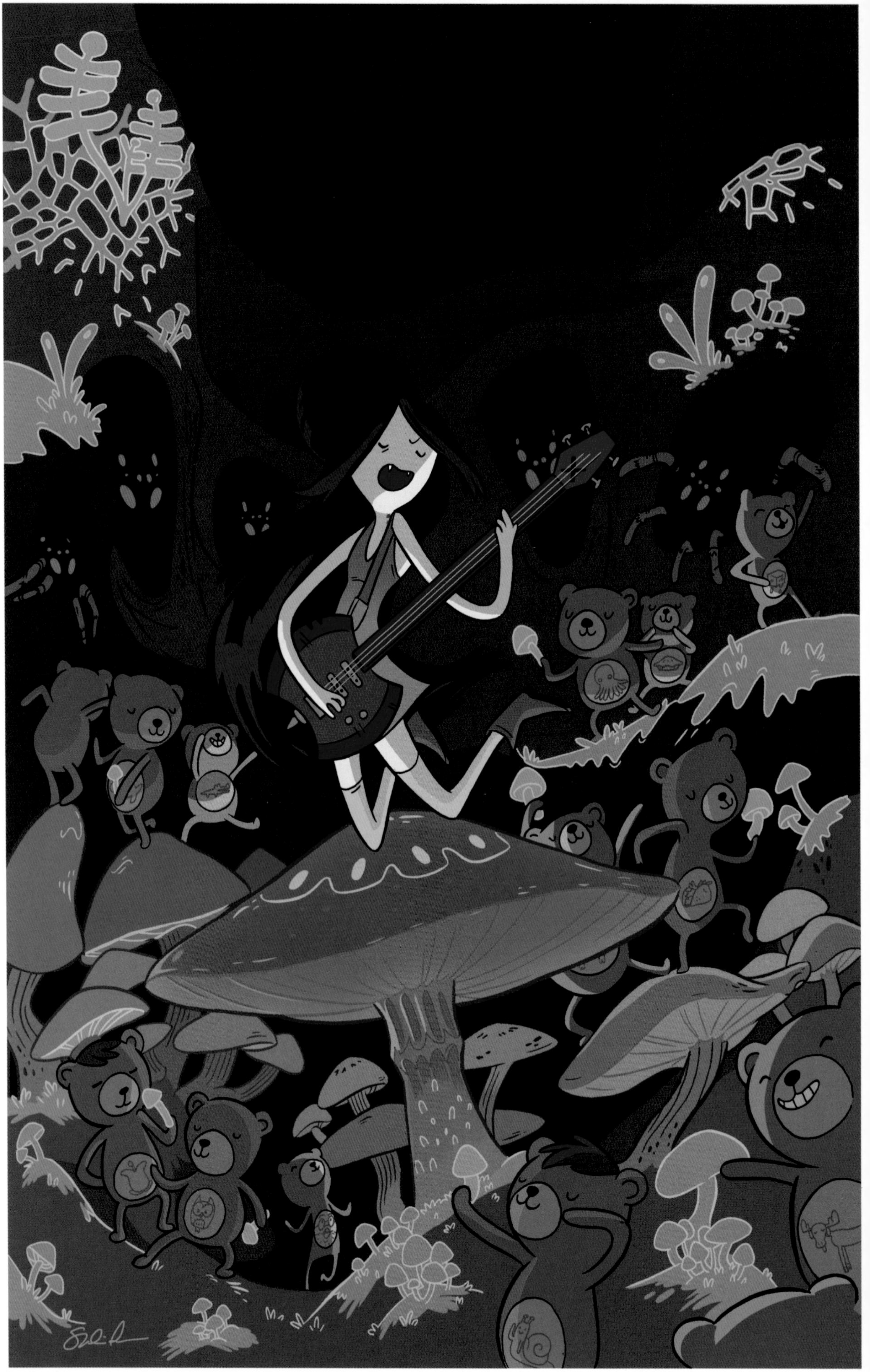

ISSUE TWO | SHELLI PAROLINE

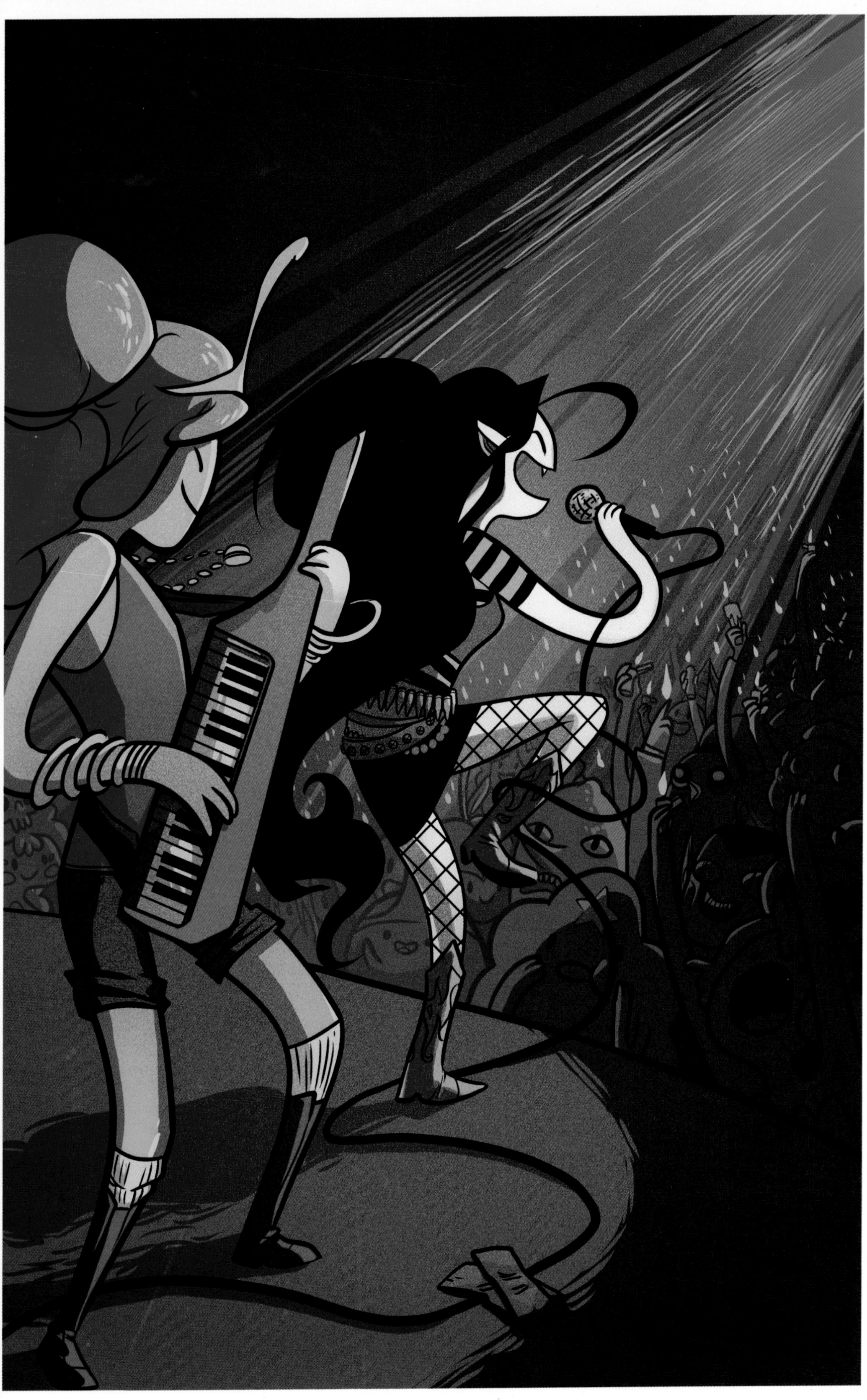

ISSUE TWO | ERICA HENDERSON

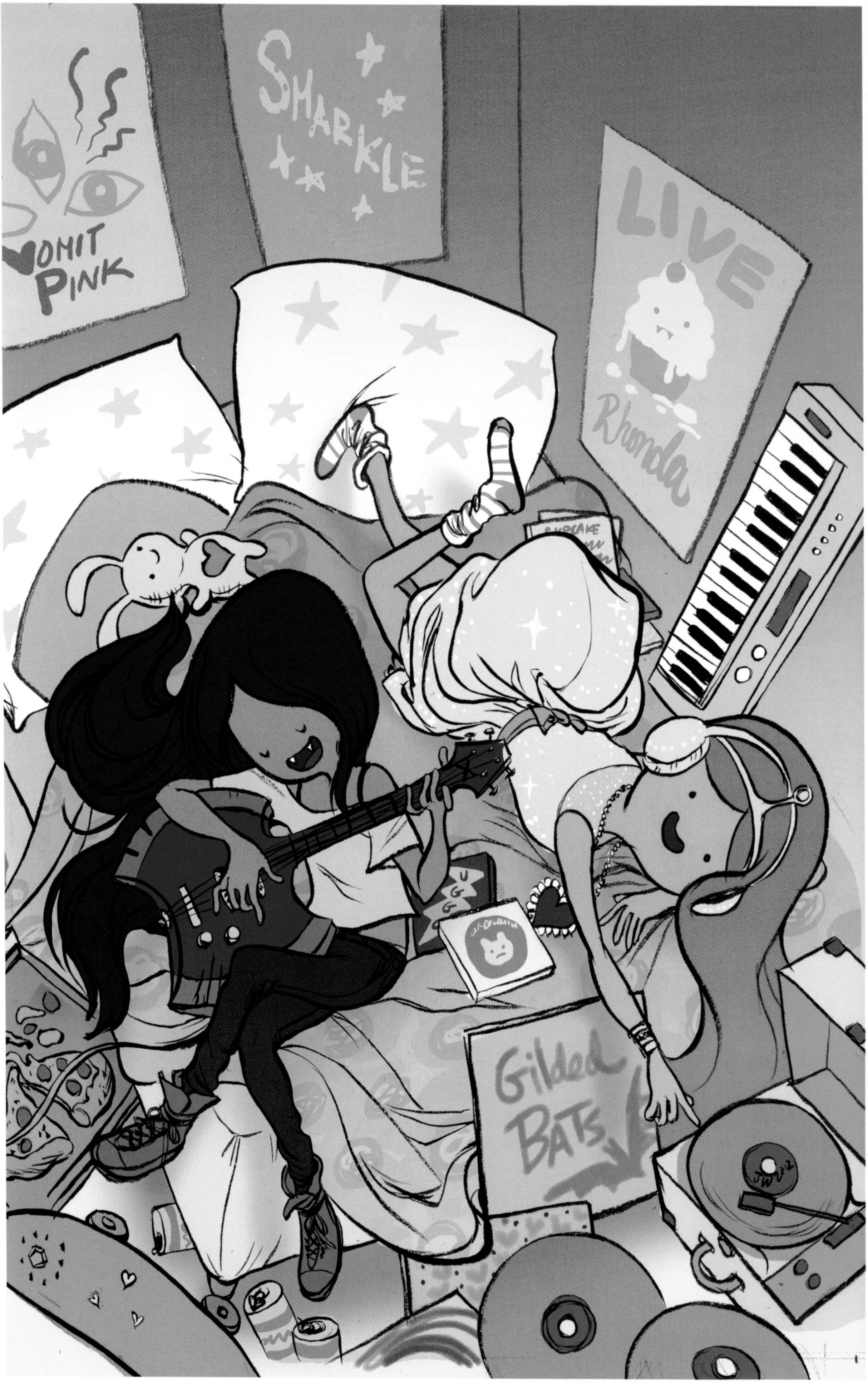
VOMIT PINK
SHARKLE
LIVE
Rhonda
Gilded BATS

ISSUE TWO | JEN WANG

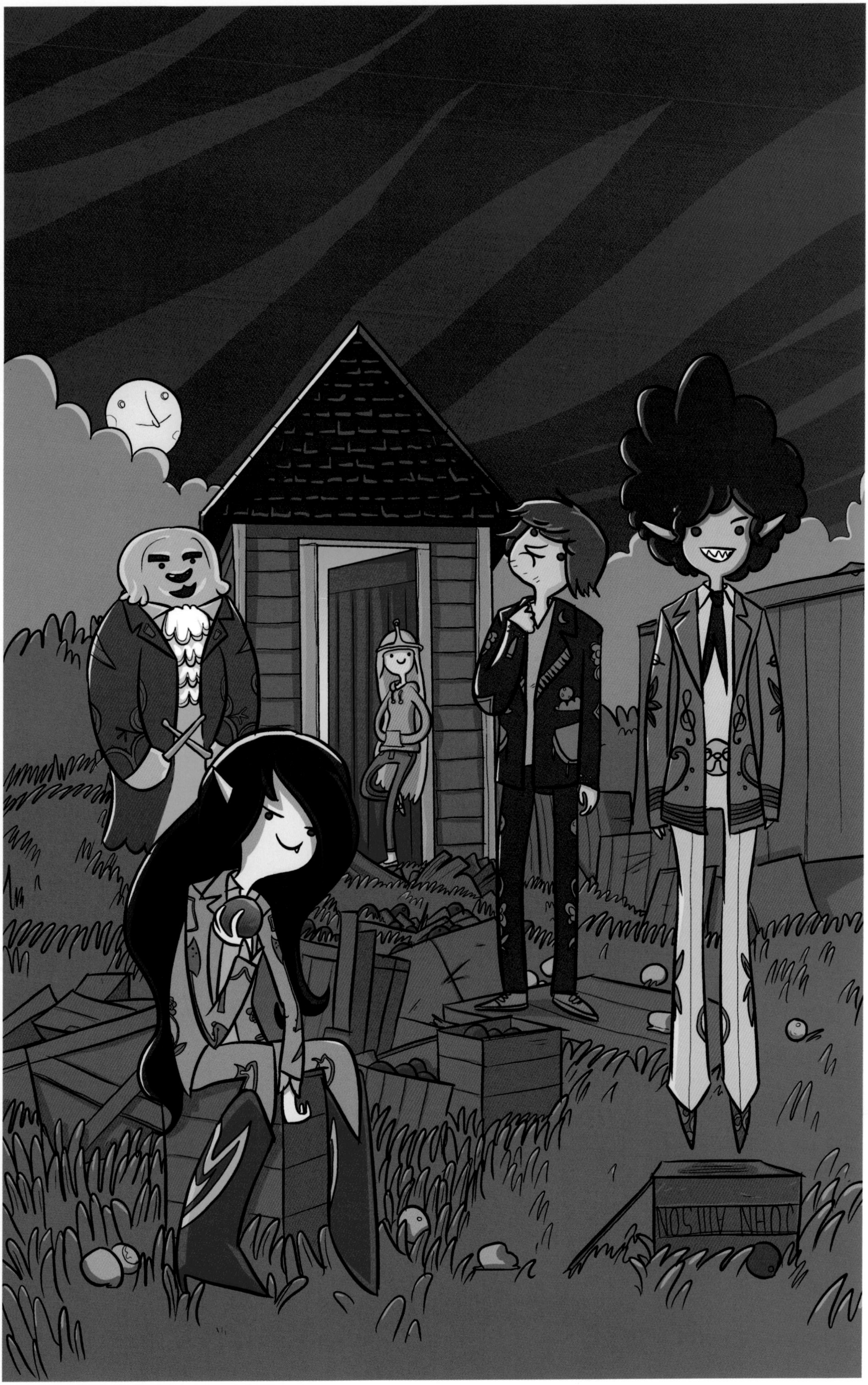

ISSUE TWO BOOM! STUDIOS EXCLUSIVE | JOHN ALLISON WITH COLORS BY STEVE WANDS

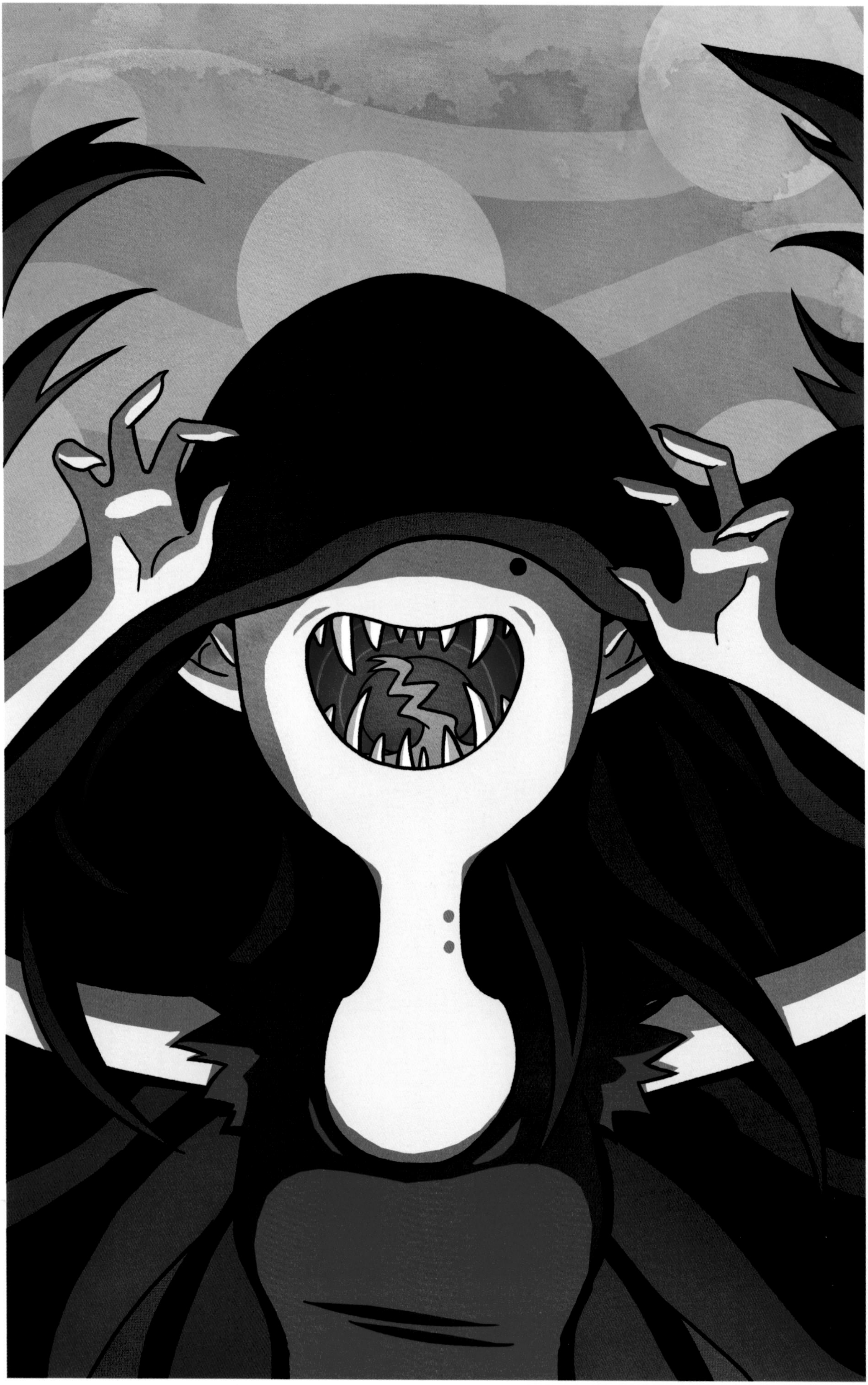

ISSUE THREE | JEN BENNETT WITH COLORS BY LISA MOORE

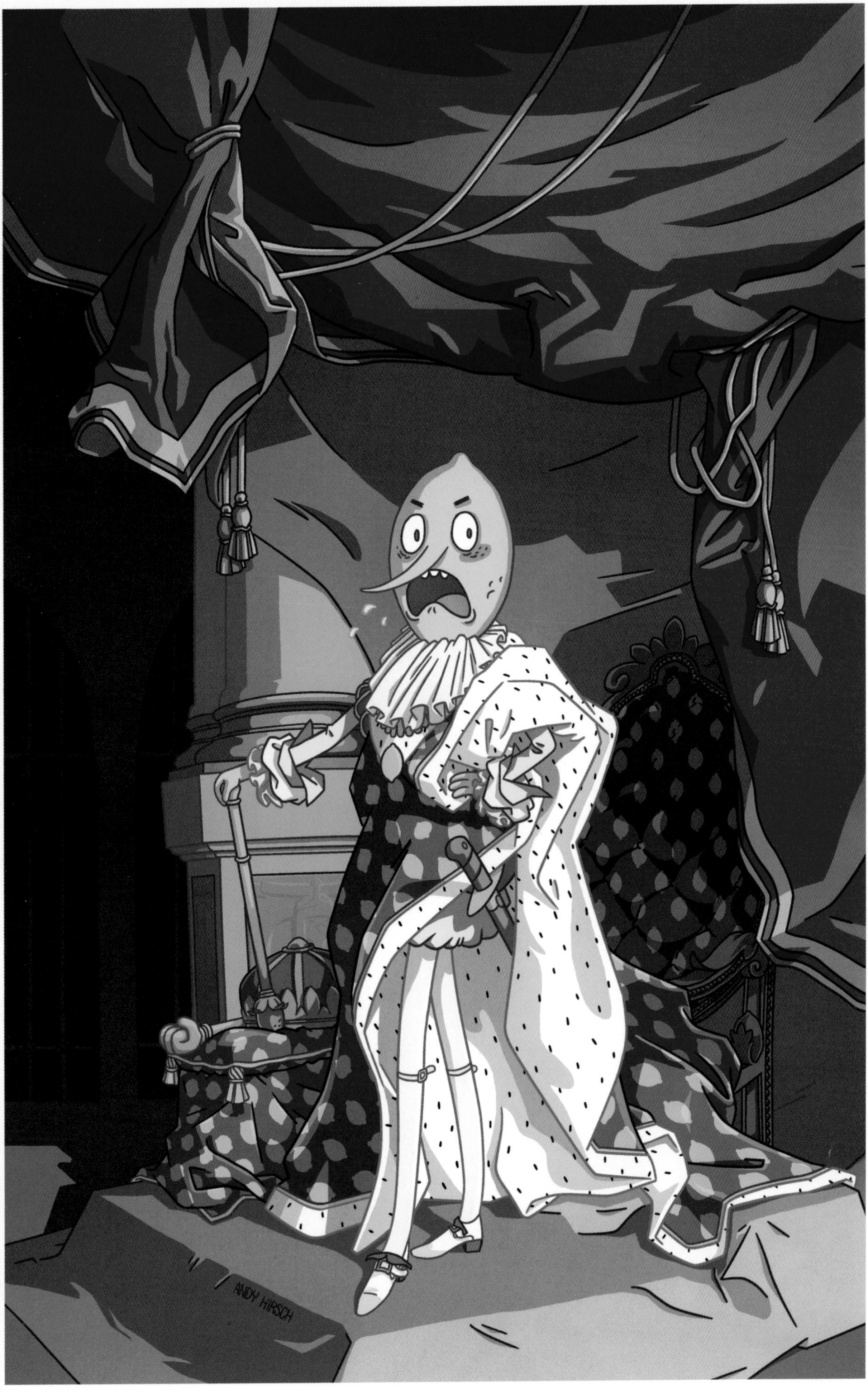
ANDY HIRSCH

ISSUE THREE | ANDY HIRSCH

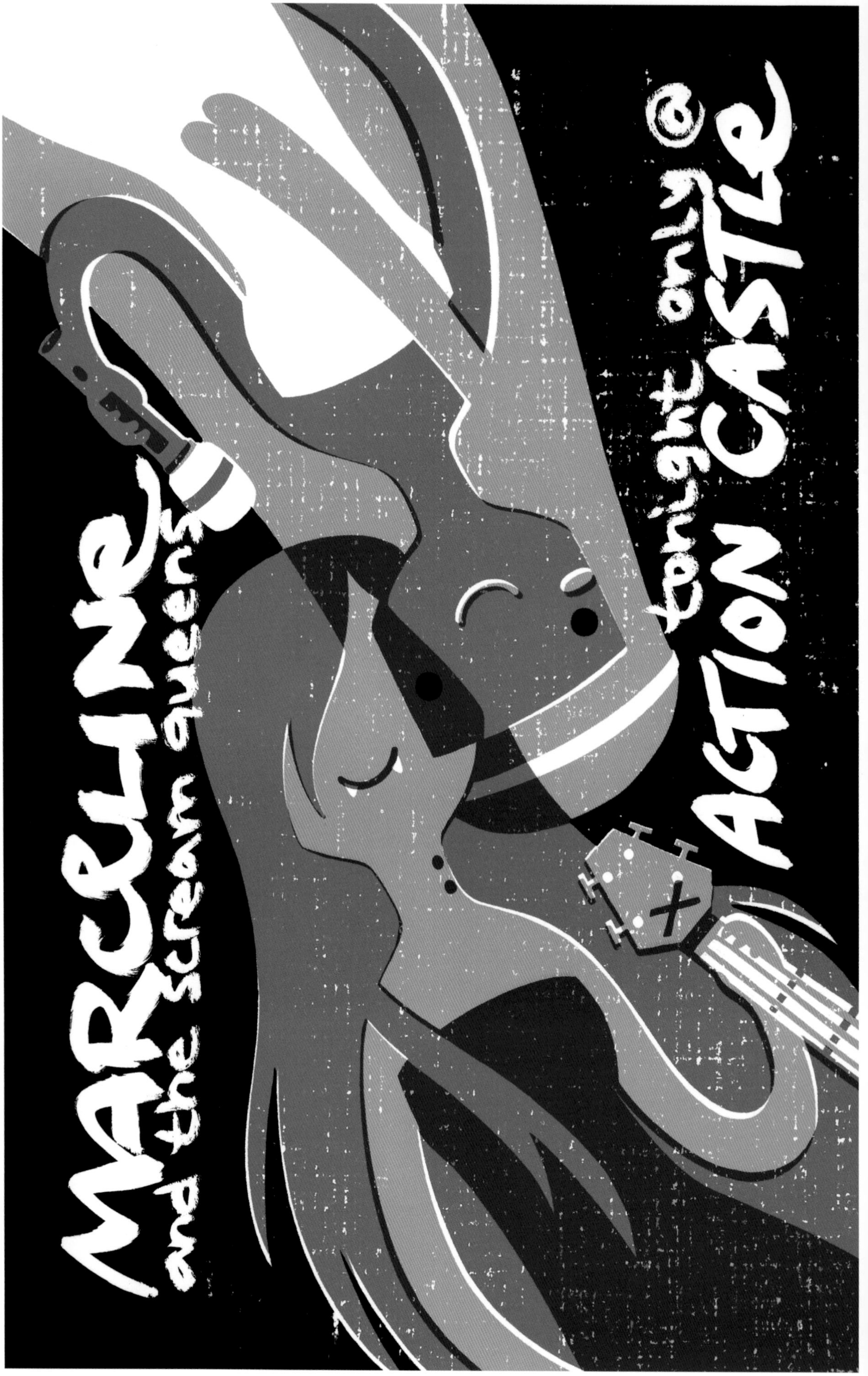
MARCELINE
and the scream queens
tonight only @
ACTION CASTLE

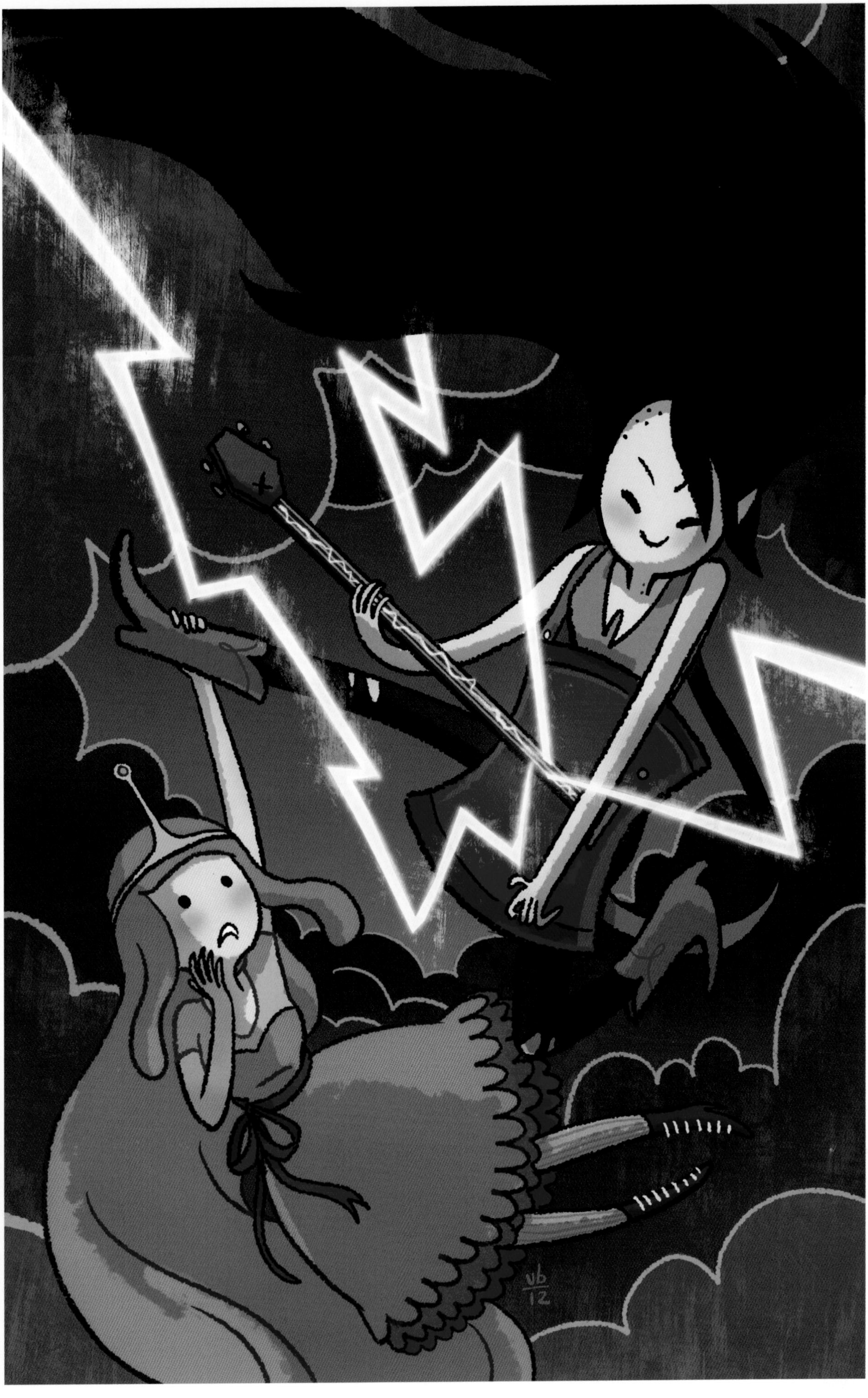
vb
12

ISSUE THREE | VERA BROSGOL

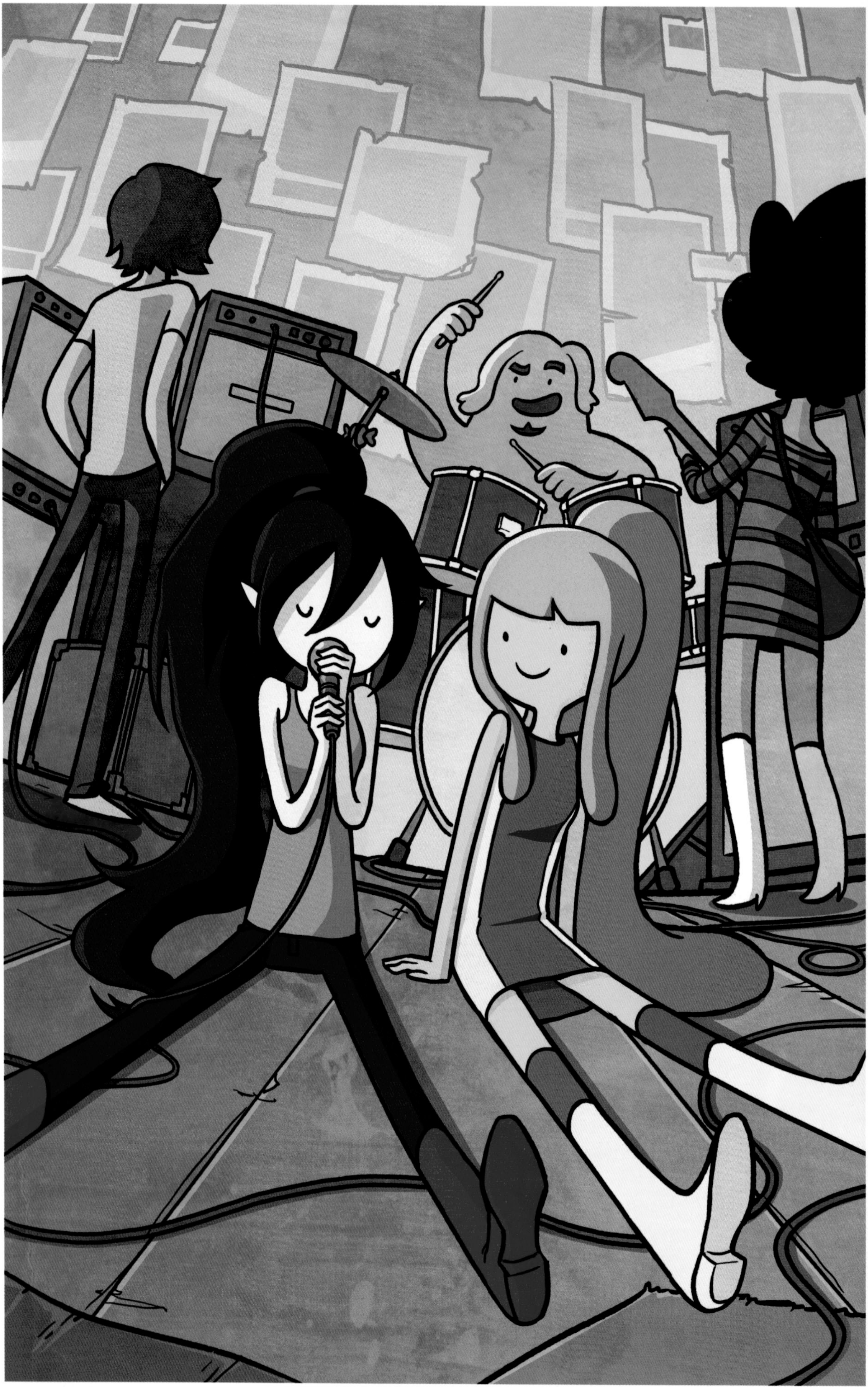

ISSUE FOUR | JEN BENNETT WITH COLORS BY LISA MOORE

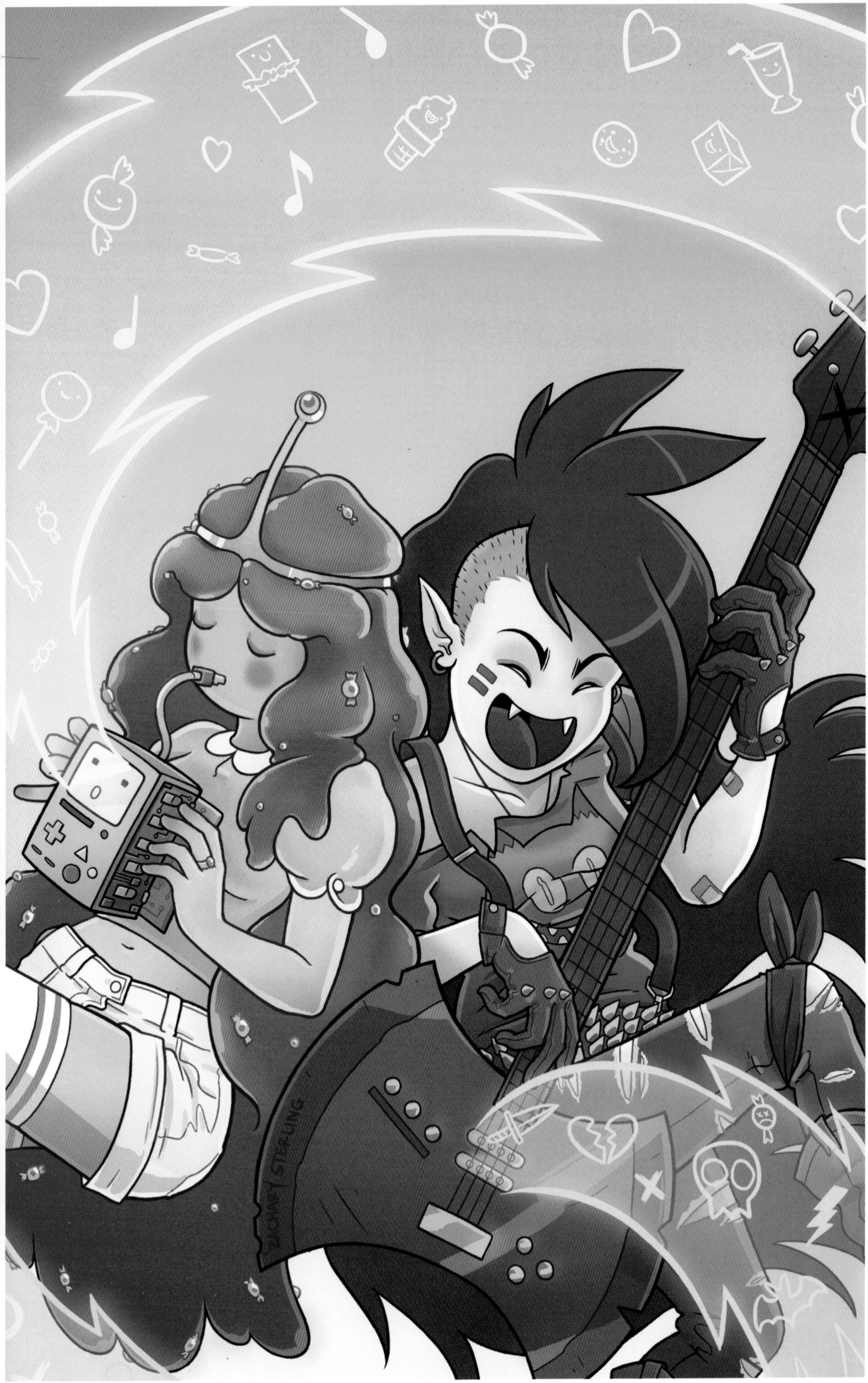
ZACHARY STERLING

ISSUE FOUR | ZACHARY STERLING

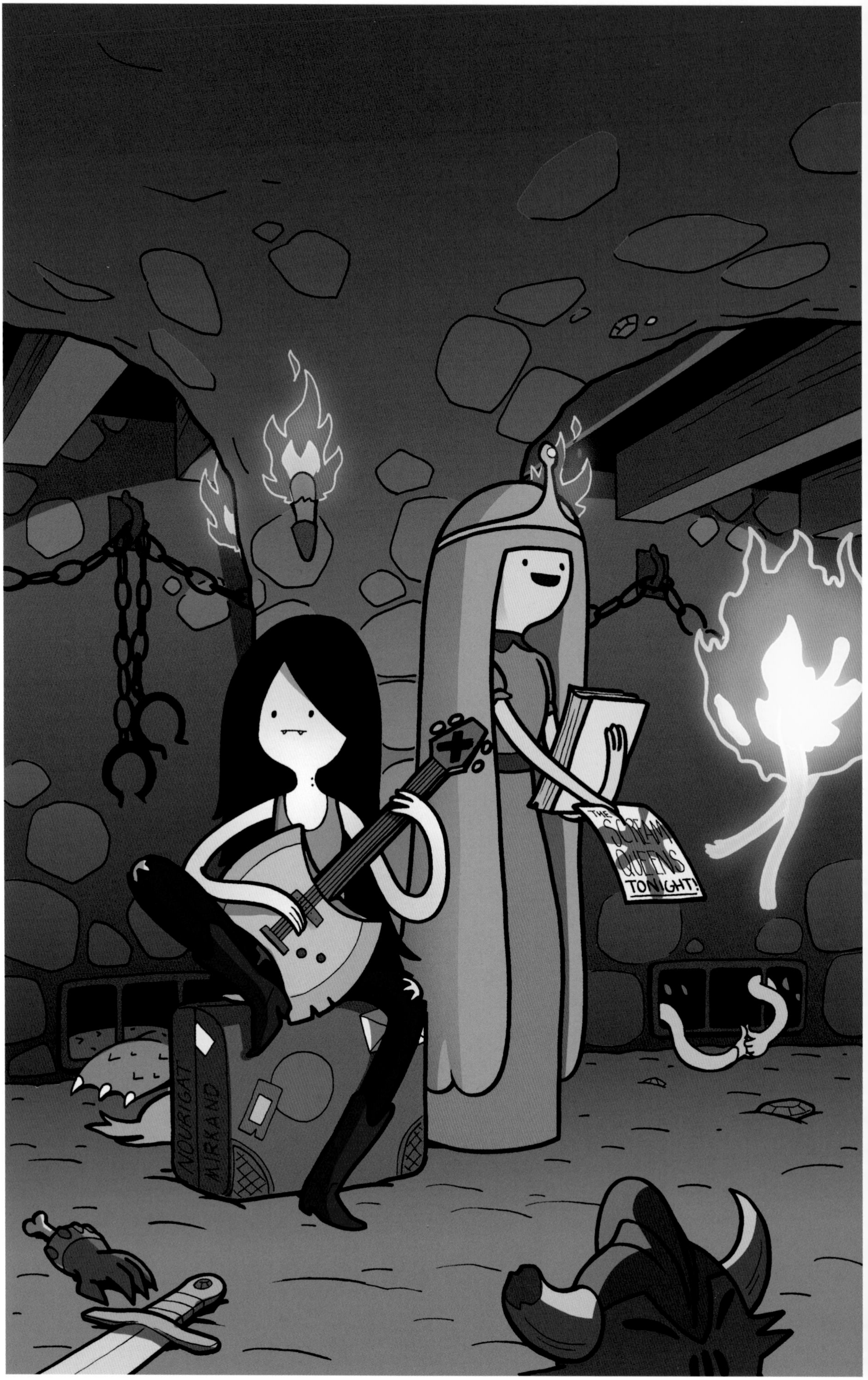
THE SCREAM QUEENS TONIGHT!
NOURIGAT MIRKAND

ISSUE FOUR | TALLY NOURIGAT WITH COLORS BY MIRKA ANDOLFO

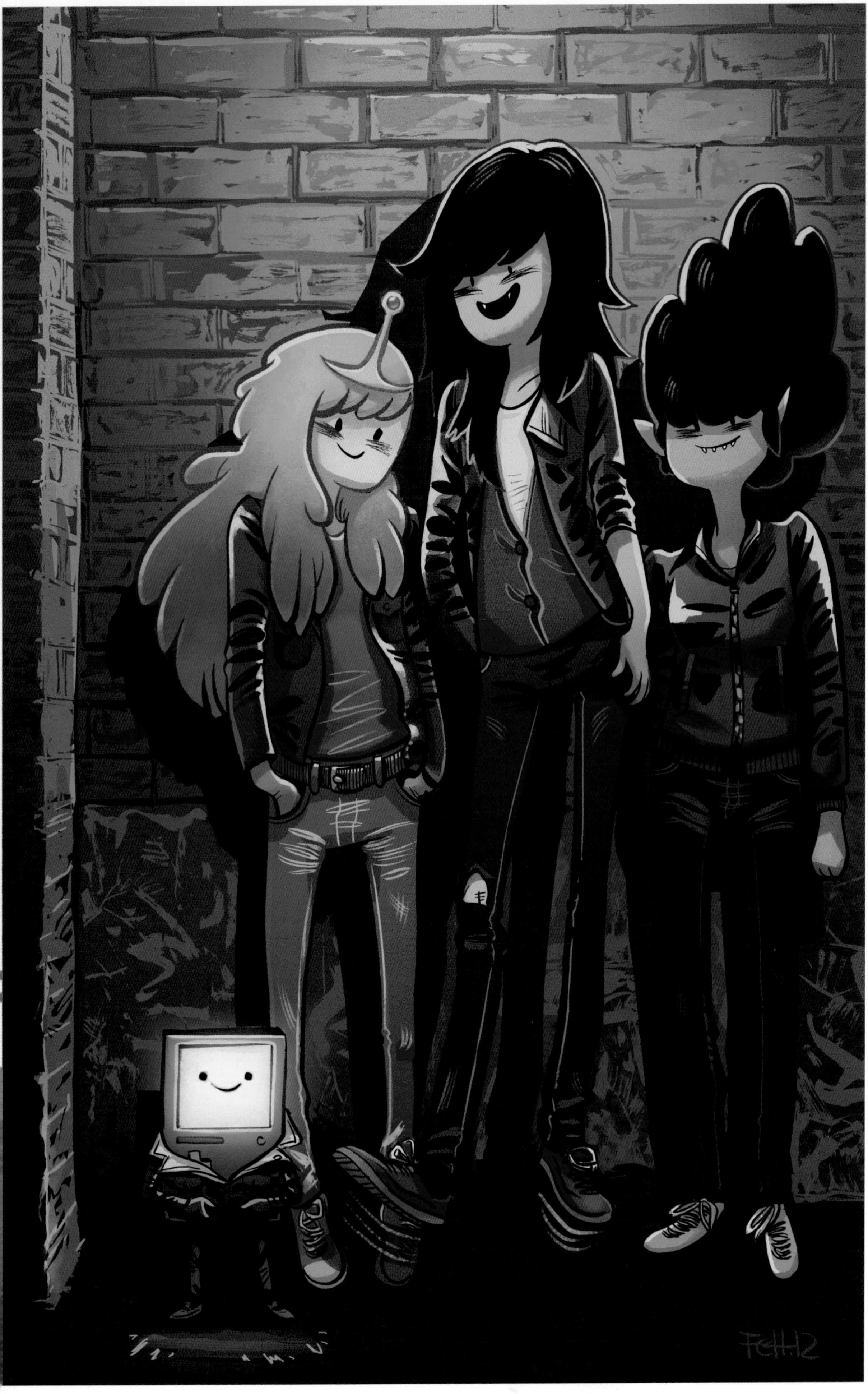
FEH.12

ISSUE FOUR | FAITH ERIN HICKS WITH COLORS BY NOREEN RANA

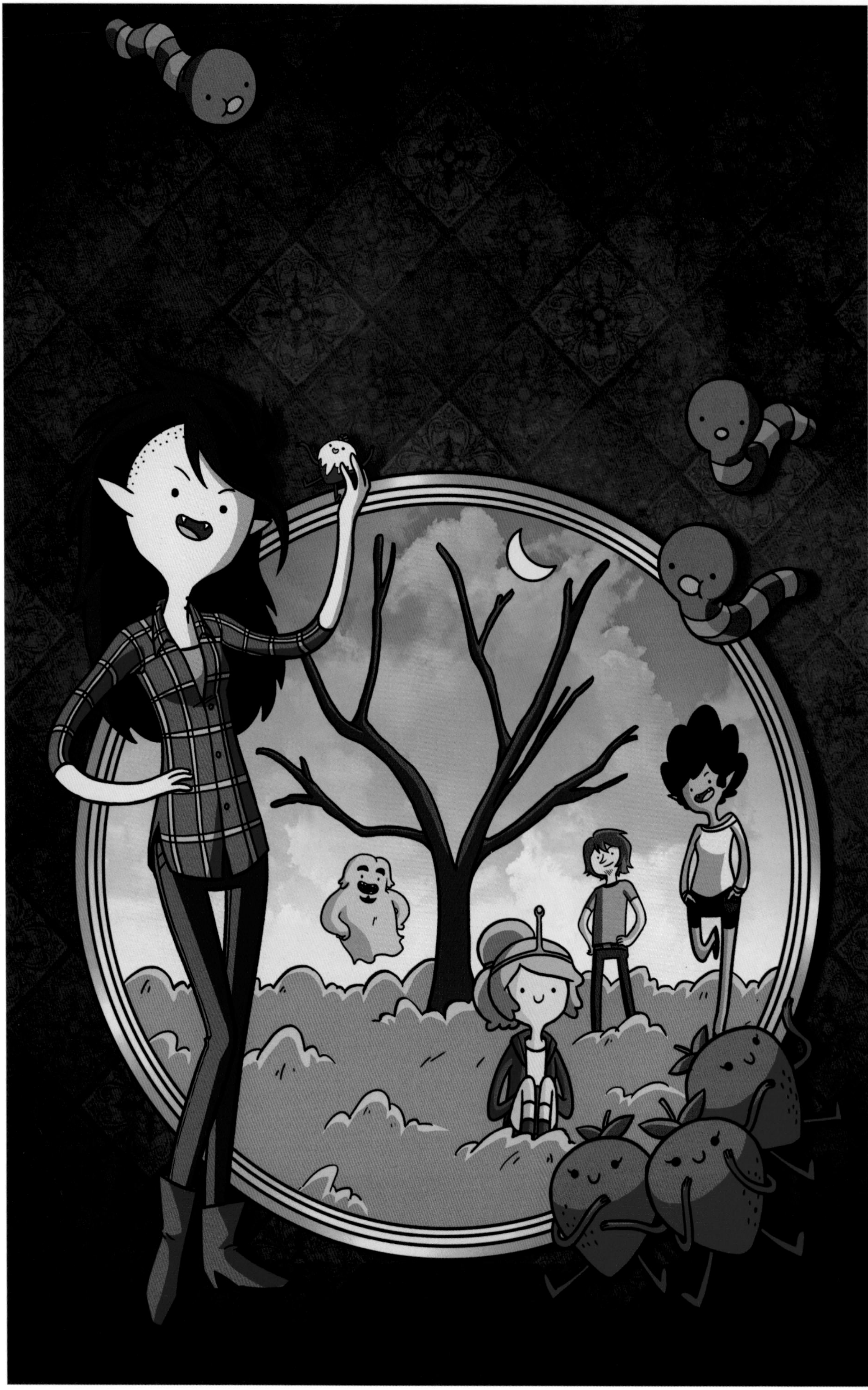

ISSUE FIVE | JEN BENNETT WITH COLORS BY LISA MOORE

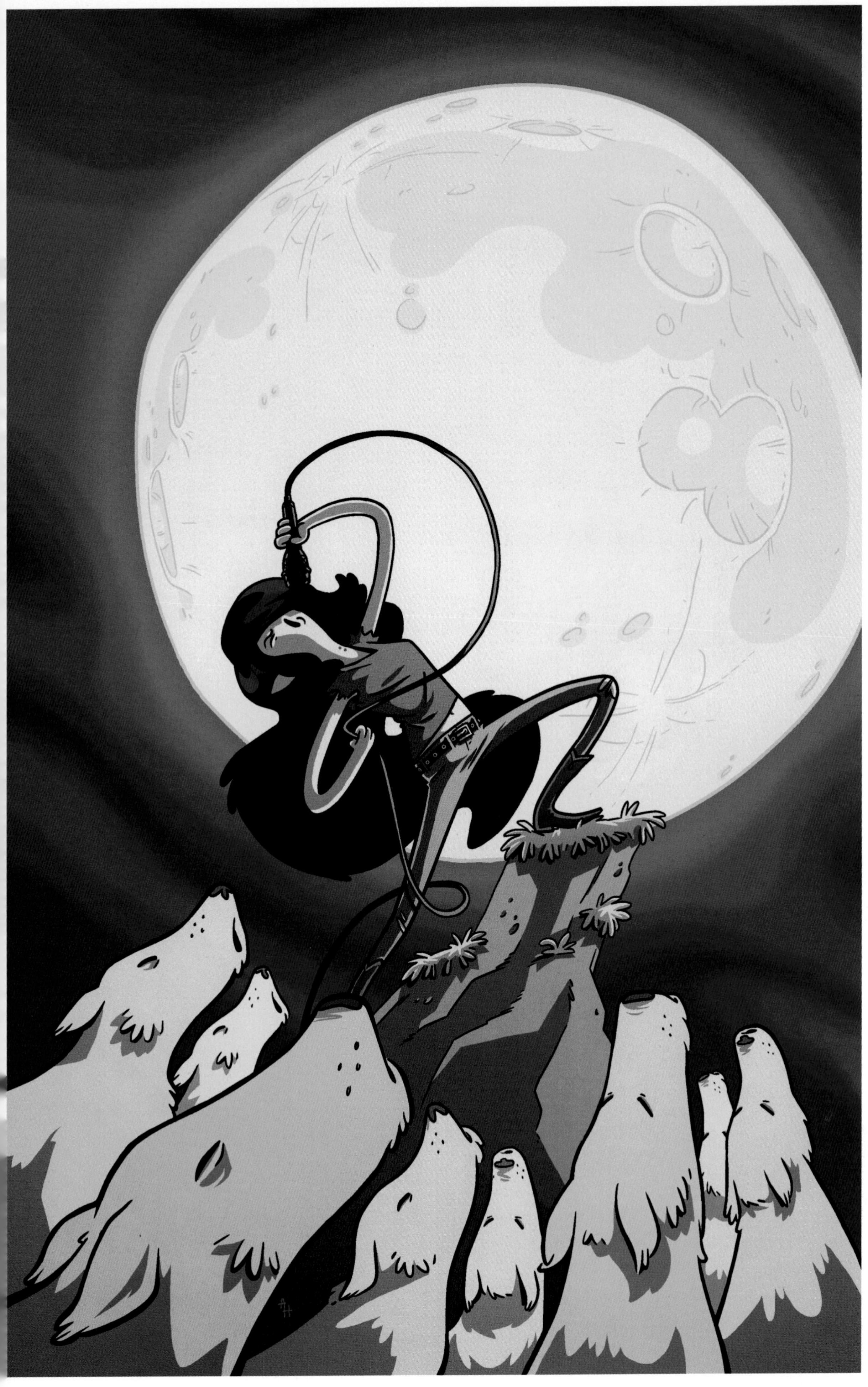

ISSUE FIVE | ANDY HIRSCH

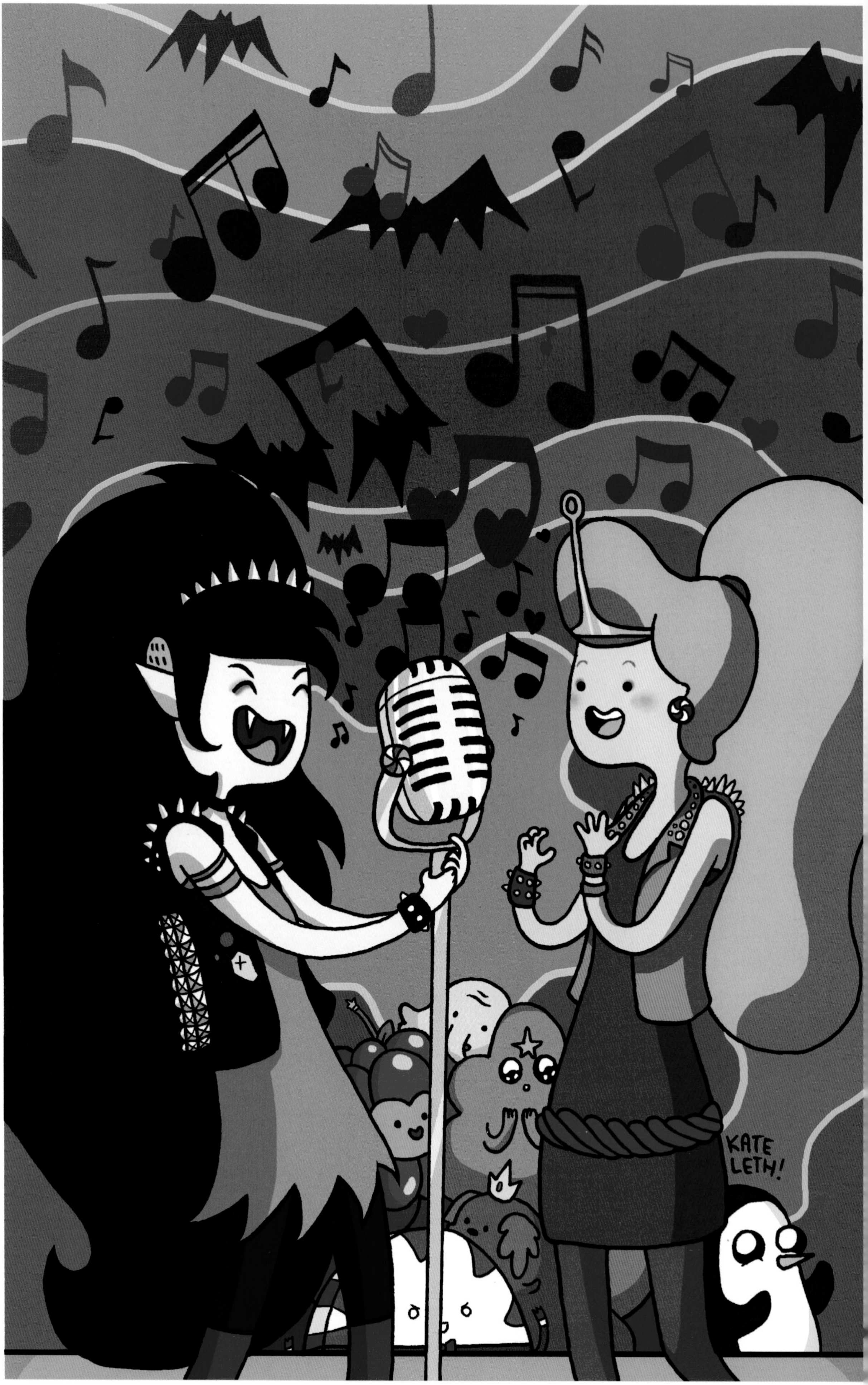
KATE
LETH!

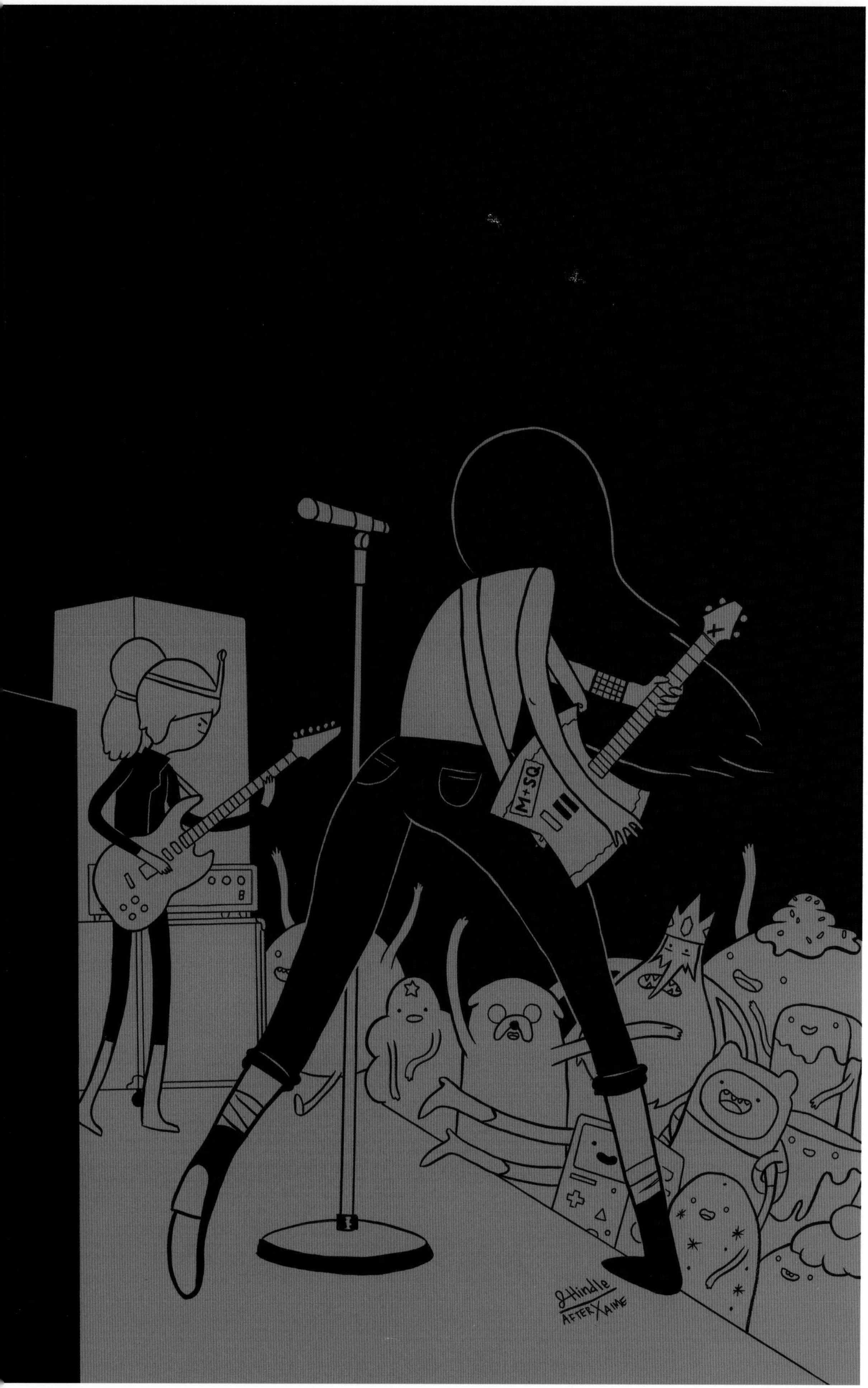
M+SQ

ISSUE FIVE | JAMES HINDLE

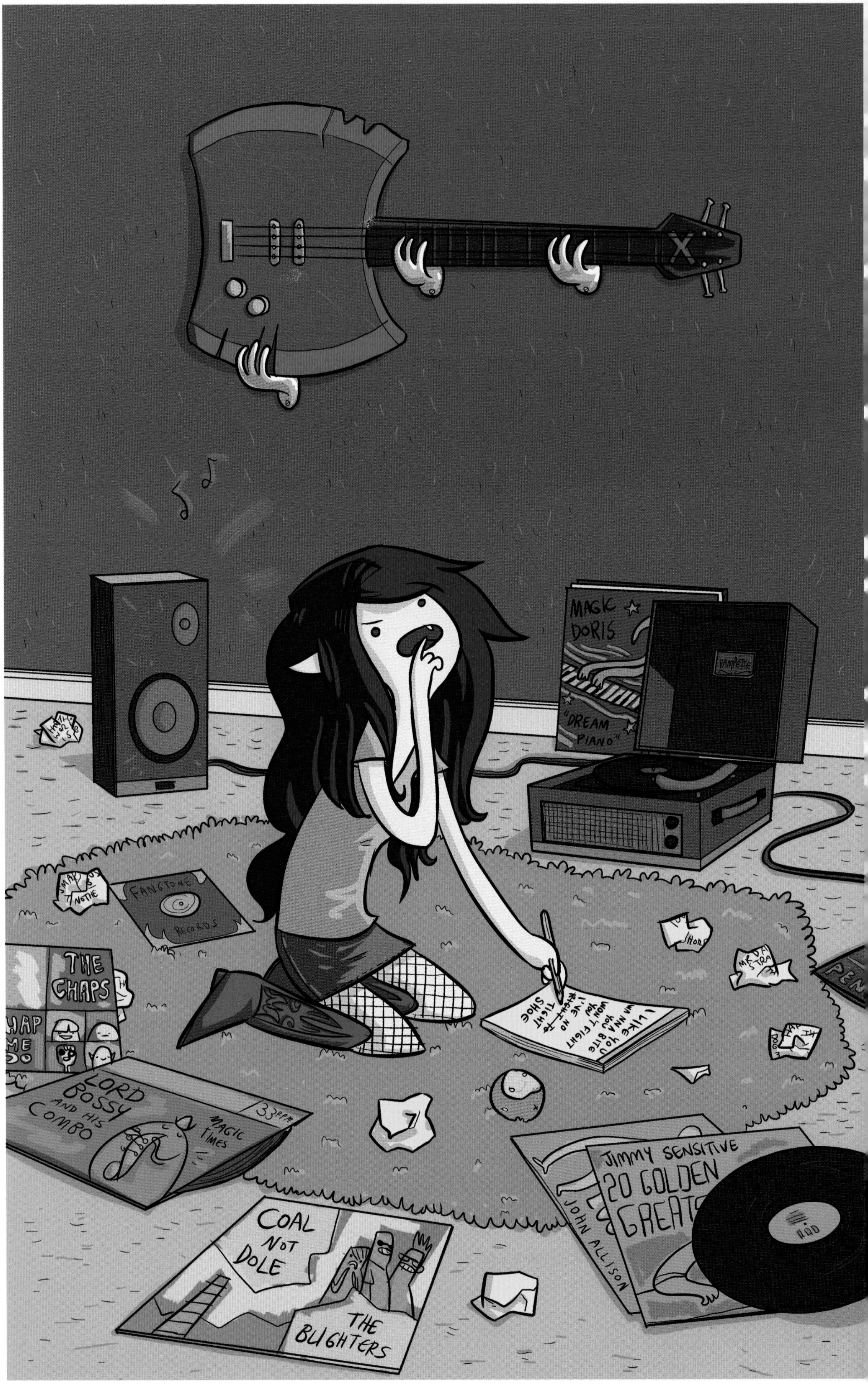
MAGIC DORIS
"DREAM PIANO"
VAMPETTE
FANGTONE RECORDS
THE CHAPS
I LIKE YOU
WANNA BITE YOU
YOU WON'T FIGHT
I'VE NO RIGHT TO
TIGHT
SHOE
LORD BOSSY AND HIS COMBO
33 RPM
MAGIC TIMES
JIMMY SENSITIVE
20 GOLDEN GREATS
JOHN ALLISON
COAL NOT DOLE
THE BLIGHTERS

ISSUE FIVE BOOM! STUDIOS EXCLUSIVE | JOHN ALLISON WITH COLORS BY STEVE WANDS

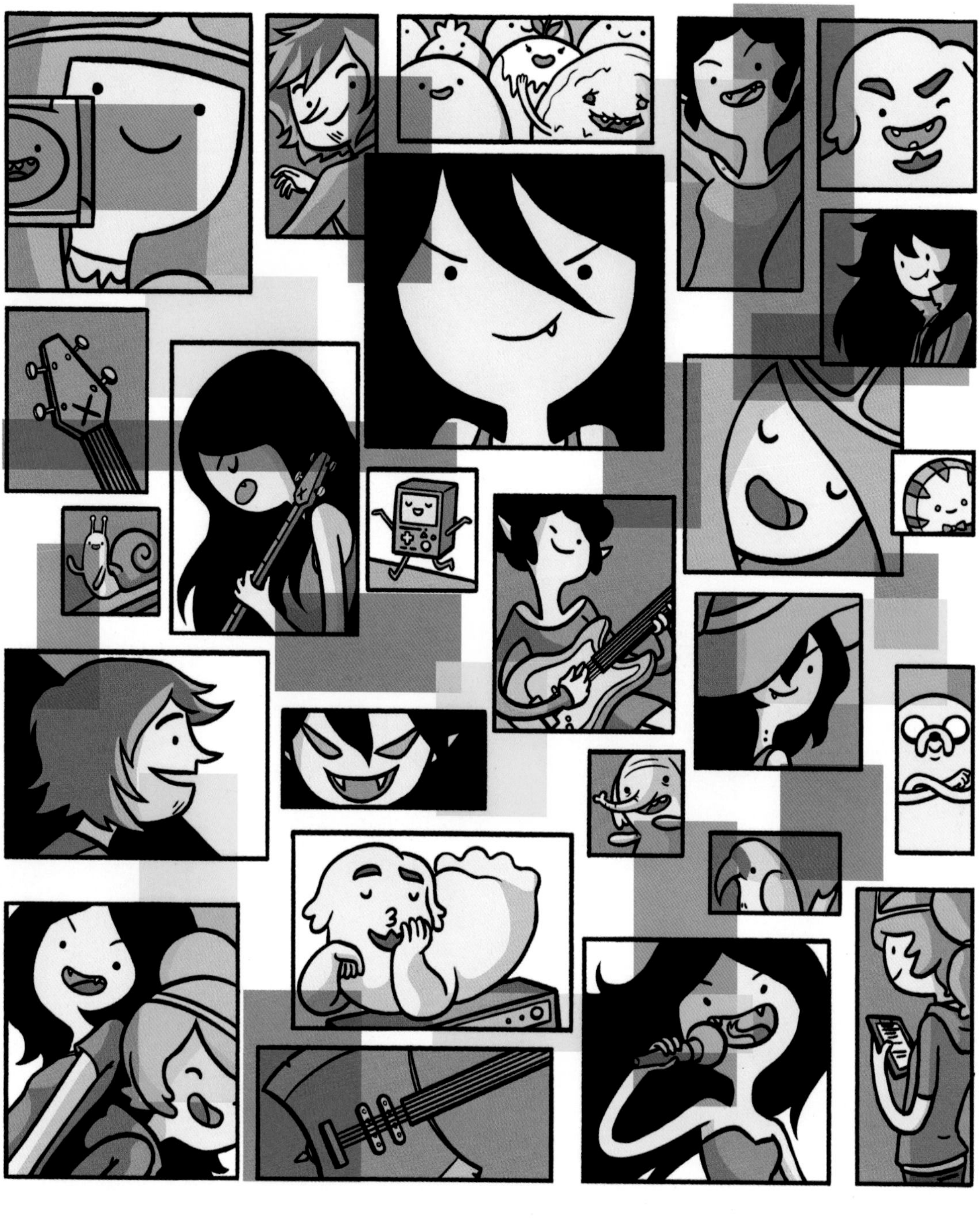

ISSUE SIX | JEN BENNETT WITH COLORS BY LISA MOORE

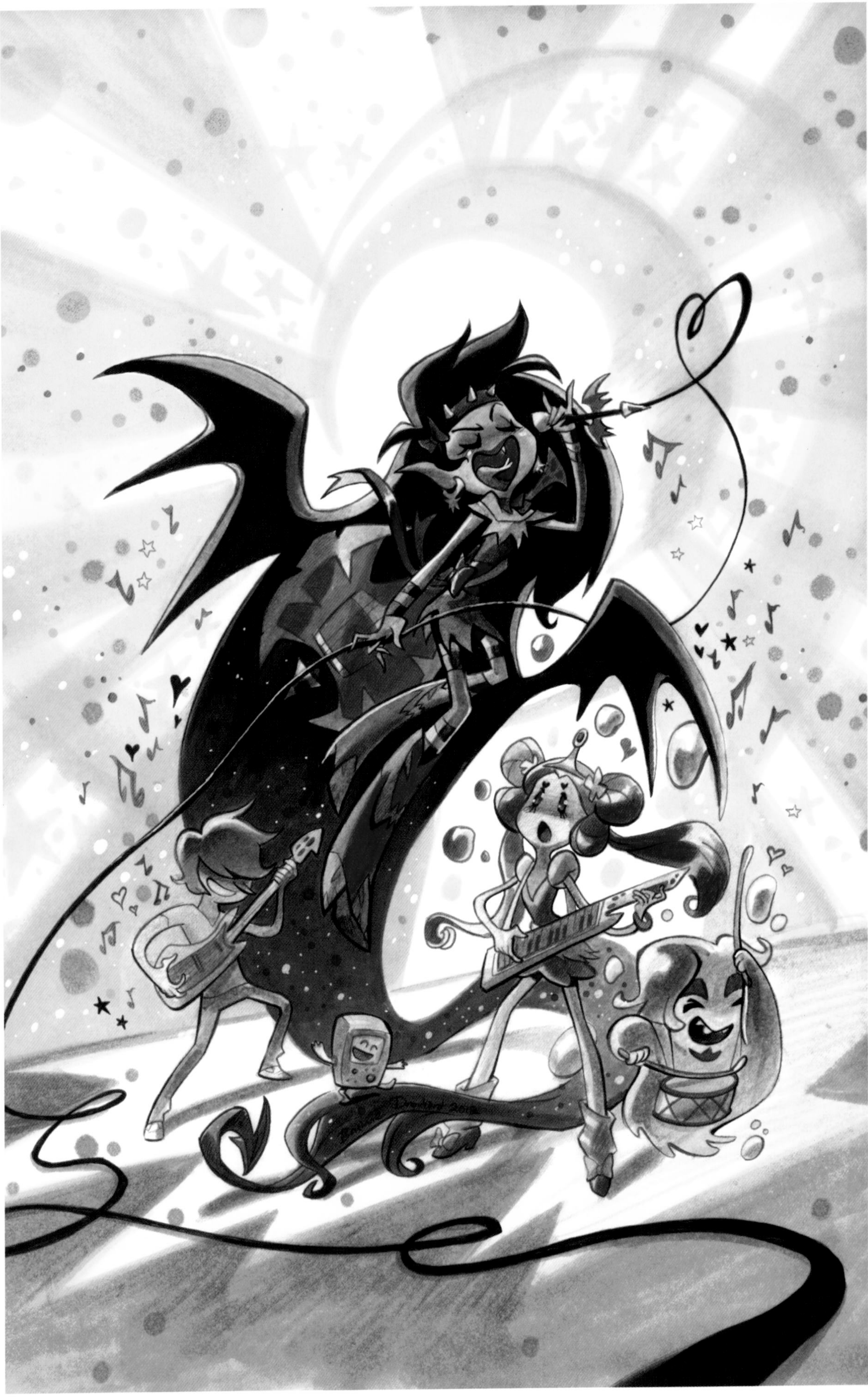

ISSUE SIX | BRIANNE DROHARD

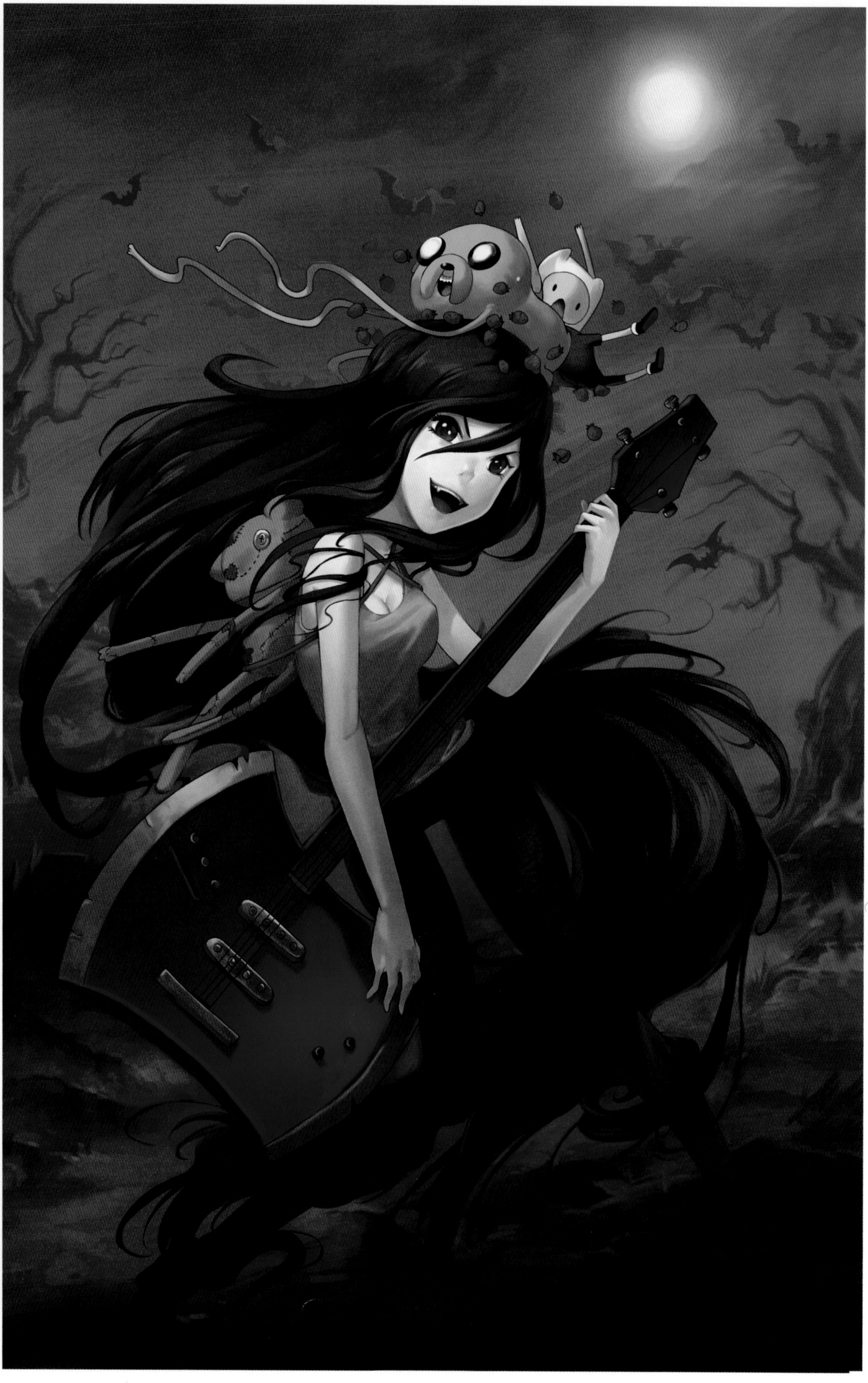

ISSUE SIX | CAMILLA D'ERRICO

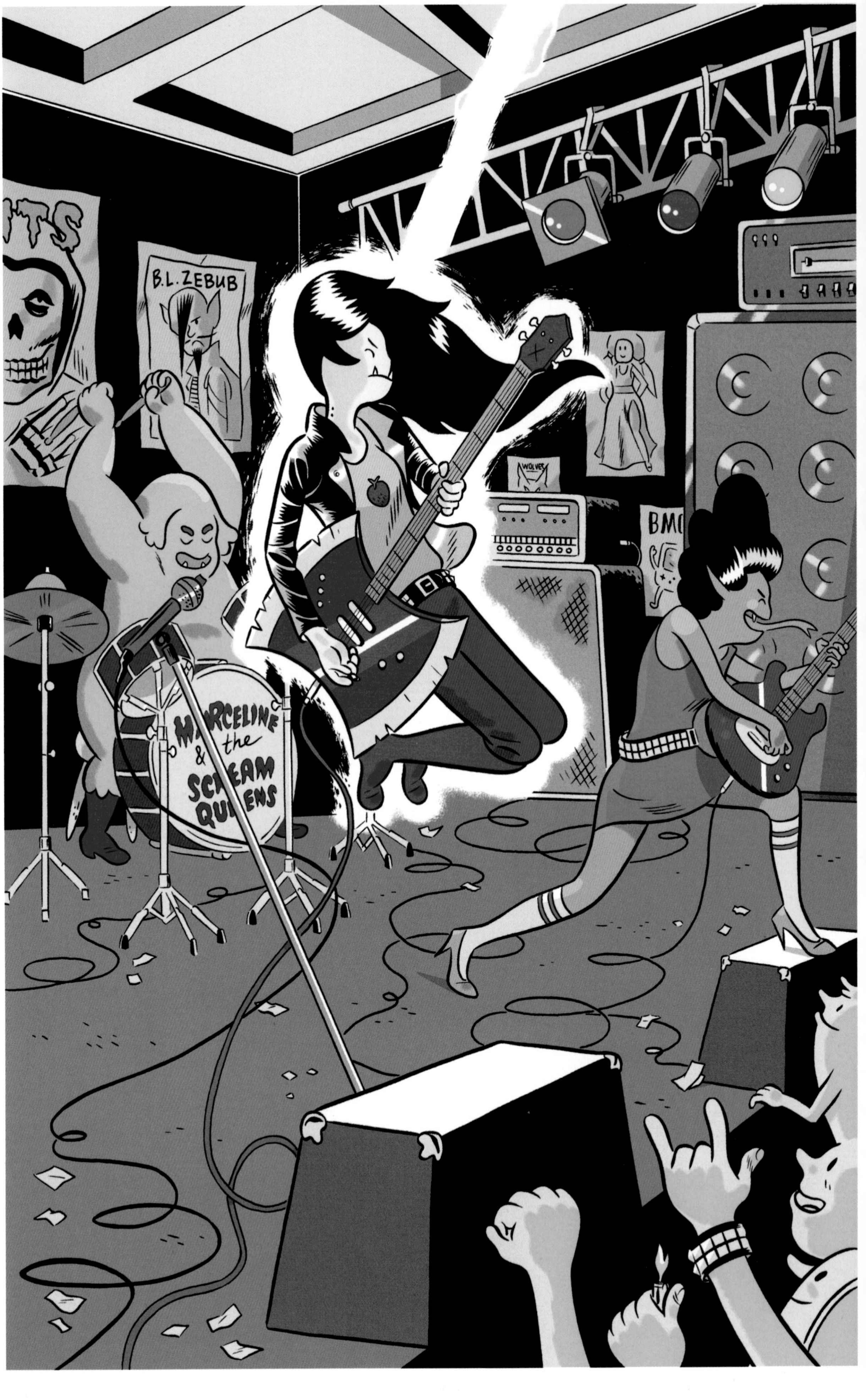
B.L. ZEBUB
WOLVES
BMO
MARCELINE & the SCREAM QUEENS

ISSUE SIX | RICH TOMMASO

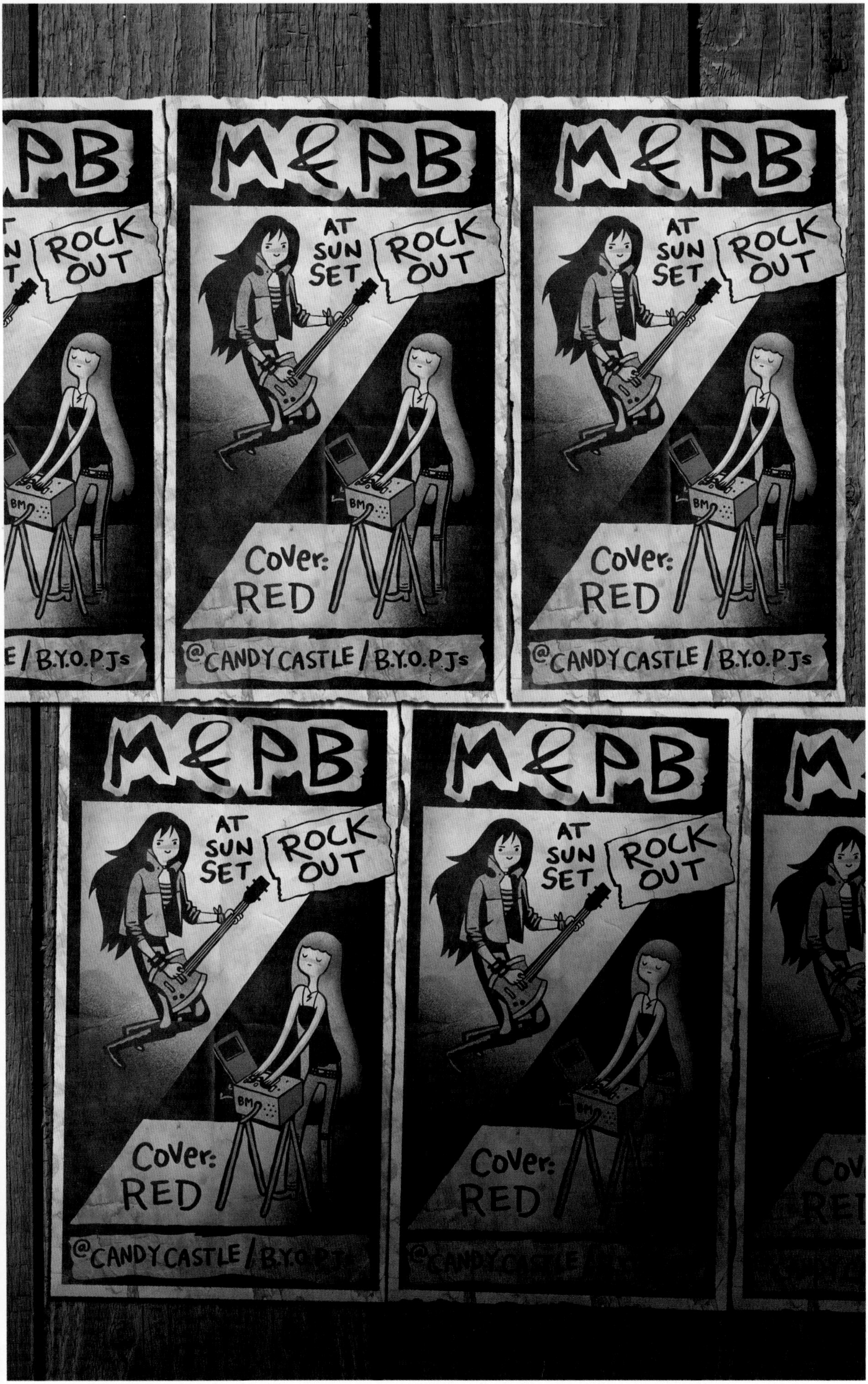
M&PB
AT SUN SET
ROCK OUT
BM
Cover: RED
@CANDY CASTLE / B.Y.O.P.Js

ISSUE SIX DYNAMIC FORCES EXCLUSIVE | LUCY KNISLEY

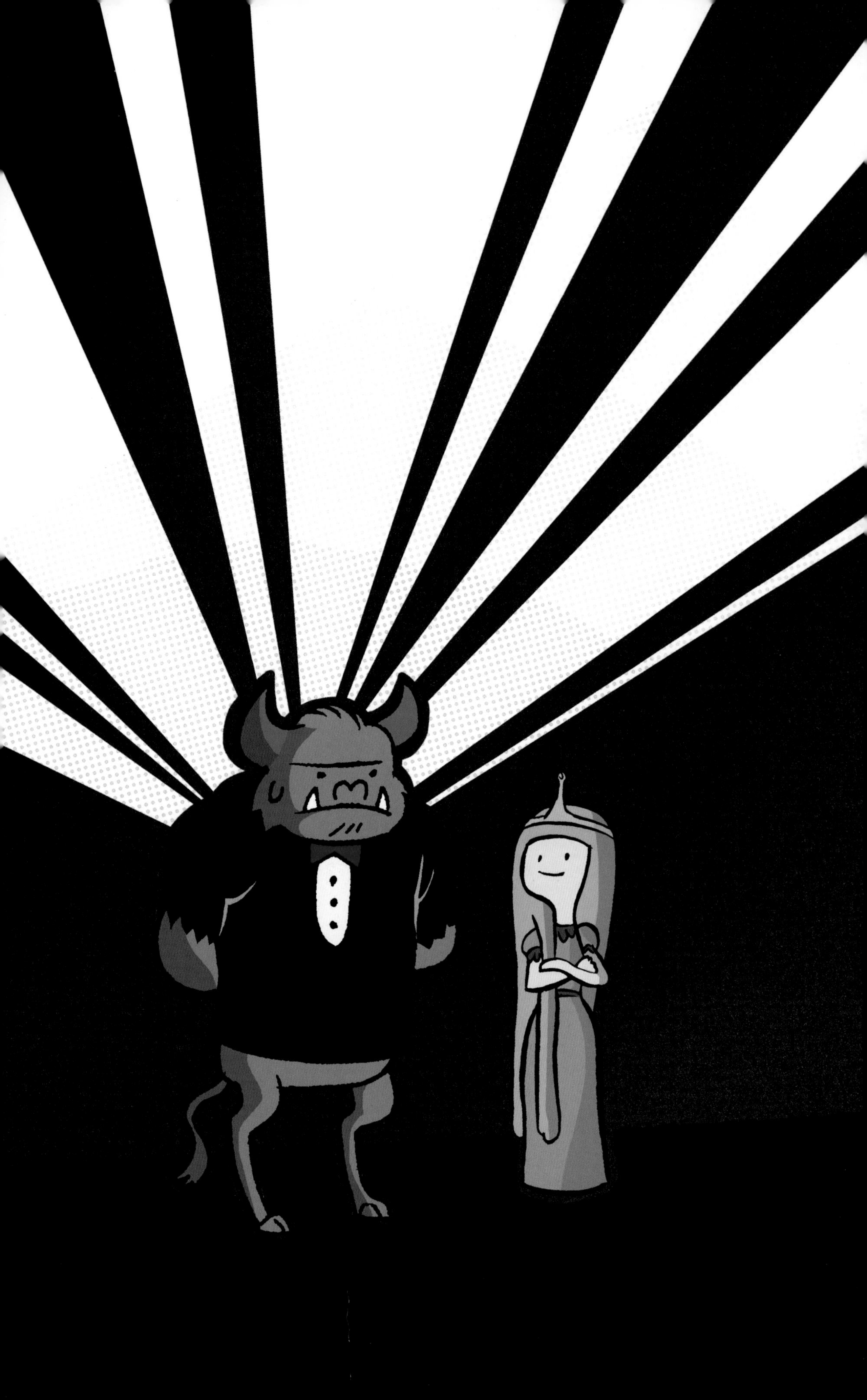

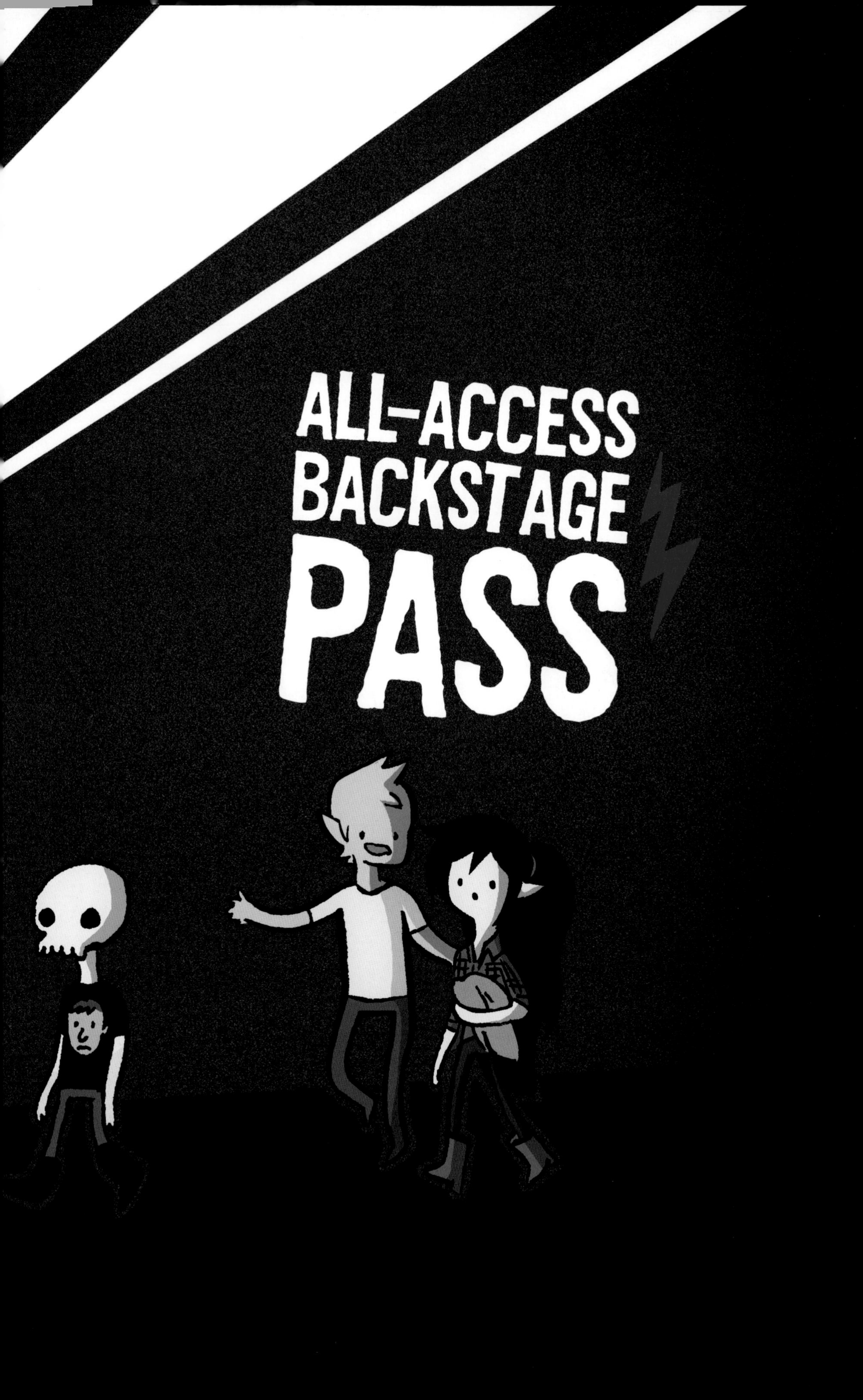
ALL-ACCESS
BACKSTAGE
PASS

BEHIND THE MUSIC

ORIGINAL LINE-UP
OF MARCELINE AND THE SCREAM QUEENS

(MEREDITH'S CHARACTER DESIGNS AND DESCRIPTIONS FOR THE SCREAM QUEENS)

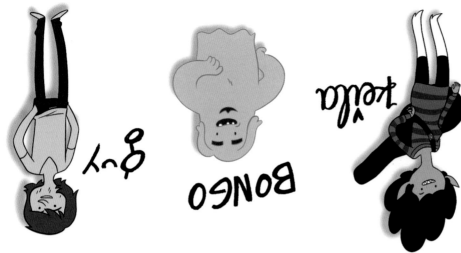

KEILA is classically trained and takes music pretty seriously. She's probably the most upbeat member of the group (especially once Marceline starts taking everything seriously) and tries to keep the peace with everyone. But being a vampire means she's a bit of a trickster like Marceline. Keila and Bubblegum can bond over rock history and music theory.

BONGO's style is kind of outdated (perhaps a ghost of the 90s??), but he's got a heart made of rock n' roll. He's strong but not in very good shape, so he's clumsy and running behind most of the time. Not much going on in his brain but he's lovable. Parties the most.

GUY is a charmer but secretly insecure and boring. His gimmick is that he tries to impress girls by having some tragic supernatural power (i.e. being a werewolf). These revelations will be falsely layered in an attempt to impress Bubblegum, before it's revealed that he's "just a guy". At which point he'll look like very bad boyfriend material. Design-wise I'd like to hide any features (like pointy ears) that might suggest he's anything but human.

PET*SONALITY CRISIS

BALLAD OF A VAMPIRE QUEEN

marceline
THE PLANET QUEEN

Vampire Blues

KICK OUT THE JAMS

SOUND & VISION

REJECTED BAND NAMES
(ALTERNATIVE TITLES FOR THE COMIC)

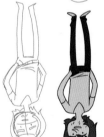

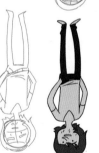

(MEREDITH'S WARM-UP MARCELINES)

MARCELINE
BEFORE THE TOUR

OUR AWESOME FINAL LOGO
(AND THE OFFICIAL BAND NAME)

MARCELINE
AND THE SCREAM QUEENS

MARCELINE
AND THE SCREAM QUEENS

MARCELINE
AND THE SCREAM QUEENS

kaboom!
ADVENTURE TIME
#1
MARCELINE
AND THE SCREAM QUEENS

kaboom!
ADVENTURE TIME
#1
MARCELINE
AND THE SCREAM QUEENS

(PREVIOUS ATTEMPTS)

MARCELINE
AND THE SCREAM QUEENS

Marceline
AND THE Scream Queens

00 YO
CITY

THE VERY FIRST SET LIST
(EXCERPT FROM THE ISSUE #1 SCRIPT)

(EARLY SKETCH)

---

maceline-ISSUE01-ver2.txt — Edited

PAGE 1
_____

A band poster featuring Marceline and the Scream Queens is being held up by a sugary set of hands (being postered over a couple other past Candy Castle-related events).

The poster reads "Marceline and the Scream Queens - Tour of a DEATHtime (heh!)" with a cool picture of the band, a list of venues (including prominently the Candy Castle Summer Festival - TONIGHT!). The poster introduces the band as follows:

Bongo - the Ghost of A Really Really Famous Drummer (Really!). Parties and drums so much it's scary??

Guy - the super MYSTERIOUS keyboardist! Moody, dreamy, a MYSTERY! What's up with him, anyway?

Keila - the bangin' lead guitarist! Classically trained purveyor of all things rock, and a snappy dresser!

Marceline - The Vampire Queen! Bassist, composer and lead singer. She doesn't stop. We can't stop her. Help!

_____
PAGE 2
_____

PANEL 1
Truck out to reveal a small pastry-shaped roadie dusting his powdered-sugar hands off in accomplishment, a rolled stack of Marceline gig posters under his arm. The ad is visible on other surrounding trees in the forest, where other candy creatures are busy postering. The postering seems EXCESSIVE. Marceline's voiceover is seen.

                    MARCELINE
This is it, you guys.

PANEL 2
Shot of Marceline and the band overlooking the postering from high up in a treehouse. Guy the pretty-boy keyboardist, Keila the afro'd lead guitarist (also a vampire), and Bongo the ghost drummer are all lounging as Marceline levitates. Keila is messing with her guitar/amp while Guy rummages through some records. Bongo is trying very hard to pull a tiny pair of boots onto his blobby, footless body.

                    MARCELINE

---

ve records and

ake their way through

                    DRUMMER
This band is such a lumping BUMMER!

                    FINN
Ooh yeah, there's a PRIMO spot!

PANEL 5
Jake fashions himself into an elevated, shaded platform for Bubblegum and Finn to sit on. He's obnoxiously huge, and blocking the view. People in the crowd behind him crane their necks and go "Hey!".

                    FINN
We'll be able to see EVERYthing from here!

                    BUBBLEGUM
(half-heartedly) All right...

_____
PAGE 7
_____

PANEL 1
Finn and Bubblegum look around as the venue darkens. Finn is looking stupidly excited.

PANEL 2
Shot of the darkened stage, looking ominous.

PANEL 3
A set of red spotlights fall on the stage, illuminating a smoky fog. People in the crowd gasp.

PANEL 4
Marceline's visage suddenly appears in the spotlight, RED eyes glowing, vampire teeth glistening.

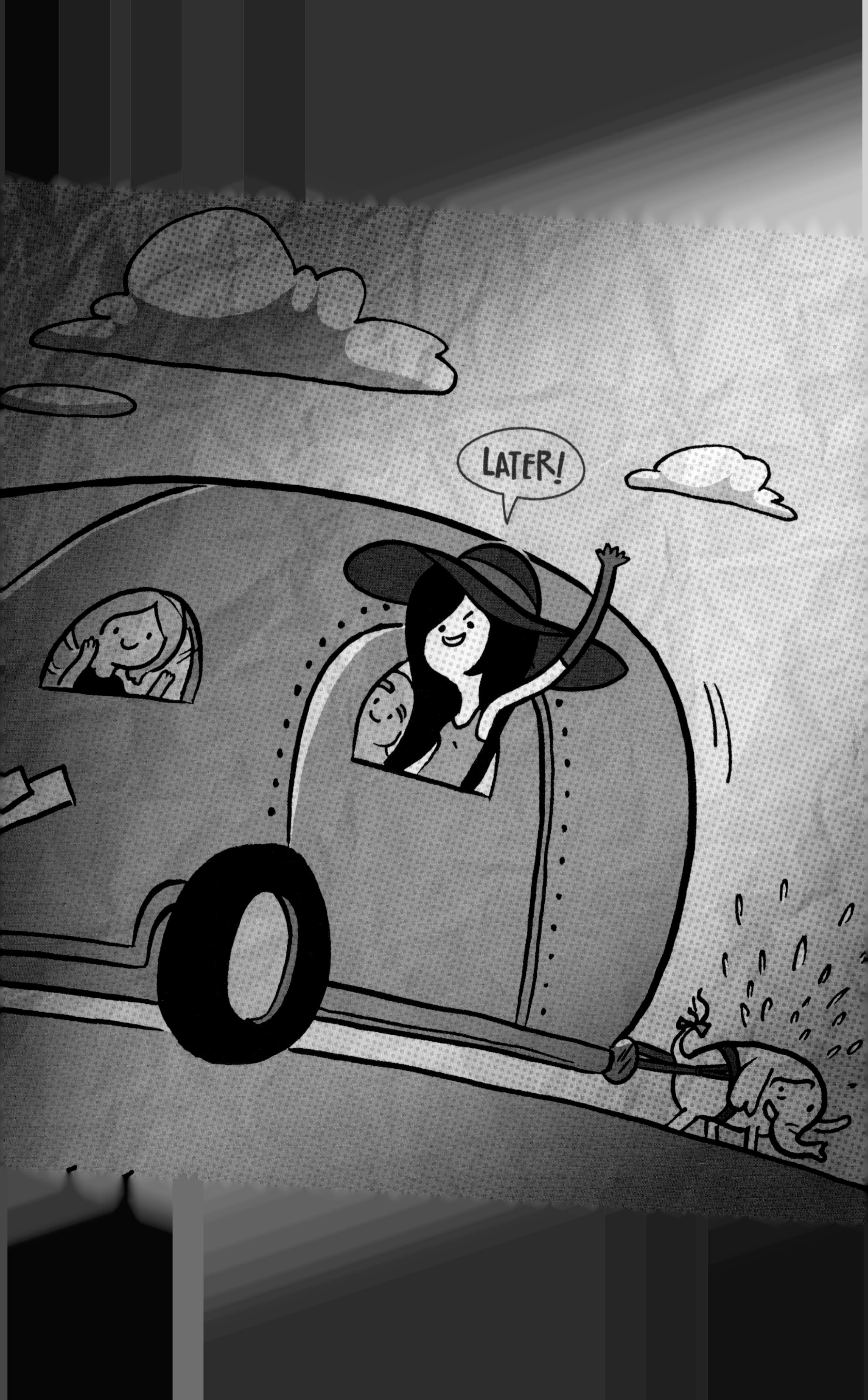
LATER!